RAIN OF DEATH

There was no way of telling how many archers stood above them.

An arrow hit the man Gift had been yelling at. Arrows landed near Gift, and he suddenly realized he was the target. The man he had directed to the wheel was trying to turn it, but not doing a very good job.

Skya had come on deck. Gift cursed softly. He didn't want her here. He hurried to her, put his arms around her, and pushed her toward the deckhouse.

"They'll kill you," he said.

She raised a single eyebrow. "Looks to me like someone is trying to kill you."

The man was still struggling with the wheel and the ship was losing momentum. If no one did anything, they'd be stuck here, easy targets for the archers above.

Some of the Fey on deck were shouting now. The Sailors were still in position, two of them with arrows in their backs. A wave came up over the deck. One of the Fey women screamed. Arrows were spraying the entire area around Gift. One of them hit a Navigator who collapsed like a puppet with its strings cut.

Skya was back on deck. She grabbed Gift and flung him aside as if he weighed nothing. She held him underneath the overhang.

"If you die," she said, "we all die. You're staying here."

THE BLACK THRONE SERIES

THE BLACK KING

Kristine Kathryn Rusch

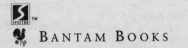 BANTAM BOOKS

New York Toronto London Sydney Auckland

THE BLACK KING
A Bantam Spectra Book / August 2000

SPECTRA and the portrayal of a boxed "s" are trademarks of
Bantam Books, a division of Random House, Inc.

ISBN 0-553-58118-X

Published simultaneously in the United States and Canada

Bantam Books are published by Bantam Books, a division of Random
House, Inc. Its trademark, consisting of the words "Bantam Books" and
the portrayal of a rooster, is Registered in U.S. Patent and Trademark Of-
fice and in other countries. Marca Registrada. Bantam Books, 1540 Broad-
way, New York, New York 10036.

PRINTED IN THE UNITED STATES OF AMERICA

OPM   10   9   8   7   6   5   4   3   2   1

For my sister, Peg Hammer, who showed me that women can be strong, courageous, and feminine all at the same time.

ACKNOWLEDGMENTS

Thanks on this book go to Anne Lesley Groell for her tremendous work on this project; Merrilee Heifetz for keeping the dream alive; Paul Higginbotham and Jerry and Kathy Oltion for their perceptive comments; my husband, Dean Wesley Smith, for loving the world of the Fey sometimes more than I do; and to all the readers who've been writing me letters and telling me what they enjoy about this world, and why.

THE BLACK KING

The Return

CHAPTER ONE

*G*IFT STOOD ON the prow of the *Tashka,* his hands clasped behind his back, his feet spread slightly apart. He wore his hair longer than he ever had, and used a leather tie to hold it back. The sun and weather had darkened his skin, making it the same color as that of the Fey around him. His hands had calluses, his body more muscles. He had learned a lot on this trip, much of it about survival.

The Infrin Sea was choppy. A wind had come up, carrying with it a light mist. The skies were overcast, the air chill, but something in it smelled of home.

If he squinted, he could see Blue Isle ahead. At first its mountainous shore had looked like a gray shadow against the gray ocean, but as the ship drew closer, the shapes were becoming clearer.

The Stone Guardians protected the only natural harbor in Blue Isle. They were huge rocks, three times taller than most ships, staggered throughout the harbor and its entry way. The Guardians created unusual currents that changed with the tides and the weather. No ship had ever made it through the Guardians without guidance. For decades, Gift's Islander father and grandfather kept Blue Isle isolated by destroying all the maps and getting rid of the people who watched the currents.

Now that Gift's sister, Arianna, was Queen of Blue Isle, she had reopened the trade routes. Maps existed again, as did the on-land watchers. Navigators learned the patterns of the currents, and some Fey had even been trained in reading the waters.

He unclasped his hand and wiped his eyes. Soon his Gull Riders would return with news of the conditions near the Guardians. Then he would put his Sailors and Navigators into action.

His stomach was jumping. He was coming home after almost a decade away. He had traveled across the Fey Empire, and then he had gone to the Eccrasian Mountains to train as a Shaman. There he had touched the Black Throne and his life had changed.

He shuddered, remembering how the Throne had clung to him, how it had tried to absorb him, and the strength he had used, both mental and physical, to pull away. The Throne was a living thing, and it wanted to make him Black King. But his sister Arianna ruled the Fey.

Arianna was a good Black Queen, and an excellent Queen to Blue Isle. Except there was something wrong now. He had Seen it in Visions. Something was wrong with her. And no one would tell him what it was.

He took a few steps forward, as if that would bring him closer to the Stone Guardians. Once he had vowed not to return to Blue Isle until he became a Shaman. But he would never be a Shaman. A Shaman couldn't practice with blood on his hands, and Gift hadn't realized that, in his youth, he had accidentally killed a Wisp.

Now he didn't know what he'd do if something was wrong with Arianna. He was the oldest, the one who should have taken the Throne, but he had renounced it. Arianna was the ruthless one, the one who had the willingness to make the hard decisions and the enemies that leadership required. He had always been the gentler of the two, the one less willing to take risks.

"Standing and squinting at the Isle won't bring it any closer."

Gift turned. Skya stood behind him, her black hair in its customary knot on the top of her head. The wind had pulled strands from it, whipping them about her narrow face. He had always thought that she looked like the perfect Fey: her features symmetrical and upswept, her chin so narrow that it looked almost pointed, her black eyes filled with life and intelligence. She was one of the most beautiful women he'd ever seen, and although he'd spent the last six months with her, he was still surprised at the depth of that beauty.

"Part of me wants to get there now, and part of me doesn't want to return," he said.

She didn't answer him. She tried not to discuss what she called matters of state. But he sometimes saw that as her way of avoiding anything personal. "The Gull Riders are back."

"I told them to report to me," he said.

"They're waiting in the hold." She put a hand on his arm. Her touch was gentle. He put an arm around her and pulled her close. Her gaze met his and in it was a warning he ignored. He kissed her, slid his hands into her soft hair, pulling it free as he had done almost every night on this trip when she slipped into his stateroom after everyone else had gone to sleep. The kiss was long and deep and he didn't care who saw it.

She did. She believed they did not belong together.

She had never told him that, not in so many words, but he knew. It was one of the few times he knew what she was thinking, and he had no way to reassure her.

Finally she pulled away. "Gift," she whispered. "We can't—"

"I thought you didn't follow rules," he said, placing his wet forehead against hers. The mist ran down their faces like tears.

"Only the rules I make myself."

"You've made up rules about me?"

She smiled and slipped out of his grasp. "The Gull Riders are waiting."

He sighed. "All right. Are you coming with me?"

She shook her head. "This is your ship, remember?"

There was a bit of rancor in that. He'd hired Skya to be his guide, to get him out of Ghitlas and to Nye. He had told her time was of the essence, and that he needed to be at Blue Isle within a month. She had laughed at him, and told him the best way was to go through Vion, and catch a ship out of Tashco on the Etanien continent, bypassing Galinas altogether. Her guidance had saved them months of travel. She was going to leave them in Tashco, but he had persuaded her to come to Blue Isle, a place she had never been.

At that point, they hadn't been lovers, but the possibility had been there. He liked to think she had made this trip for him, but she had never said that. He knew that her natural curiosity and distaste for rules might have been the thing that convinced her to come.

Also, knowledge of Blue Isle would make her much more valuable as a guide. She needed as much experience as possible. The Fey were not known as natural guides. It wasn't part of their magic. It wasn't really part of Skya's magic either, but that didn't seem to matter. She was born with a Spell Warder's talent—the ability to create spells for all types of magics, which meant that she had a little bit of all of the magics that existed among the Fey—but the Warders were also the most rule-bound of all the Fey. Such a job would have driven her crazy.

"It may be my ship," he said, "but I can always use your advice."

"I have no advice to give," she said. "I'll watch you maneuver through the Stone Guardians, but I'm still not sure they're as dangerous as you say."

He stared at her for a moment, measuring. She raised her eyebrows, then shrugged. "This is a new world for me, Gift."

He nodded. Just as everything had been new for him in

Vion and Etanien. She had been surprised at that. She had thought that the Heir to the Black Throne should have understood everything about the Empire. Now that he had traveled a lot, that concept made sense to him too.

But Arianna had never been off Blue Isle. She had no idea that women went shirtless in half the Empire or that there were still slaves in rebellious regions like Co.

To Arianna, Blue Isle had been the entire world.

It felt strange to be back here. Sometimes he questioned his own motives in returning. Was he coming back to solve a problem he didn't entirely understand? Or had the touch of the Black Throne done something more to him?

When he had wrenched his hand free of the Throne, it had emitted a white light that had triggered a series of Visions, Visions he could still see if he closed his eyes.

—His long-dead great-grandfather, sitting on the throne in Blue Isle, smiling at him—

—And his sister was standing before the Black Throne, looking at it with such longing that it frightened him. He wanted to warn her, to tell her to stand back, but he almost didn't recognize her or the look on her face. He took a step toward her—

—He was in water, thrashing, an undertow pulling him down. Water filled his mouth, tasting of brine and salt. The old Fey in the boat—his great-grandfather again? Or someone who looked like him?—reached for Gift, but if Gift took his hand, the old man would die. And Gift didn't want that. He didn't want to cause someone else's death—

—His sister, her face gone as if someone had drawn it and then wiped it away, calling his name—

—His long-ago best friend, the man to whom he'd always be Bound, Coulter, kissing a Fey woman, kissing her, and then Gift grabbing him, pulling his head back, and putting a knife to his throat. He had to—

—His sister, screaming—

—In the Places of Power, two Shaman stood at the door, preparing to find the Triangle of Might. He couldn't stop them. He was trying, trying, but he didn't have the strength—

"Gift?" Skya said.

"What?"

"You looked strange for a moment."

"I always look strange." He kissed her again, lightly, then headed toward the hold.

As he stepped into the large deckhouse, he nodded at one of the Nyeians braiding rope. This ship carried a larger crew than most ships, and it seemed as if most of the crew did nothing. But they were there for an emergency.

Gift had a cache of Weather Sprites to bring storms or to hold them back, five Navigators whose services he would probably need in a few moments, and a large group of Sailors to get him through the Guardians. Those were all magical Fey. Then there were the Tashil and Nyeian crew who actually tacked the sails and swabbed the decks, and did all the necessary manual labor. They had carried the bulk of the work on this trip.

The Bird Riders he had with him were also necessary for long ocean voyages. Most of the Riders he had were Gull Riders, although he had a few Hawk Riders for their strength and a few scattered Bird Riders from Sparrows to Pigeons to Robins who had come to him from various places on Etanien, all carrying messages from Seger.

Seger was a Healer who had served Gift's Fey great-grandfather, whom Gift's Islander father had eventually defeated in battle fifteen years before. Seger had proven loyal to Gift and his family by saving the life of Sebastian, a Golem that Gift considered to be his real brother.

Now Seger served as Arianna's Healer and sometimes advisor. The fact that Seger had sent for Gift—and by more than one messenger—told him that things were very bad indeed.

He was the Heir to Arianna's throne because, like him, she had never married and had no children. If they both died, the Black Throne would revert to his grandfather's oldest son, Bridge, whom his grandfather and great-grandfather had never trusted. That was on the Fey side.

On the Islander side, things were worse. If Gift and Arianna died without issue, the throne would go to someone who wasn't a direct descendent of the Isle's Roca.

Gift climbed down the steps, past the lower decks his hands on the rope railing. The steps became a rope ladder on the last part of the descent leading him into the darkness of the hold.

When he reached the bottom, he hurried down the narrow corridor to the mess hall. He pushed open the door to find the five Riders he had sent out. They were naked and in their Fey forms, their bird selves subsumed into their torsos. But they still had the look of birds. Their hair grew in a light feathery pattern down their backs and their noses curved like beaks.

The ship's captain, Wave—a Sailor who, at a hundred, had decided he was too old to send his consciousness into the sea—leaned against the wall. His powerful arms, tattooed in the L'Nacin tradition, were crossed against his chest and Gift could tell from the expression on his face that the news was bad.

"Well?" Gift asked.

One of the Gull Riders, a woman named Uhgse, looked over at him. Her dark eyes were beady.

"There's a lot of chop," she said, "and eddies that actually form holes in the surface of the water. The waves are hitting the stone at an incredible height. There's no clear way for the ship to make it through."

"It'd be like sailing in a hurricane," said Abdal, another of the Gull Riders.

But there was one Gull Rider Gift had come to trust more than the others. "Ace? What do you think?"

Ace, whose real name was Graceful, had taken one of the Domestic-spelled towels and was drying his hair. He stopped when Gift spoke to him.

"I think the surface always looks like that." He had a deep voice and warmer eyes than most of the Gull Riders. "I felt no wind while I was between the Guardians, but the air currents were unsteady. The weather's not bad enough to make the chop anything out of the ordinary. I think we trust our maps and go in."

Gift nodded. Ace had proven himself over and over. Originally, Ace had served Gift's uncle, Bridge. Then a Gull

Rider from Blue Isle had arrived on Bridge's ship, near death. Ace had taken her mission—to find and report to Gift about Arianna's troubles—and had completed it in record time. He had found Gift shortly after Gift had arrived in Etanien, in a place Skya insisted was impossible to locate.

"I won't go through chop and whirlpools with just a map for guidance," Wave said.

"Of course not," Gift replied. "We use all the Sailors and Navigators, and if we don't find a Ze, we don't go any farther."

"A Ze?" Ace asked.

"It's a fish," Gift said, "and it's native to these waters. Sailors have found it to be a useful guide through the currents around the Stone Guardians."

"You'd better find that Ze well away from those stones," Uhgse said. "We're not going to be able to anchor, and I'm afraid the currents'll pull us into the rocks."

"It's my job to worry about that." Wave gave her an odd look as he pushed past her. "I'll get the Sailors working."

"Good," Gift said.

Wave left the room.

"I've gone through the Guardians before," Gift said to the Riders, "and the water was as you described it. I suggest that you rest until we get into the currents, then Shift to your Gull forms and fly above us. You might see some things that will help us through."

"Are you worried about this?" Abdal asked.

"No more than any sane man would be," Gift said.

He left the room and headed back toward the ladder. The ship was rocking more than it had before, and he wondered if they were taking action too late. He'd heard that the currents of the Stone Guardians began far out at sea. Perhaps he should have sent the Riders out the day before.

He shivered once, then grabbed the ropes and pulled himself up. When he reached the deckhouse, he found Xihu.

She was a Shaman who had defied the rest of her kind to

travel with Gift. She felt the Black Family needed a Shaman, and since they had none, she had volunteered. She was younger than most Shaman, which put her in her nineties. Her face wasn't as lined as most, although she had her share of wrinkles. Her white hair frizzed around her skull, making her face look like the center of an explosion.

"What is it?" he asked. He was taller than she was, a sign that he had more magic, which always astonished him. He had been raised to believe that Shaman had the most power.

"A Vision," she said softly.

And then he saw the evidence: the tear tracks that lined her eyes, the moisture beside her mouth, the crease in her cheek where her face had rested against something.

He put a hand on her arm. She felt thinner than she had when they started this journey over six months before.

"Are you all right?"

She nodded, then led him out of the deckhouse.

Sailors were standing near the rails, holding their hands out so that their fingers could be pricked by the Navigator. Five Navigators would work with over twenty Sailors. The link between them was established through blood. Then the Sailors would send their consciousness into the water while their bodies remained on the ship. They would contact fish, and learn the gossip of the waters. In this area, the Ze had become the third part of the chain that went from Sailor to Navigator, who then imparted that information to the Captain. Other crew members would stand behind the Sailors' bodies and protect them so that they wouldn't get lost in the sea.

No one paid Gift or Xihu any attention. The Sailors and Navigators were too focused on the links; the remaining crew were too worried about failing to protect the Sailors after the links were finished. Still, it felt strange to be on deck with this many people.

"What was the Vision?" Gift asked.

"I've been seeing Blood against Blood." She was referring to the chaos that would descend on the world if Gift's

Fey family—the Black Family—fought against itself. The last time the Blood against Blood had happened, all but a handful of Fey had died at each other's hands.

If it were to happen now, the effect would be even more devastating, as the Fey Empire covered half the world.

He swallowed. "I won't attack my sister."

"It is more complex than that," Xihu said. "I am seeing your great-grandfather."

"Rugad's dead. He's been dead for fifteen years." But Gift's voice shook a little as he said that. He had Seen Visions of his great-grandfather as well—had been seeing them since his great-grandfather died near Blue Isle's Place of Power. "Maybe you've been seeing my uncle Bridge. He's on the Isle now."

At least, Gift assumed he was. That was where Bridge had been heading six months ago, according to Ace.

"Yes, I've heard the argument," Xihu said. "It could be you as well. There is a frightening similarity of features among the men in your family."

The Navigators had finished pricking fingers and pressing their own hands against those of the Sailors. The Sailors were assuming their positions against the rail. Gift looked past them. The mist was almost a rain now, but not worth troubling the Weather Sprites over. He could see the Stone Guardians in the distance, growing larger as they came closer.

"Tell me the Vision," he said.

Xihu folded her hands together. She looked toward the Stone Guardians, but seemed strangely unaffected by them. The mist dotted her face, and caught in the wrinkles, like dew.

"I heard voices first," she said. "Voices whispering that you'd come to destroy Blue Isle. Then I Saw arrows covered with blood, and I heard a woman's laughter. Then I Saw someone who looked like you, only it was a woman."

"Arianna," he said.

"With your blue eyes and a birthmark on her chin. She had a cruel face."

He frowned. Arianna did not have a cruel face. She had been impulsive and difficult, but she had never been cruel.

"Then she turned and sat in a throne that had a crest above it: two swords crossed over a heart. And she laughed. She said, 'Gift will never rule the Empire.' Her eyes were cold." For the first time since he had met Xihu, Gift thought he saw real fear in her face. "It was as if she had no soul."

A breeze rose, sending shivers through him. That didn't sound like Arianna at all.

"What else?" he asked. He knew there had to be more because Xihu was too silent.

"Assassins," she whispered. "I heard the voices of assassins, looking for you, trying to kill you to protect the Isle."

"Fey Assassins?" He had heard of them, but thought they were a myth.

She shook her head. "I could not tell."

"Who would hire assassins? Arianna, even if she has gone crazy, can't do that. And neither could my uncle. The Blood against Blood would affect them. They know that."

"Have you ever thought," Xihu asked softly, "that the messages you received were false? Perhaps your sister is fine. Perhaps someone only wants to kill you here, on the Isle."

He shook his head. "No one would want to do that."

"Why?" Xihu asked. "You've been to both Places of Power. Maybe someone is afraid you'll find the third."

Gift crossed his arms. The breeze had given him a terrible chill. "Who does that threaten?"

"All of us. Whoever finds the third Place of Power will create the Triangle of Might, which is supposed to reform the world. None of us knows what that means. There are ancient stories that say it means only the greatest of us will survive."

"And someone thinks I'm arrogant enough to place myself in that category?" Gift wiped the water from his face. "I set guards on the Place of Power here on Blue Isle. I lived near the Place of Power in the Eccrasian Mountains for five years. I never once tried to arrange a meeting between someone in Blue Isle's Place of Power and myself so that we could find the third Place of Power."

Xihu was silent for a long time. Then she closed her eyes. "It was merely a suggestion."

"Because of your Vision?"

She shook her head. "Because that is the second-greatest thing to fear about you, Gift."

"What's the first?"

She didn't answer him. She stood in front of him with her eyes closed, the mist beading on her face, and said nothing.

"What's the first?" he asked again.

She opened her eyes. There were tears in them. "That you will kill your sister."

CHAPTER TWO

ARIANNA SAT ON a small stone bench overlooking
the Cardidas River. It flowed red here, almost as if there
were blood in the water. She knew that the color came from
the stones beneath the surface and from the reflection of the
Cliffs of Blood above. But she found the water eerie anyway, considering how many people had died near here.

It was sunny, but the sunshine was not warm. Strange
that she could know the temperature but not really feel it.
She didn't feel much of anything these days. Not outside,
anyway.

Coulter and Seger had built her a body, and she had
put her consciousness inside it. The body was built out of
the same stone that made the river turn red. Only the body
didn't have red skin. Its skin was slightly grayish, very smooth
and cold to the touch. At least, that was what Coulter told
her.

From inside, it felt like her body, only wrapped in cotton
and unable to move with any speed. But it didn't function
like her body. She was a Shape-Shifter, and even though she

still remembered how to Shift form, this body wouldn't change.

Six months ago, she had thought being in the body would be temporary. Now she wasn't so sure. Rugad, the Black King, had tried to take over her mind. He had made the assault on her when she was fifteen. He was a Visionary like she was, and he had traveled across her brother Sebastian's Link into her mind. First Rugad had tried to take over her body by force, and when that hadn't worked, he had left a tiny bit of himself inside her brain.

That bit had been the equivalent of an infant then. In fifteen years, it had grown into the equivalent of a young man. It wasn't supposed to awaken inside her for another ten years, but something triggered it—a bright light with black threaded through it, a magical sending that had come from far away. If Rugad had waited another ten years, he would have subsumed her entirely, holding her body and her consciousness hostage forever.

Coulter, who was an Enchanter, had tried to kick Rugad out of her and failed. But Coulter did manage to carry Arianna's consciousness out of her body and away from the palace before Rugad could stop him.

The problem was that she lived inside Coulter's mind while her Golem body was being built. And, much as she cared for Coulter, the lack of privacy had driven her crazy. Just as this nonresponsive body was driving her crazy.

All of the people around her—Seger, Coulter, Con, Matt, and the other students at Coulter's school—treated her as if she were an invalid. She wasn't. She simply didn't have the mobility she'd had in her natural body. Or the power. Right now, all of Blue Isle—all of the Fey Empire—thought that she was still ruling the country. Her body was, but it was being guided and powered by Rugad, the most ruthless Black King of all.

She put her hands on the edge of the bench and leaned forward. It seemed to take forever to make the movement. She had to concentrate on speeding up these commands. She didn't want to move like Sebastian for the rest of her life.

Sebastian was a Golem too, but he had been formed as

an infant. He had his own personality, which was originally composed of bits of her brother Gift. Sebastian was a special type of Golem, one that Seger said was maintained by the Mysteries and Powers, a creature that had a life of its own. Whereas if Arianna left her Golem's body, it would remain immobile until she entered it again. Eventually it would revert to the stone it had once been.

Sebastian was the only one who seemed to understand how she felt. Sometimes he would sit with her and hold her while she wished she could cry.

Most of the time, though, she found herself on this bench, staring at the Cardidas. It was hard for her to believe that this river bisected all of Blue Isle. Yet right now the river seemed to be the only constant in her life.

And somehow, every time she sat here, she felt threatened. She knew that the capital city of Jahn lay only a few days from here by ship. She and Coulter, in making their escape from the palace, had left an easy-to-follow trail. Sometimes she thought Coulter did it on purpose. She thought Coulter wanted to lure Rugad to the Place of Power in the Cliffs of Blood and either kill him or trap him there.

Arianna wasn't so sure it would be that easy, but she was surprised that Rugad hadn't come. For all his power madness, Rugad believed in the Fey way. And the most important tenet of Fey Leadership was Vision. Arianna had it, and so did her brother Gift. That was how they were able to create and sustain Golems, how they were able to move their consciousness across Links between people, and how they were able to survive outside of their own bodies as long as their consciousness had a place to reside.

Rugad had had Vision when he was alive, but the bit he had left inside Arianna had none. He had told her, while they were sharing her brain, that he would force her to use her Vision to help him lead. Only she wasn't there anymore, and he was leading Blind. She couldn't believe that was something he would do for long. He had to find another Visionary or else come after her.

Maybe he had been sitting in Jahn for six months planning his attack. After all, he had waited twenty years after his son's defeat on Blue Isle before trying to take over the Isle himself. Rugad was known for his strategy, his cunning, and his patience.

She shuddered—or at least, she thought a shudder. All of Rugad's schemes looked at the long term. He had backup plan after backup plan. Rugad acted and schemed and took his time until he got things right.

Arianna had not planned anything in her life. Her decision to become Black Queen had been impulsive. She had even governed with short-term goals. First she had gotten the Fey Empire to accept a queen who was half Fey and half Islander. Then she had gotten them accustomed to peace. Then she had gotten them to develop the resources they already owned instead of conquering new ones.

She hadn't foreseen the problems that policy would bring, but she would wager that Rugad would have analyzed every aspect of it, from the results of success to the reactions of his own people. And he would have known the price of failure.

It was ironic that in many ways she had been reduced to little more than a brain. She had always been active, physically as well as emotionally. She always made the final decision— weighing options, examining cost—but she left the actual work of analysis to someone else.

Rugad never had. And right now, he stood poised to rule the Fey Empire for the next hundred years.

"There you are."

She didn't turn. Turning would have taken too much effort. She recognized Coulter's voice.

He sat down beside her. She envied his graceful movements, his unconscious fluidity. He was thoroughly Islander— short, round featured, blue eyed—and yet he was the strongest Enchanter she had ever encountered. In the fifteen years they had spent apart, he had learned how to control that magic and how to make it work.

He folded his hands together and studied the river. "Thinking of jumping in?"

He'd asked her that the first time he found her here,

months ago. She smiled and said what she had said back then. "I'd sink, but I wouldn't drown."

That was the nice thing about Golems. They couldn't really be killed.

He smiled at her. Whenever he looked at her, his expression was filled with a love so strong that she could feel it. Sometimes she wondered why he was still interested. She clearly wasn't the woman she had been.

Then his smile faded. "You're spending a lot of time here lately."

"I'm trying to learn how to think."

"You've always had an agile mind."

"Maybe. But now I need more than that." She leaned against the back of the bench and heard the grating as stone met stone. She winced, but Coulter didn't seem to notice. "Why do you think Rugad hasn't come for me?"

Coulter brought his legs up and wrapped his arms around them. He rested his chin on his knees. "I've been wondering that same thing for some time now."

"And you haven't come up with an answer?"

"Oh, I have." He continued to stare at the water. Sunlight reflected off it, creating diamonds of red light that played across his pale skin.

"Then why haven't you told me?"

He shrugged.

"Coulter," she said. "I could cross our Link and find out anyway."

They had originally designed the Golem as a place for her to go and be private. But Coulter had assumed, and perhaps she had as well, that she would keep up her residence in the corner of his mind he had set aside for her.

She couldn't tell him that she found it claustrophobic. Much as she cared for him, she became nothing when she was inside him. She had no control, no body, no freedom at all. At least in the Golem she was half a person.

"I wouldn't mind if you crossed it," he said, so softly that she almost didn't hear him.

She took his hand in her own, wishing she could feel

more than the pressure of his fingers. "Why do you think Rugad hasn't come?"

Coulter closed his eyes, briefly enough to seem like a long blink, but Arianna knew better. "I think he no longer perceives us to be a threat."

The words hurt. "I hadn't thought of it that way, but you could be right."

Coulter didn't respond. That seemed to be his way of dealing with the topic of Rugad. Saying nothing. Letting time handle it.

She stood slowly, so that she didn't overbalance and fall into the water below.

Coulter opened his eyes and looked up at her.

"I think we have to act before Rugad does," Arianna said, "and we have to be smart about it. We have to have a plan and a backup plan, and another plan after that. Fifteen years ago, we defeated him mostly with surprise. We can't do that anymore. He knows what the Isle is capable of. He knows what I'm capable of. Now's the time to be smarter than he is."

Coulter made a small snorting sound. "He's the greatest tactician your people have ever known and you believe that we can best him?"

"I do. My father beat him. We can do it if we need to. We can't hide here anymore."

"We can wait for him," Coulter said.

"How long? Months? Years? Until he finally decides to come to us?" She shook her head once. "I can't live like this that long, Coulter. He has conquered *me*."

"No he hasn't. You're right here."

"I'm more than just my mind, Coulter. In my own body, I can feel things. I can change form. I—" She stopped herself. She had almost said that she had a place of her own. She had said that to him once before, and he hadn't understood. He had thought the Golem was enough.

"We can't rush into this," Coulter said.

This time she did turn, and as she did, her foot slipped on the bank. She tried to catch herself, but the body didn't respond fast enough. She slid along the grasses and would have gone into the water if Coulter hadn't caught her.

She let him pull her back up. He cradled her against him.

"I can't even feel you touch me," she whispered.

"Sure you can," he said. "I've touched you from the back, and you felt it."

"Not like skin against skin. Not in any meaningful way." She sat up, making him release her. She brushed the dirt off her legs and back. Even that took longer than it should have.

When she finished, the words she'd been holding back for months finally came out. "When did you stop believing you could make a difference?"

He turned away, but not before she saw the look of pain cross his face. He stood up and ran his hands through his blond hair.

"I do make a difference," he said. "I teach children how to control their magic. Sometimes I'm the only parent they have."

"That's not what I'm talking about."

He didn't answer her. He stood with his back to her, his head bowed.

"It must have taken something pretty powerful to convince you to leave here, to come to Jahn and confront Rugad."

"That worked well," he said sarcastically.

"It did." She spoke quietly. "You saved my life."

Coulter shook his head. "He'd have let you live."

"While he controlled me. I couldn't break free of him. You got me out."

"And now he controls the Empire."

"As he would have whether or not you came. At least this way, he does it without my help. Without my Vision."

"Yet you want to go back there." Coulter spoke just as softly as she had.

"I don't want him to win."

"He did rule the Fey for seventy years, Arianna."

"He was a ruthless man who sacrificed thousands of lives, maybe millions, for a glory that no one needed."

"I've heard some of the Fey around here," Coulter said. "They want to go back to fighting. They think that peace robs them of their identity."

She clenched a fist. "And most of them, like Seger, are happy the generations of war are over. Why are you arguing for Rugad? Have you forgotten what he is?"

"I haven't forgotten," Coulter said.

"Then why?"

"Because—" Coulter's voice broke. "That way you stay here. You stay safe."

She felt the breath catch in her throat. Coulter had stayed safe ever since she had become Black Queen. What had he said to her then?

You can't have everything you want, Ari. Sometimes it's better to wait.

"See?" she said. "Safety. You said it again. If I listen to you, I give Rugad control over two Places of Power, the one in the Eccrasian Mountains and the one in the Roca's Cave. He'll find the third. He'll own the Triangle of Might, and if the Fey are right—if the world re-forms when someone creates that Triangle—then it'll be created in *his* image. Do you want that?"

Coulter's head was down. "We'll guard this place. Maybe he'll come here, and we can get him then."

"Maybe. Or maybe he'll go to the Eccrasian Mountains, get someone to murder Gift, and send someone else here. We'll lose everything that way, Coulter. Because you're being cautious."

He didn't answer her. She could hear his breathing, rapid and shallow as if he had been running. The river seemed faint behind it. Finally he sat on the bench. "Is this why you come here? To plan revenge against Rugad?"

"Revenge?" Arianna asked. "Against a man who violated me and who now threatens the entire world? That's not revenge, Coulter. That's survival."

Coulter's head was still bowed. He was silent for a long time.

Finally, she said softly, "Why won't you even try, Coulter?"

He ran his hands over his face. His entire body seemed to fold in on itself, and she saw, perhaps for the first time, how he must have looked as a child. Frail and vulnerable and unloved, a captive of the Fey, a curiosity that they held on to because he was Islander and had magic.

"Because I'll fail, Ari," he said.

The comment startled a laugh out of her. "You don't know that."

"Yes I do." His hands dropped from his face. He clutched his knees, staring down as he did so. "The first time I ever fought with my magic, I killed a hundred people to save five. And they didn't die fast either. I didn't do the spell right—"

"You didn't know how." Gift had told her this. He had thought Coulter a hero.

"—and they all died horribly. Then I helped your father attack Rugad's army with that beam of light, and he turned it back on us, and Adrian, the only father I ever had, died. I saw the light come back and I didn't stop it. I didn't do anything until he was already dead."

"He knew the risks, Coulter. He was fighting just like we were."

Coulter still didn't look at her. "And the spell that could still hurt us—the one that could ruin everything—is the one I did first."

She frowned, waiting.

"When your mother died, her Link to Gift hadn't been severed and he nearly died. I saved him, and wrapped us up together. We're Bound."

"I know," she said. "You've told me."

"But you don't seem to know what it means." Finally he looked at her. His cheeks were still red, his lower lip trembling so slightly that she almost didn't notice it. "It means that if I die, Gift will too. And if you happen to be inside my head at the same time, all of us will die. I'll kill you and Gift, and where will Blue Isle be then?"

Where would the Empire be then? she thought. Strange that he only mentioned the Isle.

"You're frightened," she said.

"Of course. Who wouldn't be?"

"You're frightened of yourself." She sat beside him on the bench. "You tell all the children who come to your school to trust their own abilities, to believe in themselves. You tell them that if their magic frightens them it will eat them alive, and yet you do none of those things."

"How do you think I understand them?"

She let out a long breath of air. She had let his fear infect her. Or perhaps the fact that they had shared his mind had made his emotions bleed into hers. For six months, she had been idle because she had listened to Coulter. For six months, she had let Rugad gain control of her Isle, her Empire. Her body.

It was time to fight back.

"I'm going after Rugad," she said, "and I want you beside me."

Coulter shook his head. "It's a risk . . ."

"We need to take risks."

"Some risks aren't worth it."

She stiffened. "Maybe not to you, but this is my life we're dealing with. My identity. My entire world. I have to fight for it. Whether or not you'll be beside me is up to you."

He didn't say anything. He turned back toward the river. The diamonds of light continued to play on his face.

"Fifteen years ago, you said you loved me. I've been inside your mind. I know it's true."

"Don't," he whispered.

"Would you ask me to sacrifice everything to stay beside you? Because you're afraid? Well, I can't, Coulter. And besides, you made me a promise in the palace garden the day you left me. Do you remember it?"

He looked at her. "I said I'd always be your friend."

He had, but she wasn't referring to that at all. "You said, 'Every Visionary needs an Enchanter at her side. I'll be yours.' Remember?"

His lips thinned.

"I need an Enchanter. I need *my* Enchanter. I need someone I can trust."

"You could be dooming us all."

"Staying here will doom us all. I'm going to give us a fighting chance."

He leaned back, a grimace on his face. "And what if we fail?"

"Then at least we've tried." She took a step closer to him. "Coulter, I can't *feel* anything in this body."

"I know. But I think I can find some way to fix that."

"I love you," she said and his eyes widened. She hadn't said that to him in fifteen years. "I want to be with you. I want to make love to you. I want to have children with you. I can't do that like this. Please, Coulter. If I stay here, I lose everything. I even lose you."

His face had gone white. He apparently hadn't realized what she meant, or how she felt. Or perhaps he hadn't believed it. They had shared themselves more intimately than most people ever did. He had to know, on some level, that she was telling the truth.

He swallowed, rubbed his face, then took a deep breath. "We need a plan," he said.

CHAPTER THREE

$\mathcal{B}$RIDGE TOOK THE last bite of his lunch and sipped water from the tankard in front of him. The eating nook in the family suite was large and cold, but Bridge knew better than to complain. Arianna would taunt him as she had before. She thought him weak and stupid, and she wasn't afraid to say so.

Arianna sat across from him, her posture cool and regal. She rubbed at the birthmark on her chin as if it itched, then finished the last of her bread and cheese. She hadn't said much to him all through lunch and he knew that she was wondering where his daughter was.

Lyndred hadn't come to lunch or breakfast either. She had become more withdrawn the longer they stayed at the palace. Bridge got the sense that his daughter was frightened of something, but she wouldn't tell him what.

One of the Islander servants bowed and refilled his water glass. Bridge had stopped drinking spirits here. He felt that he needed to keep his wits about him. As the weather had gotten worse, he had started drinking more root tea, even though Arianna called it the beverage of peasants, just as his grandfather Rugad used to. Sometimes Bridge got the sense that Arianna was his grandfather come back to life.

The very idea made him shudder. Rugad may have conquered more land than any other ruler, but he was an arrogant man who seemed to respect no one but himself.

"You will tell me where Lyndred is before the day is out," Arianna said. It wasn't a request. It was a command.

"I haven't seen her," Bridge said. "Perhaps the servants know."

"You haven't even bothered to look for her? Perhaps she's ill." Arianna's concern for Lyndred wasn't unusual. Arianna seemed to have taken to the girl.

"I don't think she's ill," he said. "I think she probably wanted some privacy. Lyndred's not used to life here on Blue Isle."

"Or in the palace," Arianna said. "I suppose you raised her in that awful Bank of Nye."

He started. Arianna had never been off Blue Isle. There was no way she could have known that the Black Family's palace on Nye had once been its central bank.

She startled him like that daily. There were things Arianna should not know and yet did. Things about the family, phrases that Rugad used, histories that no one should have been able to impart to her. Her mother, Jewel, had died when Arianna was born and her father was an Islander. Arianna was raised by Islanders, not Fey, and yet she seemed to be the purest Fey Bridge had met.

"I raised her in Nye, which was my mistake," Bridge said. "Nye is a weak country with little to recommend it—"

"I know. It always surprised me that you stayed there as long as you did."

"You told me to. I offered to come here when you became Queen, but you told me to stay in my position."

She raised her eyebrows slightly, something he had come to recognize as a sign of surprise. "And you listened to me?"

But he knew that wasn't what surprised her. She didn't remember sending that message. She didn't remember a lot of things. Islanders sometimes had to introduce themselves to her more than once, and then, when they left, they would remark on how poor her memory had become.

He had heard some of the servants say that she had suffered severe headaches just before he arrived, and that she had actually been in bed unconscious for several days. Her Healers had not been able to help her, and some thought it a magical attack.

When she awakened, Arianna blamed Seger, saying that Seger had tried to kill her. Seger had disappeared from the palace, but Arianna had not tried to find her. His niece was a strange mixture of ruthlessness and carelessness that he didn't pretend to understand.

"Well," she said after a moment. "Find Lyndred. She's not used to Jahn. She could have gotten herself into trouble."

Knowing his daughter, he thought that was too accurate for comfort. He stood. He wouldn't bring Lyndred to Arianna as he had been commanded, but he would make certain his daughter was all right.

He had almost made it to the door when Arianna said, "How long do you plan to stay on Blue Isle, Bridge? Until I die and you can make your daughter Black Queen?"

That had been awfully close to the original plan, until he had arrived and realized that his young daughter was no match for Arianna. So Bridge didn't answer her, nor did he turn so that she could see the truth in his face. Instead he opened the door and left.

Arianna's suite of rooms was on the farthest wing. For some reason, she had moved from the rooms she had occupied since she was a child to ones higher up and more protected. She had adopted other new habits as well, including taking most of her meals in her chambers alone or with her family.

He found the meals both inconvenient and intriguing. Inconvenient because he had to climb six flights of stairs, and intriguing because he never knew how Arianna was going to act.

He took the stairs down now, feeling the stone walls close in on him as he entered the older parts of the palace.

He reached the second floor and walked past portraits of round, blond people who had apparently ruled the Isle since time immemorial. The portraits were done in different styles, but the faces all looked alike until he came to Jewel's. His sister's portrait, done when she was not much older than Lyndred, looked startlingly like his daughter's face. Arianna had blue eyes and too much roundness in her cheeks to look like her mother.

Arianna had given Lyndred her old rooms on the second floor. They had a lovely sitting area in the front, and a bedroom in the back, all of which overlooked the garden. Not that the garden mattered much now. The winter had set in and everything was gray and bleak.

He paused in front of his daughter's door, then knocked. It took a long time before Lyndred pulled it open.

She looked drawn and tired, with circles beneath her eyes the size of fists. He didn't remember the last time she had eaten well.

"Are you all right?" he asked, his carefully planned speech abandoned at the sight of her.

She nodded.

"You don't look all right," he said. "What's going on?"

She took his arm and pulled him inside, closing the door behind them. The room was too hot; the fire that burned in the grate seemed unnecessary. The windows were closed and shuttered, making everything dark.

"Have you even eaten today?" he asked.

She shrugged, which was apparently a no. Her clothing was scattered about the chamber. A servant hadn't been in these rooms for a long time.

"What's going on?" he asked again.

"You're not going to tell her anything, are you?" Lyndred asked.

"You mean Arianna? Why should I?"

"I thought you came here because she asked you to."

"She did, but I really came because I'm worried about you."

Lyndred put a hand on his arm. "Let's go home, Daddy. Please. Let's get out of here."

There was a desperation in her voice that he had never heard, not even when he had spoken of coming to Blue Isle and she had done everything she could to stop it. She had Seen his death here, she said, and she had Seen herself having a child by a blond man, a man who somehow broke her heart.

"What happened?" he asked again. "Did someone hurt you?"

"No."

"Then what?"

"I just don't like it here. Please, Daddy. Let's go home."

He wished Lyndred was still a little girl so that he could pick her up and hold her. She was in such distress he didn't know how to take care of her now. So he did as he would with any woman who was upset. He put his arm around her, led her to one of the chairs, moved some clothes away, and helped her sit. Then he took the nearest footstool and sat on it, pulling it close.

"Tell me what you've Seen."

She bowed her head. "You sound like her. She makes me tell her all I See."

"That's normal, honey. Visionaries compare Visions."

"She's never told me what she Sees."

"That's her right."

Lyndred raised her head. "You don't understand, Daddy. I don't think she Sees anything. I think her Vision is gone."

Bridge took a deep breath. That made sense. The headaches, the long sleep, the lack of memory. He'd seen that happen to some of his older friends. Sometimes they lost the power of speech too, or the use of an arm. Perhaps something had ruptured inside Arianna's mind. And while she seemed awfully young for that to happen, she had an unusual heritage. And the Fey had never seen a cross that had resulted in a Shifter and a Visionary in the same person. Perhaps that dual magic had taken a toll of its own.

"Why does that frighten you, that her Vision is gone?"

"She can't lead with no Vision. And she can't continue to use mine."

Now they were getting to it. "Why not?"

"Because it's not right. I See my Visions, not hers."

That was technically true, but in those words there was a desperation that had nothing to do with ruling the Fey Empire and everything to do with Lyndred.

"And what did you see in your Vision?" he asked. "What don't you want Arianna to know?"

"Oh, Daddy." Lyndred bowed her head, but not before he saw the familiar look of surprise in her eyes. She was still his little girl, amazed that he could see through her.

"I won't tell her," Bridge said. "That's entirely your decision."

Lyndred rubbed her eyes with her forefinger and thumb, then shook her head.

"You should discuss it," he said. "I am a Visionary, even if I'm a small one. A shared Vision—"

"I know." She sounded irritated, but it was mostly reflex.

He waited. She gave a shuddery sigh, then said, "I watched her die."

His breath caught. "We all die, Lyndred. Sometimes we see that Vision."

She nodded. She knew that. He had made certain she was educated about her abilities. "She . . . crumbled, like sand does in someone's fingers."

He frowned but kept his hands on her shoulders, careful not to change the pressure. "Was she old?"

"She looked the same as she does now. Only grayer."

"Like stone?"

"I guess."

He didn't say anything for a moment, and neither did she. There was already one Golem on this Isle. He had heard of it long before he came. It was named Sebastian and it had been formed by Gift, but it had a life greater than Gift's. Like the Golems of old, the ones that were said to house the souls of dead Black Kings—

He shuddered, and Lyndred felt it.

"What is it?" He could hear the concern in her voice. "What did I say wrong?"

"Have you ever touched Arianna?" he asked.

"All the time. She puts her hand on my arm, or pulls me forward. It's strange, really. I mean, it's like she feels we're sisters or something."

He wasn't going to be sidetracked by that observation. He'd seen Arianna's attachment to Lyndred too, and had been unable to fathom it. But for the moment, he wanted to concentrate on Lyndred's Vision.

"How did her skin feel?"

"Like skin."

"Not too cold or smooth, like rock?"

Lyndred made a face of disgust. "No."

He let out a small breath. A Golem—even one with a life of its own—could be discovered by touch.

"Why?" Lyndred asked.

He shook his head, not quite willing to let go of the image. It would have explained so much: Arianna's oddly prescient knowledge, her use of Rugad's phrases, her similarities to him. But she was clearly her own person—and that person had a bit of Rugad in her.

None of Bridge's remaining siblings had any of their grandfather's personality. Nor did any of Bridge's children, or his nieces and nephews, at least the ones he had met on Galinas. Only Arianna seemed to have any bit of Rugad in her.

If she was like this, then how was Gift, the child raised by the Fey? He must have been very gentle, to want to be a Shaman. Or was he gentle only in comparison to his sister?

"You're being very quiet, Daddy."

"I was thinking," he said. "Was that all there was to your Vision?"

Lyndred sighed and her lower lip jutted out slightly. The expression was nearly a pout, but not quite, and not intentional. He'd seen that all her life. It was the expression she got when she didn't really want to share something, but saw no choice.

"There was a man who looked just like her, with the same eyes and everything, and he came here, to the palace. And then she crumbled, and then there was blood everywhere."

"By the Powers." Bridge's heart had started to pound.

"What does it mean, Daddy?"

"Did the man touch her? Is that why she crumbled?"

"No," Lyndred said. "It was three quick Visions. The first was of this man, coming to the palace. The second was of Arianna crumbling, and the third was of the blood. But they seemed to happen one right after another, like they were related."

Bridge knew better than to make a story out of Vision. He had been trained not to. But it seemed so easy, so logical with this one. Gift arrives, decides he doesn't like how Arianna is running everything and kills her, leading to Blood against Blood. Perhaps no one had warned Jewel's children of the dangers of war within the Black Family. Maybe they really didn't know.

Lyndred was staring at him as if she hadn't really seen him before. "It's bad, isn't it?"

"It might be," he said. "But I'm not an expert."

"There aren't any Shaman here. I've been spending all morning wishing for one. I'd like to talk to somebody who'd know, and who'd keep the secret."

Bridge wished she could. "There are no Shaman on the Isle," he said.

"Then we can go to Nye and consult one. Please? Let's leave."

He took her hands in his. They were cold and clammy, and she clung to his fingers tightly. "First, let me hear what else you've Seen. Was this the only Vision you had?"

"Today, yes."

"Have you ever Seen that man before?"

"The one who looks like Arianna?" Her lips thinned and she blinked hard. He thought for a moment that she was going to turn away, but she didn't. "He's the one who kills you, Daddy."

A shiver that he couldn't hide ran through Bridge. "He kills me— How?"

"In a boat. You drown, Daddy."

"He pushes me over?"

"He's there when you go in."

"And I drown."

"Yes."

"Does he try to save me?"

"I don't know."

Bridge's stomach twisted. "Do you actually see me die?" She shook her head.

He let out a small breath of air. Then maybe she wasn't seeing his death at all, but something important, some kind of turning point.

"And that's the only other time you've Seen this man?"

"No," she whispered.

"What else have you Seen?"

"He's holding a baby, a newborn baby, and he's crying."

Bridge wished even harder for a Shaman. None of this made any sense, and he hadn't had any Visions to compare with it. "Before or after I fall into the water?"

"I don't know," she said. "He looked the same in all the Visions."

"Were there any more?"

"No." She sounded sad. "What does it mean, Daddy?"

"I wish I knew, honey. It sounds like you're describing Arianna's brother Gift."

"The one who wanted to be a Shaman?"

"Yes."

"But I thought a Shaman can't be violent."

"You think he's violent?"

"He kills her. He kills you."

"But you never Saw him actually hurting us."

"Everything happens because of him."

Bridge froze. He'd heard that before, long ago, in his training as a Visionary and a Leader. That phrase was one to pay attention to. "How do you know that?" he asked. "Did anyone say that in your Visions? Did anyone imply it?"

She shook her head. "I just know it. He's the center of it all."

The center was different than being the cause. Rugad used to say that Jewel was a center, and Bridge was jealous of that. He hadn't understood it until his sister died. Maybe not even until Rugad had died. For if Jewel had stayed on Nye as she was supposed to, the Black King would probably still be alive. Bridge certainly wouldn't be sitting in this palace worrying about Arianna, who would never have been born.

The entire fate of the Empire had turned around Jewel, as, apparently, it would now do around her son.

"That's important, isn't it, Daddy?" Lyndred said.

For all her youth, she knew how important it was.

"You weren't hiding from Arianna because of the death Vision, were you? You were afraid it would come out that her brother is the center."

Lyndred's eyes filled with tears. He kept a firm hold on her hands. A tear ran down her cheek, and finally, he pulled her close. She was so tall now, so thin. His daughter had been just a tiny girl only an instant ago. Now he could barely hold her close, she was so lanky and strong.

After a few moments, she sniffled and pulled away. "You think I'm silly."

He shook his head. "I'm not quite sure what the tears meant, but no, I don't think you're silly."

She smiled just a little. All her life, he had said that to her, about not being sure what caused her tears. Once he had confessed that he knew nothing of girls and it had startled a laugh out of her, a laugh he could sometimes get her to repeat.

Lyndred swallowed so hard he could see her throat move. "What if," she said, and took a breath, as if just forcing the words out would make something come true. "What if I tell her this, she decides she hates him, and that's what causes all the blood?"

It was a legitimate fear. That was the dilemma with Visions after all, trying to figure out when to tell, and when not to; when to heed them and when to ignore them. It was one of the most difficult things about being a Visionary.

He thought for a moment. "There's no hurry, is there?"

"She'll want to know what I've Seen. She asks me every day if I've had a Vision."

He started. That wasn't normal. "Every day?"

Lyndred nodded.

"And that's why you're hiding?"

Lyndred nodded again, then bit her lower lip. "So she'll know, right? She'll know why I've been hiding from her."

Arianna was smart. Of course she'd know. He ran a hand through his hair. "Not if you get real sick, sweetie."

"Why wouldn't I call a Healer?"

"Because you couldn't?" He sighed. Lyndred was right. Arianna would see through that as well. He was never good at subterfuge. He ran a hand through his hair. "One thing at a time. Is there any other reason to tell her quickly?"

"You haven't heard the rumors?"

He'd heard a lot of rumors. This place seemed to thrive on them. "Which ones?"

"The ones that say Gift is coming back. They sent for him before we came."

He had forgotten. The Gull Rider who arrived on his ship had had a message for Gift, and she had told Bridge to hurry to Blue Isle. He had thought then that she was implying Arianna was going to die, and when he saw Arianna healthy, he thought no more about it. But he had sent one of his best Riders in her place to find Gift. And if the message was for Gift to return, he would be getting to Blue Isle in the next few months.

"That complicates things," Bridge said. He thought for a moment while Lyndred watched him. Usually she snapped at him when he did that, because her mind worked so much quicker than his. It was a sign of how much she needed his advice that she let him go at his own pace.

What would his father have done? Better yet, what would his grandfather have done?

They would have looked for the thing that wasn't obvious. The piece of the puzzle everyone else overlooked.

His daughter was worrying about talking to Arianna, about telling her the wrong thing as Gift returned to Blue Isle. But that wasn't the central problem. The central problem was that the Fey's great Visionary was asking an eighteen-year-old girl what her Visions were. Daily. Which meant either that Arianna was having constant Visions herself or that she was having none.

If she was having constant Visions someone would have noticed. The Visionary fell forward, eyes rolled in the back of the socket, hands twitching. It could happen anywhere. He had heard from some of the other Fey that Arianna had tried to keep her Visions private for the sake of the Islanders who weren't used to such things, but even a minor Visionary like Bridge knew that sometimes Visions couldn't be held back, and couldn't be had in private.

"Have you ever seen Arianna have a Vision?" he asked.

Lyndred shook her head. "But she saw me once."

He didn't doubt that. He'd seen Lyndred have one after they'd arrived. It seemed as if Lyndred's Visions had increased tenfold since they set foot on Blue Isle.

"You know, Daddy, she didn't want us here until she saw me. Until she discovered that I had come into my Vision."

He had forgotten that. The look in Arianna's eyes when she saw Lyndred for the first time. What had she said? *I don't believe in courtesy. I believe in expediency. And it's obvious you might have information that's useful to me.*

Bridge had always thought Arianna had meant his trip and the Gull Riders. But her cold blue eyes had become speculative when they saw Lyndred, and Lyndred had bragged that she was a Visionary.

Perhaps we could compare Visions sometime, Arianna had said. But they never had compared Visions. Lyndred had been supplying them all.

He shook himself, then clenched his fists. Acting without knowledge was as dangerous as trying to interpret a Vision, maybe more so when discussing Blindness in a Black Ruler.

"We need more information, Lyndred," he said. "Before I can help you with these Visions, we need to know if Arianna is having any. We need to know for certain."

"How can we learn that?"

Bridge squared his shoulders. He hated sending his daughter into a battle, even a verbal one, with someone like Arianna, but he had no other choice. "You'll have to ask her for some so that you can compare. Say you feel odd, not having heard anyone else's Visions since you've arrived."

Lyndred was biting her lower lip so hard the skin around it was turning gray. He leaned forward and rubbed his finger against her chin, like he used to do when she was little. She stopped biting and licked her lip as if it hurt her.

"I don't want to sound like I'm quizzing her."

"Then don't," Bridge said. "Make it casual."

Lyndred nodded, looking vaguely ill. She was afraid of Arianna; that was becoming clear. Bridge was too. Arianna could do nothing to them. They were members of the Black Family, related by blood.

Still, Rugad had found ways to get rid of family members he didn't like. Accidental ways. Oversights. Allowing someone to make a mistake that Rugad knew would result in banishment or death.

Arianna had some of that cunning in her.

"I'll do what I can, Daddy." Lyndred sighed, then ran a hand through her hair. "Though I'm not going to tell her anything until we decide."

"Until we're sure," he said. "I don't want to give her information the Powers believe she should not know."

He didn't want to give her ammunition either. If she was ruling Blind, then Lyndred couldn't be her eyes.

"Now," he said. "We need to figure out what to tell her about your absence this morning."

Lyndred smiled. "We'll just tell her I was in bed."

"She won't believe you. You didn't call a Healer."

"I'm not going to say I was ill. There are just some times a person doesn't want to get out of bed. Especially when she's not alone."

He flushed. He didn't want to think of his daughter that way, and yet he knew she'd had lovers already. That Nyeian poet who wanted to marry her was the worst, but Bridge had worried most about the Gull Rider on the trip over. Fortunately, he'd found a way to get the Gull Rider off the ship.

"Is there someone here?" he asked.

Lyndred's smile faded a little. "No. And there won't be either."

She spoke with a firmness that she hadn't had a moment ago. He believed her. Her Vision, the one of the child, had so terrified her that she didn't want to come to Blue Isle at all. Maybe that was the one good thing that would come out of this trip. Lyndred's interest in men would decline and she would finally accept herself.

"Arianna might want to know who you spent the night with."

"That's one thing not even the Queen needs to know," Lyndred said with a haughtiness that actually sounded like Arianna.

He leaned over and hugged his daughter. "You'll do fine, you know."

"I hope so." She spoke so quietly he could barely hear her. "Because otherwise, this conversation might be construed as treason."

"It's not treason. We're not talking about overthrowing the Black Queen."

"Oh, really?" Lyndred pulled back just enough so that she could look at his face. "What do we do then, if we learn that she's Blind?"

That was the question. If it was true, a bloodless coup was the only answer. And if Arianna was anything like Rugad, such a thing might be impossible.

"We'll face that if we need to," he said. "Until then, we remain loyal to our Queen."

CHAPTER FOUR

MARKOS LEANED AGAINST the waist-high stones and stared at the ocean below. Water frothed and boiled. The rain was heavier now, slanting sideways with the wind, hitting his face like small needles. He was cold too, and he had no idea how long it would be before someone relieved him.

He could barely see the Stone Guardians and he was as close to them as a man could get on land. He stood at the edge of the natural bowl where the trouble all started. In the center of the bowl, on the flat stone surface, King Alexander had set up tables and sold his son to the Fey.

Prince Nicholas had copulated with the enemy and created two demon children: a woman who now ran the country, and a son who had gone to the Fey to learn how to be Black King.

Now the son was returning, and those who knew said he would destroy the Islanders once and for all. He would wipe out his father's people and let the Fey overrun the Isle. Just as his great-grandfather had tried to do fifteen years before.

The world Markos had been born into was not the world in which his father had been raised. Blue Isle, its religion, its customs, its traditions, were no more, all destroyed at the hands of the Fey.

The Fey, it seemed, were everywhere. He'd even seen some of the most unnatural ones, the ones that were part bird, flying around the Guardians. He'd thought that suspicious, until he mentioned it to Doron. Doron had smiled.

If we know that the Black Queen's brother is coming, don't you think she does too? She'll want to give him a proper escort.

As if half-birds were a proper escort. Markos shivered. He was tempted to use his bow and arrow to pick off some of the unnatural creatures, but he restrained himself. Doron's instructions were that no one call undue attention to this mission. And so far, everyone had listened to Doron. Doron was the best leader the freedom fighters had ever had.

The Fey made freedom fighting exceptionally difficult. When Markos was five years old, the Black King of the Fey had come to Blue Isle and destroyed everything. Some Islanders had fought back, exploding a Fey weapons store, and the Black King had retaliated by burning every building in the center of the Isle.

Markos remembered that fire. He remembered watching the Fey soldiers set fire to his house, killing his father. His mother, holding Markos against her, had hidden them in the root cellar. Her hand had smelled of dirt and sweat, her fingers digging into his skin. Through a small opening in the cellar door, they had watched his father die and had seen everything they owned destroyed.

The Fey who had done it had laughed.

For years after that no one rose up against the Fey. Some said things would get better because King Nicholas's half-breed daughter ran the country. They said that even though she was Fey, she was raised Islander and would make sure all the traditions remained.

But the Rocaanist kirks remained empty. The Auds were dead. A few Danites practiced in secret, but everyone knew that to practice the religion was to court the wrath of the Fey. Occasionally the half-breed Queen would issue decrees, and while they made the land more fertile, a lot of the crops now went off Island, to places Islanders had never been. Some Fey were even marrying Islander women, destroying the purity that had been the Isle's hallmark from its very beginning.

Occasionally, there would be resistance to the Fey. Someone would stand up, refuse to do things the Fey way. Then visitors would come, usually Islander ones who would convince the rebel that the only way to do things was to play along.

Now, it was said that the half-breed brother was returning, having learned all the Fey tricks from his uncles on Galinas. He would begin where the Black King left off, destroying all the remaining Islanders. He'd been raised Fey, and he was coming here with the express purpose of making Blue Isle a completely Fey stronghold.

Doron held a meeting of all the dissatisfied Islanders he knew and asked them if they wanted to strike a blow against the Fey. Those who didn't were asked to leave. The remaining group—twenty that night, thirty by the next—agreed that this might be their only chance.

There was the risk of retaliation, of course. Doron had mentioned that too. But Queen Arianna had shown herself remarkably lenient with criminals. It was the hope they could all rely on. That, and the fact that if they succeeded, her brother—the one with all the Fey training—would be dead.

It was what kept Markos standing here in the rain, letting the cold water drip down his back. Doron's plan, the hope it provided, and that laugh—the one he still heard whenever he closed his eyes. The Fey thought they had conquered Blue Isle. They thought they could destroy it.

They were wrong.

"Hey, Markos!"

He turned. Blasse stood behind him. Blasse was a large man, but with his hair plastered down by rain, his beard dripping, he looked much smaller. He had a bow over his shoulder, and his quiver was full of arrows.

"You really think anyone'll come through the Guardians in this weather?"

"Not anyone intelligent," Markos said. "But when has that stopped the Fey?"

He moved away from his perch. Blasse came over, scanned the river for a moment, and sighed. He didn't want to be out in that weather any more than Markos did. "For the last week, there's been nothing. You think the rumors were true?"

It was the closest the group came to questioning Doron.

"Sometimes I wonder," Markos said. "But what if we give up and the next day the Fey ships come through the Guardians?"

Blasse grunted. He wasn't a deep thinker. But, like Markos, he'd lost his entire family to the Fey when he was a boy. He'd spent most of his adulthood living in parts of the Isle where there weren't a lot of Fey. Those parts were growing scarcer.

"I saw a lot of those half-bird Fey creatures," Markos said. "That Hawk with the woman on its back spent half the morning sitting on that stone over there, staring at me."

"Should have killed it."

"How do you kill those things? Shoot it through the bird heart or through the Fey heart?"

Blasse shrugged. "Maybe both."

"Besides, I'm saving my killing for the half-breed."

"The Fey'll know you did it."

"They'll know we all did it. That's why we've got to follow Doron's plan."

They weren't allowed to discuss the plan any more than that, at least not out here.

Blasse grunted again and blew some water off his lips. "I hope none of them bird creatures come around tonight. I'm getting itchy enough to make 'em into target practice."

Markos ran his fingers over his eyes. He was wet and cold. He'd be glad to get back to the abandoned kirk and sit in front of the small fire the men allowed at night. Some sleep, and he'd be back in the morning.

There were other archers stationed at other points along the river. If Markos or his group didn't stop the Fey ships with the half-breed on them, someone else would. The Queen's brother would never make it to Jahn.

As he moved his fingers away from his eyes, he turned his head toward the Guardians. Something black peeked out of the tunnel made by the tallest stones.

"My God," he said. His heart started pounding. He hadn't believed, until this moment, that the half-breed would actually come.

"What?" Blasse asked.

Markos pointed. Blasse leaned forward and squinted. The black shape that Markos had seen revealed itself as the prow of a ship. It was riding the chop, sails up, spray surging over the bow as if the water alone could wash the Fey off the ship.

Blasse stepped back, his hands shaking. He tried to pull his bow off his shoulder, but his fingers slipped on the string. It slid down his arm, but he caught it before it clattered to the ground.

Above them a Hawk with a Fey on its back swooped over the two men, uttering its distinctive cry. Markos watched it for half a moment, recognized the woman on its back, and groaned. Had she heard the remarks about target practice? If so, they might be dead soon.

But she didn't seem interested in them. Instead, she flew directly for the ship. Markos watched until she became a speck in the air, riding the currents, the tips of her wings upturned. After a moment he realized that anyone watching her from the ship itself would see only a hawk, not the Fey riding it.

He thought that strange, almost as if she were concealing herself.

"I think there's only one ship." Blasse was trying, with his shaking hands, to thread an arrow in his bow.

Markos pulled his bow down and looked too. Blasse seemed to be right. Unless the others were farther back in the Guardians. But that seemed dangerous. Ships that came through the Guardians usually followed closely in each other's wake so that they could catch the same currents.

Markos gripped his bow. His hands weren't shaking. He had waited all his life for this moment. He threaded his first arrow and watched as the ship drew closer.

It rode forward, taking the waves as if it were daring them to overturn it. At times he could barely see the ship for the spray. The ship had cleared the last of the Guardians and was making its way from the harbor into the river. The Cardidas was wide and flanked on both sides by cliffs. But the ship still had to follow a relatively narrow path to take it to Jahn.

As it came closer, he cursed the way that the rain interfered with his ability to see below him. Blasse had grown silent too, aiming at the ship, his hands still shaking. Only Markos seemed to have any chance of hitting anything.

"Don't worry," he said. "If we miss, there are others downstream who'll get them."

Blasse nodded. He rested his elbows on the stone ledge before him, and that eased his shaking somewhat. Markos decided that was a good position, and did the same.

The ship was moving into range.

Other bird-Fey were flying above it, almost as if they were leading it forward, cawing and shouting. He couldn't make out the words, not that he would have understood them if he did. He'd always made it a point not to learn the Fey's cursed language.

"How do we tell which one is him?" Blasse asked.

Good question. For some reason no one had thought of it until now. And it was an important question, too, because they didn't have that many arrows, and he didn't know how long it would take before those Gull-Fey flew up to the bowl and tried to kill them.

"Let's shoot the guy who's steering," Markos said. "That'll slow them down. If the half-breed is on the deck, the others'll rush to protect him. If he's not, he'll come up fast and then we'll get him."

Blasse nodded. They waited in silence for the ship to pull

closer. Markos felt his stomach quiver, but his hands remained steady. The cry his father had made when they set
fire to the house resounded in his memory. That and the
Feys' laughter.

The ship was in position.

"All right," Markos said. "Now."

He had the target in his sights. He pulled the arrow back
and released it as Blasse did the same. They moved in unison, reaching behind their backs for another set of arrows
from their quivers, threading them, and shooting before the
first arrows had found their marks.

They hadn't needed the second shots. The first arrows
both hit the Fey behind the wheel and he fell, startling those
around him. Markos could hear the shouts echoing off the
canyon walls. The few Fey lying oddly against the rail didn't
move—were they already dead?—but some of their sup-
porters did.

The men in the middle didn't seem to move at all. But
one, toward the front, looked up. He scanned the walls of
the cliffs, and then his gaze stopped. The ship was directly
below Markos when the man pointed to the hiding spot.

Markos had another arrow lined up. So did Blasse.

"That's got to be him," Markos said.

"We have to be sure," Blasse said.

The bird-Fey were still moving forward but a few of the
Fey on the ship had moved to the edge of the deck and were
shouting at them, and waving their arms.

"We don't have time to be sure," Markos said.

And then it seemed as if God smiled on him. Two of the
Fey grabbed the pointer's arm and tried to pull him below
deck.

"You're right," Blasse said. "That's him."

Together they aimed, and let their arrows fly.

Chapter Five

*T*HE FIRST ARROWS killed the Captain. Gift had been standing beside Wave as one of the arrows went through his throat. The Navigators around him screamed and a few seemed to lose their concentration. Some of the Fey behind the Sailors ducked.

Gift looked toward his left as two more arrows hit the deck. They had come from the cliffs. He scanned until he saw the bowl where his parents had negotiated the treaty that had united the Fey and the Islanders. He thought he saw movement.

He pointed, and as he did, two Fey grabbed him, and tried to pull him backward. He shook them off. The ship was out of control, heading toward the rocky shores.

"You!" he said, shoving one of the people away from him. "Get the wheel. Get us on course."

"I don't—"

"Do it!"

The man ran toward the wheel. The other was still holding Gift. He shoved the man away as more arrows flew, dangerously close.

There was no way of telling how many archers stood above them.

"We have to get this thing out of here," Gift said. "Get those people off the deck. They need to help the Sailors. Make sure the Navigators are working—and all of you, call to the Gull Riders."

An arrow hit the man Gift had been yelling at. The tip protruded from the man's stomach and he looked at it stupidly, as if he couldn't believe it was there. Then he fell to his knees, and watched the blood run with the rain across the deck.

Arrows landed near Gift, and he suddenly realized he was the target. The man he had directed to the wheel was trying to turn it, but not doing a very good job. Gift hurried toward him, figuring that as long as he moved, he was not in any danger.

Skya had come on deck. Gift cursed softly. He didn't want her here. He hurried to her, put his arms around her, and pushed her toward the deckhouse.

"They'll kill you," he said.

She raised a single eyebrow. "Looks to me like someone is trying to kill you."

The man was still struggling with the wheel and the ship was losing momentum. If no one did anything, they'd be stuck here, easy targets for the archers above.

Skya saw it too, and went for the wheel, but Gift held her back. "Wave died there."

"We'll all die here if someone doesn't do something."

Some of the Fey on deck were shouting for the Gull Riders. The Sailors were still in position, two of them with arrows in their backs.

Gift shoved Skya toward the stairs. "Get the Nyeians. One of them can steer."

She started to protest, but he shoved harder. He went for the wheel himself, but the man who was steering shook his head. "I'm getting it!"

The ship was listing to one side. A wave came up over the deck, washing the man with the arrow through his stomach overboard. One of the Fey women—a young one—screamed.

Arrows were spraying the entire area around Gift. One of them hit a Navigator who collapsed like a puppet with its strings cut.

Then Skya was back on deck. She grabbed Gift and flung him aside as if he weighed nothing. She held him underneath the overhang. "If you die, we all die. You're staying here."

One of the Gull Riders landed, and skidded across the wet deck. He ended up near Gift's feet.

It was Ace.

"Find them," Gift said. "Find whoever is shooting those arrows. Who sent them. Why they're here."

Ace nodded and flew off. Gift watched for a moment. The rain was coming in at an angle as the wind picked up. The drops were spattering his face, making it hard to see.

They weren't shooting anymore. They were waiting for him to come out.

On the deck at least a dozen Fey clutched wounds and moaned. A Nyeian came up the stairs at a run, saw the devastation and started down again.

Gift grabbed him by his ruffled shirt.

"You're going to steer us out of here."

"There's no steering," the Nyeian said. "We're sideways."

"Fix it."

"I'm not good—"

Gift shoved him forward. The Nyeian stumbled, and then staggered toward the wheel. He moved the Fey who'd been trying to steer, glanced nervously at the cliffs, then used his scrawny arms to turn the wheel the other direction.

Arrows rained down, one hitting the Nyeian. He fell back, screaming.

"They're not going to let us out of here," Skya said.

The Gull Riders were flying toward the cliffs. The arrows had stopped again. Apparently the archers were conserving ammunition.

Gift knew how to resolve this, but he didn't want to. It meant costing a life. But he had a shipload of people—and an entire country—to think about.

"You!" he said to one of the Fey holding up a Sailor. It was a man about his height. "Come here."

The man did. Gift pulled him into the deckhouse.

"What's your name?"

"Rudolfo."

A young man, named in the Nye tradition. His lower lip was trembling.

"Do you believe in the Empire?" Gift asked, the words sounding strange to him.

"Yes, sir."

"We're going to die if we stay here."

"I know that, sir."

"What are you doing?" Skya hissed.

Gift ignored her. "I'm a target. They're running out of ammunition above. I need to get rid of the rest of it."

"You want me to be a decoy." Rudolfo's voice had more confidence than his body did.

"Yes," Gift said. "Stay low. Act as if you're giving orders."

Rudolfo nodded. He started out, but Gift stopped him.

"Wear my jerkin," Gift said.

Skya turned away as if she were angry. Gift pulled off his jerkin, hoping they were far enough back that the archers couldn't see this from above.

"I thought you didn't believe in Black Family supremacy," Skya said.

"Oh, I only get to use it when it suits you?" Gift snapped, as he handed the jerkin to Rudolfo.

"At least I don't kill anyone."

Rudolfo winced. Then he slipped on the jerkin, and put a hand on Skya's arm.

"I'm proud to die for my people," he said, and crossed the deck.

The wood was slippery with blood and rain. Spray crashed over the side as another wave crashed into the bow.

The Nyeian slid along the surface, stopping as he hit the feet of a Sailor on the port side.

Arrows fell, following Rudolfo, but he zigzagged enough, his movement unpredictable. One seemed to graze him, but didn't hit hard.

Gift hurried to the wheel. Skya yelled at him, but he didn't stop. He had no idea what he was doing, knowing only that someone had to right this ship or they all would die.

"Skya!" he yelled. "Get the Nyeians up here. All of them. I don't care how frightened they are."

She nodded and ran below. Gift struggled with the wheel. It slid beneath his fingers, heavier than he thought. He had to put his whole weight into it to get it to move. Not that he was sure which direction to turn it.

The Navigators were no help. They issued instructions, their eyes glassy, as if the Captain were still there to hear. They probably didn't even know that the ship was under attack.

Arrows continued to fall around Rudolfo. The ship rolled and pitched, marring the archers' aim. For that, Gift was thankful. The archers were clearly good shots; they had killed Wave instantly.

The ship seemed to be turning away from the cliffs and heading toward the center of the river. Gift glanced behind him. The sails were billowing, and one had a large rip in it.

Skya was at his side again, a Nyeian beside her. The man looked terrified.

"Steer this thing!" Gift shouted.

The Nyeian took the wheel. There were other Nyeians behind him, all standing near the stairs, looking shocked. The deck was a mess of water and blood and bodies.

Rudolfo was still moving. He reached the port side of the deck and suddenly an arrow caught him in the hip. He screamed and rolled on his side, clutching his leg.

Gift braced for the next arrow to hit, but it didn't come. Rudolfo pulled himself toward one of the small emergency boats where he'd get a bit of shelter. No one else seemed to notice that he'd been hurt.

The Nyeian had the ship moving forward at a fast clip. Gift had no idea how he'd done it.

Gift glanced up at the cliffs, saw the whiteness of gulls against the sky, and nothing else. He started toward Rudolfo, but Skya grabbed his arm.

"Maybe they realized it wasn't you."

He had no idea how they would know that, but he didn't argue. Rudolfo was leaning against the boat, his hand around the arrow shaft.

The Fey who were supporting the Sailors were looking up as well, as if they expected to be hit at any moment. The waiting was almost as bad as the assault.

Then a Gull Rider landed on deck, white feathers saturated in blood. The gull's head was almost black and some of the blood had congealed, despite the rain.

The Rider shifted back to his Fey form, growing to his full height, the bird body absorbing into his stomach. It was Ace. His naked body was covered with scratches, but as he shifted, the blood started washing off, leaving a pinkish trail on the deck.

"There were only two," Ace said.

"Were?" Gift asked.

Ace nodded. "They were Islanders."

That surprised Gift. "Did they know who we were?"

"Yes." Ace's response was curt. "They were trying to kill you."

"Me?" That made no sense. He was an Islander. His father had been a beloved king.

"They think you're bringing in a new invasion force. They think you're going to kill all the pure Islanders and cover the Isle with Fey."

"Where would they get that idea?" Gift asked.

Ace shrugged.

"How did they know we were coming?" Skya asked. "Have you sent messages, Gift?"

"No." Gift ran a hand through his wet hair. "Were they working alone?"

"There's a group of them. I couldn't find out how many.

They weren't that forthcoming, and they died faster than I expected."

That last sent a slight shiver through Gift.

"But they did say that there are more archers waiting along the river."

"Wonderful," Gift said.

"It's good to know," Skya said. "At least now we'll be ready for them."

"The river narrows farther ahead. We'll be easier targets."

"I don't think the two sent any messages off before we killed them," Ace said.

"Good." Skya put a hand on his arm. "Then the others won't know we're coming. We can get them before they get us."

"Maybe along the river," Gift said. "But we need to find the source of this rumor, find out how fast it's spread, and what we can do about it. I'm not going to watch my back in my own home."

"I think you're going to have to do that anyway," Skya said. "Obviously some people don't want you here."

Gift frowned and looked at the cliffs. "Ace, get the Bird Riders together and scout the cliffsides. We need to know whether there are any more archers ahead."

Ace nodded, and shifted back to his gull state. Then he took a run along the deck, and flew off.

"You should have let him rest," Skya said.

"I don't think we're going to get a chance to rest," Gift said. "I think it's going to take everything we have to survive."

Chapter Six

*C*OULTER'S STOMACH WAS churning as he walked back to his school. The building had once been a single stone house, but over the years he'd added rooms. Now it looked like several stone houses pushed together, with a dirt magic-yard that in any other place would be a garden or a playground in the very center.

He'd left Arianna at the river. For the first time, he was glad she was no longer residing in his head. He didn't want her to know how upset she had made him.

He understood her points. In fact, he knew she was right. But to do what she wanted meant he had to ask people he cared about to risk their lives, to follow a plan that probably wouldn't succeed.

But he had known, deep down, that waiting was wrong. That Rugad was too smart to return here, the place where he had died. He would know that inside the Roca's Cave, the place the Fey called the Place of Power, he would probably die again.

There were all sorts of magics inside that cave, all developed by Rocaanists to get rid of magical beings. It was a strange tautology: magic, which helped form the religion, became its anathema. But in order to wipe out the magic, the religious had to use magic.

Coulter could only think of one tool in the Roca's Cave—or at least, the one tool he understood—that would get Rugad out of Arianna's body, and that was the Soul Repository. Somehow, Matthias, the Fifty-first Rocaan, had used one of those dolls to trap Jewel's soul. Coulter wasn't sure how he did it, but he knew there was a magic—or a religious ritual—that provided for it.

Matthias's son, also named Matthias, was an Enchanter like his father had been. But unlike his father, young Matt was receiving training so that he could learn how to control his magical abilities. Control was the essence of all magic, Fey and Islander. Without control, the most magical, like Enchanters, often lost their minds.

Coulter didn't expect young Matt to have a quick answer to explain how to work the dolls, but Coulter did know that Matt had access to the Vault beneath the Cliffs of Blood. The Vault was where the Secrets of the Rocaanist religion were stored. Matt's father had become keeper of that Vault until his death half a year ago. Now his other son, Alexander, had taken his place.

Alex, like his father, hated the Fey and feared all things magical—despite the fact that Alex had great Vision. He saw it as a curse rather than something he could control. He would never let Coulter into the Vault, but Alex probably wouldn't deny his brother entry.

Coulter opened the back door and let himself into the kitchen. It smelled faintly of baked bread, overlaid with the sharp spices from the fish stew they'd had for lunch. Three of his students were still doing dishes and laughing as they worked. They stopped when they saw him.

"Do you know where Matt is?" Coulter asked Thea.

She frowned as if surprised that he had asked her. Thea and Matt had built a tentative friendship, some of it based on their feelings of rejection. Thea was half Fey, the result, he'd heard, of a love match that the Islander family didn't approve of. They took their pregnant daughter back into the family, and when she'd died in childbirth, they had tried to hide Thea from their Islander neighbors.

Then Thea's magic started appearing. She was a Weather Sprite. She started, as most of them did, making small rainstorms in water basins, then graduated to covering herself with rays of light, even on the stormiest days.

Her abilities terrified her family and they neglected her. She finally ran away, somehow finding out about Coulter's school, and covering half of Blue Isle to arrive at his doorstep, thin, starving, and wary as a stray dog.

In the short time she'd been here, she'd fattened up and had begun to make friends. Only recently had she stopped stealing food from the kitchen when everyone else was asleep. Coulter had never mentioned it; he figured she needed to view this place as her home.

She continued to stare at Coulter as if debating how to answer him. Even he, the person she trusted most, got assessed much of the time.

"Matt's in the library," she said at last.

"Thank you." Coulter smiled and left. The library was through the dining hall and down some narrow corridors. It was Coulter's favorite room and it had become Matt's as well. Many times, Coulter had discovered Matt in there, reading one text or another, always on magic and its history.

He opened the door now. The room seemed musty in the daylight. Usually Coulter visited the library at night, when there was a fire in the grate and candles burned in the lamps set on the tables.

Matt stood as Coulter entered, looking nervous. He had an illustrated book from Nye open before him—a book of poetry.

Coulter tried not to smile.

"It's all right," Coulter said. "I was looking for you."

Matt nodded, but continued standing. He was a slender boy with a lanky build that implied he would be very tall one day. He had golden curls that surrounded his head like a halo, and distinctive features that in a woman would be considered beautiful.

"I hope you don't mind that I'm here," Matt said.

He'd become timid in the last year. Before, he'd snuck in here while his parents slept. His father had gone insane. When his father died, his family didn't bother to tell Matt, and he left home for good. Ever since then, he'd been quiet, uncomfortable, and somewhat meek.

Coulter was beginning to rethink his plans. "I don't mind. I've told you before you have the run of the place."

"Leen says books will corrupt me."

Coulter smiled. Leen was pure Fey, an Infantry soldier who had been beside Coulter since they were young. Once they had been lovers, but that ended long ago when they both realized that Coulter could never love anyone besides Arianna. Leen was his second at the school and was very good about questioning all sorts of teachings that had gotten both of them in trouble. But her attitude toward writings and books was very Fey. She believed they were unnecessary wastes of time.

"Books might corrupt you," Coulter said, "but only in a good way."

He got one of Matt's rare smiles then. It lit up the boy's face. Then Matt's smile faded as he watched Coulter. The boy knew something had changed.

Coulter waved a hand. "Matt, please sit."

Matt replaced his book and sat on one of the upholstered chairs. He sat at the very edge of it, as if his body might contaminate it.

Coulter ran a hand through his hair, and headed for the fireplace. He looked at the flames. They were small and golden, licking at the wood without much passion. "I'm going to ask you to do something. I'm not sure if I want you to do this, but I do want you to consider it. You're welcome to refuse me. If you do, nothing in our relationship will change. Everything might change if you accept it."

He turned. Matt was watching him, blue eyes wide.

"Rugad is looking for an Enchanter," Coulter said.

A slight frown creased Matt's brow. "He has been looking for a long time. You told us not to go."

"Arianna has convinced me that we need to take action

against him soon. We need to remove him from her body, and I can only think of one way to do that."

Matt threaded his long fingers together. "He'd suspect if an Enchanter tried to hurt him."

"Yes, he would. So we gain his confidence and then try an assault he doesn't understand."

Matt didn't move.

"The Soul Repositories, do you know how they work?" Coulter asked.

Matt shook his head. "My father wouldn't let me near the stuff in the Vault."

"Well, as best I understand, they use blood to lure a trapped soul into the Repository. Your father actually did that once."

Matt's face looked blank. He had learned to mask his emotions whenever anyone mentioned his father. Coulter didn't know how to get past it. Someday Matt would have to talk about his family.

"We need someone to get close to Rugad, to lure him out of Ari's body, and then, the moment that he's gone, help her back in. Would you be able to do that?"

Matt's frown returned. "I don't know the spells."

"I can teach you some. The others—how to use the Repository, for example—will have to come from the Vault."

Matt flinched.

"Actually," Coulter said, "the spells are the least of my concerns. I'm more worried about you spending time near Rugad. He's a powerful man, extremely smart, and you would have to watch yourself every moment. He might have you do things you don't want to do."

"Then I wouldn't," Matt said.

"You might to convince him that you really work for him."

"How long would I be there?"

"I don't know," Coulter said.

"What if he catches me?"

"We'll try to get you out. I have some ideas on how we can get to you."

Matt nodded, but his eyes seemed far away, as if he were

trying to picture this. "How would Arianna know that the body is empty?"

Coulter sighed. "You and I would remain Linked. You would let me know. I'd make sure Arianna is close by."

Matt was silent for a moment, then said, "This seems risky. Why can't she just stay here?"

"She's afraid if she does, she'll never be able to go back. We'll be governed by the Black King forever."

Matt frowned. "If she goes back, I'd never see her again."

Coulter put a hand on Matt's shoulder. It was rigid. Matt and Arianna had developed a strong friendship in the time she was here. "You'd see her again. You'd see her the way she's supposed to be. If you did this, you'd give her her heart's desire."

Matt looked pensive. "I'll think about it," he said.

CHAPTER SEVEN

*L*YNDRED STOOD IN the door of the North Tower, trying to catch her breath. All the stairs in this palace irritated her. She had never lived in a place that had so many stories and mazelike rooms. Her father said it was because the palace had once been a fortress that had been added onto, which was odd because Blue Isle had supposedly never had war until the Fey arrived.

Lyndred hated it here. She associated this tower with the Black Queen, who seemed to spend most of her time here, staring out the windows as if she were imprisoned in this place.

Now Lyndred had actually come to find her. It had taken most of the day for her to get up enough courage.

Arianna was standing on the opposite side of the large room, her legs spread, her hands clasped behind her back. Her long black hair was braided and fell along her rigid spine. She wore breeches and a jerkin, an outfit that suited her more than the Islander dresses. She didn't seem to notice Lyndred, but Lyndred had learned long ago that what Arianna seemed to notice and what she really noticed were two very different things.

"Are you going to hover all afternoon?" Arianna asked. "Or are you going to join me?"

Lyndred's mouth went dry, even though she had been expecting the comment.

"I've been wondering what's happened to you. Neither your father nor I have seen you all day. I suppose he found you?"

Lyndred felt a blush rise in her cheeks. It was involuntary, and it was appropriate, at least for this lie.

"He did." Her voice sounded weaker than it had on Nye. Once she felt she had the most imperial voice among the Fey, but it was nothing compared to Arianna's.

Arianna didn't turn, but she did raise her chin slightly. "How did he convince you to leave your rooms?"

"He didn't exactly."

This time, Arianna did turn. It was a sharp movement, almost a reluctant one, as if she were unwilling to stop her contemplation of the mountains in the distance. "Oh?"

Lyndred shrugged. "There are certain things a woman does in her life that she doesn't want her father to see."

"A woman?" For once, Arianna didn't seem to understand. "You had female troubles? If so, you should see one of the Healers."

The comment startled a laugh out of Lyndred, then her blush increased. "I wouldn't call it trouble. My father knows I have lovers. He just doesn't need visual confirmation."

Arianna's cold blue eyes widened slightly as if she hadn't expected this. Then an expression flitted across her face—amusement? annoyance?—it was impossible to tell before the expression vanished. "And who is the lucky man?"

"Unimportant," Lyndred said.

Arianna's gaze became hooded, and without her saying another word, Lyndred knew what she was thinking. She would ask servants, other Fey, guards, who Lyndred's lover was, and she wouldn't stop until she found out.

"Did you come to see me for advice, then, about your lover?" Arianna asked.

Lyndred smiled. She couldn't help herself. "No. I've had lovers since I came into my Vision."

"Are the two events—your getting your Vision and taking a lover—related, then?" Arianna asked.

The question was so prescient, it startled Lyndred. She had to pause before she answered.

The two events were linked. But she didn't know if she should tell Arianna that.

"What did you See that encouraged you to first take a lover?" The question was softer than the others, a bit more intimate, as if Arianna were a friend who was entitled to know.

Lyndred stepped inside the room, and closed the door. It was time to get closer, to see if she could use these questions to her own advantage. "I Saw a blond man who would give me a child and break my heart."

"And you sought to prevent that?"

Truth, then. It would be her weapon. "I want no man to have that kind of power over me."

Arianna's eyes narrowed, and this time Lyndred thought she saw a trace of laughter in them.

"You are the most independent member of my family I have met in years." It was an obvious compliment from a woman who gave none. She beckoned with her hand. "Come stand beside me, and look at this small kingdom. Do you know how insignificant it is?"

The switch in topic startled Lyndred. She crossed the room, past the columns and the tables, until she reached the floor-to-ceiling bubbled glass.

Below, the courtyard was barely visible, and beyond it, the city of Jahn extended for miles. Her great-grandfather Rugad, the Black King, had been killed east of here. This land was powerful enough to slaughter the greatest of the Fey. She did not think it insignificant.

Arianna was watching her. "You disagree with me, don't you?"

The question wasn't hostile. Arianna seemed to like Lyndred's spirit, even though Lyndred didn't know why.

"I think any place that can defeat the Black King has to have significance," Lyndred said.

Arianna's body went rigid. It seemed like an involuntary movement. Then she relaxed. "Blue Isle is part of the Fey Empire now."

"Yes," Lyndred said, "but it's the only part that entered voluntarily. You could have held this place against the rest of the Empire, and dared them to try to take it."

"I could have," Arianna said, as if that had never crossed her mind.

"Our grandfather tried to conquer this place and failed, then our great-grandfather tried and failed. That makes Blue Isle significant, don't you think?"

This train of thought seemed to bother Arianna. Lyndred felt a perverse pleasure at shaking her seemingly unshakable cousin.

"I think," Arianna said, "that the Black King ultimately got what he wanted. Blue Isle is part of the Fey Empire, ruled by Fey."

"With its own traditions intact," Lyndred said.

"Like Nye." There was a definite edge to Arianna's voice, one Lyndred had never heard.

"And if the Islanders rebelled in any way, we don't know if we can hold them down."

"Are you sleeping with a rebel, then?"

"No," Lyndred said. "You called this place insignificant. I told you I didn't think it was."

Arianna took a deep breath, as if she were trying to calm herself. Then she turned back toward the window. "What made you do so much thinking about Blue Isle?"

Lyndred felt dizzy. She could talk about Visions now, and Arianna was the one who had opened the door. Unexpectedly.

"My Visions," Lyndred said. "They've increased since we've come here."

"Do you think that's because of the Isle or because something significant has happened?" Legitimate questions, both of them, but neither were very helpful. Arianna was good at word games.

Lyndred would have to be direct. "Have your Visions increased lately?"

The skin around Arianna's eyes tightened, as if she were struggling to control her expression. "Since you arrived?"

"Yes," Lyndred said, her heart pounding.

"No," Arianna said. "My Visions have not increased."

"What about other Visionaries? I haven't talked to any. The Infantry Leaders seem too busy with maneuvers, and I don't know of any others."

"Except your father."

Lyndred always forgot that her father had Vision. It was so minor that it seemed as though he had none at all. "My father rarely Sees anything."

Arianna was silent. Lyndred hadn't expected that.

"So," Lyndred said, "if no one else has had increased Visions because of my arrival, then it must be the Isle that's doing it."

Arianna tilted her head upward. A Hawk Rider circled around the tower, and then soared toward the courtyard below. Arianna's eyes tracked it. Lyndred watched it too, wishing it were a Gull Rider, wishing it were Ace, but knowing it was not.

"You give this Isle too much power," Arianna said.

"I give it none that it doesn't deserve," Lyndred said. "It killed a Black King."

"Did it?" Arianna's voice was cool. "I still feel his power."

A chill ran down Lyndred's back and she didn't know why. "Doesn't that bother you?"

"Bother me?" This time, Arianna sounded surprised. "Why would it bother me?"

"Because I thought you helped kill him."

Arianna turned toward her. There was something alien in her eyes, something so calculating that it almost made Lyndred take a step backward. "If I had helped kill him, I would have brought Blood against Blood on our people."

Well, that was one question answered. Arianna knew about Blood against Blood.

"But . . ." Lyndred frowned. "I thought you were there when your father killed Rugad. I thought you were part of it. And proud to be part of it. That's what we heard in Nye."

"Lies," Arianna said softly.

"But you were there, weren't you?"

"Oh, I was there." Arianna's voice was completely flat. Its tone matched the strange look in her eyes.

"Then—"

"You don't understand," Arianna said. "I gain inspiration from Rugad."

The very idea took Lyndred's breath away. "I thought your goal was to create peace for the Fey Empire."

"Rugad's rule included peace."

"But that wasn't its goal. My father said that Rugad's peace was really a rest before the next stage of conquest."

Arianna smiled. "Your father is sometimes smarter than we give him credit for."

Lyndred flushed, wanting to defend her father, but knowing that Arianna was deliberately trying to change the topic. "So that's what you did? Create a rest instead of a peace?"

Arianna's smile remained on her face, small and self-satisfied. It made her eyes seem even colder. "Think about it. I had inherited a Fey army startled and shattered by the surprise at the Cliffs of Blood. An Isle that was once rich but had to be destroyed because of the recalcitrance of its own people. Two groups who did not get along. The continents of Galinas, Etanien, and Vion were fine. If we increased production there, we'd compensate for this ruined place. I put the Empire back together. In fifteen years, Fey and Islanders have intermingled, their cultures forming one. They've both accepted me, the Fey as their Black Queen, the Islanders as their hereditary Queen. The Islanders believe that I will always maintain a peace. The Fey know better. At least, most Fey do."

Lyndred felt the rebuke. "But, no, they don't. They're worried. I came from Galinas. You've never left this Isle. You don't know what they're saying about you."

"What are they saying about me?"

The door had opened all the way, and Lyndred lied without a second thought. "They say you're Blind."

Arianna stepped back as if slapped.

"They say that you're not trying to conquer Leut because you can't See. They say you're playing it safe because you don't want to harm the Empire. They say your Islander blood has ruined you for battle forever."

"How could I have been Black Queen this long and be Blind?" Arianna's temper was rising. Lyndred could almost feel it. It had a strength to it, an unnatural strength.

Lyndred paused. Should she continue, or should she back down? But she had told her father she would find out—and what could Arianna do to her? She certainly couldn't harm Lyndred, not with the Blood against Blood. She could banish her, but that would solve Lyndred's problem, make certain that her Vision wouldn't come true. At least, the Blue Isle Vision.

"I don't know," Lyndred said, "but I've heard things about severe headaches, the fact that you were unconscious for two days. Maybe you had Sight and lost it."

Arianna's eyes were flashing. "You do not know what you're talking about."

"I don't suppose I do." Lyndred clasped her hands behind her back in a conscious imitation of Arianna. "But I do know that you've never shared a Vision with me."

Arianna's right hand was clenched. Slowly the fist loosened, as if she made a conscious effort.

"We're Visionaries of equal skill," Lyndred said. "Yet you've never taken the opportunity to share your Visions. I would have thought that you would welcome the opportunity. Instead, you only wanted to hear mine."

"I don't need to share my Vision," Arianna said. "I can interpret things well enough on my own."

"My father says it was that kind of arrogance that defeated his father. He said that Rugad used to yell at our grandfather about that very thing."

Lyndred took a step closer to the window. She could see herself reflected in the bubbled glass. She looked tired.

"My last Vision," Arianna said, "was of Gift. Drowning."

Lyndred turned. Arianna was staring out the south windows, as if lost in a memory.

"We were on a small boat in the Infrin Sea," she said.

"Headed to Leut," Lyndred said.

Arianna nodded, unsurprised by Lyndred's comment.

"And Gift had fallen out of the boat. I leaned forward with an oar, to save him, and he couldn't grab it. He couldn't swim. He was going to drown."

She sounded strangely unconcerned, as if Gift meant nothing to her, as if the entire Vision meant nothing to her. It was an offering, but one that seemed to have no weight behind it at all.

"I Saw a similar Vision," Lyndred said. "Only it was my father in the water, and Gift in the boat."

Arianna was silent for a long time, as if she were weighing this information. "You never told me this Vision."

"You never told me yours. See what we can learn when we share?"

Arianna was still staring south. Down there, Rugad had burned out most of the center of the Isle. Some of the old-timers said that the fires were visible from Jahn, which meant that they could have been seen from this tower.

"When did you have this Vision?" Arianna asked.

"Before we left Nye."

"And since?"

"No." Lyndred was feeling oddly powerful, as if she were the one in control of the conversation. "When did you have yours?"

Arianna put her fingers on the glass. "What else have you Seen?"

"Tell me first," Lyndred said.

"I saw Gift standing before that burned-out building over there." She pointed to the great ruin on the other side of the bridge. The remains of the Islander's holiest building, destroyed by the Black King. "He was protecting a girl behind his back, a Fey girl." Then Arianna turned her head toward Lyndred. "Maybe it was you."

Lyndred said nothing.

Arianna looked at the building again. "Gift held a sword

to my belly, and threatened to kill me. I said, 'You can't.' And he said, 'Oh, but I can.' "

"He can't," Lyndred said. "Doesn't he know about the Blood against Blood?"

Arianna shrugged. "I Saw what I Saw."

That Vision she had recounted with more emotion. Because Gift had threatened her? Or because of another reason?

"I Saw Blood against Blood," Lyndred said. "I just don't know what causes it. When did you have that Vision?"

"Gift was in most of my Visions," Arianna said.

"Mine, too," Lyndred said. "I think he's a center."

Arianna whirled, her braid falling over her shoulder. "Like Jewel?"

How strange to refer to her mother like that. No matter how many times Arianna did it, Lyndred could still not get used to it.

"Yes," Lyndred said. "Like Aunt Jewel."

Someone knocked on the door. Lyndred's gaze hadn't left Arianna's face. There was something in it, something behind it. Arianna had described Visions, but she wasn't saying when they occurred. And she hadn't denied the headaches, the two days of unconsciousness.

The knock sounded again.

"Come." Arianna hadn't broken her gaze from Lyndred's.

"Forgive me, ma'am," a male voice said from the door, "but I have a Hawk Rider with an urgent message. She wouldn't wait."

Arianna frowned as if the interruption bothered her. Lyndred turned and saw Arianna's assistant, DiPalmet, leaning inside the door as if he worried that Arianna would yell at him. DiPalmet wore his hair in a thousand braids in the Oudoun warrior style. His face was too thin, but that might have been a function of age. He had come to the Isle with Rugad years ago, and retired until Arianna had found him and reinstated him.

Arianna walked toward him. Her stride was long, as if she were more comfortable marching than walking.

"Send her in and then leave us," she said to DiPalmet.

Lyndred gripped her left wrist tightly. Her hands were still behind her back. She wished she could become invisible. She knew, in a moment, that Arianna would ask her to leave as well.

The door clicked shut.

"Well?" Arianna said.

The Hawk Rider was the one that had flown by outside, a woman who had put on a tunic and breeches before coming to see Arianna. The Rider's black hair feathered down her back and her hooked nose made her black eyes seem cold and birdlike.

Arianna clearly knew the Rider, and she knew that Lyndred was listening. She just didn't seem to care.

Lyndred found that odd, but she wasn't going to call attention to herself in case her analysis was wrong.

"They've arrived." The Hawk Rider's voice was high-pitched and piercing, almost like a cry.

"You're certain?" Arianna asked.

"Oh, yes." The Hawk Rider's eyes glittered. "They made it through the Stone Guardians on a Tashil ship."

"Were they welcomed?"

"If you call Islanders talking of assassination a welcoming committee."

Lyndred's mouth went dry.

"Talking?" Arianna sounded interested. Too interested.

"They had bows and arrows. They were planning to attack the ship from above. I flew past their vantage. They would have had clear shots if they were good."

"Were they?" Arianna asked.

"I didn't stay. I saw a Doppelgänger on site. I figure he'll report if anything happens."

"You don't expect it to."

The Hawk Rider raised her head. "I have great faith in the Black Heir. Two Islanders with arrows won't kill a man like that, not a man with the power of the Throne behind him."

Arianna hissed, and for a moment, Lyndred thought Arianna would strike the Rider. Then Arianna inclined her head.

"The power of the Throne?" she asked in a tone so dangerous that Lyndred wouldn't have answered the question.

"You can see his heritage. Forgive me, Ma'am, but he looks like a ruler of the Fey."

"What gives him that look?"

"His stance." The Hawk Rider seemed oblivious to Arianna's growing anger, but Lyndred wasn't. She wished now that she hadn't stayed in the room. "He is no Shaman."

"He doesn't wear the garb? His hair isn't white?"

"No, Ma'am."

"But he spent five years with the Shaman in the Eccrasian Mountains."

"That is what they say, Ma'am." Now even the Hawk Rider was beginning to understand that Arianna was extremely unhappy with this.

Lyndred found it curious. She had always heard Arianna was close to her brother. Was the change in Arianna or in Gift? He was supposed to be studying to become a Shaman. He was supposed to have no interest in the Black Throne. But nothing was as it seemed here. Had he really been training to become a Shaman? Or had that been pretense? Had he really been in the mountains so that he could get close to the Black Throne itself?

"What would you think if I hadn't warned you he was coming?" Arianna asked. "If you saw that ship coming through the Stone Guardians? If you knew who Gift was by sight?"

The Hawk Rider raised her head slightly. She had been honest with Arianna so far. Lyndred had no doubt the Rider would be honest again.

"I would think," the Rider said softly, "that he was coming to claim his heritage."

"But he can't do that," Arianna said. "The stricture against striking someone of his own blood is strong."

"If he's as good at manipulation as the rest of his family," the Hawk Rider said, "that stricture shouldn't matter."

Lyndred's hands were shaking. Arianna hadn't been surprised that Islander assassins were waiting for her brother.

She had a Doppelgänger and a Hawk Rider in the same area. She had known that Gift was coming to Blue Isle, and she had known that Islanders would be lying in wait. Was the Doppelgänger there to protect Gift? Or was he there to report to Arianna when something happened to Gift?

Or was Arianna letting Lyndred listen to this as a warning? An acknowledgment that Arianna could do anything she wanted to any member of her family so long as she left no fingerprints?

Just like their great-grandfather. He had let his son go on a foolish mission, let him die, rather than report the Vision that would have saved him.

Was Arianna doing that with Lyndred? Was that why Arianna was silent about her Visions? Or were her Visions the reason she knew of the Islander assassins in the first place? And if she knew, why hadn't she stopped them? What did she hope to gain from their assault against her brother?

"Is anyone observing now?" Arianna was asking.

Lyndred had missed some of the conversation. She forced herself to concentrate.

"I have left two others there. They'll let us know if something serious happens."

"Thank you," Arianna said. "You've done well."

The Hawk Rider bowed once and left, closing the door quietly behind her.

"Your brother," Lyndred said. "It sounds as though you don't want him here."

Arianna's eyes narrowed. "He is a complication we don't need. But he is family."

"I heard he was the legitimate Heir to the Throne."

"He turned it down to become a Shaman."

"Which he is not."

Arianna shrugged. "He will not question me."

Lyndred was still shaking, but she had been bold all day. A few more steps wouldn't matter.

"I've Seen the Blood against Blood," she said. "Don't be too sure that what's between you will be settled easily."

"Gift loves his sister." Arianna's tone was mocking, as if she put no value on her brother's affection.

"You haven't seen him in five years. How do you know that?"

"Because Gift imagines himself a saint, just like his father did."

"His father killed the Black King," Lyndred said.

"His father—"

Again, that odd construction. Not "my father" but "his." Why was Arianna distancing herself from her family?

"—won a battle, nothing more. The Fey Empire still rules Blue Isle."

"And it seems as if the soul of the Black King possesses you," Lyndred said.

Arianna's eyes widened, and then she laughed. This time, the laugh was warm and infectious, a laugh that would have made Lyndred chuckle if only she had understood its source.

"It would seem that way, wouldn't it?" Arianna's eyes twinkled. "We could do worse."

"I suppose so," Lyndred said, but she wasn't sure. Arianna was not Rugad. She had been born on Blue Isle, she had no real military experience, and there was a very good chance she was Blind.

When Blindness came, madness often followed.

A mad Queen and a power-hungry Heir. No wonder Lyndred was having Visions of Blood.

CHAPTER EIGHT

A SINGLE STEP seemed to take an eternity.

Arianna was walking back from the river. Her feet thudded against the path, and even though it was flat and easy, she had to struggle for each step. She left prints so deep that water from the rains could fill them and become puddles. It felt so odd to be like this when just six months ago she could change herself into a bird and fly away, or become a cat and run as fast as the wind.

It made her feel as if she were not herself anymore. It made her realize just how much of herself was tied to her body, the way she felt, and her ability to Shift shapes.

The school wasn't that far away. She could see the edge of the magic yard just around the bend. The students were good children, mostly half Fey half Islanders like her. Only their families hadn't wanted them around. Their families had banished them or sent them away or ignored them. Frightened, apparently, by their magic. Frightened by their looks.

She had spent a lot of time with those children at Coulter's request. He had known that she would have a lot to tell them, a lot to give them. And she had. But it wasn't her life's work, no matter how tragic their circumstances were. Her life's work was in Jahn, ruling the Isle, ruling the Empire, and striving to make a closeness between Islanders and the Fey not just a matter of policy but a way of life.

Rugad would ruin all that.

She slowly brought a hand to her face and brushed away a loose strand of hair. The movement made her slightly dizzy.

Then the world tilted. She was sliding into a Vision, only it had never been this slow before. She lost her balance and, unable to recover, felt herself topple as—

—She saw Gift cradling an infant and crying. He looked as if he were inconsolable. She started to say his name when—

—A ship, its deck stained with blood, docked in Jahn harbor and Gift was there, talking to a Fey woman who wore brightly colored clothing. She was pleading with him, telling him that he was making a mistake—

And through the Vision, blood flowed . . .

—Gift grabbed the Fey woman, thrust her behind his back, and held a sword to Rugad's belly. Only Rugad looked like her, but he wasn't—

—Gift grabbed a Fey woman who looked like Arianna's mother, thrusting her behind his back, and holding a sword to Rugad's belly. Rugad looked like himself, only younger—

—Gift grabbed a different Fey woman, the one from the boat, and shoved her behind his back. He thrust a sword against Rugad's belly and said—

—"We're drowning. Ari, please!" Gift was floundering in water. Seawater. Rugad was in the boat, extending an oar, trying to save Gift. Rugad? Or someone who looked like him? Were any of them Rugad? She couldn't tell. It was as if—

—Coulter was holding her, telling her he'd love her no matter what. Even if she was stuck in this body forever, he would always be beside her—

—And Matt laughed. He was handsome, unlike his

father, but she saw bits of his father's craziness in his eyes. He was wearing the robes of the Rocaan. He came closer, holding a vial of holy water. "You should be careful who you trust," he said. "I'm not Matt. I'm his brother, Alex"—

—A beautiful map was spread out across the table before her, showing the Fey Empire and beyond. She couldn't read the language that dotted it, but the symbol at the top unnerved her: a single heart resting on top of a single sword with a crown floating on top—

—And a man she didn't recognize walked behind the fountain in the Roca's Cave. "If I stand here," he said, "one of my people will sense me, and we will find the third cave. The third Place of Power. And we will own the Triangle"—

She coughed. She was lying on the path, dirt pressing into her face. Her body didn't hurt, but it ached, as if her landing had knocked the wind out of her. As it would have felt if she had a real body, not this thing made of stone.

Someone was crouched beside her. "Ari?"

Sebastian. His voice was dear. She closed her eyes and clung to it, letting the strangeness of the Visions wash through her.

She had had one or two Visions since she left her own body, but nothing like this. Something had happened. Something had changed.

"Ari?" He sounded panicked.

"I'm all right, Sebastian." At least she didn't talk like he did, so slowly and carefully. Seger said that was because Arianna couldn't imagine herself talking like that so she taught the Golem body to speak rapidly. Sebastian never did.

"I . . . sent . . . for . . . Coul-ter . . . and . . . Se-ger."

"You sent whom?" Arianna didn't want anyone to see her like this, sprawled like a child in the dirt.

"Sca-ven-ger."

She shuddered. Scavenger had been a friend of Gift's and Coulter's. In fact, he had saved Coulter's life more than once. But he had never been kind to Arianna. Not even when they were all living in the Roca's Cave, trying to figure out a way to fight Rugad.

"He was with you?"

"He . . . saw . . . you . . . fall."

Arianna opened her eyes. The dirt in front of her was crosshatched with footprints. "How long was I out?"

"Long . . . e-nough," Sebastian said. "Was . . . it . . . a . . . Vi-sion?"

"Yes," she said. "Help me up."

He slid his hands beneath her shoulders and steadied her. She supported herself with her arms and carefully, with Sebastian's help, sat up.

"Am I all right?"

He kept one hand on her back and brushed some dirt away with his free hand. "You . . . are . . . not . . . cracked."

Leave it to Sebastian to put everything in perspective. He had literally shattered three times that Arianna knew of. Until this last time, when Seger had used some clay to repair him, he had borne the marks of the shatterings in cracks that ran through his features. Now he looked like a gray version of Gift. A slower, steadier version.

A door slammed in the distance. Arianna ran a hand through her hair. A shower of dirt fell on her shoulders.

Within moments, Coulter was beside her. Seger wasn't far behind. Matt ran behind them, looking worried. Scavenger was walking down the path, his short, squat body powerful.

Coulter knelt beside her. "Are you all right?"

"It . . . was . . . a . . . Vi-sion," Sebastian said.

"I thought so." Seger sat down. The strain of the last few months showed on her face. There were lines near her eyes where there had never been any before.

"It was several Visions," Arianna said. "Something's changed."

The fear that she was beginning to recognize filled Coulter's eyes. "Do you know what?"

Matt arrived. He looked panicked. The boy had become taken with her. He loved to sit beside her and listen to her tell stories about Jahn.

She reached toward him. He grabbed her hand and squeezed, then let go.

"The Visions were about Gift." She turned to Sebastian. "Is Gift on Blue Isle?"

Sebastian shrugged, a single movement of the shoulders. "We . . . have . . . nev-er . . . o-pened . . . our . . . Link."

As he spoke, Seger looked away. Arianna caught the movement. So did Coulter.

"You know something," he said to Seger.

Seger raised her chin slightly. "I sent for Gift when Arianna was fighting Rugad, before you arrived."

"And you didn't see fit to tell us?" Coulter asked.

Arianna looked at him. Once Coulter and Gift had been very close. What could Coulter object to now?

"With all that happened," Seger was saying, "I forgot."

Matt was watching with wide eyes. He clearly didn't understand any of this.

"Gift can handle himself," Arianna said.

"Gift . . . will . . . go . . . to . . . the . . . pa-lace, look-ing . . . for . . . us."

Coulter nodded. "And he'll find Rugad in place of Arianna."

"But will he recognize Rugad or will he think Arianna has changed?" Seger asked.

Arianna thought about her Visions, and the Blood flowing behind everything. "Gift knows me."

"He also knows Rugad," Coulter said.

"They've never met," Seger said. "Have they?"

"Rugad tried to invade Gift's mind before he left part of himself in Arianna's." Coulter looked older than he ever had before. "That alone might make Gift recognize him."

"It might make him vulnerable to Rugad too," Seger said.

"May-be . . . we . . . should . . . o-pen . . . my . . . Link . . . to . . . Gift."

"So that Rugad can come through it here? And learn all of our plans?" Coulter asked.

Matt looked at Coulter, as if he were startled by Coulter's reluctance to take a risk.

"We have plans?" In Seger's voice, Arianna heard the frustration she'd been feeling.

"Now we do," Arianna said.

"Did you get them from the Visions?" Seger asked.

Arianna started to shake her head, but before she could complete the movement, Coulter said, "We made the plans several hours ago. At the river."

"Maybe that's what caused the Visions." The voice belonged to Scavenger. He was standing behind Seger. He was staring at Arianna as if she had done something to offend him.

"Maybe," Seger said.

"It didn't feel that way," Arianna said. "It felt as if the Visions were triggered by something else."

"Maybe Gift is on Blue Isle," Seger said.

Arianna flashed on the Vision of the ship in Jahn harbor. It wasn't a Nyeian ship or anything she recognized. But there had been blood on the deck. Dried blood. And Gift looked weary, like he had when he had arrived at the Roca's Cave all those years ago.

"What is it, child?" Seger asked.

Arianna nodded. "I think you're right. I think he is here, on a ship that isn't from Nye, with a woman I've never seen before. And she's frightened for him."

"If he's already in Jahn, we can't do anything to help him," Scavenger said. "He's going to face Rugad without us."

"Let's hope he'll treat Rugad like he would treat me," Arianna said.

"He'll think you've gone mad," Coulter said.

"From his perspective," Arianna said, "I will have."

"Is . . . there . . . a . . . Fey . . . way . . . to . . . deal . . . with . . . mad-ness?" Sebastian asked.

Seger shook her head. "It's one thing magic cannot cure and often causes. We suffered through our insane Black rulers, and hoped they did no damage."

Matt looked away. His father had gone insane. Arianna tightened her grip on his hand.

"Is there an Islander way to deal with it?" Scavenger asked.

Arianna frowned, careful not to meet Matt's gaze. She remembered hearing stories of insanity in the history, but she had never paid attention to her lessons. Then her father had tried to tell her, and she hadn't listened to that either.

"As far back as I can remember," she said slowly, "we have had sane rulers."

"So Gift is on his own," Seger said.

"Let's hope he remembers he has friends," Coulter said.

"Maybe we should try to find him." Arianna looked at Coulter.

His blue eyes were haunted. "If he's already in Jahn, things have started without us."

"How did Gift get to the city?" Scavenger asked.

"I Saw a ship, with its deck covered in blood," Arianna said. "The problem is, I don't know if the ship is already there, if it will arrive soon, or if it won't arrive at all. It feels right to think that Gift is on Blue Isle, but it could be me, just wishing."

"No." Sebastian bowed his head. "I . . . have . . . been . . . thinking . . . of . . . Gift . . . late-ly. It . . . feels . . . as . . . if . . . he . . . is . . . close."

"I thought your Link was closed," Coulter said.

"You could argue that they are the same person," Seger said. "Perhaps that's how Sebastian knows."

"You should feel something too," Scavenger said to Coulter. "After all, you're Bound to Gift. Your life and his are intertwined."

Coulter shook his head. "I haven't felt Gift for years." There was a flatness to his tone that made her look at him closely. A lie? Or a denial that went so deep that even if he felt Gift, he wouldn't acknowledge it even to himself?

She suspected the second was true. Gift had hurt Coulter years ago, and Coulter had decided, after Adrian's death, that he was unworthy of anyone's affection. Even Gift's. Especially Gift's.

She slipped her hand in Coulter's. "We have to go to Jahn."

"I thought we'd wait a little. Let Matt get settled."

Matt started at the mention of his name.

"You're sending him to Rugad, aren't you?" Scavenger asked. "To be Rugad's Enchanter."

"Yes," Arianna said. "We need someone close to Rugad."

"The boy's magic isn't going to be what Rugad expects," Scavenger said.

"Matt is pure Islander," Coulter said. "Of course Rugad won't recognize the magic."

"I hope you've briefed the boy on all he needs to know," Scavenger said. "He's never encountered a mind like Rugad's before."

Matt looked nervously at Coulter.

"You should help Matt, then," Arianna said to Scavenger.

"I will," Scavenger said, but he seemed preoccupied. "You said your Visions were lined with Blood."

She nodded.

"Who causes that Blood?"

"I don't know," Arianna said.

"Rugad? Gift?" Scavenger's voice lowered. "You?"

"I will not kill Rugad," she said.

"Then what's the point?" Scavenger asked. "That's the only way to be rid of him."

"That's the only thing I can't do," Arianna said.

"He's not the real Rugad," Scavenger said.

Arianna looked at Sebastian. Sebastian, who was formed from bits of Gift's essence, years ago. "I disagree," she said softly. "If Sebastian's real, and he is, then Rugad is real. We have to operate from that premise, much as I wish we didn't."

Sebastian brushed her shoulder, almost as if he were thanking her. Matt looked confused. Seger sat with her arms wrapped around her legs, her head bowed in thought.

"There's one other thing." Seger's tone was almost regretful.

"What's that?" Coulter asked.

Arianna was watching Seger's face. She had a hunch none of them would like what Seger was about to say.

"Gift might accept Rugad as Arianna—a changed Arianna, but still the Black Queen."

Arianna stiffened. He would never do that. He would know her. But Sebastian leaned forward just enough to make her doubt it. Sebastian knew Gift better than all of them, and he was listening to Seger.

"That means," Seger continued, "if you go after Rugad, you might have to go after Gift."

"But I Saw Gift with a sword against Rugad's belly," Arianna said.

"Are you sure it was Rugad?" Seger said.

Arianna started to nod, then stopped. "The first time, yes. The second time, it looked like Rugad—like the man—only younger. And the third, I don't know."

"You Saw the same Vision three different ways?" Scavenger asked.

"Yes."

"Then the future isn't set yet." Scavenger let out a small sigh. "Arianna is right. Everything is centered on Gift. Be careful of him. If he believes that Rugad is Arianna, he could attack you—and accidentally start the Blood against Blood."

"Maybe we should stay here," Coulter said.

Scavenger looked at him. "If you choose to stay here, you choose to give the Empire to Rugad. Is that what you want?"

"No," Arianna said. "It's not what I want. We've been at peace for fifteen years. We've been prosperous."

"But our magic is based on war," Scavenger said. "And intermingling with new cultures."

"Blue Isle's magic isn't based on that," Arianna said. "We're part of the Empire now. Things change."

"Will Rugad harm the Empire by ruling it?" Scavenger asked.

"Yes," Arianna said.

"How?" Scavenger asked.

Arianna swallowed. If she didn't answer this, Scavenger might stand in her way. She might never return to her body, might never rule her people again.

"He may have all of Rugad's personality and all of his memory," she said, "but he's Blind, Scavenger. Remember what happened the last time the Fey had a Blind Leader?"

"The Blood," Seger whispered.

Arianna nodded. "Maybe that was the Blood I was Seeing. Maybe I was Seeing what would happen if we didn't defeat Rugad."

Scavenger stared at her for a long moment. She got the very real sense that he did not like her.

"Maybe," he said. "But I would feel better if you knew what was going to cause it."

"So would I," Arianna said softly. "So would I."

CHAPTER NINE

$\mathcal{A}$CE'S WINGS WERE getting tired, but he didn't want to stop. He had a feeling that someone would attack the ship here, where the river turned slightly. Bluffs jutted into the water, narrowing the passage even more, and trees bent by time and the wind reached across the divide like parted lovers.

This was a perfect ambush site.

Ace slowed and waved a small arm so that the Gull Riders following him would slow as well. He wanted to surprise the ambushers.

With a flick of his fingers, he indicated to his troop to spread out, fly carefully, and search. Eight Gull Riders could cover a lot of distance. It would be hard to see anyone in the trees, particularly Islanders, camouflaged against the wood. However, the archers would have to be close enough to the edges of those bluffs to see the ship.

Ace swooped closer to the trees. The bark was black and gray in the places where it had ripped off. Most of the trees were pines, but the undergrowth was dead or in its winter dormancy. That helped a little.

He saw a tree limb shake, an unnatural movement that had nothing to do with wind. With his right hand, he signaled his troop. He banked above the tree, then circled it, so that the others would know where he went. Then he flew under the branches.

An Islander, solid with muscle, his blond hair thinning, sat in the fork of a thick branch. He had an excellent view of the water. He leaned forward just enough so that he could grab arrows from his quiver.

Ace slipped behind him and grabbed the shaft of an arrow in his beak. Then he flew out of the branches, circled, and headed back toward the archer. The archer didn't turn, apparently not observant enough to notice the Fey man on the bird's back or the arrow in the bird's beak.

Quietly, Ace landed on the branch just behind the fork, right next to the trunk. He reached down and took the arrow out of his beak. The arrow's shaft was almost too thick to hold in his tiny hand. He'd never tried this maneuver before. He hoped it would work.

He shifted back into his Fey form. His legs sprouted from the gull's feet, and his arms grew. With his free hand, he braced himself so that he wouldn't slip on the branch. The gull's body absorbed into his stomach.

The arrow nearly fell as his hand changed size, but he managed to grasp the shaft between his thumb and forefinger. Keeping a solid hold on the arrow was proving the most difficult part.

The archer didn't seem to notice. He was leaning farther forward on the branch. In the distance, Ace could barely make out the white sails of the Tashil ship. They looked like white dots on the horizon.

Ace got a solid grip on the arrow and pushed himself toward the fork. As he moved on the branch, it bounced. The archer turned, and Ace shoved the arrow, point forward, into the man's eye.

The archer screamed, and clutched his face. His bow fell, clattering as it hit branches on the way down. Ace grabbed the man's hands with one of his own, and yanked another arrow out of the quiver.

"Tell me who you work for or I'll take out the other eye," he said in Fey.

The man was shaking his head and sobbing. He spoke in a language that Ace did not understand.

Ace cursed, and then repeated himself in Nyeian.

The man shook his head again. Useless piece of dirt. Ace couldn't get information from him because the man only spoke the Islanders' language.

Ace shoved the second arrow into the man's throat. The man gurgled, his remaining eye clouding over. Then Ace pushed him off the branch into the water below.

He landed, moments later, with a loud splash.

Ace sighed and wiped his hands on the tree bark. The blood stained it, making it even darker. Then he propped his feet on the branch and shifted back into his Gull form. He had to get one of these bastards to talk. Gift may have had an idea who wanted him dead, but Ace wanted confirmation.

The next tree was shaking as well, and so was the tree beyond that and the tree beyond that. His Gull Riders, attempting to find out who wanted the Black Heir dead.

Ace flew to the next tree.

Abdal was in his Fey form, holding an unfamiliar knife to an archer's throat. The archer's quiver had spilled arrows down the tree and onto the ground. The bow was caught in a branch just below them. There was blood on the archer's chin but he looked oddly calm.

Abdal's hand was shaking. Gull Riders were not normally soldiers. Usually they were scouts. Abdal hadn't even gone on the raid against the first archers. Now he was here, in an unfamiliar place.

"Who hired you?" he asked again in Fey.

The archer had an unlined face, kept carefully blank. Ace couldn't tell if the man understood or not.

He flew to the nearest branch and peered down. The archer saw him, but said nothing.

"Try Nyeian," Ace said.

Abdal sighed. "I already have."

"Islander?"

"I don't speak it."

But Ace had the sense that the archer was following this conversation. Something in the stillness of the man's body, something in his eyes . . .

Ace hopped down a branch and looked closer. The archer turned away. Ace's heart started to pound.

"Look at me," he said in Fey.

The archer closed his eyes.

Abdal's mouth opened slightly. With his free hand, he grabbed the archer's chin, and yanked the archer's face toward Ace.

"Look at me," Ace said again.

The archer kept his eyes closed. Ace wanted to shift, but didn't dare. He'd lose his perch on the branch. Instead he leaned closer and rested the tip of his beak against the archer's right eyelid.

"Look at me," Ace said, "or I'll remove your eye myself."

The man's eyes flew open, and Ace gasped in spite of himself. Gold flecks. The archer had gold flecks in his eyes.

He was a Doppelgänger. Doppelgängers killed their hosts and took their host's form, along with his memories. This Doppelgänger had killed an Islander who had been part of this assassination team and had taken his place without anyone suspecting. The only thing that gave him away—that gave all Doppelgängers away—was the gold flecks in his eyes.

"Who sent you?" Ace asked.

The man's mouth formed a thin line.

Ace pushed on the eyelid. "Tell me who sent you or I swear I'll disfigure you in ways you'll never forget."

"All right," the man said in perfect Fey. His voice was raspy because of the knife against his throat. "Take your beak out of my eye, and I'll tell you."

Ace took a step backward. The man sat up, carefully so as not to lose his balance. Abdal kept a grip on the knife.

"We heard talk about an uprising among the Islanders," the man said. "I was sent here to find out what was going on."

"We?" Ace asked.

The man nodded. He wiped at his chin. Blood smeared across his fingers. "I report to the palace."

Ace went cold. He had thought that Gift and his sister, Arianna, were on good terms. "To whom at the palace?"

"The Black Family."

"Queen Arianna?"

"Her uncle and cousin have joined her now."

Ace swallowed. Bridge hadn't seemed like a cunning man, but Lyndred—beautiful Lyndred—had been cunning. Would she have sent someone after her own cousin?

"What were you supposed to do here?"

"Find out what was happening."

"You're here with a group of assassins. Weren't you supposed to stop them?"

"As an Islander? With a bow and arrow? What was the chance of that?"

"I don't care about chances," Ace said. "I care about your orders."

"My orders were to report."

"And to shoot Gift if you saw him?"

The man shook his head.

"But you weren't supposed to save him either, were you?"

"I assumed there were others who were supposed to do that," the man said. It sounded like a lie.

"What's your name?" Ace asked.

"Reginald." A Nyeian name. He was young then. He had probably come to the Isle with Rugad.

Now Ace had to figure out what to do with him. They couldn't bring him to the ship. A Doppelgänger was dangerous, particularly around non-Fey like the Nyeians. With one grasp of a hand, he could bring someone close, then put his fingers in their eyes, his thumb in their mouth, and pull their essence out of them. He could transform himself into someone else in a matter of minutes.

Of course, once they found the bones, they'd search for him, but he could be long gone. And things would get worse if he tried to take over Gift.

Ace shuddered. That violated Fey code, but Reginald's presence seemed to do that anyway.

"Are you done questioning him?" Abdal asked.

Ace shook his head. His bird head stayed in place, watching Reginald. It seemed to unnerve him. "I thought Gift was popular with the Islanders."

"They don't know him." Reginald was as far back on the branch as he could be. It was bending slightly. Too much weight and it would break. Ace wondered if Reginald could survive the fall into the river.

"They're trying to kill him because they don't know him?"

"Rumors have been flying all over this part of the Isle. It's said he touched the Black Throne and now he wants to be Black King. It's said once he becomes king, he'll kill every Islander."

Ace lifted his wings, a gull sign of surprise. "You believe that?"

"I believe he's touched the Throne. I believe he went to the Eccrasian Mountains to find a way to overthrow his sister."

Ace turned his bird head toward Abdal. Abdal looked as surprised as Ace felt.

"What about the Blood against Blood?" Abdal asked.

"He could overthrow her without killing her," Reginald said. "She's peaceful. She needs someone to defend her."

"Is that why you're here?" Ace asked. "I thought your orders came from the palace."

"I didn't say they came from her."

"Wouldn't she know if someone had sent you here?" Abdal asked.

"Why would you follow someone else's orders?" Ace asked.

"I don't speak to the Black Queen directly," Reginald said. "My orders always come from someone else."

"Who did they come from this time?"

"Jair," Reginald said.

"And he is?" Ace asked.

"The head of the Fey Infantry on the Isle."

"A Doppelgänger taking orders from the Infantry?"

Reginald looked a bit guilty. "Sometimes. Things aren't as structured here."

"I guess not," Abdal said.

"You took orders from an Infantry leader, orders that could lead to the death of the Black Heir, and you didn't question them?" Ace's voice rose. He had to concentrate to keep it down slightly.

"No one said to kill him."

"No one said to defend him either," Ace said.

Reginald's cheeks flushed. "Isn't that why you guys are here?"

"Gull Riders as a defense?" Abdal said.

"You were doing pretty well," Reginald said, touching his throat.

"Better than you do when you lie." Ace hopped a little closer. "If you were ordered not to defend the Black Heir, aren't you worried that your actions could cause Blood against Blood?"

"I'm not of the Black Family," Reginald said.

"But you have three members in the palace. Arianna, Bridge, and Lyndred. What if your orders came from one of them?"

"*No one told me to kill anyone!*" Reginald scooted back just a little farther. "Besides, he touched the Black Throne."

"How do you know?" Ace said.

Reginald's flush grew deeper. "The Visionaries, like Jair, they all saw a black stream cross the sky. They all knew the power came from the Throne. Only a member of the Black Family could have done that. Only Gift was close."

"Do you know that for a fact?"

Reginald frowned.

"What of Rugan, Rugat, or Golden?" Ace said, listing Bridge's siblings. "What if it had been one of their children?"

"I don't know." Clearly Reginald hadn't thought of that. "I don't think the Shaman would have let them into the mountains."

"The Shaman, denying a member of the Black Family?"

"They can't," Abdal said. "By law. The Black Family must be allowed access to the Black Throne. You know that."

A few yards away, someone screamed. Reginald's head turned. A body—an Islander, his white skin and blond hair vivid in the gray light—broke through one of the trees and fell, slapping against the bluff with a sickening thud. He landed with a smack in the water below.

Reginald swallowed. "I'd forgotten it."

This time, Ace knew he was speaking the truth. "If you were ordered here, then why are the Islanders here?"

"I told you," Reginald said. "They believe Gift is going to slaughter them all."

"Where did that belief come from?"

Reginald shrugged. "I didn't know about it until I joined them."

"Think," Abdal said. "You have memories from your host. Use them."

Reginald glanced at the water below. He seemed to realize how close to the edge he was. "They were rumors. Everyone heard them."

"Everyone?"

"All the Islanders in my host's village."

"And who spread those rumors?"

Reginald shrugged.

Ace was feeling frustrated. "How did they know Gift was coming back?"

Reginald spread his hands. "I really don't know. My host didn't know. Someone put the rumor out there, and the Islanders believed it."

"Someone," Ace said. "Someone who knew Gift was coming."

"It leads back to the palace, doesn't it?" Abdal said.

Ace turned both of his heads toward Reginald. "Blood against Blood."

Reginald was shaking. "I wouldn't have caused it."

"But you would have let a Black Heir die."

"I thought he was going to cause it," Reginald said.

Truth at last. Reginald would have let a member of the

Black Family die to protect the Fey. Maybe they all would, if they believed it. But Ace had traveled with Gift for months now, and had never seen that kind of evil in him.

"What do I do with you?" Ace asked Reginald.

"You kill him," Abdal said. "He already said he would have let Gift die."

Ace was staring at Reginald. Reginald glanced at the water below, probably calculating whether or not he'd survive the fall. Another scream echoed, harsh and raspy. Ace's people were doing their work.

Reginald glanced at him. "I'll find out who gave the orders."

"You already told me," Ace said. "Jair."

"No," Reginald said. "Who gave *him* the orders."

"Why should I trust you?"

"Because I wouldn't bring on the Blood against Blood."

"You nearly did." Ace said.

"I didn't know." There was desperation in Reginald's voice. "Please. I'll help you. I'll help Gift. I'll make sure no one attacks him. I'll even ride on your ship if you let me."

"And kill the Black Heir yourself," Abdal said.

Reginald shook his head so furiously the branch bounced. He grabbed it in sudden fright. So he didn't think he'd survive the fall. Ace wondered if there was a percentage in killing him.

"All you're supposed to do is report, right?" Ace asked.

Reginald stopped moving. His grip on the branch was so tight his knuckles were pale. "Yes."

"Then report."

"What?" Abdal asked.

Another scream echoed, higher, filled with more panic. Perhaps Gull Riders should be soldiers more often.

Reginald asked, "Should I find out for you who was—"

"No," Ace said. "Just report."

"Report what? That the Black Heir is dead?"

Ace glanced toward the west. The ship's sails looked much larger now. "Report the truth—that the Black Heir survived. Let them know that he'll be at the palace soon."

"I can't get there before you," Reginald said.

"Of course not. You have a message system set up. There are probably Bird Riders or Wisps nearby. You can make your report."

"That gives them time to prepare for him," Abdal said.

"Do you expect them to meet him with a full army?" Ace asked.

"I don't know," Abdal said. "It's crazy here."

Ace had to agree. But if Gift didn't like this idea, then he could change it.

"How many others of you are there?"

"No Doppelgängers," Reginald said. "At least that I'm aware of."

"Archers," Ace said. "I meant archers. How many more assassins will we find?"

"There are nests every ten miles or so," Reginald said. "Only a handful of people though. Most Islanders are afraid of the Fey. Or don't believe the rumors. A few even think Fey rule is good for the Isle."

"Who are these assassins, then?" Abdal asked.

"Those who never got over losing the war," Reginald said.

"They won the war." Ace's voice was flat. "The Black King died."

"They lost," Reginald said. "The Fey are still on the Isle."

"How many Islanders believe that?" Ace asked.

"Most of them," Reginald said.

"But Arianna shares the blood of the hereditary rulers."

"And she looks Fey," Reginald said. "Some Islanders hope they can get their land back. They think killing Gift would be a good first step."

"It'll only bring the wrath of the palace on them."

"They believe it'll start the war again. They think the Fey won't survive it this time."

"Why?" Ace asked.

Reginald shuddered. "They're reviving the religion."

"The one that killed Rugar's people?" Abdal asked, speaking of the Black King's son, Rugar.

Ace looked at him. He hadn't heard this.

"Yes," Reginald said. "They're searching for someone who knows the Secrets. They believe if they find an Aud or a Danite who wasn't killed by the Fey, he'll be able to re-create all the religion's weapons. And then they can use the weapons to defeat the Fey."

Ace frowned. "So this is the first shot in a war."

"If they can bring down the Black Family and wipe the Fey off the Isle, they will," Reginald said.

Abdal's eyes narrowed. He obviously didn't believe Reginald. "You said there weren't that many of them."

"There aren't. They believe more Islanders will join their cause as they have some successes."

Ace glanced down the river. It had been too easy to defeat them so far. "Well, they won't have any success if they continue on this course."

"They're just beginning," Reginald said.

"So you have faith in them?"

Reginald shrugged. "I have faith in the Fey."

The correct answer, of course. But did that mean Reginald had faith in all Fey or those he knew on the Isle?

It ultimately wasn't for Ace to decide. "Make your report," he said. "We'll see you when you reach Jahn."

Reginald glanced at the knife that Abdal still held. Abdal grinned slowly at him. "You'll have to make it back without your weapons."

"How do I know the rest of your Gull Riders will leave me alone?" Reginald asked.

Ace shrugged. "It's a chance you'll have to take."

"I could talk to the Black Heir," Reginald said, "explain to him what I told you."

"You could," Ace said. "Or I could lose patience with you and change my mind about your survival."

Reginald nodded once, swung off the branch. His feet caught a branch below him, and he slowly worked his way down.

Ace waited until he was all the way to the bottom and starting to run before saying to Abdal: "You follow him. Make sure he doesn't take over someone else. We need to be able to track him."

"You think Gift'll want him to go free?"

"I don't know," Ace said. "But I know we can find you. If Gift doesn't like what I've done, we can always find Reginald and kill him."

"What do I do when he reaches the messenger?"

"Follow the messenger. Stay out of sight if you can. We'll meet you in the city."

Abdal nodded, set the knife on the branch, and shifted into his Gull form. Then he flew away, going low so that he could keep Reginald in sight.

Ace watched for a moment. An occasional glimpse of a Gull Rider would keep Reginald in line. He would strive to complete his mission as quickly as possible.

Still, the entire meeting left Ace unsettled. Obviously the Islanders were mounting a campaign—however small—against the Fey. But Ace was convinced that they were unwitting accomplices of a Fey mastermind. And he was afraid that the mastermind was a member of the Black Family.

He remembered how easily Bridge had gotten him off the ship. How Lyndred's black eyes had an intelligence beyond anything Ace had ever seen. How beautiful that intelligence made her.

And how dangerous.

Had the two of them influenced Arianna against her brother?

He would have to tell Gift.

The next few days wouldn't be easy. For anyone.

CHAPTER TEN

ATT HADN'T BEEN to the Vault since his father died. And he hadn't gone much before that. His father, who had once been the Fifty-first Rocaan, head of Blue Isle's religion, spent his last years in the Vault as he went mad. He usually forgot to wash and sometimes forgot to eat. The place smelled of filth and piss and his father's sickness.

Going to the Vault even now, six months after his father's death, made Matt's stomach turn.

But if Matt was going to help Arianna, he would need to go. He needed to know how the tools of the religion worked. He knew in principle. His father—when he was sane—had discussed it enough at home.

Magic is an abomination, his father used to say, and Matt often wondered how his father could believe it, considering his own powers. But his father had been a bundle of contradictions, most of which Matt still didn't understand.

The Roca understood that when he came back. He understood how magic destroyed those around it, so he devised tools that would eliminate magic from the Isle. And it worked, boys. We had no magic until the Fey came. Then we discovered, all over again, the tools the Roca had left for us, and we used them to defeat the Black King.

Not all of that was true, of course. Over the years, Matt had learned that his father, even when sane, bent the stories to his own advantage. There was magic on the Isle. There had always been magic, at least since the Roca had discovered the cave a thousand years ago. The Roca had simply taught the Islanders to fear it.

The Vault was located at the base of the Cliffs of Blood and had been there as long as the mountains themselves. It was a natural cave, blocked off and protected by a structure built by the Roca's successors. When the Roca returned, after being thought dead and rising to the hand of God, he lived in the Vault and never left it. There he wrote the Words in the form of a letter to his two sons, a letter that got misinterpreted and misunderstood as time went on.

To get to the Vault, Matt had to go through the center of Constant. He took a circuitous route so that he could avoid his mother's house. She was still alive, but she wasn't dealing well with his father's death. She had loved Matt's father, despite the man's madness, and his death had nearly ruined her.

Sometimes Matt didn't blame her for failing to fetch him the day his father decided to disappear into the mountains. His father had had one last moment of lucidity. Neither Matt's brother nor his mother had seen fit to find Matt so that he could say good-bye, or maybe even talk his father out of walking into the Cave, where the spirit of Arianna's mother lurked.

That spirit had tried twice before to kill Matt's father, and he had survived through luck the first time and skill the second. Alex said that his father wanted to die this third time and that was why he went, but Matt didn't believe that. He felt that his father had forgotten about the dangers, and was trying to reach the Roca's Cave for a reason he never stated.

The thin winter sun generated little heat, but it reflected

off the stone roads, and made the center of town seem warmer than the outskirts. The slight breeze that blew off the river wasn't getting past the stone buildings, so the air hung heavy. A storm was brewing; he could feel it. He wanted to be underground, away from everything when it hit.

He made his way through the bazaar. Only a hardy few stood outside to hawk their wares. He knew most of them, and said hello as he passed. They'd long since stopped trying to patch the breach between him and his mother.

She had actually come to the school to see him a few months ago. She had seemed diminished, somehow, her tall, angular body so thin that he could see her bones. Her eyes had sunken into her skull and the beauty that used to radiate from her was gone. Even her red hair, once her most striking feature, looked dull and almost brown.

She had tried to apologize, saying once again that there hadn't been time to send for him, saying that she had been so destroyed by his father's death that she hadn't even realized there was a rift between Matt and Alex.

Matt hadn't been able to speak to her. She had waited three months to come to him, and then she hadn't offered a real apology. No one had even told Matt his father had died until he showed up at the house, days later. Nothing would ever change how he felt.

The muscles in his shoulders were getting tight the closer he came to the Meeting Hall. A headache was starting to build, and he cursed himself. If he had studied the Words as a boy, like his father had wanted him to, he wouldn't have to come here now. Coulter said there were religious items in the Roca's Cave. Matt could have gone there. But he had studied just enough to know the overall history of the religion, and not enough to know how to use its tools.

For that, he would need to face his brother, Alex.

A man stepped out between the streets. He had long braided hair and scars all over his arms and face. He was thin and Fey, and familiar. Wisdom. He had obviously been looking for Matt.

I hear you are leaving. Wisdom moved his hands to

speak. Wisdom had lost his tongue—the source of his magic—to Rugad fifteen years before. He would not let anyone replace it, so he and Matt had developed a language of their own in sign.

"Soon," Matt said.

Don't, Wisdom said. *Stay out of their business.*

"Why?" Matt asked.

Because it will give you problems you will not want.

"Coulter asked me to help."

Say no, Wisdom signed.

"I already said yes."

Wisdom sighed. *You are too young for this.*

"Arianna was my age when she became Black Queen."

And where is she now?

"Don't. You won't get me to change my mind." Then he hurried away before Wisdom could say anything else.

Matt turned onto the street where the Meeting Hall was. It stood by itself, a windowless wooden building that had once been the center of Constant. After the Fey killed the Wise Ones inside the building, the village's rulers moved to a different location.

Matt climbed the steps and opened the door. It creaked. A smell—dampness, decay, and neglect—nearly overpowered him. He put a hand to his nose and stepped inside.

Someone had cleaned up in the last six months. The broken furniture was gone, the cobwebs had disappeared, and there were new torches hanging in the torch holders. A lamp stood on a table beside the door. Matt removed the glass bell, used a flint to light the candle inside, and replaced the glass. Then he picked up the lamp by its base, and peered around the room.

People had not only cleaned, they had refurbished. A new table stood in the center of the room, benches along the sides, just as it probably had been long ago. There were still empty corners, and the smell of disuse, but it looked as if someone had been working to revive this place as a meeting hall.

Matt's heart began to pound. He went to the door that led to the Vault. The door was closed. His father used to keep it open—at his mother's suggestion—so that he could

leave quickly if he had to. Matt pulled on the knob, half expecting it to be locked.

It wasn't. The door slid open easily.

The scent of newly cut wood greeted him. The stairs that
had been rotting away had been replaced by new ones, so
new, in fact, that the wood was still brown. The stairs went
a long way down, to a corridor that was made of mountain
stone, clean and dust-free. He had never seen this corridor
clean before.

He walked carefully, clinging to the lamp, appreciating
the thin illumination that it provided. He followed the corridor to the bend in the middle, where the stones dripped
with moisture. Here the smell and look were familiar: the
wild smell of the mountain itself, a smell that always made
the hair on the back of his neck stand on end.

He associated that smell with his father. In the days before the madness had taken him over completely, his father
used to come home smelling like this.

The stone in this part of the corridor—and from here
on—was the vibrant red of the mountain. Coulter said the
mountain was alive. He said that through it came the magic
that was bred into generations of Islanders.

Matt knew what Coulter was talking about. As a child,
Matt—attracted by the color—had chipped away at a bit of
the red stone, and a small chunk had fallen into his hand, already gray. The gray was the same kind of gray a body
turned after a person had died. Ever since then, the gray
stones of the village made Matt think of death.

The stone changed as the ground flattened. This was the
oldest part of the cavern, not made of piled stones but literally carved out of the rock. He was in the cave, the one
where the Roca had actually lived.

Matt braced himself, and went deeper. A few steps farther and he felt it: the song, as his father used to say. The call
of the mountain. It was a lure, begging him to come closer,
begging him to disappear deep into the mountain, just as his
father had done. And, as his father had taught him when he
was a little boy, he shook his head and willed the feeling to
go away.

It didn't, but it lost some of its power.

Maybe this was what his father had felt. Maybe this was what his father could no longer deny.

Matt turned a corner, and saw the door. It was standing open, and a square of light from inside poured into the corridor.

His heartbeat increased even more. He was shaking. He made himself take a deep breath. Alex was probably inside. And Matt would have to face him. He couldn't tell Alex the truth, and he didn't have a lie prepared. Maybe he would tell him a partial truth, and that would be good enough.

Or maybe his brother wouldn't care why Matt had come. Maybe he would just be happy that Matt was there. Maybe he would apologize and all would be right between them.

Matt stepped inside.

The room was warm, as usual, and smelled faintly of smoke. Torches burned in their holders. Furniture was scattered around, chairs, tables, a bed in the corner. In the last few years of his father's life, the furniture had been ripped and overturned. The entire room stank. But none of that remained.

He set down the lamp and ran a hand through his curls. The door to the Vault was closed. It was a small wooden door, unpretentious, with a single handle. It hadn't been closed in his father's day. It was always open, the unnatural light from the Vault spilling into this room.

He made himself walk toward it, made himself grab the handle, made himself turn and pull it.

The door opened, and the light covered him.

It was a white light that seemed to come from the walls themselves. It was warm and friendly and it terrified him.

It always had.

He stepped inside, and looked at the stone altar in the middle of the room. No one stood behind it. That startled him. He had expected to see Alex there, watching him, but the room was empty.

Or, at least, it seemed empty. His brother might have

gone down one of the corridors that branched off the back, the corridors their father had forbidden them to step into, the corridors their father had actually disappeared down the last day of his life.

A tear ran down Matt's face. He wiped his cheek with the back of his hand, and took another deep, shuddery breath. There was no reason to mourn his father. His father hadn't been a real father for years. He had been an embarrassment, to himself, his family, his sons.

He had had the deepest laugh Matt had ever heard.

Matt blinked hard and made himself concentrate. Nothing had changed. The beautiful tapestries still hung on the walls, depicting scenes from the Roca's life. The table was still set up for the Feast of the Living, the silver bowls in the center of the table sparkling as if they had just been polished. Vials of holy water sat on freestanding shelves, and swords lay between them. Suspended from the ceiling in an arching pattern were the globes for the Lights of Midday.

The bottles lining the wall to his left glowed redly. Inside, he knew, was blood, supposedly the Blood of the Roca, stored for hundreds of years. Drums hung from one of the pillars. Skin, supposedly human skin, was pulled across them. As boys, he and Alex were forbidden to touch everything, and the only thing they didn't want to touch was the drums.

Finally, he looked at the dolls. They were small, made of handblown glass. They seemed eerily alive, and always had. His father used to tell of the day when he took one of the dolls, placed drops of blood inside, and carried it into the cavern so that he could capture the soul of the Fey woman who had tried to kill him.

Now Coulter wanted Matt to do the same thing. To save that woman's daughter.

Matt shuddered. It meant carrying the dolls. It meant getting close to the Black King, and actually using the weapon. It meant testing himself on levels he hadn't even imagined before.

Coulter had told him that he didn't have to do this. But

Matt had thought of Arianna, whom he liked. She wasn't evil, like her mother had been. She was a good woman who meant a lot to the country. Who meant a lot to him.

He shook himself slightly and crossed to the altar. The stones embedded in the white floor glowed as his boots touched them: ruby, emerald, sapphire, diamond, and then the two his father had no name for, the black stone and the gray stone, both with the brilliance of jewels.

Matt reached the altar, but didn't touch it. He knew the gold veins running through it would glow when he did, the acknowledgment of a heritage that descended directly from the Roca. Meaning that Matt was distantly related to Queen Arianna. She was the descendant of the Roca's eldest son. He was a descendant of the younger.

He'd always thought that strange. The blood still told, all these centuries later.

The Words were open before him, the handmade paper as new as if it had just been finished. The ink on its surface seemed barely dried, even though the Roca had written the letter a thousand years before.

In Ancient Islander.

Matt had forgotten that. He knew the language, but poorly. His father had insisted on teaching them how to read it, and like everything to do with this abominable religion, Matt had learned just enough to get by, but that was not going to be good enough now. The Secrets he needed were outlined in these Words, and he couldn't read them well enough to understand them.

"It's easier to read the Words if you place your hands on the altar."

Matt looked up. His brother stood in the doorway. Matt no longer felt as if his brother were a mirror image of himself. Alex wore a robe, like his father used to. He had gotten taller, his curly hair long. He was thinner than he had ever been, almost as if he had forgotten to eat, and his eyes, once a clear blue, were hooded and dark.

"I didn't think you were here," Matt said.

"I come every day." There was an accusation in those words, although Matt wasn't exactly certain what it was.

"Are you here to steal the Words? Or have you finally come to your senses and left your Fey friends?"

Matt stayed behind the altar. It felt like protection. "Actually, I'm here to learn more about the religion."

"So that you can learn how to protect your friends from it?" Alex crossed his arms.

Bile rose in Matt's throat. "Why do you hate me so much?"

"I don't hate you," Alex said. "I hate the company you keep."

"Why?" Matt asked. "They're good people. They've helped me. They wanted to help you."

"They're turning you into an abomination."

"How do you know? You haven't seen me in months."

"I've been waiting for you to come home."

"You kicked me out of the house."

"You left on your own."

"After you and Mother made it clear I was no longer wanted."

Alex's eyes glinted. "You're still angry about the day Father died? Mother and I both told you that there was no time to get you. She went all the way to the horrible place you're living just to talk to you."

"She talked," Matt said. "She didn't apologize."

"There was nothing to apologize for. If anyone needed to apologize, it was you. You left her when she needed you the most. And if you'd been here more often in Father's last year, you would have known how sick he was. How unhappy."

Matt stared at his brother. Once they had been so close they seemed to know each other's thoughts.

That had been a long time ago.

"What do you want?" Alex asked.

"An apology," Matt said. "An attempt at understanding me."

"I understand," Alex said. "You're on a path that will lead you to the same madness that took our father."

"You've Seen that?"

"Yes."

"With Vision, like the Fey have."

Alex's lips pursed. "It was a divine message."

So that was the explanation now. "A message from God?"

Alex shrugged. "Mother says I lead the religion now. Father wanted me to do that."

"Father was crazy."

"Not at the end."

"So you say."

"If you're not going to steal the Words, what are you here for?"

"Answers," Matt said softly.

Alex's eyes narrowed. "Answers about what?"

"I need to know how these things work. I want to do what the Roca said, take some power away from those who misuse it."

"You're going to attack the Fey?"

Matt nodded.

Alex took a step closer. His right foot brushed the ruby, sending a red glow throughout the room.

"You'd betray your friends?"

"Not all Fey are bad," Matt said.

"Just the ones your friends point to."

Matt swallowed again, trying to keep the bile down. "Please, I can't tell you any more."

"Then I can't help you." Alex's face looked odd in the red light. "If you decide you want to leave them, I'll do everything I can for you."

"Alex." Matt put his hands on the sides of the altar. Golden light flared like a thousand candles. "The world isn't as black and white as you make it out to be. Come meet some of my friends. Get to know a few Fey. Please learn how some Islanders can hurt people, and some Fey would never think of it. Come experience more of life than this tiny room."

"It's not tiny," Alex said. "The whole world exists in here."

Matt closed his eyes. It didn't help. He still felt as if something were breaking inside him.

When he opened his eyes and dropped his hands, he saw Alex peering at him. There was a familiar gentleness in the look.

"What do you need to know?" Alex asked.

"How the Soul Repositories work," Matt said before he could stop himself.

"Why?"

Matt couldn't answer, at least not directly. "Our father used them."

"Yes," Alex said. "He told us about them."

"But not about anything else." Matt waved a hand toward the pillar. "What do the drums do? The Lights of Midday? The vials of holy water?"

"Your friends know. Coulter was present when our father killed the Black King. Or doesn't he remember?"

"He knows some of it," Matt said.

"Why does he need to know the rest?"

Matt licked his lips. "Alex, please—"

"He needs the help of a religion he despises?"

"He doesn't despise the religion," Matt said.

"He doesn't practice it."

"No one does."

"Because the Fey killed all the leaders."

Matt shook his head. "They didn't kill Father. He was the one who said the religion had to change."

"He said I was the one to do it. I won't do it by helping Fey."

"I'm not Fey," Matt said.

Alex's eyes darkened. "But you're trying to be."

Matt shook his head. "I'm trying to discover how to use my gifts. You could do the same thing. The Visions you have, there are ways of making them clearer, of making them work for you."

"Fey ways."

"Alex . . ."

"I will do things as I see fit." His brother sounded just like their father. Matt remembered those words from arguments with their mother, back when Matt was little.

"And somehow you can't even see your way toward helping me?"

"What do you want me to do?" Alex asked. "Read the Words to you? Or have you finally learned how to decipher Ancient Islander?"

Matt flushed. "I can read it."

"Enough to misunderstand," Alex said.

"Then tell me what I need. It'll help all of us."

"So you say."

"Yes." Matt's voice had an edge to it that he hadn't even realized was there. "So I say. Trust me, Alex. We used to be more than brothers. We used to be friends."

Alex nodded. He took another step closer, his foot landing on an emerald, sending a green light up his leg, making his face sickly pale.

"Yes," Alex said. "We used to be friends. Now it's you who doesn't trust me. I know what it's like when you're lying, Matt. You won't tell me what you're going to do, and it's big, isn't it? It would have to be to bring you here."

"I can't tell you. I can't tell anyone. I promised."

"Who?" Alex asked. "Your Fey friends? Coulter?"

Matt nodded his head once.

"A promise made to the ungodly is no promise at all."

"Really?" Matt asked. "Does it say that in the Words or is this wisdom according to Alex?"

Alex let out a small groan. "I thought we were actually talking."

"We were, until your ignorance got in the way."

"My ignorance? I'm not the one who can't read his people's original language."

"I'm not the one who claims to be a man of God, and yet manages to hate everyone around him."

They were both breathing hard, each breath in rhythm. They used to do that as little boys when they fought.

"Get out," Alex said. "You're not welcome here."

"I need the information, Alex. It'll benefit all of us."

"Get out." Alex's inflections remained the same. Flat. Toneless, as if he were feeling nothing.

"Our father wouldn't want me to be kicked out."

"Our father is dead. You didn't even love him enough to visit him in his last two weeks of life."

"He would have wanted me to complete this mission."

"He would have wanted you to stay away from the Fey." Alex took another step forward. His boot brushed the sapphire and the light turned blue. "In fact, he forbade us from going anywhere near that place where you live."

"He was a sick man, Alex. He didn't know. And it looks as if his sickness infected you."

"He was right about the Fey."

"If he was right, then why did he help put Queen Arianna on the throne? She's half Fey."

"Nicholas left him no choice. All of Nicholas's children were part Fey. It was either them or the Black King."

"Either way, they're Fey. And our father was the one who helped her become Queen."

"Get out," Alex said.

"Tell me what I need to know," Matt said. "Give me one of the repositories and help me get it ready. Then I won't bother you again."

Alex shook his head.

Matt's stomach twisted. He would have to help himself. He couldn't steal the Words, but he could take the knowledge—in a way that not even Coulter would approve.

Matt put both of his hands on the Words. He uttered a spell he had only read about, from a book in Coulter's library. A Fey spell as reported by the L'Nacin.

The unfamiliar words spilled off his tongue and he hoped he was pronouncing them right. He hoped the L'Nacin reported them correctly. He gripped the book, careful not to touch the altar, and he held on tight.

Alex lunged toward him, but Matt picked up the Words and hugged them to him, finishing the spell as he did so. His fingers tingled.

Alex brushed the altar, and it flared gold. He reached for the Words, and Matt turned away, so that his brother missed once again.

The tingle continued up Matt's arms, into his shoulders, his neck, and through his face. Finally it reached his skull, and he knew what the Words said as if he had written them himself. A splitting pain ran through his head, and he cried out, dropping the Words.

Alex caught them, and collapsed on the ground, holding them close.

Matt clutched his head, and leaned forward, using the altar for support. The golden light bathed him, hurting his eyes. Tears of pain ran down his face. It felt as if someone had shoved a torch into his brain, burning its way into his mind.

The Words would never leave him. They were part of him now, so deeply embedded he could feel each word like a brand.

"What did you do?" Alex opened the book. The writing was still on the pages, but it seemed fainter now. "What did you do?"

Matt wiped his face with the back of his hand. "I learned the Secrets you were hiding from me."

Alex looked stricken. "You weren't ready for them."

"Actually," Matt said. "I don't think either one of us is ready. But it's too late. I know them now. Let me have a Soul Repository and a bit of the Roca's blood, and I'll leave you."

"No." Alex struggled to his feet. "You know the Words. You can build one yourself if you want it that badly."

"Alex, I need it now."

"I'm not going to help you, Matt. You want to use this for blasphemous reasons."

"When did you stop trusting me?" Matt asked.

Alex looked at him, blue eyes filled with sadness. "When you chose to follow the path our father forbade."

"Have you ever thought that Father might have been mistaken? Mother did. She gave us permission to go to Coulter's school, remember? Before Father died?"

"She was wrong." Alex kept one hand wrapped around the book and extended the other. "Come home, stay with us, renounce the Fey magic. I'll teach you about the Roca and the religion our father practiced, and I'll show you how life should be lived. Together, we can reestablish Rocaanism. Together, we can build the religion in the image the Roca wanted."

Matt stared at his brother's hand. Rebuilding a religion that most considered dead held no appeal for him. The Roca's words, burned into his brain, showed no great desire for religion. Instead, they showed—at least to Matt—so much remorse that the Words were choked with it.

"I don't think the Roca wanted a religion," Matt said. "I think he wanted to undo the grief he'd caused, take away the magic he'd unleashed on Blue Isle. Only he wasn't able to close the bottle. It was too late."

Alex shook his head.

"We have magic, given us by the Roca." Matt spoke softly. "The Fey have magic too. We're part of their Empire now. We need to learn how to behave in this new world. If you and I work together, as our mother once believed, we can make an impact. You can help establish the Roca's morality on the Isle, and I'll make sure—"

He stopped himself before he finished the sentence. Because he was going to say he would make sure the right people ruled.

"You'll make sure what?" Alex asked.

"That we'll get the message to the right places," Matt said.

"We're too far gone for that. I can no longer trust you, and you obviously don't trust me." Alex let his hand fall. "You're not welcome here anymore, Matt. And neither are your friends."

"That doesn't seem very charitable."

"It's not about charity. It's about protection. The Words have always been protected, and now you've tampered with them. I can't let you touch anything else."

Matt glanced at the glass dolls, the drums, the jewels glowing on the floor. What would Alex do if Matt just took a doll, grabbed a bottle of blood, and fled?

Matt couldn't bear to do it. It would be the last straw, the final degradation of his father's memory.

"All right," he said. "I'll leave. But I want you to know one thing, Alex. I'm not the one who separated us. I tried to keep you beside me. I talked to you. It's you who rejected me."

Alex said nothing. Matt made his way around his brother, stepping carefully on the jeweled floor. Each flaring light from the gems seemed to pull him farther away.

"Have you ever thought," Matt said when he reached the door, "that maybe it isn't the magic that drives people like Father crazy? Maybe it's this place, this Vault. Maybe if you spend too much time here, the light and the heat and the stones destroy your mind. Have you ever thought that?"

But Alex did not answer him, and Matt did not turn around. He left the Vault for the final time, the Words newly embedded in his mind, and his brother's silence shredding his heart.

CHAPTER ELEVEN

*D*INNER WAS LATE. And served in the dining hall, as if Arianna were planning some sort of ceremony. Yet when Bridge arrived, he found the table set for three. Himself, Lyndred, and Arianna.

He hated the dining hall. The servants called it the Great Hall. It had old floor-to-ceiling windows on one side, and swords on the other. It was drafty and colder than any other room in the palace, and sound echoed here, making him feel as if he were eating in an audience room.

Lyndred came in one of the side entrances. She was wearing breeches and a jerkin, her hair braided down the back as if she were preparing for battle. Her skin was gray and her mouth pinched. She looked even more frightened than she had when he had seen her that afternoon in her room.

She slid her arm around her father's back and pulled him close. He put his arm around her. She leaned her head on his shoulder.

"I think I was right," she whispered.

"The Blindness?" he whispered back.

"She's being cagey, and I can't figure out any other reason why." Lyndred was leaning against him hard. "But I don't think that's our biggest problem."

At that moment, Arianna swept in. She was wearing a pale blue gown and someone had piled her hair on top of her head. The gown accented her unusual eyes, and the hairstyle narrowed her face so that she actually looked like a traditional Fey beauty.

But there was something masculine in her manner, something uncomfortable in her stride, something that suggested a gown was unnatural to her.

"Sit," she said as she reached the table.

A Fey servant scurried ahead of her and pulled back a chair. She didn't even seem to notice, although she did sit down. Another servant pulled a chair for Lyndred and then for Bridge. Bridge murmured his thanks.

The servants were now mostly Fey. Most of the Islanders—some who had been with the palace since Arianna was an infant—had been let go.

The wine steward entered, cradling a bottle to his chest. He poured a bit into Arianna's glass. She tasted, then nodded her approval, and the steward poured into all of their glasses. Bridge took a sip: it was a good red with a fruity dryness. Lyndred didn't touch her glass. Arianna twirled hers between her fingers.

"Have you told your father yet?" she asked Lyndred.

Lyndred started as if caught in a lie. "I haven't seen him until now."

"You were looking so peaceful just now, I thought maybe you had."

Bridge frowned. Was this the greater problem Lyndred had referred to?

"It seems," Arianna said, "that Gift has returned to the Isle."

"I would think you'd be happy to see him," Bridge said.

"The circumstances are odd. We thought he was going to become a Shaman."

"He hasn't?"

"If he were, he would still be in the Eccrasian Mountains."

A team of servants entered, some carrying bread, another carrying a tureen of soup, and the rest with bowls. The bowls were set down before them, the bread placed in the center of the table along with a knife, then one servant ladled the soup into the bowls while the other held the tureen. No one spoke until they left.

"Why would he come back?" Bridge asked.

Arianna stared at him as if he were the stupidest thing she had ever seen.

"The Black Throne, Daddy," Lyndred said. "Arianna thinks he went to the mountains to consult the Throne."

Bridge felt cold. "He wouldn't. He gave the Throne to you."

"He has no other reason to come back." Arianna bent over her soup and brought the spoon to her lips. The movement should have been delicate, but was not.

"I thought you were close." Bridge picked up his spoon. The soup smelled of winter vegetables and heavy spices. "And isn't this his home?"

"He would have notified me, don't you think?" Arianna said.

"Islanders knew he was coming," Lyndred said. "They were trying to kill him."

Bridge lost his grip on the spoon. It clattered against the table. "How did the Islanders know and we didn't?"

Lyndred bit her lower lip. Arianna continued to eat. Had he missed something?

"You knew?" Bridge asked Arianna.

"I suspected."

"A Hawk Rider confirmed it," Lyndred said. "Today. Arianna didn't even seem surprised by the Islander assassins."

"What did they do to him?" Bridge asked.

"We don't know." Her coldness shocked him. He had heard how close she was to her brother. She should have cared that Islanders were trying to kill the Black Heir.

Unless she put them up to it.

"You knew they would try to kill him." Bridge sounded like the boy who used to confront his grandfather.

And, to his surprise, Arianna smiled like his grandfather used to. Her blue eyes, so cold, twinkled. "They use bow and arrows. It's so inefficient."

This was a warning. She wanted Bridge to know that she would allow her own brother to die so that she could remain on this Throne. She wanted him to know that he was no match for her, for anything she came up with. He knew that he was no match, but he hadn't expected this ruthlessness. Not from a woman who had been raised Islander.

What if all of his information had been wrong? What if the reason the Islanders defeated his grandfather had been because they hid their ruthlessness beneath a religious veneer? What if Arianna, as part Islander, was more ruthless than any previous Fey had been?

He shuddered.

"You're not eating, Bridge," she said.

"Sorry," he said, picking up his spoon. "This is just so unexpected."

"Yes, well." Arianna finished her soup, leaving the spoon in the bowl. "I have cause to worry and so do you. Gift has not seen fit to notify me of his return. And he has been to the Black Throne."

Bridge had taken a mouthful of soup. It was good and rich, but he could barely swallow. "How do you know?"

Her eyes appraised him. Lyndred sank back in her chair as if she didn't want to be part of this discussion.

"I believe Gift will try to destroy me," Arianna said.

Lyndred looked at him sideways, and this time, he understood what she was trying to silently say. She wanted him to notice that Arianna hadn't answered his question.

"I just heard from another Hawk Rider a few moments ago," Arianna said. "Gift is on the last part of the river. He'll be in Jahn by morning."

Bridge set down his spoon. "What are you going to do about that?"

Arianna smiled. "I'm going to make certain we keep an

eye on him. And if he doesn't come to the palace immediately, I'll invite him. He does need to meet you. He didn't stop in Nye on his way to the Eccrasian Mountains, did he?"

"No," Bridge said. She should have known that. Wasn't it by her orders that Gift did not stop? Or had that been a lie too?

"He needs to know that family sticks together."

Bridge nodded. The servants had entered again. One collected bowls while another set down plates. The scent of roast beef wafted in from the hallway. Bridge's stomach growled. It was the constriction in his throat that was preventing him from eating. "I thought you said that family didn't matter."

Arianna glanced at the servants. She didn't seem upset by his comment. "When would I have said that?"

"The day that I met you."

Another group of servants entered with roast beef, gravy, and roasted potatoes. Some cooked carrots were placed along the side, adding color to the meal. There was too much food for the three of them, but no one seemed to notice or care. In Nye, Bridge always made certain the portions were right, so that no food was wasted.

A servant started to carve, but Arianna waved him away. She stood, grabbed the knife, and cut the meat herself. Then she served Lyndred and Bridge as if it were something she had always done.

Her hand on the knife looked so sure. Her grasp was correct, her movements easy.

"Is that enough?" she asked as she set a slice on his plate.

"It's fine," he said.

She set the knife down and returned to her chair. He got the sense that everything she did, she did for a reason, even down to cutting the meat.

The servants had all left. Bridge found himself staring at the knife.

"I don't believe I said family doesn't matter." Arianna spoke conversationally. "I believe I said I only extend courtesy to those who deserve it. That's a different thing."

"Does Gift deserve courtesy?" Bridge asked.

"I'm not certain. He hasn't informed us that he was coming. But perhaps there's a reason for that. What do you think?"

Bridge wasn't going to make the mistake of answering that. Instead, he said, "Someone sent for Gift. You know that. We told you when we arrived."

Arianna ate a bite of meat, chewed, and leaned back in her chair. "So your point is, if someone sent for Gift he's entitled to courtesy?"

That hadn't been his point, but he was willing to claim it. He nodded.

Lyndred was eating silently beside him. She kept her head down, as if she wanted to remain invisible.

"I wonder," Arianna said. "I was ill, so someone sent for Gift. I suspect it was Seger. I suspect Seger of many things. Have I told you?"

"You think she harmed you."

"It seems logical, especially with her quick disappearance." Arianna cut her meat with the side of her fork. "Then she sends for Gift. She has known him for years. What if she and he have concocted a way to get me off the Throne, a way that won't involve the Blood?"

"How could you know that?" Bridge asked. "I mean, how could you find out?"

"I wouldn't have, if you hadn't told me about your Gull Rider all those months ago. And if your daughter hadn't been Seeing Blood."

Lyndred brought her head up. Her skin was even grayer. "I don't know what that's connected to."

"I know," Arianna said. "That's why Visionaries share their Visions, so we can figure these things out."

"It's still speculation," Bridge said. "Not proof."

"I know. But I no longer trust Gift, and I don't think you should either."

"I don't know him," Bridge said.

"None of us do any longer." Arianna ate another bite of meat. She chewed slowly, watching him. "You once asked me about the swords."

He glanced involuntarily at the swords behind her. So that was why they were eating here. She wanted to make a point.

"A Black Robe, a young one, came in a secret door when Rugad held this palace, and killed twenty Fey with a sword he pulled from the wall. Because he had this power, he diverted the Fey's attention from guarding their Black King. Rugad nearly died that day. Later I heard that Rugad had taken a Red Cap and had him place his finger on all of the swords. Most didn't even break the skin, but a few sliced off fingers with no effort."

"Magic?" Lyndred asked.

"Of the Islander sort. Theirs seems to be concentrated on items rather than on people. But that's not the point."

"What is the point?" Bridge wanted this discussion to end so that he could eat.

"The point is that a single sword wielded by one man nearly toppled the Fey Empire. Everything about this Isle is unexpected. Our people were repeatedly defeated by believing that something was impossible only to be shown it wasn't."

"Our people?" Lyndred said so softly that for a moment Bridge wasn't sure if Arianna heard her.

Arianna smiled. "I am half Fey, Lyndred."

"And half Islander."

"And when I talk to Islanders and say, 'Our people,' they know that I mean Islanders. I am speaking to Fey."

"So you claim both?"

"I rule both, although it is, really, a specious distinction. I rule the Fey Empire. It happens to include Blue Isle. Keeping that distinction makes the Islanders happy and costs me nothing."

But Bridge felt as if she weren't really keeping that distinction at all. It seemed that she had become more Fey. Perhaps that was the inevitable consequence of being Black Queen. Or perhaps it was something else.

"I'm still not sure of the point," Bridge said.

"The point is," Arianna said slowly, as if she expected Bridge to have trouble understanding, "that surprise, not the Islanders, was our greatest enemy. All of this started as a discussion about Gift and what you consider to be my strange reaction to him."

Bridge set his fork down. Arianna still held hers. Lyndred had stopped eating a while ago.

"You may think I'm cold to Gift," Arianna said, "but I'm not. I simply can no longer afford to trust him. And I will not let anyone surprise me."

Bridge frowned. Maybe he was as dense as Arianna thought. "Why are you telling us this? We can't do anything about your relationship to Gift one way or another."

The smile vanished from Arianna's face. Her expression was hard and ruthless. For the first time, Bridge thought he was seeing the person that lurked deep down inside Arianna, the one that controlled her every thought and movement, the one she rarely let anyone see.

Arianna studied him for a moment, then looked at Lyndred. Her gaze fell so intensely on Lyndred that his daughter squirmed and looked to him for help. He didn't move. Something else was playing here, something very important.

"Why am I telling you this?" Arianna was talking to Bridge without moving her gaze from Lyndred. "Because your daughter believes I'm Blind."

Lyndred flushed. Inwardly, Bridge cringed.

"And since she believes that, I think she might ally with Gift. He might come here, tell her tales of the Black Throne and his hereditary rights, and convince her that I'm unfit to lead the Fey Empire. Oh, he might say I can remain Queen of Blue Isle, but he wouldn't think someone who has never been off the Isle should rule the Empire."

Lyndred was shaking. Bridge wanted to put his arm around her, but couldn't. Not yet.

"Makes for a good argument, doesn't it? I can think of a dozen others. And if he uses them, he might convince everyone that I'm unworthy."

"He won't kill you," Lyndred said.

"No," Arianna said. "He's too smart for that. But if he convinces you that I can't rule, and convinces your father, and convinces everyone else, what choice would I have but to step down?"

"You would do that?" Bridge kept his voice low and dry.

Arianna turned that piercing gaze on him. "Probably not. And then what would happen? A crisis of confidence as the Fey believe they are ruled by an incompetent. The Islanders are already rebelling. Imagine if the Fey joined them. Gift doesn't have to give the order to have me killed. There are a thousand ways to avoid the Blood against Blood and still manipulate the Empire. The last Black King knew them all."

"Except in the end." Lyndred spoke quietly. Bridge smiled at her. She had courage, his girl.

Arianna's eyes narrowed. "You've said that to me before. I think you fail to realize that Rugad achieved his goal. He wanted Blue Isle in the Fey Empire, ruled by himself or a member of his family. He got both of those things. That is not failure."

"He didn't live to see it."

"No one lives forever, Lyndred."

This time Bridge shuddered. Arianna's comment almost sounded like a threat.

Lyndred obviously heard it too. She squared her shoulders. "Forgive me, Arianna. I made a mistake. I always look on death as the ultimate failure."

To Bridge's surprise, Arianna smiled. "That's because you have limitations, Lyndred. To the most talented Visionaries, death is only the end of one road, not all of them."

Bridge felt his mouth fall open. He had heard such things, but had never seen them. What did Arianna know that he didn't?

"Are you saying Rugad's not dead?" The words came out before he could stop them.

"Oh, he's dead," Arianna said. "His body burned near the Islander Place of Power. But his spirit lives on."

"As a Mystery?"

"I don't think the Powers consider a man killed in battle to be the victim of a murder." Arianna cut more meat with her fork.

"Then how?"

"A man doesn't die until his dreams die." Arianna cut the last bit of meat on her plate. "And Rugad dreamed of extending the Empire to every part of the world."

"You're going to fulfill that dream?" Lyndred asked.

"Are you surprised because I've kept the Empire at peace for fifteen years or because I'm part Islander or because I share the dreams my family has always had?"

"All of that," Lyndred said.

"Peace," Arianna said, "is simply the resting time between battles. Islanders fought each other until one culture took over the Isle. And I believe a person should always pursue the dreams that make the most sense."

Bridge was staring at her.

"Don't look so shocked, Bridge." Arianna ate the last bite of meat. "Wasn't this what you came to Blue Isle to convince me to do?"

He flushed and silently cursed.

"Well, it's true, Bridge. Our people will go back to war, just as they're supposed to. I've been training Infantry, preparing armies, working with Foot Soldiers. You have Vision. Rather limited, but still good. You've also fought in several campaigns. I can make you a general and send you on the first wave to Leut."

"Like Rugad sent my father to Blue Isle? To get me out of the way?"

"If only you were cunning enough to be in the way." Arianna chuckled. "Lyndred, on the other hand, could become one of my most clever adversaries. When she grows up, of course. And since I'm currently without issue, I need to keep her here. You understand that, don't you, Bridge?"

Lyndred frowned. Bridge recognized the look. He didn't want his daughter to say anything more. He put his hand on her knee.

"I understand," he said, barely keeping his anger in check, "that any Blind leader would keep the best Visionary beside her."

Arianna's face came alive as it never had before. Bridge

could feel her anger. It was so powerful that he could barely prevent himself from sliding his chair away from the table.

"You will not say that again." Her tone was low and threatening.

Lyndred's knee was taut beneath his hand. His daughter was tense, maybe more tense than he was.

"Are you afraid of the truth?" Bridge said. "I've seen no evidence of your Vision, and everything you do shows me you have none."

"I don't have to share my Vision with someone like you."

"Probably not," Bridge said, "but you are talking about my daughter's future, and I disagree with your choices for her."

"I make my own choices," Lyndred said.

Bridge continued as if she hadn't spoken. "My grandfather Rugad, the man you claim to admire, believed that everyone should experience war, even future Leaders. My daughter never has. She should be in her own troop, following someone else's leadership, until she understands the impact battle has on everyone."

The color in Arianna's cheeks had grown darker. She shoved her plate away with such force that the rest of the dishes scattered across the table. Bridge's almost landed in his lap. He didn't try to catch it, thinking that would be exactly what Arianna wanted. Instead he slid back just a little and watched as the dish hung on the edge.

"Your daughter," Arianna said in a voice so soft that it seemed at odds with her latest movement, "should be beside me. I learn from mistakes. And that judgment, that insight about war, was a mistake. Jewel died because of that whole idea that Leaders must experience war. I will not make the same mistake with Lyndred."

"I thought it was Fey tradition to send Leaders into battle," Lyndred said. "So that we could be warrior rulers."

"You want to rule the Fey?" Arianna rose from her chair. Each movement had a power that astonished Bridge. It was as if she had more hidden reserves than any other person he'd met.

Lyndred looked up at her. It was a lazy movement, one that made all the threat Arianna was projecting seem ridiculous. "Of course I want to rule the Fey."

Bridge's breath caught in his throat. Lyndred didn't know what she was doing. She couldn't. She had no idea how Arianna would treat her.

"But," Lyndred said, "I'll do so only if the Throne comes to me. And I'm what? Fourth? Sixth in line? Then again, you were second. So anything can happen."

The color had drained from Arianna's face. Had no one ever challenged her before? "You mock me."

"Yes, I do." Lyndred stood. Bridge's hand slid off her knee, unheeded. He wanted to grab her wrist and pull her back to her seat as if she were still a little girl. "I think you're paranoid and dangerous. I think you have no idea how to rule our people. You tried peace, found that it wasn't trouble-free as you thought, so now you seek to divert us with war. You're not following any plan. You have no Vision. All you're doing is trying to make sure no one dislodges you from a Throne you do not understand."

"I would kill anyone else for saying that." Arianna took a step closer to Lyndred. Lyndred didn't move.

Bridge stood. He'd seen flashes of this woman in his daughter before, and he had a hunch that the little girl he'd nurtured would be gone forever after this night. The woman would have completely taken her place.

"Yes," Lyndred said. "You would have killed anyone not of your family. And if you were as smart as our great-grandfather, you'd find a *successful* way to manipulate my death. Unlike the things you tried with Gift. Too nebulous. People don't follow nebulous orders—and you can't give an obvious one. Such a bind you're in."

This time Lyndred was the one who took the extra step. She was so close that she and Arianna nearly touched.

"You can't kill me." Lyndred's voice was as soft as her cousin's. Bridge had to strain to hear. "You can only banish me, and you won't do that, will you? You want my Vision. You need it."

Arianna didn't move, but Lyndred smiled.

"Isn't it amazing how much of our intelligence is based in our Vision? We rely on it so much. Even my father, who doesn't have half the Vision I do, relies on it."

Bridge frowned, not sure why Lyndred brought him into this.

"Of course, you can't kill him either. He's a blood relative as well. Is this the kind of rebellion you were afraid of from your brother? He has Vision too, doesn't he? He probably knows all about your Blindness. He has probably come home to save the Empire. You know the rules. Any Blind Leader should step aside."

"I am not Blind," Arianna snapped.

"I don't believe you," Lyndred said.

Bridge's heart was pounding. His daughter was standing up to the Black Queen. Fearlessly. He had never had that kind of courage. He wondered where Lyndred got it from.

"It's not something I can prove in an instant," Arianna said.

"I suppose not," Lyndred replied, "and that puts you in quite a bind. I don't believe you, and you can't prove me wrong. Now your brother is coming. Perhaps you should get me out of the way so that my prejudices don't influence him."

"You're free to go anytime you like," Arianna said. "It was your wish to stay here."

Lyndred's shoulders stiffened. She obviously hadn't expected Arianna to acquiesce. "It was my father's wish."

"I'd be happy to leave this place," Bridge said.

"You don't get a vote." Arianna spoke to him without looking. "It's Lyndred's choice."

His intervention had given his daughter enough time to think. He could see the difference in the set of her back. Her confidence had returned.

"Good," Lyndred said. "If it's truly my choice, then I make this one. When you proceed to Leut, I want my own Infantry unit. I want to be a traditional Fey Leader. I have little hope of getting the Throne, but I do have hope of heading a country or an area. I want Leut. And I'll take it."

She paused as if considering something. "Unless you feel you need me here."

Trapped. Arianna had to admit to the Blindness or she had to let Lyndred go.

"All right," Arianna said. "You're free to make your own mistakes. As soon as I have the troops ready to go to Leut, you'll be with them. It does mean you'll need to train."

"Training's fine," Lyndred said.

"And what of your father?"

"I don't need training," Bridge said. "I'm the only one here who has fought in a war."

"Ah, yes, the Nyeian campaign. Your actions were so effective." Arianna turned toward him. She obviously knew how poorly he had done as an Infantry Leader.

He wasn't going to defend himself, so he deliberately misunderstood her. "Thank you."

Arianna made a soft sound of disgust. She stepped away from Lyndred. Bridge's daughter didn't move at all. Arianna studied them for a moment, then she said, "No matter what you choose to believe about me or my warnings, my brother will be here shortly and everything will change."

"I know," Lyndred said. "I've Seen it."

And then she walked away. Bridge watched her go.

"Your daughter is headstrong," Arianna said.

"Like my sister used to be."

Arianna nodded, watching as Lyndred disappeared into the corridor. For a moment, the Black Queen of the Fey seemed almost lost.

"Your lecture on surprise," Bridge said, "applies to my daughter. She will never do what you expect. And she certainly won't do what you want. Not unless she sees value in it. Right now, she believes you're Blind, and she will act on that."

Arianna was still watching the hallway. "She knows about the Blood."

"She knows. But she's smarter than I am. Cunning and manipulative, just like the best of my family. If you are Sighted, figure out a way to prove that to her, or she will stand against you."

"You'll tolerate this sort of disrespect from your child?"

Bridge smiled. "She's not showing disrespect to me."

"Disrespect to the family affects all of us."

"Really?" Bridge said. "Rugad never believed that. And isn't his the model you claim to be following?"

She turned to him, her expression flat. "Sometimes you accuse me of being like Rugad, and then you accuse me of not being like him at all. Which is it?"

"Does it matter?" he asked.

"Yes."

He shrugged, disliking the chill that was running up and down his spine. "Every person is different, Arianna. You can be like him and unlike him in turns."

She stared at him a moment longer. "I suppose."

"You can't run your government on an old model." He stopped, unused to giving anyone advice. But she was silent, as if she were listening. "Things are different here. You're different. You don't take advantage of those differences."

"What do you mean?"

"You're part Islander, and yet you talk of them as if they're another people. You can control them. You can stop this rebellion, and give Gift a chance. You've been apart from him long enough that your mistrust of him is coloring everything. Perhaps he's coming back because he's worried about you."

A slight frown creased her forehead. "Why are you doing this?"

"Advising you?"

She nodded once again, a curt half movement that urged him to get on with things.

"It seems to me that no one has, and you're floundering. Maybe if you have someone beside you who can offer insights, you'll be better off."

"Why would you help someone you believe to be Blind?"

"You say you're not. I have to believe that. You rule my people. And you are my niece."

"I never thought kindness a Fey attribute."

"That's because those of us who have it aren't that successful as Fey."

"Yet you would give me advice."

"Presumptuous, I know," he said. "But you're being impulsive. My father was impulsive. My grandfather used to say that's what got him killed."

"I'll bet your grandfather was impulsive when he was young."

"Probably," Bridge said. "But you're not young any longer. You have to make decisions based on what's best for our people. Not on what will keep you as head of the Fey."

"You believe I should step down."

"Only if you're Blind."

They stared at each other for a moment. Then Arianna said, "I will never step down. I will rule the Fey for the rest of my life."

Chapter Twelve

*T*HE *TASHKA* SLID into Jahn harbor as the morning sky was lightening in the east. Traces of yellow were barely visible above the river; the mountains were gray shadows in the distance.

Gift stood on deck, hands clasped behind his back, legs spread slightly. He had been unable to sleep. He had helped his Healers tend to the wounded, and he had found places for the dead. He would bury them here on the Isle, and send notices to their families.

Nyeian sailors were handling the ship now. The remaining Fey Sailors were below. The entry into Jahn harbor was easy enough to be handled by people without magic.

Skya was asleep below. She had stayed beside him as long as possible, but in the end, he had finally told her to get some rest. He knew that she had never seen slaughter like that.

He had. His entire life seemed filled with violent death. Reflecting on it now, he was astonished that the Shaman had only found one incident wherein he had caused someone to die.

Things were much different than he had expected. A

Doppelgänger among the Islanders, ready to send a message back to Jahn when he arrived. Islanders trying to destroy the Black Heir to prevent the Fey presence from taking over the Isle. Talk of reviving the deadlier parts of his father's religion, the parts that would kill any Fey who came into contact with it.

This was not the Isle Gift had left. These were the sorts of things his sister had avoided in the early years of her reign. She hadn't forbidden Rocaanism. She had accepted it, and asked that the destructive parts of it be modified so that the Fey could participate. Everything Arianna stood for had been about acceptance, not hatred.

What had happened on the river had all been about hatred.

Someone wanted him dead, and he knew that someone had Fey blood. His uncle Bridge, as the Doppelgänger had implied? Or Bridge's daughter? Or was there someone else, someone that Gift didn't know or expect?

The light in the eastern sky was getting brighter, and he could see more of Jahn. The city had changed while he was gone. The houses were painted, and there was a look of prosperity to the place.

He had often thought of the city as he had first seen it, when he was eighteen. Jahn had been a startlingly white city then. When sunlight fell on its streets, the brightness hurt the eyes. The stone bridge over the river was the same, its graceful arch the center of the city. But the matching buildings on either side of the bridge were no longer there. The Tabernacle had burned that year. Its shell still remained on that side of the river, a blackened, sunken remnant of the magnificence that once had terrified him.

The palace now appeared to be the heart of Jahn. The palace had three towers—the fourth removed a century ago, replaced with a kitchen and a ceiling that vented to the sky—and still looked shiny white. The eye went to it immediately, but somehow that made the skyline seem unbalanced, as if something were missing, something that was essential to the Isle itself.

Warehouses had been constructed by the water's edge,

and there were more ships in the harbor than he had ever seen. Arianna had opened trade with Galinas again, and Blue Isle's riches were sent all over the Fey Empire, just as the Empire's wealth returned to the Isle. Her peaceful policies had increased the quality of life all over the Empire.

He wasn't sure what had happened to his sister. Seger's message had been so urgent. What if Arianna had died? What if the changes were caused by his uncle Bridge, acting as ruler until Gift returned?

"It would be better if you slept before you left the ship." The voice behind him was soft.

He turned. Xihu stood there, her robe falling gracefully around her. Her shock of white hair formed a soft cloud around her head.

"I can't sleep," he said. "I keep seeing blood."

"Real blood?" she asked. "Or is it a Vision?"

"The deck," he said. "From yesterday afternoon."

She put a hand on his shoulder. "You have forgotten."

He shook his head slightly. "I haven't forgotten. This is my home. It just looks strange after years away."

"No," she said. "The Visions."

He stepped away from her so that he could see her face. Her brown eyes held a sorrow they hadn't had before.

"The Visions we had before we left Protectors Village," she said.

He suddenly felt light-headed. She was right. He hadn't been thinking of those at all.

"They Saw your sister give the Throne to a Fey man with coal-black hair, a man that Madot mistook to be you."

He nodded. He had thought then that it couldn't have been him, but someone who looked like him. Madot, his teacher at Protectors Village, had said that all of the Fey men in his family had the same look.

"Perhaps," he said, "she gave the Throne to Bridge."

"If she did," Xihu said, "it would not have been willingly. Remember the Warning."

The Warning had come to most of the Shaman the night before Madot had taken Gift to the Black Throne, the night before he rejected his heritage.

" 'The hand that holds the scepter shall hold it no more,' " he said, quoting the Warning as if he had received it from the Powers himself, " 'and the man behind the Throne shall reveal himself in all his glory.' "

"The Warning makes no more sense to me now than it did when I first heard it," he said. "There are a thousand interpretations. I could be the man behind the Throne. Or I could be the man Arianna hands the Throne to. Or Bridge could be."

"One thing is certain from all of these Visions," Xihu said. "Your sister will not hold the Throne forever. She may not be holding it now."

"I know," Gift said.

The ship continued to move forward, very slowly, looking for a place to dock near one of the warehouses.

"I have Seen nothing of her death, have you?" Xihu asked.

Gift shook his head. "Although what I have Seen is strange. Sometimes she doesn't seem like Arianna in my Visions. Once, I even saw her with black eyes."

"Eyes so deep that they seem to reflect nothing."

"Yes." Gift turned to her in surprise.

"The traditional eyes of a Black Ruler."

"You've Seen that too."

Xihu nodded.

"Your Vision came true," he said. "The arrows covered with blood."

She shivered. "I should have seen that for the Warning it was."

"You didn't know Islanders used bow and arrow. I did, but I didn't think anything of it."

"The eyes, Gift, were not from that Vision. In that Vision, her eyes were blue. And cold."

"You said she had a cruel face."

"Yes."

"These dark eyes, the eyes of a Black Leader, when did you See those?"

Xihu took a deep breath. "Only a few hours ago."

He felt a jolt run through his body. "You had a Vision?"

"Yes." Each time her voice got softer. "But you did not."

"I haven't had one in months." Until that moment, his lack of Vision hadn't concerned him. Now it made him wonder. "Do you think that's a problem?"

"I do not know," she said. "I wish you would See something."

"Why?"

"Because I keep Seeing the Blood, Gift."

"And the Triangle?"

She shook her head. "Just the Blood."

He stared at the palace. Theoretically, his sister was inside. Arianna, whom he had loved and trusted. "Your Visions have grown stronger the closer we've gotten."

"Yes."

"Do you think that's because I'll trigger the Blood?"

"I don't know what else has changed."

"Should I leave?"

She stared at the city. The dawn was turning orange and pink, the colors soft on the water. Jahn looked like a peaceful place, a beautiful place, not the city of terror that he remembered.

"Can you leave?" she asked gently.

The palace reflected the light. Whenever he looked at it, he thought of Sebastian, made of stone yet full of life. He thought of his father, a kind man who had a core so strong that he could beat the most powerful ruler the Fey had ever had. He thought of his mother, who had died within those walls.

"I have to see Arianna first," he said. "Then I can go."

Xihu folded her hands and placed them across her stomach. "If you're going to go, you should leave now. Before you see her."

"I came here because Seger said she was in trouble. If I go now, I might make things worse."

"You know that Seger's message could have been false, that the assassins could have been waiting for you on the riverbank because they knew you would arrive. Your presence here might be enough to trigger the Blood."

"You believe it is."

"My Visions have grown worse."

"I haven't Seen this at all. I thought a man was supposed to See his own death."

"You won't recognize it," she said. "You will think it's something you can change."

He looked at her. He had Seen a lot of things. He thought of the most vivid Vision he'd had recently, the one in which he'd been in water, feeling an undertow pull him down, wondering if he would drown, when an old man who looked like his great-grandfather tried to save him—a man whom Gift did not want to die in his place.

But as a young man, he thought he'd Seen his death. He'd actually had a Vision in which someone stuck a knife into his back. The Vision had come true, but not in the way he'd expected. It had altered drastically, through actions that were probably not his own. And he had not been the one who had been stabbed. That had been Sebastian.

He frowned. "Maybe I've Seen my death. But I thought I Saw my death once before, and it didn't come true."

"Perhaps it would have, if things had been different."

"Perhaps."

The ship brushed against the dock. Gift felt a small shudder beneath his feet, hearing the scrape of wood against wood. At that moment, the sun appeared on the horizon, bathing everything in light until the entire city was golden. Then the sun rose higher, and the light changed.

Gift was holding his breath. It was almost as if Jahn were blessed, as if there were a specialness to this place that he felt in no other. Perhaps because it was the closest thing he'd had to a home in the last fifteen years.

"I'm going to see her," he said. "And then we'll figure out—"

The sky turned black and he pitched forward, hitting the deck. For a moment, he thought something had happened to the sun, and then he realized that he was having a Vision. That everything was changing.

—A Fey woman with a perfect, narrow face and snapping black eyes touched Coulter's cheek. He tried to pull away, but she would not let him. She turned, looked at—

—Gift cradling a newborn in his arms. Tears ran down his cheeks. He didn't know how she could give this child up and return to a life without it. Without him—

—And the blood flowed—

—He was in water, thrashing, an undertow pulling him down. Water filled his mouth, tasting of brine and salt. The old Fey in the boat—his great-grandfather again? Or someone who looked like him?—reached for Gift, but if Gift took his hand, the old man would die. And Gift didn't want that. He looked up, expecting to see Arianna in robin form. Instead, he saw Ace, circling, concern on his bird face—

—Arianna wrapped her hands around her skull. She was screaming—

—Skya looked at him, her face bathed in sweat, her hair limp against her head. "I can't live like this," she said. "I do not belong here." He reached for her—

—And the blood flowed—

—His great-grandfather said, "You will never defeat me. I know more about Fey magic than you ever will."—

—"Of course he does." Gift's mother stood before him, her hands on his face. Her hair was half silver, just as it would have been if she had lived. He had never seen her look this old. "But you are your father's son. You are the center, Gift. The heart of everything, and you always have been. Your father and I were right, thirty-four years ago. Only you can bring peace. Only you."—

—And the blood flowed . . .

He opened his eyes. His right cheek was pressed into the wood of the deck, his left was hot in the morning sun. The air smelled faintly of river mold, a scent that always got worse around the Cardidas in the winter.

He was faintly dizzy. He blinked, wondering if Xihu had been felled by a Vision as well. He looked for her, saw her feet, then pushed himself up.

She was staring at the river. The Nyeian sailors were staring at the river too. And Skya, who was standing inside the deckhouse door, was staring just as they were.

"What?" It was as if his voice didn't work properly. It

scratched against his throat, almost as if he hadn't used it in a week.

Xihu stared at the water. He thought for a moment that she hadn't heard him, then she crouched beside him and extended her hand. He took it, and let her help him up.

She still hadn't taken her gaze off the river. Her expression was sadder than any he'd seen in a long time.

"It was an Open Vision," she said.

He swallowed against that dry throat. An Open Vision was rare. He'd had two before, once when he was a little boy and once when he was fighting the Black King.

"What was it?" he asked.

"Blood," she said and shuddered visibly. Her hand, so warm and dry within his, quivered.

"What kind of blood?" His Visions had had blood flowing through them, behind them, like the river itself, but there had been no specific images of blood.

"The whole river was blood. The surface was covered with it."

He looked. The early morning sky was reflected in its waters: reds and oranges and deep pinks, all of it looking fresh and wonderful and not like blood at all.

"Blood against Blood?" he asked.

"I hope not," she said.

But this time it was he who shuddered. He had Seen blood in all the Visions. He knew what it meant.

Xihu hadn't let go of his hand. "Is that what you Saw? Blood on the water?"

He shook his head. The Nyeian sailors were looking at him oddly, as if he were some kind of strange creature, something they had never seen before. He couldn't talk in front of them.

Skya hadn't moved from her place at the door. She had a hand over her stomach and she looked vaguely ill. For the first time since he had known her, he saw fear on her face. When his gaze met hers, she looked away.

The words she had spoken the day they met rose in his mind: *I don't like Shaman. They get in the way with their*

Visions and pronouncements and rules. And the look on her face when she discovered that he was a Visionary. Not fearful, not exactly. But not very happy either.

"Everyone Saw this, didn't they?" he asked Xihu.

"Yes," she said. "It was an Open Vision."

"Like a great battle had been fought?"

"Like a hundred people had died and the river was turning to blood."

He frowned. He'd seen that before, when his great-grandfather died at the Cliffs of Blood. There were dead all along the mountainside, and the water itself, always the color of blood, looked even redder.

"Was the water covered in blood or the color of blood?"

"You Saw it too," she said. "It was an Open Vision."

He shook his head. "I didn't See that. I had seven Visions. You Saw only one."

She leaned back on her heels. "I wonder what that means."

Gift frowned. When he'd had his last Open Vision, Scavenger had explained it. *Open Visions occur with firm destinies, when the parties are tied together by an event of such importance the fate of the world rests on it.*

He and Coulter had been in that first Open Vision, standing on a barge in the Cardidas, looking at the burned-out Tabernacle. Only when the Vision had come true, they weren't on a barge, but on the banks of the Cardidas, and it was after the Black King had died.

Gift had had seven Visions, eight if he wanted to count the blood running beneath it, but Xihu and the others had only Seen the blood.

Was that the only part with the firm destiny?

What if he wasn't supposed to bring peace? What if he was the center because he was the one who destroyed everything?

"What does it mean?" he asked.

Xihu ran her fingers along his cheek, a soft caress, almost a lover's touch. Then she leaned forward and kissed him on the forehead.

She walked away from him without answering, moved to the edge of the ship and stared into the water. He sat in the center of the deck, alone. Skya had disappeared. The Nyeian sailors were still staring at him.

The Visions disquieted him, as they always did. But it was Xihu's silence—her way of answering his question—that disturbed him most of all.

THE BLACK HEIR

CHAPTER THIRTEEN

COULTER WATCHED MATT pick his way across the broken steps that led to the Place of Power. In all the years that Coulter had made his way up these steps, he hadn't bothered to fix them. Somehow, changing this place seemed like a sacrilege, even if he were to make an improvement.

The morning was chill. The storm promised the day before never happened, and now the sky was clear. Sunlight reached this part of the Cliffs of Blood, but it was not warm. He could see his breath.

He pulled his heavy coat closer and wished he had remembered gloves, even though he knew he wouldn't need them once he went inside. His stomach was jumping. In all the years he had guarded this place for Gift, he had never tampered with it. Now he was going to.

Arianna had given him permission. With a wisp of a smile on her stone face, she had said, *Even though it doesn't seem like it, I'm still the Queen of Blue Isle. Whatever I say is more important than my brother's wishes.*

But Gift had impressed upon Coulter the importance of keeping the cave untouched. It had a power that Coulter could sense every time he stepped inside. King Nicholas and Matthias had tapped that power to defeat the Black King, but even then Coulter had sensed that the two men were touching only one small part of the cave's power.

Yet, here he was, introducing someone new to the cave's magic. He wouldn't have done it if it weren't necessary. If Rugad weren't still alive.

Matt took the final step and walked onto the stone ledge. Coulter could hear Matt's gasp, even though he was still several steps away. Then he heard Leen's voice. She had guard duty that morning. It was a tradition more than a necessity. Coulter had set up a single guard to make sure no one wandered accidentally into the place. At first, he had been the only guard. Now several of his trusted companions stayed here, rotating their shifts and maintaining constant vigil as if it were the most important thing in the world.

Perhaps it was.

Coulter climbed the remaining steps and walked onto the stone ledge. Leen had placed her chair away from the edge as she always did. She was standing, her hand on Matt's shoulder. He was looking at the giant swords embedded in the stone. They were huge and made of varin, just like the smaller swords inside the cave. Large jewels were embedded in the hilts, jewels that took and focused magic.

Matt stared at the swords, his mouth hanging open. Coulter hadn't warned Matt what he would see and, apparently, Matt's father had never described the place. These swords—this cave—had to have triple meaning for Matt. He was raised by the man who had once led this religion. He also knew that the cave had a magical center, just like the Place of Power in the Eccrasian Mountains, the place where the Fey themselves had originated. And this was the place where Matt's father had helped defeat the Black King.

If things worked right, Matt would complete the job his father had started.

Leen glanced over Matt's shoulder at Coulter. She had known they were coming up, but she hadn't approved of it. She felt that there had to be another way—teaching Matt a

Lamplighter Spell, perhaps—rather than using the tools of Rocaanism.

Coulter wanted to use the most powerful tools he had. He figured they would only have one chance at removing Rugad, and he didn't want that to fail.

He walked across the ledge—the place where he had sat countless times, the place where his adoptive father had died—and stopped beside Leen and Matt.

Matt was still staring at the swords. They formed a pattern: a sword in the front, two swords behind it, and two swords behind them. They formed a triangle, a way to focus power. His father had moved the swords from their positions around the cave's mouth to the positions they were in now. He had done it with the force of a magic he hadn't really accepted or believed in.

"They're so big," Matt whispered.

Leen nodded. Coulter didn't say anything. Maybe Matt knew the story after all.

"I always thought they were regular swords. My dad never said they were this big."

And impossible for one man to lift. Impossible for a dozen men to remove. It was only possible for these swords to move through an Enchanter's magic.

Matt looked at Coulter. "I'm just like him, aren't I?"

Coulter shook his head. "You have his skills. That doesn't make you like him."

Matt had turned back to the opening of the cave. There was something different in his manner, something in his eyes—a wisdom, a knowledge—that hadn't been there before. It was as if he were seeing more than anyone else when he looked at the entrance.

He had been different when he came back from the Vault. He was shaken and saddened by his encounter with his brother, but Coulter had expected that. He hadn't expected any help from Alex, but had sent Matt anyway, hoping that they wouldn't have to come up here.

But Matt had done something unexpected. Matt had used a spell that even Coulter wasn't familiar with to absorb the Words. Late last night, Coulter had stayed in the library, reading about the spell in the few books that mentioned it. One book described how the spell was performed. Another discussed the goals of the magic, and a third mentioned the fact that the spell was not something that should be used lightly.

Then Coulter had sent for Seger and told her what Matt had done. She sat down abruptly on a nearby couch, as if her legs couldn't hold her.

Let's hope there's nothing harmful in those Words, she had said, *for they're a part of him now.*

A visible part. Seger seemed to think the personality of the writer would seep into Matt's mind, the way a touch of an aromatic spice changed the taste of food.

Coulter felt as if he could already see those changes. But he wasn't sure if what he saw was because he expected a change, or because a change actually had occurred.

He put a hand on Matt's back. "Are you ready to go inside?"

Matt nodded, his mouth a thin line. His chin trembled.

Leen looked at Coulter. She had become more reserved since Arianna's arrival. "I'll stay out here."

"Thanks," Coulter said.

Matt didn't even seem to hear her. Coulter kept his hand on Matt's back, guiding him around the swords as they walked to the mouth of the cave.

Matt hadn't commented on anything yet, which Coulter found unusual. When he'd first come to the Place of Power, he'd seen the cave as a point of magic. At the time, he hadn't been able to identify what that strangeness was, but he had found it compelling. Matt had grown up beside the Cliffs of Blood and probably accepted that feeling as normal. His father would have prevented him from going to the cave, and Matt probably didn't think a thing of it.

But the compulsion to go inside grew as Coulter got closer to the cave. He had to think that it felt the same way to Matt, only Matt said nothing.

As they passed the last sword, Matt reached up and placed his hand on the jeweled hilt. A little shock ran through his back. Coulter knew this feeling too, the way the swords hummed with power. It was always unexpected to touch an inanimate object and realize that it felt alive.

He braced himself for Matt's questions, but again Matt said nothing. Instead Matt let his hand fall and continued forward.

They stopped at the mouth of the cave. Heat radiated from the interior, a heat for which Coulter had never found the source. A pale pink light came with the heat. It looked as if a sun burned inside the cave. Once that light had been a brilliant white, but it was no longer.

Coulter felt his heart pound as he stepped inside.

The walls and ceiling were white as they had always been. But the floor had changed. The once-white surface had turned red. The redness flowed forward, dripping down the stairs that led to the fountain burbling below.

The fountain was the same. The water flowed into a basin and then disappeared again in the wall. The power in this place concentrated around that water.

Coulter had a theory about the fountain. He believed its water was the source of Islander magic, but he hadn't discussed that with anyone else. It was one of the many reasons he guarded the mouth of the cave.

Matt was staring at the floor. He did know the story then: how his father and Nicholas, their hands joined, had dripped blood onto the floor, and that blood had remained, coloring everything. Matt crouched, touching the surface with a reverence that made Coulter slightly uncomfortable.

He let the boy alone, though. Matt had never had the chance to say a proper good-bye to his father. Perhaps he could do so here.

While he waited, Coulter focused on the walls. Behind him were swords. In another section were chalices. In a different area, vials of holy water. Toward the back were the tapestries that Adrian and Nicholas had studied to determine how many of these items were used.

The balls that created the Lights of Midday were depleted, nearly used up in the battle against Rugad. Coulter doubted any of them would work again.

He remembered how those globes felt beneath his hands, smooth and hot. When he held them, light flared, a powerful killing light that seemed to touch the Fey in the heart of their magic. He had stood beside Nicholas, holding the globes, the light finding the jewels and focusing it on the army below.

How many people had died that day? He didn't know. He had tried to back away from those globes, tried to stop when he realized that the screams from below had come from his magic—his hands—but Nicholas wouldn't let him.

Coulter shook off the memory. He never wanted to touch those things again.

Matt stood. "Where are they?"

He meant the Soul Repositories. Coulter knew that there were dozens up here, along with the blood of the Roca, blood that Matt now assured him would attract any magical soul into one of those Repositories.

That's what they're designed for, Matt had said, his voice sounding more authoritative than usual. *They are designed to capture the soul of your enemy.*

"They're by the tapestries," Coulter said.

Matt glanced down at the fountain. He'd already been instructed to stay away from it, but he wasn't looking at it with longing. He was looking at it as if he heard something.

Then Coulter sensed it: the presences he'd felt before. He knew that these were Mysteries or Powers. When Jewel had come to visit her family, he could never see her, but he could sense her, just as he had been able to sense all the Powers that were unleashed when Nicholas had drunk the water.

"What is that?" Matt whispered.

Coulter waited a moment, sensing several different personalities coming up the stairs toward them. "Mysteries, probably," he said. "They feel more like people than Powers do."

"Mysteries?"

"The Fey say that's where Vision comes from. The Mysteries are the souls of people who've been murdered. They are visible to three people and three people only: the person they love the most, the person they hate the most—who is usually the person who killed them—and another person of their choosing."

Matt backed up. He grabbed Coulter's arm and tried to pull him toward the entrance.

"What are you doing?" Coulter asked.

"One of those things killed my father."

Jewel. Matthias had murdered her, and she had sought revenge.

"You don't know that," Coulter said. "Your father probably died of exposure in the back corridors."

He was sorry to speak so harshly, but he couldn't let Matt leave, not now.

"My father said if he came into this place, he would die. The thing grabbed him by the throat and tried to choke the life from him once. Then he was ready for her the second time—"

"Using the Soul Repository." Coulter had seen the first attack, and saw the Repository where Matthias had briefly imprisoned Jewel.

"Yes." Matt was pulling on Coulter's arm. "Come on. Let's get out of here."

Coulter put his hand over Matt's. "They won't harm you unless you've killed someone. They probably just want to see you."

Matt had stopped moving but his body was rigid. "Why?"

"I don't know," Coulter said. "I've never been able to talk to one. But Gift tells me they're just like regular people. They're probably curious."

Matt inclined his head backward, then ducked behind Coulter. "Something's touching me."

"Let him alone," Coulter said. "Please. He's just a boy."

He held Matt against him, as if he were defending him. Coulter had never been with anyone before who could feel the presences as he did. The presences crowded around them, but didn't seem to move. After a moment, the feeling of them eased. They weren't gone, but they weren't close any longer.

"Are you sure they won't hurt me?" Matt whispered.

"Have you harmed any Fey?" Coulter asked.

"No."

"Then I'm sure they won't hurt you."

Matt let him go and stepped beside him. Matt's face was flushed and his eyes were too bright. "Why Fey?"

"I don't know," Coulter said. "It's just that I don't know of any Islanders—" Then he paused and corrected himself. "Any modern Islanders who've become Mysteries."

"There are ancient ones?"

Coulter looked at Matt sideways. "You tell me. You're the one who's absorbed the Words."

Matt looked down. "The terms are different."

"But the effect is the same," Coulter said.

"There've been Islanders murdered since the Roca's time."

"Yes," Coulter said. "But not by you, right?"

Matt smiled as if the idea of killing anyone was ridiculous to him. Coulter felt a slight twinge because he was sending an innocent to do a job no innocent should ever do.

"Not by me," Matt said.

"Then you'll be fine." Coulter put his hand against Matt's back again. "Come on. Let's do this."

Matt looked down the stairs, past the fountain, to the darkness of the corridors beyond. "Do you think my father was one of those Mysteries?"

Coulter frowned. "I don't know. I don't know what the rules are for that. We're not even sure how he died."

Matt nodded, but didn't look satisfied. "If I went down those corridors, do you think I could find him?"

Coulter pushed Matt farther forward. "You're not going into one of those corridors."

"Why not?"

"Because you can lose time in there. What feels like an hour can be a day. What feels like a day can be a week."

"So my father could still be wandering down there?"

Coulter shivered. He couldn't help himself. He didn't want to think about Matthias alive. "I don't pretend to understand this place."

"But—"

"Matt." There was more anger in Coulter's voice than he had expected. "Don't make me regret bringing you here."

Matt's lower lip trembled. "He's my father."

"I know," Coulter said. "But you're here against orders from King Nicholas, against Gift's wishes. They never wanted anyone to come into this cave, and they certainly wouldn't approve of a member of your family being here."

"But Arianna said it was all right."

"Yes. She believes in you and knows what's at stake. Don't destroy that trust."

"My father—"

"Your father has been gone for six months. Even in the best of conditions, he could not be alive. We've always known that, Matt. Don't let the magic in this place seduce you into believing otherwise." Coulter put his hands on Matt's shoulders and turned the boy toward him. "If you can't withstand the magic here, you'll never be able to face the Black King."

Matt's eyes filled with tears.

Coulter pulled him close. Matt's entire body was shuddering. He rested his head against Coulter's shoulder, and Coulter realized he hadn't really held the boy since his father's death.

Matt snuffled for a moment, then backed out of the embrace. He wiped his face with the back of his hand, then used the sleeve of his jacket.

"I tried to talk to Alex about my father," Matt said. "He wouldn't listen. He thinks I'm betraying my father's memory."

Coulter brushed one of Matt's curls off his forehead. "Your father came here where he wasn't wanted, and helped Nicholas kill Rugad. His biggest accomplishment was to protect his home from Rugad's ambitions."

"I know." Matt's voice sounded choked.

"If you get the Repository and go to the palace, if you defeat Rugad once and for all, you'll have done more for your father than Alex ever could."

Matt looked at Coulter, and for the first time there was hope in Matt's eyes. "You think?"

Coulter's heart ached. He was manipulating this boy by telling him the truth. "Yes."

Matt blinked twice, a single tear running from the corner of his left eye. He brushed at his cheek impatiently. "I hadn't thought of it that way. But you're right. My father said getting rid of the Black King was the best thing he'd done after marrying my mother."

And fathering his sons fell beneath that. Coulter mentally cursed Matthias. The man had done so much to hurt his boys, and almost all of it through carelessness.

But was that worse than what Coulter was doing? He was sending Matt into danger. Matt, with his pure heart.

Coulter put his hand on Matt's arm and said softly, "You don't have to go through with this, you know. We can come up with some other plan."

Matt frowned, as if he hadn't expected the change in direction. "No. I've come this far. I can do this, Coulter. Do you think I can't?"

"I know you can," Coulter lied. "I just want to make sure you do it for your reasons, not mine."

Matt ran a thumb beneath his eyelid and sighed. "If I stayed here, knowing what I know, I'd never respect myself again. My only choice is to go forward."

Coulter understood that too well. He had backed off at the wrong moment and had berated himself for years. That was why Arianna had had to push him to act this time. And deep down, he was afraid he had waited too long.

"Then let's do this," he said.

Matt shot one more uncertain glance at the fountain, then walked to the corner where the dolls rested. They were made of handblown glass and seemed amazingly lifelike. Matt was staring at them as if he had never seen anything like them. And that was impossible, since he had seen the dolls in the Vault. He had said so.

"What's wrong?" Coulter asked.

"They're full," Matt said. "There are souls in them."

In spite of himself, Coulter shuddered. Years ago, when they were trying to figure out the cave, Adrian and Nicholas had opened one of these and released the soul of an Ancient

Islander. But they had not tried to open the rest. Coulter had always believed that to be a sign.

"How can you tell?" Coulter asked.

"I don't know." Matt crouched beside him. "They just seem different."

Coulter glanced at him from the corner of his eye. Was this one of the things that Matt had absorbed from the Words? Coulter wasn't going to ask. Not yet.

"Are all of them full?"

"I can't tell." Matt was biting his lower lip.

"Then I guess we need to find out. We only need one of these."

"And the vials of blood." Matt looked at them. The old blood glinted redly inside the glass vials. That was supposed to be the Roca's blood, although Coulter wasn't sure he believed it. Still, anything was possible up here.

"We'll get those last." Coulter reached for the dolls. They were very small, about the size of his hand. He saw at least twenty in front and more behind.

Matt hadn't moved.

"If you're going to do this," Coulter said, "you're going to have to help me."

Matt grimaced. It was almost as if he didn't want to touch a full Repository. But Coulter wasn't going to wait for Matt to get over his squeamishness. Coulter grabbed the nearest doll by the arm, surprised at the smoothness of the glass. He couldn't tell if the doll was supposed to be male or female, but it was very delicate.

The doll stirred as he touched it. Its eyes opened, and its face, which had been clear glass a moment before, was light gold. Its lips pinkened as he watched, and its cheeks flushed with color. Then its eyes became a hard, focused blue.

Matt gasped. The doll reached for him, then pointed at the vials. Coulter set the doll down. It reached again, opened its mouth, and froze in that position. Slowly, the color leached out of the glass and the movement ceased. The eyes were the last thing to disappear.

"It cursed you," Matt said.

Coulter's hands were shaking. He couldn't pick them all

up to move them, searching for an empty doll. He couldn't bear to refuse them all, and he didn't dare release them, not knowing why they were imprisoned.

"Can you see which one of these are empty and which ones are full?" Coulter's voice wasn't as steady as he wanted it to be. He wiped his hands on his breeches. He could still feel the glass beneath his palm, warming to his touch.

"I can see the ones in front," Matt said. "They're all full."

"What about behind?"

Matt shook his head. He hadn't taken his eyes off the doll that moved. Its face had frozen in a different position, in the position of the curse.

Coulter sighed. He hated to waste magic on small tasks, but he saw no other choice. He wasn't going to touch any more of those things. He pointed a finger at the dolls and lifted them one by one, moving them to an empty spot in the wall.

Matt watched as Coulter moved the dolls. Apparently his magical touch didn't create the same response as his nonmagical one. The dolls clinked as he moved them, and he was careful not to hit them too hard. That glass, smooth as it was, felt fragile. The last thing he wanted to do was break one of them. He didn't know if that would release the spirit or destroy it.

Finally Matt said, "Stop."

Coulter clenched his fist. The last doll he moved leaned against the rest. There were still five in their original positions.

"I think those are empty," Matt said.

"I don't want to pick one up and have it move on me."

"It won't," Matt said.

Coulter took a deep breath, then reached forward. He grabbed the nearest doll. The glass was just as smooth as the first, but that was the only similarity. The doll was lighter, and it did not move, even though the glass warmed beneath his touch.

Coulter swallowed hard. He had been more nervous than he had thought. He handed the doll to Matt.

"This is yours," Coulter said. "You'll need to take it with you to Jahn."

Matt held it as if it were an undersized baby. He stared at it for a moment.

"Would you like more than one, just in case?"

Matt shook his head. "I can always make another," he said absently. Then he gasped and looked at Coulter as if Coulter had caught him in a lie.

Coulter didn't speak for a moment. Then he asked, keeping his voice calm, "Is making one of these easy?"

Matt flushed. "I didn't know I could until I touched it. Honest. I wouldn't have come here otherwise."

His eyes were tear-lined again, as if he were afraid Coulter was going to punish him for the omission. Yet Coulter believed Matt's last statement. Magic didn't work in a linear manner. Just because Matt had absorbed knowledge didn't mean that he had gone through it all.

"Well?" Coulter asked.

"No, it's hard," Matt said. "I need to use a special recipe for the glass, then I have to find someone who can blow it smooth."

Coulter reached forward and grabbed another doll. "Just in case. Keep them separate from each other."

Matt nodded.

"You're probably going to have to carry one of them at all times. You'll have to make it invisible. It'll be a drain on your magic."

"I'd already thought of that. I thought I wouldn't hide it until I got inside of Jahn."

"Maybe even inside the palace," Coulter said.

Matt sighed. He glanced at the vials of blood. "How much of that should I bring?"

"I don't know. Tell me how to use these things."

Matt stared at the one he held. "You take off the head. Then you put some of the Roca's blood inside. Two drops is enough to lure a loose soul."

"All right." Coulter couldn't resist a glance at the full Repositories. "Take as many as you can carry just in case Rugad proves more difficult."

"All right." Matt's finger traced the doll's features. "There's no way you can come with me?"

"Rugad knows me. He saw me when we fought for Arianna. He'd know right away who I am."

Matt nodded. He didn't look happy.

"You're going to have to set up a block inside your mind," Coulter said. "You can't let him look inside you."

"Can he?"

"I don't know. He was a Visionary, although that Vision is gone now, so I'm not sure he can do anything. But we should always prepare for him to be smarter than we give him credit for."

Matt wrapped his hand around the doll and brought it close to his chest. "How powerful can one man be?"

"Your father killed him once," Coulter said. "And Rugad was prepared for that. He was prepared for his death by leaving part of himself in Arianna's mind. His voice was in Sebastian, and that could have brought him back. He might have even left a bit in Gift's mind as well."

"You mean, even if I destroy him, this isn't over?"

"It's over if we find a way to warn Gift," Coulter said.

"And if we don't?"

Coulter glanced at the three remaining empty dolls. "We'll have to do this again."

Chapter Fourteen

$\mathcal{L}$YNDRED STOOD AT her windows as she had since dawn. Something had drawn her out of her bed. She had grabbed a fleece robe for warmth, wrapped it around her, and pushed the windows open.

The garden below was barren. The tree branches, empty of their leaves, reached to the sky. The magnificent flowers that she had seen when she first arrived were long gone, their stems brown and dead, the hedges on which some of them grew mere sticks jutting out of patches of dying grass. The rich smell of decay reached her on the cold morning breeze.

But that wasn't what caught her attention. What had drawn her from her warm bed to the window was a disquiet, as if something had gone horribly wrong.

She had awakened from a dream in which a Fey man with blue eyes—a man who looked like a male version of Arianna—was standing before her. She touched his face. His skin was warm. He leaned back, trying to move away from her fingers, but she put a hand on his shoulder, holding him in place. He seemed uncomfortable with her, as if he didn't trust her. As if he never would. She stepped closer to him, and then she heard her name being called. She turned—

And woke up.

The dream had the clarity of a Vision. She had to go to the window, and as she did, she had a sense of blood.

It was that feeling that had her standing at the window long after the sensation had left. Her hands were numb from the cold, her feet chilled. The skin on her face was icy, and she was sniffling. But she hadn't moved.

For the briefest of instants, she thought the Cardidas was covered in blood.

A movement in the corner of the garden caught her eye. A gull swooped, then landed on the gate, its body partially obscured by a thick tree branch. Gulls were rare in the garden. They usually ventured away from the river only when they were certain of food, and since they were scavengers, they rarely killed their own. This gull looked as if it was here for a purpose.

The gull hopped onto the nearby branch and she gasped. A Fey man rode on its back. A Gull Rider. Lyndred leaned out the window farther, and the Rider's Fey head turned toward her.

Ace.

It took a moment for her to realize she had said his name out loud. He hopped closer, the gull's head tilted. Then he flew toward her. She moved away from the open window, and he landed on the floor inside. He shifted to his Fey form, his legs appearing first, then the gull's head receding into his body. Finally he stood before her, naked.

She had forgotten how tall he was, how trim and muscular. But she hadn't forgotten the feeling of his skin against her fingers, how rough it was, almost like scales, and the fineness of his featherlike black hair.

Somehow she had always imagined that when she saw him again, she would run into his arms and hold him, but his eyes held her back. They seemed as cold as the bird's.

"How did you get here?" she asked. "My father sent you on a mission."

"I completed it." His voice was deeper than she remembered, and very familiar. "I see you're comfortable."

She shrugged. He was beautiful. This time, he didn't try to hide his nakedness, and she didn't pretend that she had never seen a naked man before. But the flirtatiousness that had been between them was gone.

"Is there something wrong with that?" she asked. "You knew that's where we were headed."

"You've been here a long time."

"Things are not quite as we expected."

He studied her for a moment, then he reached out and took her chin between his thumb and forefinger. His nails were long, almost like talons, and could have scratched her, but his touch was gentle. The way he studied her reminded her of her dream, of the blue-eyed Fey whom she had held in just the same way.

Then he brought his lips to hers. In all their flirting, he had never kissed her. His lips were soft like other men's, but the slight brush they gave hers sent a warmth through her and made her realize how long it had been since anyone had held her.

He started to move back, but she followed him, parting her lips and catching his, deepening the kiss. His hand on her chin kept them apart. It was almost as if he couldn't help himself, almost as if he had a compulsion to kiss her, a compulsion he wanted to deny.

She tried to step closer, but his fingers dug into her skin, exerting a mild force to hold her back. He broke the kiss and lifted his head. His eyes were hot, passionate, the opposite of what they had been a moment before. He was as aroused as she was. She grabbed the ties of her robe to open it, but he caught her hands with one of his own.

"No," he said.

She pulled her chin from his grasp, but let him continue to hold her hands. "You want to. I want to. What's wrong with that?"

His fingers brushed the hair behind her ear.

"I missed you," she said.

For a moment, he stared at her, and she could see the

longing on his face. Then he let her go, whirled, and grabbed a blanket off her bed. He wrapped it around himself.

"We can't," he said.

"My father already knows I'm an adult." She untied her robe and let it fall open as she walked toward him. "He might be upset, but he's no one to be afraid of."

Ace grabbed the ties on her robe and fastened them, pulling it tighter than she would have. "It's not your father that has me worried."

Lyndred waited. Something had happened. Something much more significant than the passage of six months.

She ran a hand through her hair and turned away from him, walking back to the window. The river of blood. The dream that had been like a Vision. And now Ace. Then there was all of the turmoil of the day before. Arianna and her Blindness. Lyndred's father and his foolishness. And the decisions Lyndred had made about the Throne itself.

The passion she had felt a moment ago had disappeared. The cold wind felt good against her skin. "How did you get here?"

"To your room or to the palace?"

"Onto the Isle."

He didn't answer.

The river glinted in the thin sunlight. She could see only bits of it through the buildings on the bank.

"The last time I saw you, you were headed toward Galinas. What brought you to Blue Isle? Your loyalty to my father?"

He swallowed so hard that she heard it. "The mission I took was to find Gift. But you knew that."

There it was again, that thread of accusation. She wasn't sure she had heard it the first time, when he had said, *I see you're comfortable*. But this time she recognized it for what it was. He blamed her for something she didn't yet understand.

"Of course I knew," she said. "Why else would anyone send a Gull Rider across the Infrin Sea?"

She turned then. A frown appeared on his forehead and disappeared just as quickly. That hurt expression in his eyes grew. He knew she had lied to him. Her father had told her about the mission—or at least, what he had guessed about it.

"But why would you come to Blue Isle?" She put her hands on the sill, then leaned on it. "For some reason, I can't believe you came here because of me."

He flushed and came toward her, his face open and very vulnerable. "I missed you too, Lyndred. I just didn't expect to see you. I thought maybe you'd be gone already."

This time she was the one to step away from him. "I'm still here."

"I know."

"Is that a problem?"

He glanced out the window, almost as if he were looking for someone. "Aren't you cold?"

"No." She crossed her arms. "What are you doing here, Ace? And who did you come with?"

She already knew. He had come with Gift. And he was doing reconnaissance for Gift. Was Gift more interested in the Black Throne than he was in his sister? Had Arianna been right?

"How's Arianna?" Ace asked.

He wasn't answering her questions. "Fine."

"So what are you still doing here?"

Lyndred had had enough. She walked toward him and put her hand in the middle of his chest, shoving him back toward the bed. "I'm done answering your questions. Now you get to answer mine."

The force of her hand made him trip on the edge of the blanket. He caught himself too late, and fell into a sitting position. He let the blanket drop, thinking, apparently, that she was going to try to seduce him. But she was too angry for that now.

"Are you traveling with Gift?"

Ace took a deep breath, glanced at the window again, and then said, "Someone tried to kill him when he came through the Stone Guardians. There were Islander assassins waiting for him."

"Maybe he's not well liked on the Isle."

"Maybe. But we found a Doppelgänger living among the Islanders. He said that he was to report back to the palace."

Like the Hawk Rider. So Arianna *was* trying to kill her brother. She was going to allow the Islanders to do it, and when they succeeded, she wanted one of her people to report.

"Are you sure that's all the Doppelgänger was doing?" Lyndred asked. "Wasn't he supposed to influence the Islanders so that they would attack Gift?"

That wounded look crossed Ace's face again, but he hid it quickly. He didn't suspect Arianna of attacking her brother.

He suspected Lyndred.

"He said"—Ace spoke carefully, his tone dull and flat—"that he was supposed to report back. He denied taking any action. He said the Islanders were already going to attack when he joined them."

"Hmm." She walked to the window, bent down, and looked into the garden. It was still empty. Fortunately, there were no gardeners tending things as there had been all summer. She reached for the edges of the windows and pulled them closed. Then she pulled down the tapestry that blocked the light. The room wasn't quite dark. Still it took a moment for her eyes to adjust so that she could still see Ace's face.

"Why did you do that?" he asked.

She had trusted him once. "I want to meet my cousin Gift, and I don't want Arianna to know."

"Why not?"

Two different answers crossed her mind. In the first, she imagined herself telling him everything. But he was a lowly Gull Rider who had never learned anything about Leadership. He wouldn't be a good confidant, even if he did have insights. In the second, she thought of blackmailing him, promising to tell all if he made love to her. But she wasn't that desperate.

"You don't have a need to know," she said. "You're just the messenger."

He remained motionless for a moment. Then he looked down, nodded once, and gathered the blanket tighter around him.

"I'm sorry for the way I acted a moment ago," he said softly. "I wasn't lying when I said I missed you."

"I'm not going to give you any information, Ace. No matter how sweetly you talk to me." No matter how much she wanted to.

He stood, looking awkward in that blanket. "I'm supposed to find out how Arianna is. I'm supposed to see if I can catch a glimpse of her."

"Why?"

"Because Gift wants to be careful. Someone tried to kill him."

Very smart. She would do the same under similar circumstances. "Tell him his sister is fine."

Ace shook his head. "I can't. I have to see her for myself."

"Why?"

"Gift has some questions and I want to be able to answer them honestly." Ace was still using that flat, cautious tone.

"I'll answer them," Lyndred said.

"No. I have to do it myself."

Even the small trust they had had was gone. Unless Lyndred had been making it up out of her own neediness.

"Then you'll die," Lyndred said.

"I can be discreet."

Lyndred smiled. It was a reflex; she knew the smile didn't reach her eyes. "I'm sure you can. But you don't know our Black Queen. She'll find you, break your bones into fine twigs, and then find out everything you know and things you didn't know you knew. Is that what you want to do for your friend Gift?"

Ace's dark eyes studied her. His face remained completely still. It was a birdlike expression, measuring, cautious, and completely without emotion.

"I thought," he said, "that Arianna was our compassionate Queen. Lover of peace and things humane."

"I thought the same," Lyndred said. "And then I met her. She's none of those things."

"But we've been at peace for years."

"She calls it a rest between wars."

Only Ace's eyes moved. "How do you know she'd kill me?"

"If you think I'm lying to you, test me. Risk your life." Lyndred crossed her arms and lowered her voice. "Or do you think I'm the ruthless one? Do you think that I'm trying to wrest the Throne from my cousins?"

"No." But his dark gaze slid away from hers. He was lying.

"You still want to see her yourself?"

"I have to."

"Then the best way to do it is to come through the front gates, by foot, and say that you must report to my father. Everyone will testify that you were on the ship, and Arianna already knows about the other Gull Rider. You'll get to meet Arianna. But I won't be able to guarantee that you can rejoin Gift."

Ace ran a hand through his feathered hair. He turned away from her and touched the tapestry with his taloned fingers. She wondered if her decision to shut the window made him feel trapped.

"I will talk to Gift," Ace said without turning. "I will tell him your proposal. But I can't guarantee anything. He makes his own decisions."

"I would worry about him if he didn't." Lyndred bit her lower lip. She was more concerned about Ace than she wanted to admit. "You're not going to try to see Arianna, are you?"

"I'll let Gift make that decision as well," Ace said.

"Tell him what I said."

Ace nodded. She didn't like the fact that he wouldn't look at her. She wanted to go to him, to touch his arm, to pull him against her. She didn't want him to be punished for spying on the Black Queen. But she had already warned him, maybe too many times. And he would make up his own mind.

She didn't like men she couldn't control.

Her hands became fists, tucked within her crossed arms. "Tell me," she said, "is my cousin Gift as ruthless as his sister?"

"You can decide for yourself when you meet him," Ace said. He pushed aside the tapestry, and unlatched the windows. Then he climbed on the ledge, keeping the blanket clutched around him. He turned and looked at her. His dark eyes remained cold, birdlike, assessing. There was nothing of the man who had introduced himself to her aboard ship. No playfulness, no warmth.

Then he leapt into the air, letting the blanket fall. By the time she made it to the window, he had shifted. The gull was lower than her window, his head and torso barely visible on top.

He didn't wave to her. He didn't even look at her. Instead he flew over the wall and toward the river.

She watched until she could no longer see him. Then she closed and latched the window, and prepared herself for the day ahead.

CHAPTER FIFTEEN

*G*IFT DECIDED TO walk the short distance from the Cardidas River to the palace. He started out shortly after his meeting with Ace. Skya was beside him, Xihu behind him. Ace flew above, looking worried. Other Gull Riders were already in place, ready to protect him. Gift also brought a few Foot Soldiers to act as bodyguards. He hadn't thought such a move necessary until that morning when Ace returned looking upset and more than a little frightened.

Gift swayed as he walked. He hadn't gotten his land legs back. He kept his hands at his side more for balance than for readiness. Although he did carry a knife, and so did Skya.

She hadn't wanted to go with him, but he had convinced her. She had been cool to him since the Open Vision—cool and distant and sad. He wasn't sure what was causing the sadness. The coolness and the distance he could attribute to the fact that the Vision had reminded her exactly what he was.

Someday he would have to find out what it was about Visionaries that made her so wary.

The walk felt familiar. He had been on this path a hundred times in his life. The first time he had actually run, with Arianna in pursuit. She had been angry enough to kill him that day.

It had been the day they met.

He smiled at the memory. Over time, they had become close. No one would have been able to tell the boy who fled his sister that they would later become close.

He still trusted her, despite what he had heard from Ace, despite what he had seen as the ship had traveled inland. Arianna had been mercurial and difficult, but she had been the best choice to rule both Blue Isle and the Fey. It had been Gift's decision fifteen years ago to place her in that position. He hadn't wanted to be a leader. He had known what it entailed, and at the time, he hadn't thought he had the stomach for it.

This trip had shown him otherwise.

Skya was watching him. She wore her purple, red, and gold silk robes—the outfit she had worn when they first met. The robes fell in layers. She had a sword tied to her waist, and the knife was in a holder beneath her left arm. Around her neck was a small collar of bells. She jingled as she walked. Her hair was pulled away from her face, accenting the sharpness of her features. She looked beautiful and exotic, clearly a creature who did not belong in Blue Isle.

She had done this for effect, and he suspected the target was not Arianna but him. He wasn't sure about the message, though, and he wasn't ready to ask.

Ace kept swooping down, as if to call attention to himself. Gift ignored him. Ace had wanted to come back to the palace alone, to enter as Lyndred had told him to do. Gift was worried that Lyndred had planned some kind of trick, and Ace acknowledged the possibility.

Gift knew that Arianna would never kill anyone for spying on her, but he was wary as well. He had received warning after warning, some from Visions, some from Legends, and one from the spirit of his mother, that there was something wrong with his sister.

He also didn't like the fact that his uncle Bridge was here, or the things he'd heard about his cousin Lyndred. Yet Ace claimed that Bridge was a decent man—the most decent man in the Black Family, Ace had said, and then flushed. Apparently, he thought Bridge more decent than Gift. To Ace's credit, though, he didn't apologize.

Ace had also admitted, in this morning's meeting, that he was deeply attracted to Lyndred. He had offered that information as an acknowledgment that his judgment might be clouded. Gift found it interesting that Ace seemed to feel she was untrustworthy in all matters, not just those of the heart.

Gift had decided, long before Ace revealed his feelings for Lyndred, that he would not visit his cousin—at least, not until he had seen his sister. He had a feeling more would come of this meeting than he might like.

He had told no one of his mother's words. *Arianna has been infected with dark magic. She is becoming what the Black Throne needs.*

And the Throne, which his mother considered a live thing, needed someone who would continue the Fey's conquering of the world. The Throne wanted the Fey to have the Triangle of Might.

"Gift?" Xihu asked softly.

Gift shook his head. He wasn't going to discuss this. Not with anyone. He had to see for himself.

Even though his mother had warned him against that too.

I fear for you if you go to Jahn, she had said. *Sometimes dark magic triggers other dark magic.*

But, he had said to his mother, *Ari needs my support.*

It will take you months to reach her, his mother replied, *and by then she will be gone.*

Dead?

I chose my words carefully, his mother had said, and explained no more.

He had believed her then, and part of him believed her now. But he also knew that there were many things she hadn't been allowed to tell him. She had conveyed to him, in that brief meeting, that she believed he and Arianna were corrupted, and that he had to have children to allow his parents' Vision to continue.

Children.

His whole life had been about learning until six months ago, when Madot had taken him to see the Black Throne. And only then had he realized he had been walking the wrong path.

He still wasn't sure of the right one. Perhaps that alone was reason to stay away from his sister. But he couldn't shake the feeling that something was wrong. He didn't take prophesies and warnings from Mysteries—even if the Mystery was his mother—as literal truth. He had to see for himself.

"Gift?" Xihu said again.

"What?" He had to struggle to keep the impatience from his voice.

"There are other ways. She could come to you."

They were halfway to the palace. It gleamed ahead of them, its white walls untouched by the colors that had sprung up all over Jahn.

"We've discussed this, Xihu. I want to go to the palace. I want to see all that's changed."

"The palace is the place your sister controls," Xihu said.

"She controls the Empire. And I don't like having the same discussion more than once, especially if the sole purpose is to make me change my mind."

Xihu raised her chin slightly. "You used to listen when a Shaman spoke."

"I used to be an apprentice." The words were more bitter than he had intended.

Xihu sighed, and said no more. Skya studied him, frowning. He did not meet her gaze. She was coming as his companion, not his guide, and he had told her that. When she had opened her mouth to deny the relationship, he had placed a finger over her lips.

You have been my companion all the way across the Infrin Sea, he had said. *I didn't need to be guided home.*

She had moved her face away from his hand. *The word*

companion *makes me feel like an extension of you. It diminishes me.*

Nothing diminishes you, he had said, but she hadn't believed him. And when she had appeared on deck, just before his party left, she had been wearing her exotic robes. She had walked beside him, and said nothing until now.

No one else spoke. Ace continued to dive, and Gift continued to ignore him. The only sounds were their footsteps on the cobblestone and the jingle of Skya's bells. Even the town around them was silent.

He straightened his shoulders and focused on the palace. He was almost there. The wall that protected it rose to his left, and ahead, he saw the gates. They were open, and Fey guards stood outside. The guards wore uniforms from his mother's time. They were holding ceremonial spears he had never seen before on the Isle—although he had seen them in Galinas—and they wore swords.

The disquiet he had been feeling grew. His sister had continued Islander traditions. She had used Islander guards, and had retained the palace staff. Even though she looked more Fey than Islander, she had always felt more comfortable with their father's people. For some reason, this change made all the warnings seem more real.

Gift left Skya's side and moved slightly ahead of the party. His own guards flanked him. He ignored them. He reached the open gate, saw the Fey guarding it, and noted that they were older Infantry, not tall enough to have significant magic. He met the gaze of one and then the other. He nodded to them. They did not nod back. As he stepped inside the gates, they crossed their spears before him.

Gift stopped. Skya reached him, and so did the rest of the party. They waited for him.

"My name is Gift," he said. "I am the Black Queen's brother and the Heir to the Black Throne. You will let me pass."

No Fey dared refuse an order from a member of the Black Family unless they had higher orders rescinding it. But Fey rarely got in the way of disputes between the Black Family members. It was too dangerous. Arianna should have had Islander guards if she wanted to prevent Gift's entry. They would have had no qualms about turning him away.

Slowly, the guards raised their spears. One of them nodded to him.

"Forgive us, Sir," he said, using the Fey form of address. "We had orders not to let anyone into the palace without prior approval."

"I'm not changing those orders. I'm merely trying to bring my friends into my home." Then he smiled at the guards. "Carry on."

The one who had spoken gave him a tentative smile. The other did not meet Gift's gaze.

Skya was watching him as if she didn't recognize him. Xihu looked thoughtful. His own guards had moved even closer, as if the encounter had unnerved them. Gift could no longer see Ace. As per instruction, his Gull Riders had made themselves scarce.

He walked through the gate as if he had left only an hour ago. He tried not to stare at the changes. And there were changes.

The hay that was often stacked near the wall was gone. The stables were larger and seemed to be better cared for than ever. There were more horses than Gift had ever seen, tended by Fey grooms. The dogs that usually ran loose through the courtyard were gone. There were dogs, but not the rangy mutts that once had control of the place. These dogs were controlled, sitting along the wall as if waiting for a command.

Their silent vigil made him nervous.

The kitchen door was open, and from it he could smell fresh bread. He did not enter that way, although he would have in the past. Now he was going to use the entrance to the main hall, the one the Black King had used when he had taken the palace from Gift's father, Nicholas.

As Gift walked along the path toward that door, he saw a Fey Infantry unit practicing its sword-fighting technique near the west wall. The unit had divided itself into pairs and was working on individual combat. There was no sound of metal on metal, though. They were using a technique he hadn't seen since his grandfather was alive: silent practice, with more than a foot between the swords and a referee on one side.

This unit was young, then, and not that experienced. It would be a matter of days before they could progress to actual contact between the swords.

Arianna had never learned that sword-fighting technique. But Gift's uncle Bridge had fought in the Nyeian campaign. Had he been the one to instigate this?

More guards stood by the arched doors that led into the Great Hall. When Gift saw them, he nodded, then pulled the doors open before they could say a word. He strode through the doors as if he were part of an invading army.

He was beginning to feel as if he were.

One of the guards followed his party inside. The guard was thin and Fey. Scraggly hairs grew on his chin; a young man's attempt at a beard.

"Sir, I—"

"Announce me," Gift said. He sounded so much like his grandfather that it startled him.

"Sir—"

"In case you don't recognize me, my name is Gift. I am the Black Queen's brother. And I must say, the welcome I've had since I've come to Blue Isle has left something to be desired. Now, find my sister and announce me."

He didn't raise his voice, not really. He just emphasized the words as he reached the final sentence. It was his grandfather Rugar's method, one he had used often with his troops when Gift was a boy, and it had the same effect with this young guard. The boy bobbed his head in acknowledgment, then hurried down the corridor, twisting his hands as he went.

Gift turned slightly to make sure his party was with him, then he asked one of the Foot Soldiers to close the doors. Without waiting to see if his order was carried out, he turned around.

He hadn't been in this hall in a long time. The swords still hung on the walls. The arched windows with their bubbled glass made the entire place seem airy. He had often envied Arianna growing up here. Where Gift had grown up there had been no light at all.

Gift was tempted to cross the corridor and enter the audience hall, to see if his Islander family's coat of arms still hung or if someone had replaced it with the Fey's. Instead, he stood, silently, hands clasped behind his back, and tried not to feel as if someone else had moved into his home.

A Fey man who wore his hair in Oudoun braids came through the corridor that the guard had gone down. He walked without hurry, as if a group of visitors who had disregarded the rules was as common as the evening meal.

When he reached them, he stopped before Gift, peering into his face as if to confirm Gift's identity. First the man looked at Gift's eyes. They told his heritage more than anything else. No other Fey of his age had blue eyes. Then the man's gaze fell to Gift's chin. Gift suppressed a start of surprise. The man wasn't looking for blue eyes or a resemblance to Arianna. He was making certain Gift wasn't a Doppelgänger or a Shape-Shifter.

"I am DiPalmet," the man said, "assistant to Arianna. She is waiting for you. She will see you alone."

Gift felt the muscles in his neck tighten. "She will see me with my entourage."

His tone, sharp and commanding, seemed to have no effect on DiPalmet. "I have strict instructions."

"I'm countermanding them."

DiPalmet stared at Gift. Gift wasn't sure what he would do if DiPalmet didn't listen. Then DiPalmet nodded once, more an acknowledgment than in any kind of agreement.

"Such matters are for the Black Family to sort out," he said.

Gift made no reply.

DiPalmet led Gift toward the stairs. For a moment, he thought DiPalmet was going to take him to Arianna's personal apartments, but they climbed right past the second floor. They continued up, the stone staircase narrowing, and it took Gift a while to realize they were climbing one of the towers.

He had thought that Arianna would at least see him in the audience room.

When he finally understood where they were going, he hoped he was wrong. They were heading toward the North Tower. Arianna had hated the tower, wanted to close it off, even though she knew that wasn't practical. She and Sebastian and their father had been captured by Rugad's forces in that tower, and she had had a particularly nasty set of Visions there. Then Rugad had used it as his base of operations because he had been able to see the entire area. Arianna had said that the tower had a stink nothing could get rid of.

The stairwell was cold, the stones cracked. A water stain ran down one side, and there was the slight smell of mold. Arianna used to keep the palace in good repair. Had she stopped? Or were most people forbidden to come to the tower as they had been in Rugad's day?

The higher they climbed, the more he noticed shadows on the walls. A lot of the military decorations from times in the Isle's past were gone.

Just once, he glanced back. Skya was holding her robes up so that her distinctive slipper boots wouldn't get stuck in the hems. Xihu had one hand on the wall as she climbed. The Foot Soldiers were bringing up the rear, looking solemn.

When they reached the tower door, DiPalmet entered first. "Your brother insisted on his entourage."

"Did he?" Arianna's voice sounded cold. "Then fetch one for me. Guards and the rest of the family. We may as well make it cozy."

Gift couldn't see her yet, but he felt an odd sort of disconnection. He recognized her voice and didn't at the same time. It was almost as if someone were mimicking her—a good mimic who didn't understand the emotion constantly flowing through her tone.

DiPalmet stood aside and Gift entered. The North Tower looked the same as he remembered it: a smattering of chairs arranged for convenience instead of comfort; a long table that looked dwarfed in the center of the room; and the columns that broke up the line of sight and made him feel as if someone could be hiding in the room and no one would be the wiser.

Arianna had her back to him. She was gazing out the east windows. Through them, he could see the Cardidas.

She wore her hair braided down her back Fey style. Instead of the gowns she had worn in deference to her Islander heritage, she wore a Fey military uniform—pants and a jerkin. She looked stronger than he remembered, more muscular, although the Arianna he had spent the most time with had been twig-thin from stress and lack of food. He had never grown accustomed to her looks after she had gone back to her normal weight.

He turned to his party and waved at them to scatter throughout the room. He wanted them here, but didn't want them in the way. Skya stayed by the door. Xihu moved toward a column as if she didn't want to be seen. The Foot Soldiers waited for Gift to move first.

He wasn't quite sure why he was so reluctant. He hadn't seen Arianna in years. Normally, he would have hugged her, but something about her posture held him back. That and the coldness he had heard in her voice. He was no longer sure of his welcome. And he wasn't sure of his emotions. He certainly didn't feel like hugging her.

If he crossed the long expanse of floor between them, it would feel as if he had lost the first battle in a protracted war. So he clasped his hands behind his back, and said softly, "Arianna."

She didn't turn right away. In fact, she didn't move at all. He would have spoken louder, but that, too, would seem like some kind of surrender. What kind of game was she playing?

"I thought you were going to stay in the Eccrasian Mountains until you became a Shaman." She used that cold, cold voice again and she spoke in such a flat tone he had trouble distinguishing the words.

"Apparently I am not Shamanic material," he said.

"Because of your Black Blood?"

"Because I killed someone."

She turned then, an eyebrow raised. It was Arianna, right down to the birthmark on her chin, the mark that showed her to be a Shape-Shifter. She looked slightly older, a few lines around her mouth that hadn't been there before, but pretty much the same as the woman he had left—except for her eyes.

They were startlingly different, their blue the color of ice on a frigid morning. If he didn't know better, he would have said this wasn't Arianna at all. Perhaps it was her twin or a Doppelgänger. But Arianna had no twin, and there were no telltale flecks of gold in her eyes.

"I thought you were too gentle to kill." There was mockery in her voice, so slight that he wondered if the others had heard it.

"I guess war makes soldiers of us all."

She raised her chin. "The Shaman threw you out?"

"I left them."

"Because they didn't want you?"

If her eyes hadn't been so alien, he would have answered her honestly. He would have told her about the Shaman's insistence that he take the Black Throne. He would have explained what he saw there, what he learned. Instead, he said, "I left because I heard you were in trouble."

"From a Gull Rider?"

"From a Vision."

She made a small sound of acknowledgment. Then she shrugged one shoulder and smiled. "As you can see, I'm fine."

"Actually, Ari, you don't seem fine to me. This greeting has been unusual. I thought we were family."

The smile remained on her lips as if it had been sewn there. "We are."

"I thought we were close."

"We were."

The words hurt more than he wanted them to. "What changed?"

"You. You have no business on Blue Isle."

He let out a small breath of air. "It's my home, Ari."

She said nothing. Those blue eyes remained on his, steady and unconvinced.

He couldn't quite believe this. Whatever he had imagined his reception to be during the long journey, it hadn't been this. "You're actually afraid that I want your throne?"

"What other purpose do you have here?"

"Besides seeing you and Sebastian?"

She said nothing. His words seemed to make no difference to her. Then she looked over his shoulder at something beyond him, and he turned. Two Fey stood in the door. The man was as old as Gift's parents, and had the look of Gift's grandfather Rugar. The woman was tall and very young. Her sharp, angular features made her look more like Gift's mother than Arianna did.

"Bridge, Lyndred," Arianna said. "You may enter."

They came in side by side. They walked around the Foot Soldiers and stopped by the south windows, as if they didn't want to be noticed.

Lyndred was staring at Gift, her gaze as cool and appraising as Arianna's had been. Bridge's expression wasn't quite as sharp. He seemed uncomfortable.

Gift looked back at his sister. Had she used them to answer his question? Or had she used them as a dodge? He couldn't tell.

"We have to finish this discussion, Arianna."

She crossed her arms. "It was your idea to have your entourage join us. I have no idea who these strangers are. Bridge and Lyndred, at least, are family. And family seems to mean so much to you."

He couldn't believe this was his sister. Something had happened to her. Dark magic, his mother had said. And his mother had said that it threatened him as well.

"All right. Let's talk, just the two of us."

Arianna looked at the others in the room. "You are all dismissed."

"Gift." It was Skya. He turned. She shook her head slightly. What did she see that he hadn't?

"I'll be all right."

Her face shut down. She nodded once, then left the room. The others followed. Arianna frowned when she saw Xihu. Did the Shaman make her nervous? Gift couldn't tell.

Lyndred was the last to leave. She paused at the door, holding its frame with one hand, and looked over her shoulder at the two of them.

"Sure you want to do this alone?" she asked Arianna. But even though the words were an offer of help, they had that same undercurrent of mockery that Arianna had been using with Gift. Something was going on here, something he didn't entirely understand.

"You're dismissed, Lyndred." Arianna actually sounded annoyed.

Lyndred smiled, as if the reaction were the one she wanted, and then left, pulling the door closed behind her.

Gift walked toward Arianna. He was going to try to repair the damage the words had done, but he didn't know how. Her arms were still crossed, and he found he didn't want to touch her at all.

He stopped an arm's length away from her. "What's happened here, Ari? What have they convinced you of?"

She grinned. "Bridge and Lyndred? Bridge has convinced me that he's as incompetent as everyone says. Lyndred has her eye on the Throne."

"Like I do?"

"You are the firstborn."

"I gave up the Throne. I told you that fifteen years ago. I am a man of my word."

"You no longer have a future. You are a Visionary. What else would you want?"

Her assumptions were startling. This was the sister who had once understood how much Gift disliked command. She had once called him too gentle for leadership, and in those days, she had been right.

"You told me I would always be welcome here."

"I've grown up."

They were of a height. His father had once said that they looked like the male and female sides of the same coin. But

Gift wasn't seeing that now. He was seeing how Fey Arianna had become.

"Is that why you sent the assassins after me on the Cardidas?"

She didn't seem shocked at all. "I would never send assassins after you. I know about the Blood against Blood."

"Well, someone used Doppelgängers to plant the idea that I was bad for the Isle in the Islanders' heads. It can't be traced to you. Maybe it goes to that young viper you've let live in this palace. Has she been trying to get rid of our family?"

"That's twice you've made accusations against Lyndred. Do you know something that I don't?"

"Perhaps," Gift said. "I know that the Spies and Doppelgängers among the Islanders who tried to kill me were supposed to report back to the palace. As I see it, that means they were reporting to one of three people. Lyndred, Bridge, or you."

"That's quite an accusation."

"Someone wanted me dead, and in a way that wouldn't start the Blood against Blood. You're being hostile, Ari, in ways you never would have before. What's changed?"

She lowered her gaze. Without the intensity of those eyes, her face softened. She sighed. "I've been leading the Empire for fifteen years, Gift. That's what's changed."

"No," he said. "You've changed. Why is this palace full of Fey? Why are you wearing Fey clothes? What happened to the Islanders who've worked here their whole lives? And what happened to the idea of blending Fey and Islander traditions?"

"It didn't work. The Isle is part of the Empire. It's time to stop pretending that's not true."

"You were supposed to rule both," Gift said. "That was our agreement."

"And you've come to enforce that?"

"No!" He spoke louder than he intended. She was deliberately not understanding him. "I came because I heard you're in trouble."

She raised her eyes. "Now that you see I'm all right, you can leave."

He stared at her for a long moment. Arianna had never had this cold streak. She had been difficult and flighty. But she had never been cold.

He got a firm sense that he was talking to someone else, but he didn't see how that was possible. He'd already checked for a Doppelgänger. He supposed she could be a different Shape-Shifter, one who made herself look like Arianna. But that would take years of practice, access, and some way of getting rid of the real Arianna. It seemed unlikely to him.

"Why are there Infantry units practicing in the courtyard?" he asked.

"Because we've been idle too long. Do you know what happens to Fey who don't fight, Gift?"

"Oh, I don't know," he said. "It seems to me that Fey who don't fight are doing quite well all over Galinas."

"The Domestics. Those who were never meant to fight. The others are restless, aren't they?"

In every country he visited, he had seen Fey in trouble with the authorities. Foot Soldiers whose blood lust had gotten out of control. Dream Riders who banded together and terrorized the locals. Dog Riders who stayed in their animal form so that they could eat their meals raw.

"Our people were made for war, Gift. When the warrior magic isn't used, our people suffer." She sounded as if she believed it.

"Our people, Ari?" he asked. "Who might that be?"

"We're Fey," she said.

"I'm part Islander. So are you."

"All Fey are part something, Gift," she said. "It's time you see yourself as one creature instead of two."

"I do see myself as one creature," he said. "A man who had a Fey mother and an Islander father. The shared heritage makes me stronger."

"It makes your magic stronger. It makes your spirit weaker."

He stared at her.

"Islanders are weak people, Gift, and they're only a small part of the Empire. They are no more important than the Nyeians or the L'Nacin."

"We have our own magic," Gift said. "We are as important as the Fey. We're just different."

She shrugged. "Believe it if you want. But—"

"I don't believe it," he said. "I know it. And so did you. Islander magic defeated the Black King. Islander magic put you on the Throne. Islander magic is what's important here. Fey magic lost the battle for Blue Isle."

Her face didn't move, but her eyes seemed to grow colder. "The battle for Blue Isle will be but a footnote in Fey history. What matters is that the Isle became a part of the Empire. In that, the Fey won."

He took a step toward her and reached out his hand. Somewhere inside that impassive face was the sister he had known. Something had changed her and he was determined to find out what.

"Arianna," he said, "what happened here? What changed you?"

She looked at his outstretched hand, then lifted her gaze toward his. "You touched the Black Throne."

He felt the blood drain from his face. He hadn't discussed that with anyone. How had Arianna found out? Had she Seen it? He wasn't sure if he should deny it or if he should tell her the truth.

But she took the decision away from him. "It wanted you."

"I rejected it."

"No one rejects the Throne."

"I did," Gift said. "Just as I did when we were young."

"You don't understand what it takes to lead the Fey. You will not help the Empire if you find a way to overthrow me."

"I don't want to overthrow you, Arianna. You are the Black Queen and have been from the beginning. I simply wanted to make sure that you're all right."

"And now you are convinced that I'm not. It's a short step from there to believing that you need to take over the Throne to protect the Empire."

"I won't take the Throne," he said. "That hasn't changed."

"I think it has."

His hand was still outstretched. He lowered it, then curved his fingers into a fist. "I'm interested in the Throne, Lyndred is interested in the Throne. The only one whom you haven't accused is Sebastian."

"Sebastian is no longer a factor."

His nails bit into his palm. "What does that mean?"

"It means that Sebastian has left the palace."

"Why?"

"Because his spirit is yours, Gift. He was a doorway, a way for you to get to me. He didn't belong here."

"He's our brother."

"He's made of stone."

Another chill ran down Gift's back. Arianna had always believed that Sebastian was a real person.

"Have you destroyed him?"

"Of course not," she said. "He's on his own now."

"Where?" Gift asked.

"I believe he lives with Coulter."

Gift frowned. "He's at the Roca's Cave?"

"I think so."

"You don't know?"

"I don't want him here any more than I want you here. You threaten the Empire."

"Arianna, I am not interested in the Empire. I don't want the Throne. I came here for you."

"All right," she said. "Let's pretend I believe that. I don't need you, Gift."

"Then why is Lyndred here?"

"Because she amuses me."

"That's a lie."

Arianna clasped her hands behind her back. "All right, then let me tell you the truth. She's not ready to be a threat. She's too young and inexperienced. Bridge is too stupid."

The harshness grated, but Arianna had always spoken plainly. There had just never been such obvious deviousness behind her words before. Seger had been right; there was something wrong with Arianna. Gift just didn't know what it was yet.

"I need a Visionary beside me, Gift," Arianna said, "and Lyndred was the only one. I can't trust you. You've touched the Throne, and now you have your own pet Shaman. You came here, ready to take over the Empire, Shaman in hand, and Enchanter beside you."

"Enchanter?"

"Isn't the woman who traveled with you an Enchanter?"

"Skya is my guide."

"You needed a guide to get back to Blue Isle?"

"I needed a guide to get out of Vion in a hurry."

"You're out. Why do you need her now?"

He looked at Arianna for a long moment. "I should think that would be fairly obvious."

"Do you love her?" Arianna asked. It sounded like a business question.

"No," Gift lied. "But one of us needs to give this Empire an heir, don't we?"

"Is she pregnant?"

"Not yet," he said. "I thought we would make our home on the Isle, and you would have a hand in raising the child. After all, the child would inherit if something happened to you. I thought that you and I were a team."

"There is no room for a team to rule the Empire, and no need for you to groom one of your children as an heir to my throne."

"I saw Mother," he said, "in the Place of Power in the Eccrasian Mountains. She said having an heir was the most important thing."

"Mysteries often mislead," Arianna said.

"Mother never has, and you know that. She's the one who trained you."

"I abandoned that training long ago," Arianna said. "It wasn't right."

"It's what made the Fey follow you in the first place. You had no clue how to rule the Fey. You were raised Islander. If you just remember who you are, and who I am—"

"You are the Heir to the Black Throne."

"I'm your brother. I care about you."

She turned away from him and went back to the east windows. It was as if she were looking for answers at the end of the Isle, as if she were trying to see the Roca's Cave.

"A ruler cannot care about anyone, Gift." This time, the voice sounded like Arianna's. The mixture of sadness and regret in her tone was what caused it. "I can't care for anyone. It will become a weakness. You know that. People have crossed your Links in the past, just as they have crossed mine. It's better not to have any Links at all."

Gift felt cold. Coulter had told her to close her Links fifteen years ago. Was that what made Arianna this cold, unfeeling person now?

"Our father loved us," Gift said. "He loved our mother. And he was an effective King."

"A King of a small island. He could afford to have weaknesses."

"Even with the Black King of the Fey pressing down on him?"

"Even then," Arianna said.

Gift took a step closer. She raised her head, and her eyes, reflected in the glass, met his. She had been watching him just as he had been watching her. "You can't mean this."

"But I do. Our mother's love for our father made her trust him. Our grandfather's love for our mother brought her to the Isle in the first place. Only Rugad seemed to see things clearly, and that was because he didn't have his emotions engaged."

Gift felt his breath catch in his throat. "You're using Rugad as a model for how to rule?"

"Of course."

"You hated him. You were going to set up your rule so that you never made the same mistakes he did."

"His mistakes were minor. They were recoverable."

"Dying? Losing the battle to us and our father? That's recoverable?"

"Yes." Her smile was secretive, almost as if she were inviting him to guess at something, as if they were playing a game with rules he didn't understand.

"Arianna, you can't mean this. Tell me it's all a joke."

"I mean it," she said.

"Rugad is the worst model you could have chosen."

"Rugad was the greatest ruler the Fey ever had."

"Rugad died in the middle of losing a battle."

"In a war he won. Why do you keep forgetting that Blue Isle is part of the Fey Empire now?"

"An independent part. The first part to join voluntarily, just as our parents wanted. And they wanted us to rule in a new way. They said that to you the day you decided to become Queen."

"Yes, they did," she said. "They were wrong."

Gift frowned. Her words played in his mind. *What changed?* he had asked her and she had immediately said, *You touched the Black Throne.* He had thought it an accusation, but what if it wasn't? What if it was an admission? What if the light that shot out from the Throne was what had changed her, infected her somehow? What if Rugad hadn't become the ruthless man Gift remembered until he touched the Black Throne?

"Mother said you were infected with a dark magic."

Arianna started. For the first time since he arrived, Gift thought he had seen a real emotion from her. "She said that in the cave?"

"In the Eccrasian Mountains, just before I came here."

"What else did she say?" There was an intensity to Arianna's question now, as if a lot rested on Gift's answer.

"She said that I shouldn't see you. That sometimes dark magic ignites other dark magic."

"Did she?" Arianna asked. "What did you take that to mean?"

"Nothing then. I wonder now if something didn't happen to you, fairly recently."

"Because I have changed my way of ruling?"

"Because you're so cold and bitter."

She threaded her hands behind her back. "You sound like Bridge, making everything about emotion, not logic."

Gift's cheeks grew warm from the rebuke, but Arianna didn't stop.

"I've been on my own for years now, Gift. I've had time to think about this. I know what's best for the Empire. I've studied it. I know what should and shouldn't be done."

"Based on what? The past behavior of Black Rulers?"

She nodded. "We have been the most successful people in the history of the world."

"Successful? The Isle was successful. It had been at peace for a thousand years before the Fey arrived. That's just a different way of measuring success."

"And not a good one for the Fey." Her words echoed in the large room. Apparently they had both raised their voices.

They stared at each other in the silence. Then Gift said, "So that's why you're training the military. You're going to invade Leut."

Her features became still. It was as if the mercurial Arianna had learned how to wipe all emotion off her face. He would never have believed that possible.

"You don't have a large enough military to invade a new continent. And you're not a war leader. You don't know what you're doing."

"You do?" Arianna asked.

"Ari," Gift said. "This isn't for us. You've made incredible strides in peacetime. You've doubled food production throughout the Empire. You've expanded trade among the member nations. You've made us rich through our own means, not through conquering others."

She nodded. "It was an oversight that needed to be corrected. Now that it has, it's time to return our attention to the things that made the Fey the people they are."

He stared at her. She looked the same. She was his sister except for those eyes. It was as if someone else looked out of them. But he didn't know how someone else had gotten in. He didn't know anyone strong enough to cross her Links and take her over. Besides, Coulter had had her close her Links years ago.

The thing he kept coming back to was the light that had flared from the Throne. It had gone searching, the Shaman had said. Maybe it had found fertile ground in Arianna. Maybe that was what his mother had meant by being infected by dark magic.

But if Arianna was infected, he had no idea how he could prove it—or what he could do.

"Ari," he said, "the day we met, do you remember it?"

"Of course," she said coldly. "I tried to kill you. I didn't know about the Blood against Blood then."

"Before that, though, what did I offer you?"

Her blue eyes twinkled. "Are you testing me, Gift?"

"Humor me."

"You can tell I'm not a Doppelgänger. There are no gold flecks in my eyes."

Gift waited. His heart was pounding.

"Of course, if I'm some rogue Shape-Shifter who has taken Arianna's place, you can kill me and assume the Throne and no one will be the wiser. There won't even be Blood against Blood."

His palms had grown damp. He wasn't sure what he would do if she didn't answer him. Were there spells that made Shape-Shifters revert to their original forms? Skya would know.

Arianna inclined her head toward him. "If I were a Shape-Shifter, though, one with normal gifts, I would have had to practice this shape from birth. I would have chosen the shape of the Black Queen. Wouldn't my own people have thought that odd?"

Gift said nothing.

"I suppose they could have wanted to overthrow the Black Family, but that would have taken a special Fey. Unless I'm really Islander, or half and half. Imagine if I were. What kind of creature would I be then? Or maybe I had the same Shape-Shifting ability the real Black Queen does, able to take dozens of forms."

Gift's mouth was dry. He wasn't sure he wanted her to be able to answer him, or not. He wasn't sure he wanted to know that this sarcastic, bitter woman was really his sister.

"A new Shape-Shifter would, naturally, have studied

everything possible about me, but wouldn't know all the details. And unlike a Doppelgänger, wouldn't have absorbed my memories."

She wasn't dumb. She understood his test too well.

"On the day we met," she said, "you wanted to take Sebastian away from the palace. You thought he was going to die. When I found you, you offered to take me with you. I had no idea who you were, so I refused. I tried to prevent you from kidnapping Sebastian and it wasn't until later that I finally understood you were my real brother, and that killing you would have been a disaster of untoward proportions."

A chill ran down Gift's back.

"Interesting test. Most people know that I tried to kill you the day we met, but they don't know the other reasons behind it. They don't know that you had come to the palace with good intentions and that I was the one who was ill-informed."

The chill stayed with him. He wasn't sure how to move. The memories were Arianna's, which meant he was not looking at an imposter Shape-Shifter. Could a person's basic nature change so much in fifteen years?

Or had something changed it, warped it, had some kind of magic made her something else? Was this what the Black Throne needed? Was this what it wanted? Was this what he would have become if he had accepted it?

"There were so many memories you could have chosen," she said. "That one was particularly apt. You wanted to remind me of the Blood against Blood, didn't you? And you wanted to remind me that you have never meant me harm while I nearly brought the Blood on both of us. Marvelous. You do have a proper Fey mind. You simply choose to waste it."

Gift's breathing was shallow. He didn't want this person to be Arianna. He wanted the sister he had known back.

"It's too bad, really," she said. "If you didn't have such a soft-hearted philosophy, I could have used you. But you're too dangerous, Gift. You have several advantages that make things too difficult for me. You're the eldest, and for that reason alone some believe you should be Black King. You've touched the Throne and it wanted you, even though you claimed you rejected it. You've given up your Shamanic training, so you have no future, no plans for a life outside of these walls. And you've already found a mate to breed heirs."

He stared at her. He wished he had listened to his mother now. Had she known this was going to be the result of his visit?

"Even if you don't try to overthrow me, someone might in your name. And then what will we have? Blood against Blood?" She shrugged. "It's not something I want to test."

"I'm not going to overthrow you."

"You believe that now," she said. "But people change over time."

"Like you did."

"It's possible." She walked toward him, then reached out a hand and put a finger under his chin, lifting it slightly. She was inspecting him as if he were a horse. Her fingers were cold. "They say you're the greatest Visionary the Fey have ever known. Is that true, Gift?"

"I don't know." When he spoke, her fingernail dug into his chin.

"How many Visions did you have when you touched the Throne? Three? Five?"

"Seven," he said.

Her finger dropped away. Her eyes grew even colder. "Seven. That is impressive. Were any of them about me?"

"Some," he said.

"Are you going to share them?"

Three of them were about her. In the third, she stared at the Black Throne longingly, the expression on her face alien to him then, but familiar now. This was the woman he had Seen in that Vision.

"No," he said. "I'm not going to share them."

Arianna frowned at him. "It's a Visionary's duty to share Visions."

"And I already have. With all the Shaman in Protectors Village." Gift crossed his arms. "You can't have this both ways, Ari. Either I'm your brother or I'm your enemy. You've spent the last hour telling me that we have no obligation to each other and now you want to claim one."

"You're trying to blackmail me into resuming a relationship that will harm our people?"

"I don't see it that way."

"As blackmail?"

"As harmful."

She shook her head. Her lips had thinned. She seemed suddenly unsure of herself. "So the Shaman, after hearing your Vision, sent one of their kind with you, to take care of you when you became Black King?"

"Actually, she volunteered to come with me to serve the Black Family."

"She would become my Shaman?"

"I don't speak for her. Ask her."

Arianna turned away. She walked to the window, the south window this time, and he couldn't see the reflection of her face. She seemed almost disturbed by the idea of having a Shaman.

"You know," she said after a moment, "I can't have you stay on the Isle."

"You've made that clear."

"It's customary to give lesser members of the Black Family a military commission."

"If we're at war." Gift didn't want a military commission, but he'd see what she offered.

"That's right. Otherwise, you might get the leadership of a small country. You're quite shrewd, Gift. Giving you a military commission or a position of leadership would be inviting trouble."

"I don't understand why you don't trust me. I haven't done anything to you."

"Yet." She clasped her hands behind her back and spread her legs slightly. That stance disturbed him as well. It was a military posture, one Arianna rarely used. Their mother had used it. Their grandfather as well. But Arianna had been more fluid. Rarely did she hold herself so still.

"I had hoped you would keep your monastic ways. I had hoped your studies would have kept you busy for the next thirty years. I did expect you to become a Shaman."

"So did I," Gift said. "But the war with Rugad disqualified me. I am not able to use Domestic magic."

"That's what worries me. If you had remained a Domestic, you would not have been a threat."

He sighed. There was no convincing her otherwise, no matter what he said. He wished he had stayed beside her these last few years. He wished he knew what had caused the changes.

"So," she said, "I want you to leave the Empire, Gift."

His breath stopped in his throat. "You're banishing me?"

"I think that's my only choice."

"And what will you do if I don't agree?"

She turned, looking at him over her shoulder. "I don't have to kill you to remove you as a threat. If you want to stay in the Empire, I'm sure I could find a nice cell for you. The dungeons below the palace are adequate, but I know there are better places in L'Nacin."

He'd heard about L'Nacin prisons. They were renowned for their brutality.

"Mother was right," Gift whispered. "Something's got a hold of you. This is not you, Ari."

"It is now," she said. "And if you don't think I mean what I say, then test me."

He wasn't going to. "The only place I can go, then, is Leut. Aren't you afraid I'll warn them that the Fey plan to invade?"

She shrugged. "They have probably been preparing for that for years. One more warning won't hurt. They won't be able to do anything."

"You've studied their culture? You know how they make war?"

"I'm learning," she said. "Maybe I should send you as my ambassador. Does that have a better ring to it? Stay there for a dozen years, Gift, and send reports to me."

"No," he said.

She smiled. The look didn't reach her eyes. "How did I know you would say that?"

"Rethink this, Ari. I can stay out of your way—"

"No. Think of it as a compliment. Past Black rulers have manipulated their heirs to get them out of the way. You're not easily manipulated. So I'm telling you, directly, that I want you and your little entourage gone. Or I will make certain that they die, and you're miserable for the rest of your life."

Gift was shaking. "My ship is damaged. Several of my crew died in your assassination attempts."

"I didn't do anything."

"Don't lie to me. I understand now. If you've become ruthless enough to threaten me with prison, then you are ruthless enough to manipulate Islanders into trying to kill me."

Her smile grew a little wider.

"I need time to hire more crew. I want you to let some of my people return to their homes. They don't deserve to be banished because they were serving the Black Family. I want time to find replacements for them."

"You'll take your woman."

He would have to now. His lies had trapped Skya as much as they had trapped him. He didn't regret having to take her with him, but he did regret the fact that he caused her loss of freedom. She would hate him for that.

"I'll take her," he said.

Arianna nodded. "You have two weeks. You'll be watched at all times. If you take longer than that, I will take action. Is that clear, Gift?"

"Very," he said.

"Good." She waved a hand. "Now, get out of my sight. I never want to see you again."

Chapter Sixteen

*E*VERY MUSCLE IN his body hurt. His spine ached, and his butt had never been this sore. At least his teeth had stopped rattling. Matt clung to the horse's sides with his thighs, the reins tight between his fingers. He had ridden before this, but never for any distance, and never without an instructor. Now he'd been on a horse for two days straight, taking only a few hours to sleep on hard ground before he continued.

The road wound along the Cardidas River. Coulter had told him it would take him directly to Jahn. Matt had asked how he would recognize the city, and Coulter had smiled. *It's the only place of its type in all of Blue Isle,* he'd said.

Matt wished he could see it now. But all he saw was the narrow road, barely wide enough for the horse. There was a sheer drop on his right side, and if the horse should slip, they would plunge down to the Cardidas. On his left was a steep mountain wall.

He had never been away from home before. He hadn't even had time to tell his mother he was leaving, not that she would care. After he and Coulter had left the Roca's Cave, Matt had gotten on this horse and headed out.

Packed over the back were blankets, changes of clothing, food, and hidden in it all, the vials of the Roca's blood and the dolls. Matt hated them, but they were the point of his mission. He just had to time it right, and make sure he didn't get caught.

He pulled his coat tighter around him, almost losing his balance in the process. The horse shook its head, as it often did when he made some kind of error. At least he wasn't bouncing anymore. He seemed to have found some kind of rhythm. Coulter had told him to let the horse have its head and it would take them down the road. That was proving to be true. All Matt had to do was feed, water, rest, and groom the horse, and it seemed to do fine.

Better than he was doing.

He had spent the first day reviewing all the instructions he had received. The last disturbed him the most. Coulter had pulled Matt aside just before he left and had given him an instruction he wasn't supposed to reveal to anyone. *We need to stay in touch. I will keep my Link open to you. If you need me, just shout.*

Matt had nodded. Coulter had explained Links before. Matt had never used his, but he understood what to do. He also understood why Coulter wanted him to keep this quiet. Arianna wanted the Links between Coulter and Matt closed so that Rugad couldn't travel across them. Coulter had said he agreed. It was only at the last moment that Coulter seemed to change his mind.

But reviewing plans wasn't helping today, and the Words Matt had absorbed offered no comfort. *Even a farsighted man,* the Roca had written, *cannot see the future well enough to make an informed choice.*

Matt shook his head. He now knew Ancient Islander well enough to speak it like a native. On the first day of his ride, he had gone through the front section of the Words, trying to understand them. Then he'd had the nightmares, dreams of betrayal and of locking beloved old friends in

Soul Repositories, and on the next day, he had tried instead to focus on his surroundings.

But the Words still haunted him. Sometimes he thought he could see shadows of ancient armies, fighting the battles that the Words had caused. Sometimes he felt a hopelessness that was not his own.

He wished that Scavenger were with him so that he could ask about the Fey Mysteries and Powers. Sometimes Matt felt as if he had picked one up in the Roca's Cave, and it hovered around him, sharing its emotions and its memories. But he couldn't see it, and he wondered if his loneliness caused the feeling.

Something crashed behind him, and the horse shied. Matt fell forward, grabbing the horse's neck, and it whinnied in distress. It didn't shake him off, though, and it didn't run in panic, although it did increase its stride enough to hurt his balance.

They were already around a corner by the time Matt was able to look behind him. He thought he saw another horse. He reined his up, and dismounted, heart pounding.

He reached into one of his pouches and removed an apple for the horse. It deserved a treat for not throwing him when it shied. He patted its neck and spoke softly to it, all the while looking back along the trail.

The horse was calming, its tail twitching as it ate. The river gurgled below, flowing over some large rocks. The water was white and frothy, and looked nothing like the bloodred water he knew from home. Thin grass and a twisted pine tree grew on the hill behind him. He leaned against a dirt crack in the hillside and was as quiet as possible, but he heard nothing more than his heart, the horse, and the river.

Maybe he should walk back and see if someone was waiting just around the corner. But that was silly. A rock had probably dislodged—there were fallen rocks all over this trail—and that was what had spooked the horse.

If there had been someone else on the trail, he would have passed by now. Besides, why would anyone hide from him? Only a handful of people knew where he was going. Rugad had no idea Matt was coming. And Alex wouldn't leave the Vault.

Matt sipped some water from one of the skins that Seger had prepared. She had asked the Domestics to make him a number of provisions. Even if it took him extra days to get to Jahn, he wouldn't go thirsty. The water replenished itself, and would for a week. He would be hungry though. Food didn't replenish itself, and if he took too long to reach Jahn, he would have to rely on people he met for food and companionship.

He took a deep breath and then mounted the horse. He still had a long trip ahead of him.

The best thing he could do was stop making up problems, and focus on the trials ahead.

CHAPTER SEVENTEEN

*G*IFT'S SHIP LOOKED out of place in Jahn harbor. Even though its sails were down, the masts were taller than any others. It was longer, too, and sat deeper in the water. It probably held more people than the average Nyeian ship.

Lyndred stood at the end of the gangplank and squared her shoulders. She didn't see any guards on deck and she thought that odd. Still, she was nervous about going on-board. The look her cousin Gift had given her in the North Tower had been cold and dismissive. She wasn't sure she could trust him.

She wiped her hands on her breeches, then started up the wooden ramp. A rope handhold had been woven on one side to help her keep her balance.

Lyndred hadn't expected Gift to leave. She had thought that Arianna would find him a place in the palace and he would join them for meals. Lyndred would be able to watch him, to see what kind of person he really was, to see if he were trustworthy, and then she would be able to go to him if she had to. But the servants were already talking about the way Gift had left, his face dark with anger. Arianna had said that he would never come back.

Lyndred hadn't expected such bad blood between them. It made her nervous. It reminded her of the dreams she had had, and the way she had thought she saw the Cardidas covered in blood.

When she reached the deck, a Nyeian sailor barred her way. He was slight and had the delicate features of most Nyeians. He reminded her of Rupert and she wondered what she had ever seen in that kind of man.

"I'm here to see Gift," she said.

"He sees no one."

"I'm his cousin Lyndred."

"Sorry."

She was gripping the rope so hard that it burned against her palm. If he were Fey, she could order him aside. Perhaps that was the beauty of a Nyeian guard. Even though he had more to be frightened of than a Fey, he was too stupid to know it.

"At least tell him that I'm here."

"Why is that, Lyndred?"

She turned in the direction of the voice. Ace stood just to her right, half hidden by thick ropes. He was wearing a loose Nyeian shirt, drawn at the wrists and open at the throat, and tight Nyeian pants. The white shirt accented the darkness of his skin and hair.

"It's important that I see him."

"Important to you, to him, or the Black Queen?"

"I asked you to tell him I wanted to see him."

"I did tell him. He obviously chose not to see you."

Lyndred could order Ace, but she wasn't going to. "Please. I'll stay right here. I won't even get on his precious ship. Just let me see him for a few moments."

Ace's eyes narrowed. "I suppose it's not my decision." He pointed at the Nyeian. "Don't let her move until I get back."

"Aye, sir," the Nyeian said.

Ace disappeared.

Lyndred swallowed against a dry throat. Her dream brought her here, more than anything. She knew when she saw Gift that he had been the man in that dream. There was something about him that reassured her, just as there was something about Arianna that frightened her. The fact that he didn't want to see her seemed to confirm the emotions of the dream. It seemed right that Lyndred had to seek him out. That was the way it ought to be.

Ace reappeared at the railing. He didn't look at her. "Let her by," he said to the Nyeian.

The Nyeian moved aside. Lyndred walked the last few feet up the ramp and stepped onto the ship.

She hadn't been on a ship since she had arrived in Jahn. The bob and sway of the deck even on the Cardidas's relatively calm waters brought back the trip she had made across the Infrin Sea.

Ace took her arm. "Try anything, and I'll be the first to slit your throat."

She smiled at him. "Nice to see you too, Ace."

He led her belowdecks. There were doors leading off the narrow corridor, and the familiar scents of sweat, sea salt, and fish. At the end of the corridor was a large door. Ace opened it and pushed Lyndred inside. She almost lost her footing and reached for him, but he escaped her grasp. He went back out the door and closed it behind him.

The Fey woman she had seen with Gift leaned against a cabinet built into a wall. She had changed into a jerkin and breeches—the same outfit that Lyndred wore—and she no longer looked quite as foreign. She was, quite possibly, the most beautiful woman Lyndred had ever seen.

The Shaman stood to one side, her black eyes taking in everything. She had her hands threaded before her as if she were trying to maintain a calmness she didn't feel. Despite her white hair and lined face, this Shaman struck Lyndred as young. Perhaps it was the expression on her face or the way that she faded into the background as if she weren't sure she belonged.

Gift stood near a porthole. He had his back to Lyndred and didn't turn even after Ace had shut the door.

Lyndred took a step into the cabin. It was larger than any she had seen before. It was in the front part of the ship, and its ceiling was low. A wide bunk, cabinets, and a desk were built into the walls. Two portholes showed views of the harbor; one that Gift stood in front of, and one that was on the opposite wall. There were also free-standing chairs that could be stacked and stored and a table that someone had placed there as a secondary workspace.

Lyndred bit her lower lip, then realized what she was doing. She walked deeper into the cabin. She wasn't quite sure how to open the conversation without apologizing, and she didn't want to start that way.

Then Gift turned. His blue eyes were flat but they weren't cold, not like Arianna's. It seemed instead as if some of the life had left them. He crossed his arms and leaned against the wall. "Are you here to corrupt me the way you corrupted my sister?"

Lyndred took an involuntary breath. He blamed her for Arianna's reactions? "I haven't corrupted anyone."

"Really." Gift stood up and walked toward her. Neither the woman nor the Shaman moved. "Ace tells me I can't trust you."

Lyndred's heart twisted. She cared about Ace, and she wasn't sure what she had done to earn his distrust.

"Well," Lyndred said. "I'm going to trust you."

Gift stopped directly in front of her. He was as tall as she was and had a muscular thinness that spoke of great strength. "Should I feel honored?"

There was anger beneath his coldness. Lyndred could sense it more than hear it. She remembered the dream, the way he kept pushing away from her, and the way she held his shoulder, making sure he stayed. Perhaps that dream wasn't prophecy. Perhaps it was a warning. Perhaps it told her how to speak to Gift.

"I've been here six months," Lyndred said. "Your sister's been the same the whole time."

"Now you're defending her?"

"Defending myself, actually. My father and I—she tried to kick us out of the palace when we first arrived."

The woman turned toward Gift. The Shaman didn't move. And something—interest?—flickered in Gift's eyes.

"But then my father told her who I was, and what my magic was."

"Vision," the Shaman said softly.

Lyndred nodded, not taking her gaze from Gift. "It's not as great as yours, but it's there. And it's strong. Stronger than it's been in my father's branch of the family. Like your mother's, my father said."

"He's guessing. My mother came into her Vision on Blue Isle."

Lyndred wanted to reach out and take Gift's hand. "When Arianna found out I had Vision, she offered to let my father and me stay at the palace. And every day, she has asked me to tell her what I've Seen."

"You have daily Visions?" the woman asked. She had an accent that Lyndred didn't recognize.

This time, Lyndred faced her. "I'm sorry. We haven't met."

The woman glanced at Gift as she answered. "I'm Skya. Gift's woman."

The words had a nasty twist, as if she didn't like saying them.

"She's my guide," Gift said. "She got me out of Vion safely and back here. She's—"

"Banished, just like he is." Skya's tone was so bitter that Lyndred almost recoiled.

"Arianna banished you?" Lyndred asked.

Gift shrugged. The movement seemed casual, but wasn't. His skin, lighter than her own, was slightly flushed, his eyes bright with anger. "Apparently, she thinks I will try to take the Throne from her, and bring the Blood on us all."

"The Blood," Lyndred whispered.

The Shaman took a step forward. "What did you See, my child?"

Lyndred felt her own skin flush. "Blood on the river, yesterday morning."

Skya gasped, but neither the Shaman nor Gift looked surprised.

"What else?" the Shaman asked.

"Blood everywhere. It was a single, horrible Vision."

"What caused it?" the Shaman asked.

Lyndred shook her head. Gift made a slight, disgusted sound, and backed away. Lyndred caught his arm. She could feel his muscles through the softness of his shirt. "I know you blame me for what's going on, but you have to understand how much I'm trusting you. I Saw you kill Arianna in a Vision. I don't want you to do that."

"I can't do that," he said, pulling his arm free. "It would bring the Blood on us."

"I know," Lyndred said.

"Is that why you're here, to find someone to kill Arianna?"

"Gift." The Shaman took a step forward. "Let the girl talk. What did you See, child? Tell me your Visions."

No one had spoken to her with that kind of gentleness in a long time. Lyndred blinked hard so that the tears wouldn't fall. She took a deep breath and looked only at the Shaman. "I've had three major ones, really. All of them about Gift."

"You're sure it's Gift?" the Shaman asked.

Lyndred nodded. "Now I am."

"What were they?" the Shaman asked.

The other two were staring at Lyndred with an intensity that made her flush. In some ways, these people unnerved her more than Arianna did, but not because she was afraid of them. Because she wanted to impress them.

"There were three quick Visions," Lyndred said. "One's already come to pass. I saw him enter the palace with a group, as if he were invading the place."

"This morning," Skya said softly.

"Then I saw Arianna crumbling."

"Crumbling?" the Shaman asked.

"Like a dirt rock that someone squeezed. And then I saw all the Blood."

Gift hadn't moved. The Shaman's mouth was open slightly. Skya was frowning.

"That's all?" the Shaman asked.

Lyndred shook her head. This time, she turned to Gift. "You have to understand that I'm trusting you and I'm only doing it because I don't know where else to turn."

He was watching her, his features smooth, as if he were

holding himself rigid. Only his eyes had changed. They were darker, their blue almost black.

"What else, child?" the Shaman asked.

"I Saw you," she said to Gift, "holding a baby and crying."

Skya closed her eyes and turned her head away, but no one else seemed to notice. The Shaman continued to watch Lyndred.

Gift hadn't moved, but all of the color drained from his face.

"And," she said, her voice trembling, "I Saw you kill my father."

"What did you See?" Gift's tone was low and menacing. Maybe she could believe that he meant to harm her and her father. Maybe she had been wrong.

"My father is drowning. You're in a boat. You do not save him."

"That's not killing him," Skya said.

"He's in the water because of you," Lyndred said, not taking her gaze off Gift's face. "Everything happens because of you."

He shook his head. "That's not how I Saw it. I was the one drowning. A man—he looks like Rugad—reaches for me."

"They could be part of the same Vision," the Shaman said.

All of them looked at her. The silence in the room was so profound that Lyndred felt as if everyone could hear her heartbeat.

"You could have fallen overboard," the Shaman said to Gift. "Her father, who has the look of Rugad, could have reached you. Somehow you tip the boat. You get aboard, but he drowns. Or perhaps starts to drown. Did you actually see him die, child?"

Lyndred shook her head.

"Or it could have happened in reverse," Skya said softly. "Maybe it's a death Vision for Gift."

Gift turned to her, his expression filled with surprise. "I thought you knew nothing about Visions."

"I told you I didn't like Visionaries," she said. "That's different."

"You told me," he said softly, "that you didn't like Shaman."

"Because of their Visions."

Lyndred felt as if she had walked into the middle of a private conversation. The Shaman put her hand on Gift's shoulder. He straightened, nodded toward Skya as if they would finish the discussion later, and then glanced at the Shaman.

"You said, child, that everything happened because of Gift. Do you mean the drowning?"

Lyndred swallowed against a dry throat. "I meant everything I Saw."

They were all silent, as if they didn't believe her.

"You have to understand why I came to you, why I would risk all of this," Lyndred said.

"Because you believe Gift is the center, the one who should rule," the Shaman said.

"No."

"Because you hope you can pit me against my sister, and the door will open for you to take the Black Throne," Gift said.

"*No.*" The room was getting close, stuffy. A bead of sweat ran down Lyndred's back.

"Then why, child?" the Shaman asked.

"Because Arianna's Blind." Lyndred spoke louder than she wanted to. "Don't you understand? That's why you frighten her. Because she can't *See* anything. She asks me for my Visions and doesn't share hers. I've never seen her fall prey to a Vision and neither has anyone else, not since she's been ill."

"Arianna was ill?" Gift asked.

Lyndred nodded. "She was unconscious for more than two days, and she had horrible headaches before that."

"After you arrived."

"Before," Lyndred said.

"Then how do you know?"

"My father found the Islander servants. They told him. She released most of them after she awoke. She's been different since then."

Gift glanced at the Shaman. The Shaman took a step toward Lyndred and then stopped. "When was this?" she asked, as if she were afraid of the answer.

"More than six months ago," Lyndred said.

"When exactly?"

"I don't know," Lyndred said.

"You have Vision." Gift spoke with a calmness that sounded forced. "Six months ago, did you see a light threaded with black?"

"No," Lyndred said. At least, not that she could remember. All she remembered was that coldness that swept over her, a coldness that had worried her father. "But right about the time we left Nye I had the oddest feeling, as if everything had changed."

"Changed?" the Shaman asked.

Skya was looking as confused as Lyndred felt. Why was this important?

"As if I had been touched by a darkness in my magic," Lyndred said. "And then the feeling went away."

"Darkness," Gift repeated. He put a hand to his face and closed his eyes. Then he turned away. "Darkness."

"What is it?" the Shaman asked.

"Gift?" Skya asked.

Only Lyndred watched without saying anything. Gift had gone to the bed and sat on its edge, his face hidden by his hands.

"Gift?" Skya asked again.

"My mother had said that Arianna had been infected by a dark magic." Gift's hands made his voice sound muffled.

"You think it was the Light from the Throne?"

Gift nodded.

The Shaman frowned. "That wouldn't Blind her."

"Islander magic is different. It changes Fey magic. Maybe, in seeking her out, the Light hurt her." Gift stared at Lyndred. "Are you sure about this Blindness?"

"She won't tell me her Visions. No one has seen her have Visions. She seems to want to know about any kind of Vision. She's almost ravenous for them."

"Then that's what it is," Skya said.

They all looked at her. She held out her hands as if in explanation. "I had the funniest feeling looking at her, as if she were two people, one overlaying the other."

"What's your magic?" Lyndred asked.

"She's a Warder," Gift said.

"Could you see these people?" the Shaman asked.

"No," Skya said. "But if she had gone Blind, she would be two people. The woman she once was with Vision and strength, and the frightened person underneath who knows that she lost it all."

Gift shook his head. "The woman I saw wasn't frightened."

"She was frightened enough to banish you," Skya said.

"No," Gift said. "It's not as if she's afraid of me. It's as if she's trying to control me."

"Because of what you might do," Skya said.

"Because of the Blood," Gift said. "She thinks I'll unleash it."

"You might," the Shaman said, "if you discover that she's Blind."

Gift looked at Lyndred.

"I might be wrong," Lyndred said, "but I was raised to believe that a Blind ruler was the worst thing the Fey could have."

The Shaman stared at Lyndred as if she didn't quite know what to make of her.

Gift ran a hand through his hair. "What do you expect me to do? I can't overthrow her. That's what she expects, and that will bring on the Blood."

"Will it?" Lyndred asked.

"You know it will."

"There have been bloodless coups in Fey history."

He raised his head. Those blue eyes were intense. "Is that what you're advocating? A coup?"

Lyndred shook her head. "I'm not advocating anything except that you should find out what's wrong. You don't seem pleased by today's events. I just don't want you to close any doors."

"You might be the one who is provoking the entire crisis," Gift said. "It could be your meddling that causes the Blood."

Lyndred flushed again. She had never put herself on the line like this before, and had never been treated this way. She was beginning to get tired of it.

The Shaman apparently noticed that Lyndred was getting angry. She held up a hand. "You said everything happens because of Gift?"

"Yes," Lyndred said.

"I've Seen that too. I've told you, Gift, you are the center whether you want to be or not. And we now have another Visionary confirming it."

"Arianna has banished me from the Empire."

"Her threat is idle," the Shaman said.

"Is it?" Gift looked at her. He seemed quite young, suddenly, almost a boy. "She threatened everyone on this ship if I don't leave."

"Because she knows you have attachments. Because she believes she can use them against you. And if you let her, this tactic will work."

"What if she is Blind?" Skya asked. "What then?"

"We can't force her to step down," Gift said.

"I'm sure we could find a way," the Shaman said.

"It would be impossible to prove."

"Actually," the Shaman said, "it's quite simple. Lyndred could have done it on her own if she wanted."

"How?"

"By asking her to make a Shadowlands."

Only Visionaries could make Shadowlands. They were like boxes of air made in the sky, only an entire army could hide in them.

"I don't know how to make a Shadowlands," Lyndred said.

The Shaman shook her head. "Then your father committed a grave oversight in your education. You should know how. In fact, when you return, ask Arianna to teach you."

"She'll see through that."

"She might," the Shaman said. "She might not."

"You're advising me to stay?" Gift asked.

"She gave you two weeks," the Shaman said. "A lot can change in two weeks."

Gift stood. The frown on his face was deep. "I'm curious about one thing. You Saw Arianna crumble, like dirt. Have you touched her?"

Lyndred nodded. "You think she's a Golem, right? My father asked the same thing. Her skin is warm and soft and feels like mine."

"A Shape-Shifter Golem can't shift its skin, can it?" Gift asked Skya.

"No," Skya said. "Golems feel like stone. And a Golem that lives on its own is very rare."

"I know," Gift said. "My brother Sebastian is a Golem."

Skya shook her head once, as if she hadn't known that.

"I've seen no trace of your Golem," Lyndred said. "The Fey servants said he tried to harm Arianna and fled the palace months ago."

"Did she destroy him?" Gift asked.

"No."

"Do you know where he went?"

"With a Healer named Seger and someone called Coulter. They took a carriage east."

Gift shook his head. "This makes no sense. Arianna says she asked Sebastian to leave the palace."

"Maybe she did," Lyndred said. "I'm only telling you the gossip."

"It can be easily checked," Skya said.

Gift nodded. He turned those sharp blue eyes to Lyndred. "What's your interest in all of this? What do you want?"

"I once thought I could live a small life in Nye," she said, "but my father made sure that wasn't possible. Then as we were coming here, I thought maybe I could find a way to take the Throne. Now, I just want to be free of this place. Arianna watches me. She guards me as though I'm something that she owns, and I don't want that. And there are so many blond men—"

"What?" Skya asked.

Lyndred swallowed. She had done that to herself. "Blond men," she said softly. "One of them will hurt me badly someday. It's a Vision."

"Visions," Skya said. "Visions and prophecies and warnings. This is why I said I didn't want to come on this journey, Gift. When you're with a Visionary, these things dominate your life. You don't seem to have the ability to make any choices without them. And the worst part about it is that those Visions don't always come true."

"Sometimes we avert them," Gift said.

"And usually you misunderstand them. Your sister has banished you from your home. Stand up for yourself." Skya's eyes narrowed. "Stand up for me."

"It's not that simple," Gift said.

"It is simple. You're the Black Heir. You're the one who has touched the Throne. You've been all over the Empire. Arianna hasn't. Establish yourself as the Black King. The people will follow you."

Lyndred held her breath.

"If I do something like that," Gift said, "I'd have to watch my back at all times."

The room had grown unbearably hot. Lyndred felt another trickle of sweat run down her cheek. No one else seemed to notice. All she knew was that she couldn't stay here any longer. "I'm going to go. I'll be at the palace. If you need me, just send for me."

"I think Arianna will have something to say about that. You know that she's put someone on me, to watch me?"

Lyndred hadn't known that, but it didn't surprise her. She shrugged. "Arianna expected me to ally with you."

"She did?" the Shaman asked. "Was that Vision?"

"No," Lyndred said. "She knows I think she's Blind."

"You told her that?" the Shaman asked.

"Yes."

"Was that wise?"

"She's smart," Lyndred said. "She would have figured it out on her own. Just as she'll figure out that Shadowlands thing."

"I don't know if we should let you go back, then," the Shaman said.

"She can't kill me any more than she can kill Gift. Unless, of course, she manipulates it."

Gift's mouth narrowed. "It's your choice, Lyndred."

They were kind to think about her. Even in their mistrust, they were kind. "My father's there," she said. "I'll go back."

"Be careful," the Shaman said.

Lyndred nodded. "I'll do my best."

CHAPTER EIGHTEEN

ARIANNA SAT ON the stone bench and watched as Dash prepared the carriage. He knew horses and was an excellent carriage driver. He was the one who had helped them escape Jahn six months before.

Con was helping him. Con would be going with them as part of the team. He was bringing his sword, the one that had helped put Sebastian back together. The unspoken idea was that if Arianna shattered, Con had the means to re-assemble her.

Dash was securing bedrolls and food to the back of the carriage. They were taking more supplies than Arianna thought necessary, but Coulter wanted them to be able to hide for a long time if they had to. Matt was supposed to send them a message when he felt they should come to the palace. Coulter thought that might take weeks.

She didn't want to take weeks. She wanted to face Rugad and get him out of her body. She wanted to be able to move again.

The last few days had been torture. She had wanted to leave as soon as Matt had, but she knew she had to wait.

If anyone saw them coming into Jahn so soon after, word might get back to Rugad. He would figure out what was going on. Coulter said he wouldn't, but Arianna had decided underestimating Rugad was the worst thing they could do.

Dash went back into the kitchen for more supplies. Arianna stared at the carriage. The trip would be a long one. She wasn't looking forward to it. But she was looking forward to seeing Jahn. She had missed it more than she wanted to admit. And she was going to take it back.

Coulter was worried that their plan wouldn't work. Coulter was worried that they'd get caught, maybe even killed. He was also afraid he would have to use his magic, as he had in the first battles against the Black King. And Coulter was afraid he'd freeze, just as he had then.

Arianna had her own concerns about that. But she was different from Coulter. The first plan might not work. It might cost some lives, but they were at war. They had to expect some risks.

So she had come up with a secondary plan that she told no one about. It wasn't one she liked much. She liked her third plan better, but she wasn't sure she could pull it off, not yet.

She had lived too long in this body thinking it immutable stone. She was trying to change that. For the last two nights, she had come to the magic yard after everyone else had gone to bed and she had held out her hand, trying a simple Shift that infant Shifters could do in their sleep—literally. It was why so many infant Shifters, born to non-Shifter parents, died.

She tried to turn her fingers into flame.

Both nights nothing happened and she had finally given up, going to bed angry and upset. She was trying to do something easy, but it was also something that had come so naturally to her and had first happened when she was so young that she had no memory of learning it. So she spent a lot of time imagining her fingers in flame, trying to remember the feeling, trying to control the body.

She was trying to convince herself that Shifting was as natural to her as walking. If she could walk in this stone body, she could Shift it.

The problem was that she knew some of the theories of Fey magic. No one knew whether the magic resided in the soul or in the body, but some believed that certain magics— Shifting being one of them—resided more in the body than others. Still, no one had proven that. She had to control her own thoughts. Until she believed she could Shift in this body, she wouldn't be able to.

If she could Shift, she suddenly had a variety of options open to her. She could walk into the palace as herself, skin feeling like flesh and blood, and show the Fey around them that there was at least one imposter in their midst. Or she could appear as Gift—she had done that before—or even, if she practiced, Rugad himself. That would scare him.

She smiled. That would scare everyone.

Behind her, she could hear Coulter giving last-minute instructions to Leen. Leen and Scavenger would run the school while Coulter was gone. Leen would be in charge, but Scavenger would handle much of the magic instruction. His knowledge made him invaluable.

She heard footsteps and slowly turned her head. Sebastian was making his way down the path. She sighed softly. She had been trying to avoid him all day.

He sat down beside her and took her hand in his own. Their skin scraped as it touched, the screeching sound of stone against stone. She winced. Sebastian didn't seem to notice.

"I . . . want . . . to . . . go," he said.

"We've talked about this, Sebastian."

"I . . . un-der-stand . . . your . . . con-di-tion . . . better . . . than . . . any-one . . . else. I . . . can . . . pro-tect . . . you."

She sighed. "I think it's too dangerous for both of us to be there. He took me over and he almost had you once. What if he tries again?"

"The . . . voice . . . is . . . gone. I . . . am . . . my-self . . . on-ly."

He sounded so sad. He still regretted taking Rugad's

voice years ago. Seger had managed to get the voice out of him, but it had nearly cost them Sebastian.

"I know that. But I don't want to worry about you. I want you here and safe."

"I . . . am . . . not . . . as . . . eas-i-ly . . . killed . . . as . . . most."

She knew that too. And that probably applied to her now as well. These stone bodies had advantages. They could be shattered and they could be reassembled.

"Ari?" Sebastian asked.

She turned to him and put her hands on his dear face. She loved his slate-gray eyes, the way they showed the gentleness that was such a part of him, even now, even after all the things he had lived through.

"You have to stay here, Sebastian."

"No. You . . . need . . . me."

"Yes, I do." She leaned her forehead against his. There was a faint clink as the stone surfaces met. "I do. But I haven't told you how before."

He raised his hands and grabbed her wrists, pulling her palms away from his cheeks. Then he moved back so that he could see her. "How?"

"Remember how Seger said it could be argued that you are part of Gift?"

"She . . . is . . . wrong. I . . . am . . . my-self."

"Yes, you are. You have lived separately from Gift for decades now. But you can't deny that you two started as the same soul, living in two different bodies."

"That . . . was . . . a . . . long . . . time . . . a-go."

Arianna put a finger against Sebastian's lips. "It was. But that's not what I'm talking about. I know you no longer know Gift's mind. I wish you did. It might make life easier."

Sebastian took her wrist again. "Ari . . ."

"I want you to listen to me. There is a chance that I won't live through this. It's a fairly good chance."

"The . . . Black . . . King . . . can't . . . kill . . . you, Ari. The . . . Blood . . ."

"He knows. But he's arranged deaths before. He could

find a way to arrange mine. And I'm afraid he might do the same for Gift."

"No . . ." Sebastian closed his eyes.

Arianna took his hands. "Look at me. Please, Sebastian, I know you don't want to hear this, but you have to. I need contingency plans."

"Contingency plans?" Coulter was standing just behind Sebastian. "Why would you need contingency plans?"

Arianna glared at him. It was difficult enough to discuss this with Sebastian. She didn't need Coulter here with his worries and his doubts. "I thought you had things to do."

"I thought you were going to keep an eye on Dash."

"He was putting things in the carriage."

"Well, I can't find him." Coulter leaned against the wall, his arms crossed. "I want to hear these plans."

Arianna swallowed. Since she had left her own body, she hadn't made a single decision without Coulter. But she didn't want him involved in this one.

"No," she said. "I'm talking to my brother, and I'm going to do it alone."

"He's not coming with us."

"He wants to. I'm trying to talk him out of it."

"I . . . am . . . still . . . here," Sebastian said. "You . . . do . . . not . . . need . . . to . . . talk . . . a-bout . . . me . . . as . . . if . . . you . . . are . . . al-read-y . . . gone."

He sounded almost angry. Arianna could hear tears in his voice. He was feeling abandoned, her poor, sweet brother Sebastian, and she could understand why.

"Will you go away?" she asked Coulter.

"I'm only going to ask you what this is about later," he said.

"Fine. You do that." She wouldn't answer him. Or maybe she would lie. But he didn't have to know that.

Still he stayed a moment longer, as if he expected her to change her mind. Then he sighed and pushed off the wall, heading toward the kitchen door.

She waited until he went inside before returning her attention to Sebastian.

Sebastian's lower lip was jutted out slightly. Arianna hadn't realized until she, too, had become stone how much Sebastian compensated for his lack of subtle movements by making exaggerated expressions. She took his hand in her own and squeezed it.

"You are part of us, Sebastian. You are, as Seger says, a part of Gift. You have as much right to the Throne as Gift or I do."

"I . . . am . . . not . . . real."

She closed her eyes. She had always known Sebastian felt that way, but she hadn't realized how much it hurt her to hear it.

"You're real. You're just different."

"No . . . one . . . will . . . ac-cept . . . me."

"They'll have to. You'll be all that's left of our father."

"But . . . the . . . Black . . . Fa-mi-ly—" Sebastian started.

"I don't know what will happen there," Arianna said. "I don't know what this world will be like if something happens to me or Gift. But I assume that Rugad will still be in my body. You'll have to get him out, Sebastian."

"I . . . do . . . not . . . have . . . Vision."

"I know. But it's only a qualification for ruling the Fey. Someone needs to rule Blue Isle. If something happens to me or Gift, that someone is you."

"I . . . can-not . . . have . . . chil-dren."

"Talk to Seger about that. There may be magic that'll help."

"Ari, I . . . do . . . not . . . like . . . this . . . plan."

"Neither do I."

"Then . . . let . . . me . . . come . . . with . . . you."

She shook her head. "You have to guard the Place of Power, Sebastian. Whether it's as ruler of the Blue Isle or as a member of the Black Family, it doesn't matter. You must protect this place. If Gift and I are gone, then Coulter will be gone too. And I don't want any power-hungry Fey to get to this place. It's too easy now to find the Third Place of Power, and that'll create a magic storm that could destroy everything."

"I . . . am . . . not . . . strong . . . e-nough."

She brought his hand up to her mouth and kissed it. "You are stronger than all of us."

"I . . . love . . . you, Ari. I . . . do . . . not . . . want . . . to . . . live . . . with-out . . . you. I . . . al-read-y . . . do . . . not . . . have . . . Gift."

She frowned for a moment before understanding him. Sebastian felt Gift's loss not as a physical presence, but as a mental one. When Coulter closed their Links fifteen years ago, he had set Sebastian adrift. Sebastian struggled almost daily to reopen that Link and could not. Coulter would not help him. That probably explained the slight mutual suspicion between them.

"I don't want to be without you either, Sebastian," she said. "But if something happened to me, I would rest easier knowing that you are taking care of things."

He closed his eyes and shook his head slowly, like a child who did not want to hear what he was being told.

"Sebastian, you can do this."

He opened his eyes. "It . . . would . . . be . . . better . . . to . . . let . . . me . . . pro-tect . . . you."

She pulled him closer. "That's what I'm asking you to do. I'm asking you to guard my back. Protect this place, even if I die. Please, Sebastian. It's the only way."

"What . . . if . . . you . . . die . . . and . . . then . . . Ru-gad . . . comes . . . here? What . . . do . . . I . . . do?"

She stared at Sebastian for a moment, feeling slightly cold. It had to be a trick of her emotions and not her body. The answer was so simple. She didn't know why she hadn't told him before.

"You take my body away from him," she said. "You switch places with him, and you rule Blue Isle."

"What . . . a-bout . . . the . . . Fey?"

"And the Fey, until you find a Visionary from our family, one you trust."

"Ru-gad . . . would . . . be . . . in . . . my . . . stone?"

"Maybe," Arianna said. "If you don't imprison him out-side both bodies."

"It . . . would . . . be . . . hard,"

"Yes, but you can do it easier than anyone else. You almost did it once before."

He smiled then. "I . . . did."

"You can do this, Sebastian."

"More scheming?"

Arianna turned. Her hearing wasn't as good in this body as she wanted. Scavenger was behind her. She wondered how much he heard. "I want Sebastian to stay here."

Scavenger nodded. "His presence would make yours too obvious. Still, he could be a decoy for you."

"Yes," Sebastian said.

"No. We've settled this." She kept a grip on Sebastian's hands, but looked up at Scavenger. "What did you want?"

"Do you know where Coulter is?"

"He went inside. Why?"

Scavenger bit his lower lip as if he were deciding to tell her. Finally, he sighed and said, "Wisdom is following Matt."

"Wisdom?" She had to think for a moment, before she remembered the Fey man she had met on a handful of occasions. Scavenger said that Wisdom had once been Rugad's Charmer, but Rugad had cut out his tongue for some heinous crime.

When Wisdom had arrived at the school shortly before Arianna, the Healers had offered to fix his tongue and that had put him in a horrible panic. He had been afraid of Rugad's retaliation, which they had thought silly. They had thought Rugad dead.

Now they knew better.

"Why would he follow Matt?" she asked.

"Matt was the one who brought him here," Scavenger said. "He was the only one who seemed to understand Wisdom."

"So he invited Wisdom to go with him?"

"No," Scavenger said. "I think Matt knows better. But if Rugad sees Wisdom, he'll know that Matt is not there to serve him."

"What can we do?" Arianna said. "They've already left."

"How..."

She looked at Sebastian. That was the closest he had ever come to interrupting her.

"... do ... you ... know ... that ... Matt ... is ... being ... fol-lowed?"

To Arianna's surprise, Scavenger flushed. "I sent a few people to watch him. They've reported back."

Arianna glanced at Sebastian. Sebastian looked almost angry. "Was this Coulter's idea?"

"No. It was mine."

"Then you're getting in Matt's way as effectively as Wisdom is. Recall those people at once."

"But you have to know what's happening to Matt."

She glared at Scavenger—or at least, she tried to glare. "We sent Matt alone because we trusted him."

Sebastian stood. "I ... will ... tell ... Coul-ter ... a-bout ... Wis-dom."

"Why?" Arianna asked. "We can't do anything."

"May-be ... he ... will ... want ... to," Sebastian said.

Arianna shook her head. "You just want to get Coulter to contradict me. Don't ask him to take you along."

"I ... have ... made ... you ... a ... pro-mise, Ari," Sebastian said. "I ... al-ways ... keep ... pro-mises."

"I know you do. I'm sorry. Warn Coulter about Wisdom then, but tell him I don't think we can do anything."

"I ... will." Sebastian gave Scavenger a cautious look, and left.

Arianna watched him go. Her brother seemed uncertain, frightened for her, and unhappy. But she couldn't change that. She needed him here. She needed him to think about the future.

"So," Scavenger said. "You're making contingency plans. You don't believe in young Matt after all."

If she could have stood up quickly, she would have. As it were, she settled for clenching a single fist. "We are fighting the Black King of the Fey. My father barely managed to defeat him using all the magic the Isle had."

"And you lost to Rugad. That's why you're afraid of him."

"I'm not afraid of him." But the words came out quicker than she wanted. It sounded like an automatic denial instead of something she believed.

"You're afraid of him. That's why you stayed here so long." Scavenger glanced at her clenched fist as if it gave away secrets. Perhaps it did. "You should never have been here this long. You've let him get entrenched. Now you'll never get him out."

She peered at Scavenger. "Who's afraid of the Black King now?"

His dark eyes met hers. For the first time since she'd known Scavenger, she thought she saw embarrassment in his face.

"You never made a place for me in all your plans." In traditional Scavenger fashion, he had tried to turn the blame back on her.

She smiled. "I did. I want you here with Sebastian. You have to help him if something happens to me."

"Help him how?"

"If I die, and Gift dies, Sebastian needs to protect this Place of Power from Rugad."

"How do you propose he do that?" Scavenger asked.

"By taking back my body."

"Sebastian?"

"You know he can do it, and you know the magic needed even if you can't perform it. You can help him."

"But he won't be able to rule the Fey."

"That's right. But he can take care of Blue Isle, and find someone in my family—one of my cousins maybe—with enough Vision to take over the Black Throne."

"That's assuming there's no Blood against Blood."

"I think Rugad is smart enough to get rid of me and Gift without resorting to that," Arianna said.

Scavenger frowned. He glanced up at the mountains, toward the area where the Roca's Cave glinted its magic light. She knew he couldn't see that light, but she could. She could also feel its pull, a pull she didn't really want to answer.

Then he turned to her. She thought he was going to ask if she was smart enough to get rid of Rugad without starting the Blood herself. Instead he asked, "Do you really think you're going to die?"

She stared at him. This strange magicless Fey was the only one she could answer honestly, the only one who would know a half-truth or a lie if she presented it to him.

Still, she couldn't bring herself to say the actual words. "I think we waited too long. I think he's got too much power now."

"So why go?"

"You know why."

Scavenger grinned. "So you have another contingency you haven't told any of us."

She frowned at him, not quite understanding what he was saying.

"You expect to die getting rid of Rugad. You're the only one who can take out your own body without igniting the Blood."

She was relieved this stone skin didn't blush. It would have given her away.

"You will die as you kill Rugad, opening the door for Gift," Scavenger said. "That's why you're preparing Sebastian. You hope he'll take over until Gift arrives. If Gift isn't already here."

She sat before him silently for a moment. She hadn't put those thoughts into actual words, but she had known that option was there—and that it was probably the only possible option.

She had known it for a long time.

Scavenger leaned forward and, to her surprise, kissed her cheek. It was the gentlest thing she had ever known him to do.

"I never thought you'd be the courageous one, but I'm glad you are." He stood. "I'll do whatever I can to keep Rugad out of the Roca's Cave."

"Thank you."

He glanced over her shoulder at the door, as if making sure they were alone. "Don't thank me. Listen to me instead. We have had several Blind Leaders, not just the ones you've heard of, the one who went crazy."

Arianna felt her breath catch in her throat. "How do you know this?"

"I've studied, remember? All of them went Blind after years of Sight. They knew how to interpret Visions, and they kept powerful Visionaries, usually family members, at their side, interpreting those Visions. The last part of their rule wasn't the best part, but it never hurt us."

"You think Rugad will do that?"

Scavenger nodded. "Don't expect him to be crazy. Don't expect him to be frightened or insecure. Expect him to use the resources around him to protect himself."

She remembered Rugad's plan, how he was going to keep her a prisoner in her own mind, and use her Visions as his own. "Do you think he'll try to capture me again?"

"It would be the most logical thing he could do."

Her gaze met his. Her heart was beating hard. "Has a Fey leader ever committed suicide?"

"I don't know."

"Will it bring on the Blood?"

"I don't know that either. But there's never been a Shifter ruling the Fey."

She saw it in his eyes. He was giving her a way. Shifters, even practiced Shifters, sometimes got stuck in a Shift. And if a Shifter got stuck between forms sometimes the halves were not compatible. She knew exactly how to do it too. She would start a Shift, get it to the proper spot and then stop the Shift, leaving it to Rugad. He controlled her Shifting mechanism—he had proven that to her—but he had never had to deal with a crisis. And if she waited for the right point, he might not be able to.

"Would the Powers believe it was an accident?" she asked.

"I think the Powers take a liberal approach to Blood

against Blood," Scavenger said. "I think they want to avoid it as much as the rest of us do."

"You think?" she said.

He shrugged. "There's no way to know. It all involves risk."

"Yes," she said. "But I wish the risk were mine alone."

"So do I," Scavenger said. "So do I."

CHAPTER NINETEEN

*G*IFT STOOD ON the deck of the *Tashka*, watching as his cousin made her way through the streets of Jahn. He gripped the railing, the polished wood cool beneath his palms. The air was chilly and smelled of rain. Clouds threatened in the distance. Soon he wouldn't be able to stand here and stare at the palace. Soon he would have to go belowdecks.

He had asked for some time alone. Lyndred confused him: she saw him as someone who threatened the family, someone who might kill Bridge and Arianna, and yet as someone who might save them all. He wasn't so sure.

These Visions of the Blood that he had unnerved him. Were they being caused by Arianna's strangeness or by his presence? Or a combination of both? And was Lyndred's purpose to push Gift toward destroying his family or to prevent that?

There was no way for him to tell. But he did know that her Visions were true when she mentioned seeing him holding the child. He'd had that Vision himself and it haunted him.

Lyndred had disappeared down the cobblestone streets. The clouds had grown even darker, and a mist dampened the air. Beads of water had formed on his arms and face.

He had had advice from Skya and Xihu and his mother. He had Seen countless Visions, and heard even more from the Shaman. He knew the history, he knew the prophecies, he knew the warnings. And he still felt as if he didn't know where to turn. He could slink to Leut, and stay out of the Fey Empire. Or he could try to convince his sister that he could stay out of her way.

Or he could openly defy her.

The clouds to the west looked as if they had been smeared against the horizon. Rain was coming down in sheets. He would have to go below. He remembered Blue Isle's rainstorms. They were cold and nasty and usually chilled one to the bone.

The rain pelted the water downstream. He could see the wall of the storm coming. The wind had picked up and it carried a deep chill. He debated standing there, letting the water wash over him. He had felt numb since he had come back from the palace. Maybe the rain would prove to him that he was still alive.

Then a few needle-sharp pellets of rain caught him in the face, and he hurried for the stairs that led belowdecks and to his cabin.

Skya was inside. She sat on the edge of his bed, her legs crossed at the ankles and tucked against the wooden frame. She was staring at the storm through one of the portholes. He closed the door, and she didn't turn at the sound.

The rain pounded the deck above. The sky, through the porthole, was almost black. Skya had lit the lamps that hung from the walls—regular Nyeian oil lamps. Gift had insisted on Fey lamps during storms. They prevented accidental fires. This small act of defiance on Skya's part rankled him more than anything else.

"Skya," he said. "I need to be by myself."

"Oh, yes," she said. "The great Black Heir needs to think about the best route to Leut."

The numbness he had felt a moment earlier had fled;

behind it was a dark anger. He took a deep breath, fighting to stay calm. "You like to travel."

"On my own terms." She turned. Her face glistened, almost as if it had been washed with tears. He had never seen Skya cry. He would have thought that it would have endeared her to him. Instead it made the anger worse.

But he had enough Shamanic training to know the power and destructiveness of anger. He also was wise enough to know that he wasn't angry at Skya; he was angry at Arianna.

If he listened, he might have a chance to calm down. If he listened, he could avoid the fight he was spoiling for.

He grabbed one of the loose chairs and pulled it over. He sat, feet flat on the floor as he had been taught, body grounded. "Skya," he said, his voice as gentle as he could make it, "why do you hate Visionaries so?"

She blinked as if she hadn't expected the conversation to go this way. And why would she? They rarely talked about her past or his. She was the one who had stopped that sort of discussion, the one who had insisted that they live in the present and not worry about the past or, by implication, the future.

"It's not important," she said.

"It is. You haven't trusted me from the start, and you claim it's because of my Vision. Is it?"

Her eyes were black and bottomless and very sad. "I do not want to go to Leut."

"Neither do I."

"Then do something about it."

"I'm trying." He swallowed, willing himself to remain calm.

"You're hiding in this ship."

He shook his head. "I didn't expect Arianna to behave the way she did today. I didn't expect Lyndred. I'm not sure—"

"And yet you believe your Visions. You believe that all will be revealed to you and you don't realize that with all your ability to See the future, you missed the most important thing."

He felt the attack as if it had been physical. It took him a moment to catch his breath, to keep himself from yelling at her as he sensed she wanted. "What is the most important thing?"

"This isn't about your appearance here or your being some sort of center or even the Blood itself. Those are all pieces to a puzzle you don't understand. You're guessing and second-guessing yourself. You're making this worse, Gift." She was gripping the side of the bed, the blanket wrapped in her hands.

"What would you have me do?"

"Confront your sister. Overthrow her if you have to. She won't kill you any more than you will kill her. She's as worried about the Blood as you are."

He shook his head. "Once I might have agreed with you. But I don't know this woman—"

"Of course you know this woman. She's Black Blood. She acts like all Black Blood."

"Like me?"

Skya's eyes narrowed. "You're learning. I've been watching you learn how to use your heritage. I watched you use someone to save yourself on the Cardidas because you deemed your own life more important."

He flushed. "Rudolfo understood."

"I understood too. I also know that the older you get, the more you will become like her."

"And that's why you don't want to talk of the future?"

She raised her chin slightly. "I don't want to be the Black King's wife."

He felt cold. Colder than he had on deck, maybe colder than he had ever been before. "I'm not the Black King."

"No," she said. "But you will be."

"How do you know? I didn't think Warders had much Vision."

"We have enough to design spells for you. Who do you think invented Shadowlands?"

He stared at her, realizing that she hadn't answered him. "How do you know?" he asked again. "Have you Seen it?"

"I've been listening," she said. "You touched the Black

Throne. You are the center. You've had three Open Visions. You are the eldest. Your sister is Blind. Do you want me to go on?"

"No." He was more relieved than he wanted to admit. He didn't want Skya to have Seen him as the Black King. He didn't want that destiny. He never had. "Even if I were to become Black King, I haven't asked you to marry me."

Her lower lip trembled. "No, but you would have if I had allowed you to talk of the future."

He leaned back, no longer pretending calmness. "You're right. I would have asked. I do love you, Skya, and I want to marry you no matter what happens here, whether I become Black King or some renegade always hiding from my own people. I want you beside me. I have from the moment I met you. And I think you feel the same about me."

"No," she whispered. "I don't."

Her hand was clutching the blanket so hard that he could see the strain in her fingers.

"Why are you lying?" he asked.

She shook her head.

"You at least owe me an explanation. I've been following your rules. I've been living in the present as you asked, and now I have to make choices, not just for my future but for ours. I'd like you beside me and you refuse. At least tell me why."

"You're a Visionary."

"You knew that when you met me."

"And I should have left you in Tashco."

"Yes, but you chose to come here."

She closed her eyes. Her skin was taut with strain. Above them, the rain still pelted the deck, the steady drum so loud Gift could barely hear himself breathe.

"My father," she said so softly he had to strain to hear her, "was the military governor of Co."

"He was a Visionary."

She opened her eyes and studied him for a moment. "A minor one compared to your family."

"Not that minor. A governorship is usually given to someone who shows strong ability in the field." Gift knew that much from his time with the Shaman. Yes, his family were strong Visionaries, but other families had similar powers. The Shaman kept those families under close watch, in case the Black Family destroyed itself as it once did in the past. Then the Shaman would take a leader from one of those families to the Black Throne, to see if they could become the new Black Ruler.

"My mother was an Enchanter," Skya said, "and I was their only child."

"A Visionary and an Enchanter. What a powerful combination to have in a small country."

"Co is the most rebellious of all the Fey conquests."

"You told me that on the day we met."

She nodded, looking distracted. It was as if she had to concentrate to tell this story, as if he only had one chance to hear it.

"All his life," she said, "my father Saw a rebellion in Co. He said it would destroy the Fey. He was convinced it would. So whenever a rebel force sprang up—and they did often—he destroyed them. He had anyone who spoke badly of the Fey imprisoned or killed. He destroyed young men, old men, women, children, anyone who seemed as though they would hurt the Fey."

Gift's mouth went dry. Even his grandfather, Rugar, hadn't been that ruthless.

"My mother would use her powers to help him. If he couldn't get Foot Soldiers or Infantry to a rebel cell, she would create a fire spell and burn them out. She was as terrified as he was, afraid that the Co might destroy the entire Empire."

Her eyes were flat, her tone so dispassionate that it hurt. She wasn't looking at him. Instead, she was staring at a spot on the wall.

"I was a precocious child and a bit rebellious myself. My parents wanted me indoors and watched all the time. I hated being inside. I escaped as often as I could."

The rain beat against the deck. It sounded as if the world were being pounded into submission.

Gift's anger at her was gone. He wanted to hold her, to

tell her it was no longer necessary, she didn't have to finish the story, she didn't have to remember. But he needed to hear it, so he said nothing.

"By the time I was ten, I could see what his 'Vision' was doing. It was making things worse. The rebellion he had tried to quash was growing stronger with each life he took. Even our servants were talking about my father as a horrible man, and sometimes, it seemed they dared me to tell him." Her voice shook slightly. "I did tell him. Not names or anything, but what I saw, how I believed he was the one making the Vision come true. The Shaman—our family Shaman—told him not to listen to me, that I was just a child with no understanding of magic, and that he was following the only path. He believed her. Her Visions confirmed his. I was just an untrained Warder with no real Vision, just the edges of it so that I could create spells. And I was a child. A child who didn't understand the world."

Her voice had gotten hoarse. She cleared her throat, then glanced at Gift. He kept his gaze on her, making it steady. He still wasn't sure she really saw him.

"I wouldn't be quiet," she said. "Finally, the Shaman convinced them that my problem was the untrained magic, so they sent me, years early, to apprentice with the Warders in Nye. They hoped I might someday serve the Black Family. My father had had a Vision about that too. That I would be invaluable to the Black Family when I grew up."

This time she did focus on him. He held out a hand, hoping she would take it. She stared at it as if it would hurt her. Finally, he curled his fingers into a fist and pulled back.

"Six months after I left, the entire country of Co revolted against the Fey. My father and mother were slaughtered while they slept. Entire Infantry units were destroyed— burned—but most of the Fey survived. Rugad came, put down the rebellion, and destroyed most of the country. The people were too devastated to fight again. They've only now finished rebuilding. And they've started to rebel again, but the local governor learned from my father's mistakes. He is having his people commingle with the Co, making their blood ours, and conquering them slowly, a generation at a time. It is still a rebellious place, but not the hothouse it was under my father."

"And the Shaman?" Gift asked, knowing that was an important thread.

"I saw her years later, when I was guiding some people through the Eccrasian Mountains. I asked her if she had ever compared Visions with my father, and she had. He had Seen his Infantry units die. He had Seen Co in his bedroom. He had assumed a worldwide rebellion based on those incidents, incidents he had caused himself."

Her hand shook. She clasped it with her other hand. Gift watched her, uncertain what to do.

"The Shaman believed he had been right. She said he had had no other choice, and sometimes Visions went that way. At least, she said, he had had enough foresight to get me out of there."

"Sometimes," Gift said softly, "Visions do go that way."

"*No!*" The power behind her voice startled him. She was finally looking at him directly. She blinked, as if she had startled herself, then repeated, "No. That's a lie they tell you, Gift. A lie you're raised with. So that you will go in the directions of the Vision. The future is not preordained. If it were there would be no purpose to life. My father created that rebellion. It was as if he needed it to reaffirm his Vision."

"Skya, I had my first Vision as a boy of three. I had nothing to prove. Visions aren't voluntary things. They aren't something I make up at will."

"I know. I've seen your Open Vision. I've seen you have Visions. And my father too. I know all that." Her face had closed as if his words had somehow shut her down. He had no idea why. "But Gift, Vision comes from somewhere, like every other spell. Yes, it's a natural ability like all magic, but the way we interpret it is taught."

He felt his shoulders stiffen. "So?"

"So what if we're taught wrong?"

"We're taught that Visions are possible futures."

"And usually the Visions are bad, right?"

He blinked, then frowned. He had had very few good Visions. He had had some that were neutral, some that he didn't really care if they had happened or not. "Yes."

"And we always try to avoid bad things. It's part of our nature as living creatures. We try to avoid the bad and embrace the good. But most Visions, no matter how hard you try to avoid them, come true. Isn't that right?"

Her entire face was flushed, her eyes were sparkling. She looked more alive than he had ever seen her.

"That's how you can tell a good Visionary," he said, "from the power of his Visions, and from how many of them come to pass."

"If you can't change them, why have them?"

"You can change some and not change others."

"Like the death Vision, the one every Visionary has and never realizes until it's too late."

He nodded, feeling confused.

"What if," she said, "the good Visionaries, as you call them, are the ones who follow the paths laid out for them, creating the very bad things that they try to avoid?"

"What purpose would that serve?"

"Your family has taken us closer to the Blood than any other family in my memory. Your family has captured the second Place of Power." Her eyes were bright, almost too bright. "What does the Triangle of Might do?"

"We don't know."

"But what's the prophecy?"

He took a deep breath and recited, *"There are three Points of Power. Link through them, and the Triangle of Might will reform the world."*

"Reform the world," she said. "What does that mean?"

He shook his head.

"What did your grandfather think? Or your great-grandfather?"

He stared at her, not really wanting to answer, knowing that she knew and was using him to make a point he wasn't quite sure he wanted to hear. "They believed it would give them dominion over everything."

"Complete power."

"Yes."

She stared at him. "What if it doesn't do that? What if it frees the Mysteries from their positions as spirits? What if it allows the Powers to take physical form? What if it does create more power, but only for those it deems worthy like Shaman or even, horror upon horror, Red Caps?"

Gift shook his head. "That can't be possible."

"Why not? Because you can't imagine it? I can."

"How?" he asked softly.

"That's what Warders do. We think of everything in new ways. That's how we create new magics."

He never considered how Warders thought or what gave them their powers. He never realized it was their perspective and their imagination as much as their magic.

He hated the logic of this. He hated to believe that Skya might have a point. "All right, let's assume that I believe you, that I believe the Powers are using Visionaries to manipulate a future we don't want. We started this conversation talking about *my* Visions and my choices. What do you believe?"

Her face softened as if he'd asked her something that she'd been waiting all her life to hear. And perhaps she had. "Here's my guess. If you go to Leut, you will drown at sea, probably with Lyndred's father. The Visions of the Blood might simply be a way to keep you from taking the Throne from your sister, a way to keep you away from the Places of Power. Maybe even a way to get you to go to Leut."

"Why?" Gift asked. "The Throne wanted me."

"The *Throne* did," she said, "but we don't know what the Powers want. Maybe they want someone to use the Places of Power to find the Triangle. From what I saw of your sister, she will."

Gift felt cold. "You think the Powers want that."

"The Powers or the Mysteries. Something that controls the magic," Skya said. "Yes, I do."

"And if Arianna doesn't do it, do you think I will?"

Skya looked away from him. "You've made choices that do not fit with the compassionate man who wanted to be a

Shaman. You will continue to do that. You'll get harsher and harsher because you have to, and it'll take a toll on you. It'll make you someone with no heart at all."

"Like your father?"

Her eyes teared. She blinked hard, and the tears disappeared. "That's not fair. I told you that so that you would understand."

"I think I do," Gift said.

She shook her head.

"That's what you're afraid of. You're afraid that I'll be like him, that I'll misuse my Vision the way he did."

"I think you already are."

Gift's chill grew worse. "I haven't ordered people to their death."

"But would you?" she asked. "If you believed it would prevent the Blood against Blood?"

He dropped his gaze, unable to look at her. He didn't know the answer to that. If he had to spend ten lives to save a million, would he? It was the leader's conundrum, the thing his father agonized over, the thing they all agonized over. The thing Gift had always wanted to avoid.

He probably would. And he would hate himself for it.

He looked at Skya. Her face seemed shrouded, cold, as if she had read the answer in his silence. "What about Lyndred's other Vision? The one of me with the child?"

"I think it symbolizes the choices you have to make."

"What choices?"

"Do you raise a child with love and warmth, to live in a secure world? Or do you raise it to lead the Fey?"

He stood. He didn't see those as choices at all. "My father raised Arianna with love and compassion and taught her leadership."

"Your father wasn't Fey," Skya said. "And besides, look at Arianna. Where's that training now?"

Gift didn't know. That training had been one of the many reasons he had trusted his sister as ruler instead of himself. "You realize what I'm risking if I try to get my sister to abdicate?"

"Yes."

He ran a hand through his hair. "If you're right, and the good Visionaries are the ones who lead us in the wrong direction, then wouldn't it be better to have a Blind Leader?"

Skya didn't answer him at first. He turned. She was studying the backs of her hands as if they held a secret.

"Skya?" he asked.

"Maybe if the Leader believed that Blindness was better, and maybe if the Leader strove to— I don't know. I just know that there's something seriously wrong with your sister, and she's not capable of the kind of leadership she's given for the last fifteen years."

"Maybe we should take the third option," Gift said. "Maybe we should use your guide's skills and find a place to hide within the Empire, raise a family, and stay out of politics forever."

"You won't be comfortable," she said. "You'll always wonder if you're doing the right thing. And you're still going to be plagued with Visions, Visions that will test your resolve every single day."

He couldn't deny that. He would wonder every day, and the Visions would make things worse.

"You need to get your sister to abdicate," she said. "You need to take your rightful place as Black King."

"I can't."

Skya rose slowly to her feet. "Why not? And don't tell me it's because of promises you made to your sister. She doesn't care about those promises anymore. She doesn't care about you anymore."

"It's not that," Gift said, even though that was still a factor.

"Then what?" Skya asked.

"You don't want to be the Black King's wife."

She moaned softly and sank back onto the bed. "Gift, what I want shouldn't matter."

"It does." He went over to her, sat beside her, and took her hands into his own. Her fingers were icy cold. "I love you, Skya."

"I know. But what you want doesn't matter. It's who you are that's important."

His heart twisted. "I thought you didn't believe in destiny, in preordained futures."

"I don't believe in much, but I know you'll make a better ruler than your sister ever could."

He wanted Skya to have faith in him, but not like this. Not in a way that might separate them for good.

"That's not enough," he said. "We're talking treason here. We're talking of overthrowing the ruler of the Empire. We're talking about something that could destroy everything."

"And if it doesn't, it could prevent something we can't even imagine." Skya's fingers felt limp, as if there were no will in them at all. "What if your Visions are the Powers misleading you, manipulating you? What if you have nothing to do with the Blood? What if your taking the Throne is what prevents the Blood? What if your sister, through her Blindness or her power-madness, causes the Blood? You will have saved us."

"There's no way to know, Skya."

She grabbed his fingers suddenly. Her grip was so hard it hurt. "That's how the rest of us live, Gift. We have only our hearts and our minds to guide us. We make our own choices and we live with them."

He slipped his own fingers around her hands. They were clutching each other like drowning people. "But what if you chose wrong, Skya? What then?"

"You live with that too," she said. "Somehow, you live with that too."

CHAPTER TWENTY

*B*Y THE TIME the summons came, Lyndred's stomach ached. She had come back from her visit with Gift and had expected Arianna to meet her at the palace door like a worried mother. But there had been no meeting. Lyndred and her father had eaten alone, and Lyndred had told him what she had done.

He had not been pleased, but he had been curious. He had never spoken to his nephew, and he didn't know what kind of man Gift was. Neither did Lyndred. All she knew was that Gift wasn't sure if he could trust her, and seemed uncertain about what he would do in the future.

But it wasn't until Gift had said he was being watched that she even realized what a risk she had taken. After hearing part of Arianna's interchange with Gift, Lyndred knew that Arianna saw Gift as her enemy. Lyndred had gone to the enemy. What kind of punishment did that deserve?

The summons didn't come until mid-morning of the following day. By breakfast, Lyndred had been so nervous that she couldn't eat. Her father watched her as if her nervousness were contagious. He had already said his piece the night before, so they had nothing to talk about.

When the page brought the summons, he wanted her to go directly to the North Tower. She begged a few more moments alone. He waited outside the door as if she were a prisoner while she changed into a Nyeian gown. It was blue, and it had a high ruffled collar, a cinched waist, and long bell sleeves. She put on her best jewelry and pulled her hair into a chignon. If she was going to be reprimanded by the Black Queen of the Fey, her appearance would at least remind her cousin that they were both of noble blood.

When she and the page reached the North Tower, Lyndred swept past him and handed him the skirt's narrow train. She walked into the tower unannounced. Arianna didn't seem to notice.

She was wearing the leather jerkin and breeches she'd been favoring lately, her black hair in its familiar braid. Her hands were clasped behind her back and her legs were spread shoulder-length apart. Lyndred wondered if Arianna had stashed the customary knife in her boot.

The page peeked around the skirt and started to announce Lyndred's presence, but Arianna dismissed him with the wave of a hand. The page dropped Lyndred's skirt and fled. It seemed that everyone was afraid of Arianna these days.

As the door clicked shut, Arianna turned. Her gaze took in Lyndred's clothing. "Trussed up like a Nyeian. How very unusual."

Lyndred straightened her shoulders. Her stomach was churning. She didn't know quite why she was so afraid of her cousin. Arianna couldn't hurt her—not physically, anyway. And if Lyndred was right, Arianna couldn't banish her either. She needed her Vision.

"So," Arianna said as she walked toward Lyndred. "What do you think of Gift?"

"He looks like you," Lyndred blurted.

"Does he?" Arianna walked around Lyndred, still looking the dress up and down. She stepped over the trailing skirt. "Is the way he looks important?"

Lyndred shrugged. "I've just never seen such a resemblance before."

"Because you're too young," Arianna said. "The features in the Black Family are consistent generation to generation. You look remarkably like Jewel. You could have been sisters."

Lyndred had heard that before, and had even stopped at Jewel's portrait on the second floor. She didn't see the resemblance.

"Of course, Jewel would never have allowed herself to wear such confining clothing."

"I'm not Jewel."

"That's obvious enough. Jewel, at least, had the gift of subtlety."

They were going to play a round of stupid verbal games, then. Lyndred hated that. If she had to play, she'd at least make the rules. "I've always wondered why you call your own mother Jewel."

Arianna stopped in front of her. A half-smile touched her lips, as if she actually approved of Lyndred's barb. "Because I never knew my mother. She was just a name to me."

"You don't speak of her as if she were just a name."

"I know my history, child. I know more about my ancestors than most Fey ever could."

Lyndred didn't doubt that. "You summoned me up here for a reason."

Arianna nodded, then walked back to the south window. Through the bubbled glass, Lyndred saw the brownish-red waters of the Cardidas and remembered her strange dream of the waters covered in blood. "Tell me what you observed on Gift's ship."

Lyndred picked up her skirt and walked forward. As she approached Arianna, she saw the Tabernacle, a burned shell in the distance, and beyond it, the white buildings of the southern part of Jahn. In the distance, she could see the winter brown of land that Arianna was now turning into farms.

"I didn't see much," Lyndred said. "A Nyeian met me on deck and took me below. There I saw Gift, his Shaman, and that strange woman."

"Yes," Arianna said. "The Co."

"She looked Fey to me."

"She is Fey. Her clothing was Co. It carried an interesting message, I thought. Perhaps Gift hasn't understood it. This is a woman who cannot be tamed or owned."

Lyndred hadn't understood that either, and she hadn't recognized the clothing. But Arianna had, just as she had recognized Lyndred's Nyeian garb. How did Arianna know so much even though she had never left Blue Isle?

"How many troops did he bring with him?" Arianna asked. "What was the military power of the ship? What kind of ship is it, exactly, Tashil or a Nyeian copy? It doesn't look like a warship from here, but it could be a newer model, something I haven't seen before. Or were there stores in the hold, enough for trading?"

"I don't know."

"Weapons?"

Lyndred shook her head.

"What type of Fey came with him? I noted Foot Soldiers. But were there Beast Riders? Red Caps? Infantry?"

Lyndred almost mentioned the Gull Riders, then thought the better of it. "I don't know. There was a large group of Nyeians, but I think they were there to sail the ship."

"Nyeians." Arianna shook her head as if they were not important. "So you did not go to spy for me. You went to tell Gift that I was Blind."

"I felt he should know."

"And all of this talk of the Blood did not stop you?"

"I think Gift is smart enough to make up his own mind about what to do."

"You don't believe that you're pushing him toward a challenge that would be bad for the Empire?"

"Do you believe that?"

"I banished Gift. I gave him two weeks to leave Blue Isle. That should be an answer to your question." Arianna pivoted so that she no longer faced the window. She stood only an arm's length away from Lyndred.

Lyndred hated the closeness. She had to hold herself rigid to prevent herself from backing away.

"Do I believe you provoked him?" Arianna asked. "Of course I do. What is a Fey's normal response to a Blind Leader? Ask her to step down. Or force her to."

"Believe what you want," Lyndred said. "You've already made up your mind. Nothing will change it."

Arianna's eyes narrowed. "Rather like you."

Lyndred raised her chin. She wasn't going to answer that.

"I have a sense," Arianna said, "that you haven't been honest with me for a long time. What makes you trust Gift more than me? You haven't known him very long, and you haven't seen him before. So what is it? The fact that he's been to the Black Throne? Or did he come to Nye years ago, and talk with your father? Has this been planned for years? Or is it merely coincidence that you and Gift have become such instant good friends?"

Lyndred's heartbeat increased. "Gift and I aren't good friends. We haven't met before. He doesn't trust me at all. I don't even think he likes me very much."

"But you trust him."

She did. There was no lying about it.

"Did you tell him your Visions?"

"Of course," she said. "He's a Visionary too."

"And he told you his Visions as well."

"Yes," Lyndred lied.

"I thought you said they didn't trust you."

"Gift doesn't. He thought you sent me. To provoke him."

Arianna threw her head back and laughed. Lyndred remained very still. She had no idea what was so funny.

"Well, then," Arianna said. "You did your job perfectly. If you want to get rid of Gift and me, you've done very well."

"I don't want to start the Blood," Lyndred said. "I'd never plan anything that would start the Blood."

"I know that. That's why you'll let us take care of each other. You believe that we can do it subtly, without provoking the Blood. Some members of the Black Family were good at that. It looks as though you are as well."

"No."

"Certainly," Arianna said. "If you want the Throne, the best way to get it is to make certain Gift and I are gone. Your father won't take it, and your uncles aren't organized enough. But you are, aren't you?"

"No."

"Of course you'll deny it, because if you believe it deep down, you think the Powers will know and they will see that as Blood against Blood. But that's not true. The stricture is quite narrow. I can't kill you or Gift or anyone in my family, but if you happen to die in a battle I sent you to, there will be no Blood."

Lyndred stared at her. "Why are you telling me this?"

"Because I want you to know that I think you're smarter than they are. You'll achieve whatever you want to achieve. Except killing me."

There was a faint knock. Lyndred felt relieved at the sound. It meant she didn't have to respond to that accusation.

"Come," Arianna said.

The door opened. A man wearing a dark woven gray cloak with the hood up, obscuring his face, slipped inside. His movements were stealthy. Lyndred wasn't even sure she would have noticed him if she hadn't seen him come in.

Gloved hands emerged from the open sleeves. He brought them to his face and let the hood fall. His features—indistinct a moment before—coalesced into a face very similar to theirs, as if he were a member of the family. But Lyndred knew he was not. She wasn't even sure if he was really male. That had been her assumption, and perhaps he had known and catered to it.

"It took you long enough," Arianna said.

"The Black Family has not used my services for more than fifteen years." The man had a deep voice, but it was not an unusual one even though Lyndred felt it should be. "I have to find other employment to keep me busy on this small Isle."

"You could have left," Arianna said.

The man's lips curved into a smile, but nothing else on

his face moved. "Of course. But I thought the Empire was at peace. I thought there would be no need for my services."

"Unless someone decided to come after me," Arianna said. "Is that why you stayed? Because you expected work here on the Isle?"

"Tricky question, milady." The smile fell away. "And I can answer it honestly. No. I stayed because I chose to. I saw no point in returning to Galinas. I made a bargain with your great-grandfather. He offered to give me the proper training if I vowed never to touch a member of the Black Family. I have kept that vow."

Lyndred gasped softly. Arianna looked at her, and grinned. "So, now you realize what our friend is."

He was an Assassin. Assassins had started as Spies. But a Spy's magic left him if he tried to kill anyone. The Spell Warders tampered with the magic of young Spies several generations ago, trying to see if they could develop a spell that allowed them to kill and keep their magic. Apparently they'd found one.

"I thought Assassins were a myth," Lyndred said.

"Of course you did," the man said.

"There are only a few," Arianna said. "I'm not even sure how many still live."

"I have lost track, milady."

Lyndred had heard that Assassins had almost no magic, and what magic they did have simply enhanced their physical skills. They had to use tools—knives, swords, bare hands—to kill; there was no magic in that. But their magic allowed them to sneak in and out of buildings, to move silently, and to make themselves nearly invisible, even in the open.

She had heard all of this as a child, and then asked her father, who had laughed. *No one has ever seen an Assassin,* he had said, which, she now realized, was not an outright denial.

"Well," Arianna said, taking a step forward, "I have a task for you. Are you out of practice?"

The Assassin smiled. "Of course not."

"Good, because this one will be tricky. There is an Islander Enchanter who lives in a town called Constant at the base of the Cliffs of Blood. Do you know where that is?"

"I've been there," the Assassin said.

"His name is Coulter. He's a short blond man with a tremendous amount of magic. If he senses you, he can destroy you with a flick of a finger."

"Will he know what I am?" the Assassin asked.

"He's not familiar with Fey magic," Arianna said. "But he may know more than I give him credit for."

"How much time do I have?"

"As much as you need. Although the best time would be three weeks from now."

The Assassin used his gloved hands to raise the hood. His face was hidden once again. "It will be done."

He glided out of the room, closing the door behind him. Lyndred's empty stomach was queasy. "You wanted me to see that. Why?"

Arianna turned back toward the window. "I made a mistake."

Lyndred froze. She'd never heard Arianna say that before.

"I had thought, when you and your father arrived, that I would be able to use you. I believed that we would share Visions and become stronger. I needed another Visionary since I did not have the benefit of a Shaman. I got two. You, a strong and powerful Visionary, and your father, whose little feelings sometimes helped."

This was what Lyndred had been expecting. This was the moment when Arianna would punish her.

"But now, in your distrust of me, you have stopped telling me your Visions. I am not sure, when you do tell me, that you are telling me the truth. You are no longer useful to me."

Lyndred was breathing shallowly. Had Arianna brought the Assassin here as some kind of veiled threat? But she had made it clear that the Assassin could not, *would not,* touch the Black Family.

"Your father and I discussed a military commission for you, and one for him. But I think after your actions yesterday, giving you a military berth would be tantamount to inviting my own death."

"I told you," Lyndred said. "I would never start the Blood."

"After a few years of service, you would know how to achieve your ends without resorting to that," Arianna said. "No. Your little visit to Gift yesterday, no matter how much I expected it, reminded me of lessons I learned years ago. You should always expect the worst of the people around you, Lyndred, because then they'll never disappoint you."

Lyndred stiffened.

"I want you and your father to leave Blue Isle. You can return to Nye if you like, but your father will no longer run it. You will hold no positions at all. And if you feel as if you're being shadowed, you're right. I'll make certain Spies and others will keep an eye on you. I'll make certain that you don't cross any lines."

Lyndred took a small breath. This wasn't as bad as she had expected. "Don't you think you should consider this more? After all, you're all but inviting me to join your brother in whatever he chooses."

"If he chooses wisely, he'll go to Leut."

"And if he doesn't?"

"I am better equipped to take care of myself than he is."

"I will join him," Lyndred said.

"I expected as much. If he decides he can trust you. I certainly can't."

"It doesn't worry you to have me and Gift together?"

"Why should it? At least then I'll know what you're doing. Here, you could sabotage me quite easily."

Lyndred crossed her arms. "You were going to do this anyway."

"No. I would have worked with you. The test was whether or not you would see Gift. You did. And you told him everything, despite my warnings. Despite the Visions of Blood."

Lyndred took a step toward her. "Aren't you afraid that by doing this, you're the one who is going to bring the Blood down on us?"

"The battle lines were drawn the moment Gift touched the Black Throne," Arianna said. "It doesn't matter how many people stand on either side. I don't believe this will be a physical war. It'll be a war of cunning. And in any war based on that, I will win."

Lyndred stopped. She was close enough to Arianna to see the fine lines around her eyes. "How can you believe that? You've never been to war. You have no experience with battles."

"Neither do you."

"But Gift does and so does my father."

Arianna's smile was small. "Minor experience. And it won't really matter when the time comes. Soon Gift will be gone, and you will understand by then what lengths I will take to defend myself."

"Why don't you banish me like you're banishing Gift?"

"I don't need to," Arianna said. "And besides, someday you might be useful."

"After all this," Lyndred said, "why would you expect me to serve you?"

"Because," Arianna said, "you'll have no other choice."

Chapter Twenty-One

*J*AHN WAS NOTHING like Constant. The streets were cobblestone, worn and flat with time. The buildings on the outskirts were white and had windows. The river ran through the center of town instead of the outskirts, and there were no mountains nearby. Matt could see them in the distance like shadows against the horizon. He couldn't even make out the edges of the jagged peaks.

The light here was dazzling and intense, even in the winter's chill. And the city sprawled forever. When he stopped his horse at the eastern edge, he couldn't see the other side. He couldn't even see the center. There were buildings everywhere. A man could disappear along those streets and no one would ever know.

He shuddered and glanced over his shoulder. The sense that he was being watched had lessened in the last two days, but sometimes he still thought he saw movement out of the corner of his eye. Now he had an explanation for it—he was in a city, where there were hundreds, maybe thousands, of people—but the sensation of movement had been much worse in the countryside, down the mountain passes, and on the narrow trails.

The horse hadn't spooked since that moment four days ago. Matt used that as an indicator; if someone had truly been behind him, the horse would have known it. He also figured that if people had meant him harm, they would have already attacked. He had been extremely vulnerable as he traveled alone.

Matt had ridden for half a day just to get to the center of the city. Still, he felt stunned as he came over a rise and saw the bridge ahead of him, its arch curving gracefully over a calm Cardidas River. The midday sun glinted off the water and nearly blinded him. He followed the road down the rise into a group of warehouses. The river smelled fishy here, and the water seemed sluggish. It was also brownish-red, not the rust-red that he was used to.

His mother had once lived near here, in a small house where she had embroidered for the King and healed wounded people. One of the wounded had been Matt's father. They had fallen in love, and never been apart from that day.

Matt knew all the stories. But he had difficulty imagining his parents here. They had seemed overwhelmed by the demands of Constant. This city, with its continual movement and abundance of people, would have dwarfed them. Yet his father had lived here from boyhood on, and had risen through the ranks of the now-dead religion to become its national leader.

Matt's heart pounded and he kept an eye on the opposite bank of the Cardidas, hoping to see the Tabernacle where his father had served. It wasn't until Matt was nearly to the bridge that the buildings at the water's edge parted enough for him to see the other side.

The Tabernacle rose like a ruin out of the flat ground. It had four towers, now a smoke-scorched white, and the shadows of swords were visible on the walls. The windows were gone, and in several places the roof had collapsed.

Matt stared, wondering what it had been like when his father lived there. The fire that consumed it must have been spectacular, but his father had already been gone then.

Matt wondered what his father would think of this mission now. Coulter had said his father would be proud, and that was probably true. His father had never approved of anyone with Fey blood on Blue Isle's throne. Now that Rugad, the Black King who had nearly killed Matt's father and who had almost destroyed the Isle, was hiding on the throne—masquerading as his own great-granddaughter—things were much worse.

His father probably would have gone into the palace with holy water hidden in his sleeves, hoping to murder the man himself. He wouldn't have tried for something this complicated, or that required this much finesse.

The wide road leading off the bridge went from the Tabernacle to the palace. Finally Matt turned and saw his destination.

The palace was the twin building to the Tabernacle. He could see some of the Tabernacle's past glory in the palace's current structure. Someone had ruined the symmetry by taking down one of the four towers, but the other three rose over the city. Glass glinted in the top part of all three towers, a sign of great wealth.

He hadn't expected that wealth, or the obvious difference in the way people lived. There were no white homes in Constant, nor were there homes painted in bright colors. Fey lived in the town, but in their own section. Here they mingled with Islanders. There were soldiers and merchants and ships and indoor shops, something he had never seen.

He started up the road. His horse was the only one not attached to a cart or a carriage. People who walked by looked at him as if he were committing some sort of crime. He passed them, feeling more conspicuous than he wanted.

The palace got larger the closer he came, and the towers seemed impossibly tall. A large wall surrounded the palace, and over it he could barely see other buildings that seemed to be part of a larger complex. Dozens of people and carts and Fey streamed in and out of the nearest gate.

His stomach cramped and he suddenly wished he had eaten more. His hands were clammy and he felt light-headed.

He could turn around, say that he never got inside, and Coulter would be none the wiser.

But they were depending on him. Everyone was depending on him. And it was a job only he could do.

When he reached the gate, he tried to ride through, but the Fey guards on either side crossed their spears in front of him. He had to pull up his horse to prevent himself from being knocked off.

He sat as straight as he could. "I'm here to see the Queen," he said. He almost said "the King," which would have ruined everything.

"She is not holding audiences this month," one of the guards said. "You must wait until you hear the general announcement before coming to the palace."

"You don't understand," Matt said. "It's not about an audience. She's been wanting an Enchanter. I'm an Enchanter. I want to see her."

The guard who had spoken laughed. The other guard said, "She doesn't need an Islander who thinks he has magic."

Coulter had warned him that this might happen. Matt let go of the reins, and crossed his arms at the wrists. The position mimicked the spears. Slowly, he swung his arms at the elbows until his hands were parallel with his body, fingers pointed to the sky. The spears separated in exactly the same way, the guards struggling to control them and failing.

Matt didn't move. The guards couldn't bring the spears back down.

"I'd like to see the Queen," he said. "Can you get someone to announce me?"

"It doesn't work that way," one of the guards said. His face was dark with strain. "She doesn't do what you want. You must come when she's ready to see you."

"I think she's probably ready now." If he were going to ride through, he would only have a moment. Once his hands were behind the gate, the spears would fall into place. He hadn't thought of that with his particular spell. "Ask her."

The guards glanced at each other. Then one of them

shouted something in Fey. Matt's Fey was adequate, but he didn't catch the words. A tall, slender Fey woman walked toward the gate. She was wearing a jerkin and breeches, her dark hair falling softly around her shoulders. Matt looked at her chin as Coulter had told him to do. She did not have a birthmark.

She stopped beside his horse. Her posture was relaxed. She grabbed the bridle and looked up at him. "You believe that you should see the Black Queen?"

"I've come because she wanted to interview Enchanters. I'm an Enchanter." He felt ridiculous with his arms in the air, but he didn't want the guards to regain control of their spears.

She looked at her guards. "You're doing that?"

"Yes, ma'am."

"I didn't realize Islanders had such talent. Have you Fey blood?"

"No, ma'am."

"Then why would you want to serve the Black Queen of the Fey?"

He flushed. If only Arianna could hear that, she would be so angry. So would Coulter. "I thought she's also Queen of Blue Isle."

The woman's black eyes narrowed. "I guess she is."

"I'd like to serve the Queen of Blue Isle," he said. "I've always wanted to."

He was pushing the edges; he could feel it. But the woman sighed. "Let them go and I'll bring you inside."

It was a risk. If he let the spears drop, she could move him into harm's way. Or she could bar him from the palace altogether. Still, this was his first chance.

He brought his arms down. They tingled slightly. They had been starting to fall asleep.

Both guards staggered toward him, as if the movement of their spears unbalanced them. The spears tumbled to the ground. Laughter rose from behind the wall.

The woman kicked the spears aside and led Matt's horse into the palace grounds. There were dogs everywhere, and a stable full of horses. Carriages were parked near the stone

wall, and in the distance, Matt saw an entire unit of Fey
practicing maneuvers, their swords glinting in the sunlight.
He was out of his depth. He resisted the urge to pat his
knapsack with the dolls inside.

The woman stopped just outside the nearest stable. A
groom came out. He was Fey too, but not as tall as the
woman. He had green eyes.

"It's all right," she said. "You can dismount. We'll take
good care of your horse."

Matt hoped so. The horse had carried him a long way.
He dismounted and grabbed his knapsack. She put her
hand on his.

"You won't need that. We'll clean you up before you
meet the Black Queen."

Arianna had prepared him for this. *Refuse them politely,*
she said, *and promise that someone can search the sack if
they need to. You can make the dolls invisible if you must.*

He had practiced that with Coulter over and over again.
He hoped it would work with these people, while he was
this nervous.

"I do need it," Matt said. "Everything I own is in here.
You can search it if you want. I don't have any weapons."

She gave him an odd look. "If you are an Enchanter, as
you claim, you are a weapon." Then she sighed. "I suppose
it doesn't matter what you have in there. You're more dangerous than any knife."

Matt had never thought of himself that way, but he was.
His magic had more power to it than anyone else's, even a
Visionary's. It also carried more risk.

The woman took his arm and led him through a small
door on the side of the palace. It was cool and dark inside.
They had entered into an antechamber. She took him up a
flight of stairs and down a long narrow corridor made of
stone. There, she opened a solid oak door. It led into a small
room that had no windows. It wasn't a cell, but it felt like
one. There was a cot with a straw-stuffed mattress against
one wall, a Fey lamp hanging from a peg, and nothing else
in the room.

"Wait here," she said. "I'll have the Domestics come and

tidy you up. I'll also let the Black Queen know you've arrived."

He nodded. He glanced at the cot. He didn't really want to be trapped in here, but he saw no other choice.

"Are you hungry?" the woman asked.

For the first time in days, he was. He nodded.

"I'll have them bring you something to eat as well." She studied him for a moment. "You're very young, aren't you?"

"I'm fifteen," he said, drawing himself to his full height.

"What's your name?"

"Matt."

"Where are you from?"

"A small village in the mountains."

She nodded. "You've come a long way. Why now?"

He had to give her the practiced answer, the only one that Coulter believed she would accept from someone his age. "I ran away."

"Why?"

"Because my family hates me." The words were too close to the truth. He shook just a little.

The woman studied him as if she were trying to see through him. "I'm Zayna. If you need anything, ask for me. I will be your sponsor. But if you do any harm, I will be the first to kill you. Do you understand?"

He couldn't answer her. The words were stuck in his throat. Instead, he nodded.

"Good. I'll send Ling to you. She is a Domestic. She will feed you, clean you up, and make certain you have the proper clothing."

"All right." The words came out as a whisper.

Zayna nodded once, crisply. "Normally, you would not receive this kind of treatment. But the Black Queen does need an Enchanter, and I have been instructed to let her know whenever an Enchanter approaches the palace."

Matt swallowed. "I understand."

"Good." She went out the open door, and then closed it behind her. Matt waited for the rasp of the lock, but it never came. Her footsteps disappeared down the stone corridor.

He could let himself out. He didn't see doorways into any other part of the palace, but he would wager if there were any, they would be locked. But he didn't want to get deeper into the palace. If he walked out this door, he would get his horse and leave Jahn for good.

He walked to the cot and sat down. The straw poked through the mattress cover. He was filthy and extremely tired. He had made it farther than he imagined, and he had gotten himself inside. Now they claimed they would let him see the Black Queen.

Matt sighed. If only Coulter and Arianna were already in Jahn. Then he could go after Rugad right away instead of going through this entire farce. But he didn't have that kind of choice. He only had two: leave or continue forward.

He wasn't going to leave. No matter how uncertain he was, he wouldn't leave. But he would take precautions.

He picked up his knapsack and opened it. The dolls were in a special sack of their own, along with the vials of blood. He wished he had the ability to create a Shadowlands like the Visionaries did, but that was not an Enchanter spell. So he pushed the sack as far into the knapsack as he could, and then, with a wave of his hand, built a small wall of cloth in front of it, a wall that looked as if it were part of the sack itself.

Still, the sack was bigger on the outside than on the inside. Anyone touching it would know. So he put a visual spell over the sack itself, so that it looked shorter than it really was.

The dolls were safe, for the moment.

He only wished he were too.

CHAPTER TWENTY-TWO

THE SUMMONS STARTLED Xihu. A Nyeian sailor had knocked on her door and called to her. When Xihu opened the door, he had told her that the visitor was from the palace, and she had felt a strange light-headedness, as if this were the confirmation of a Vision she didn't remember.

She had gone to see Gift first, who told her to go, and reminded her that she had promised to serve the Black Family. She hadn't needed the reminding, but what she hadn't said to him was that she had thought of the Black Family as him, and him alone. She didn't feel that was worth confessing to anyone.

The sun had risen and was a small ball on the eastern horizon. It was a pale sun, giving little warmth and even less comfort. Xihu was used to the chill of Protectors Village, a dry cold that contained the smell of the mountains and a crispness that made even the air seem sharp. Here the cold was damp. The buildings were bright and colorful—a Fey addition, Gift told her—but their structure was plain, a sign of their Islander roots.

The marriage between Fey and Islander cultures wasn't

usually so easy. She had felt a strain ever since the ship had arrived in the harbor, a strain that wasn't connected to the assassination attempts or Gift's Open Vision. The strain was part of the air, part of the very land that surrounded her. It was as if she could feel a discomfort that emanated from every part of the Isle.

The messenger had led her through a different gate than she had gone through the day before. He had taken her in through a different door, and brought her to an audience room that was so large, it could have housed a dozen supplicants and another dozen guards and not seemed crowded.

There was a throne on the dais before her, a simple sturdy throne with ornate carvings on the arms. It was nothing like the Black Throne, which was actual stone, built into the wall of the mountain. This was a simple throne for a simple ruler who had no pretensions, no thoughts of world conquest.

The swords and spears that decorated the walls surprised her. She had heard that the Islanders were a peaceful people, even though Gift had once told her that the symbol of their religion was a small sword. She also knew that the Islanders had proven themselves strong fighters. Still, she had not expected such a warlike place.

She walked toward the throne and stopped, looking up at the coat of arms emblazoned against the wall. Two swords crossed over a single heart. Gift had mentioned that as well, but seeing it mesmerized her. It looked as if it had been created by the same person who created the Fey crest, which was a sword piercing two hearts. No wonder Gift had been startled when he had gone into the Black Throne Room.

Two peoples with magic. Two peoples with Places of Power on their homelands. Two peoples with inverted crests. There was a message here that she felt she should understand.

A door closed behind the dais, and then a person swept into the room. For a moment, Xihu thought she was looking at Gift's identical twin—and then she saw the braid running down the back, the birthmark on the chin, the feminized features, and knew that she was looking at Arianna.

Arianna wore breeches and a jerkin, and thick boots. She had muscular arms and a trim, athletic figure. Her eyes were blue like Gift's, only unlike Gift's they had an edge to them, a darkness that seemed to be threaded through them.

Xihu remembered Gift's suspicion, that Arianna had somehow been tainted by the Throne's dark magic, and wondered at it. It certainly seemed possible. She knew that the Light had gone Seeking. She just didn't know what it had found in Arianna—if it had found anything at all.

Arianna did not sit on the throne. Instead she stepped off the dais and walked across to Xihu. Arianna extended her hand in the Nyeian fashion. Xihu stared at it a moment before taking it, knowing that it was some kind of test.

Arianna's hand was warm and dry. Xihu was surprised at the warmth and the fleshy feel of the fingers. She had half expected, after the Visions and the comments she had heard, that this Arianna would be a Golem.

"Do I pass?" Her voice was throaty and filled with a dry irony.

"I thought I was the one being tested," Xihu said.

Arianna smiled faintly. It was a cool, appraising smile, almost appreciative, and Xihu remembered the feeling she had had in the tower room, that Arianna seemed to play emotions for effect, not because she felt them.

"You are," she said. "I need a Shaman. I'm not thrilled with having one from the Eccrasian Mountains, nor am I thrilled with having one who is my brother's choice, but here you are. I do have some issues that I wouldn't mind discussing with a Shaman."

"Issues?" Xihu asked.

"Yes." Arianna did not elaborate. "I suppose Gift has already convinced you that I'm not the woman I once was."

"He says you're different."

"What do you think?"

Xihu shrugged. "I did not know you before."

"But you have an opinion."

Xihu folded her hands into her robe. "I believe that the

course you have led us on during the last fifteen years is an appropriate one. I do not think that moving to Leut, as you outlined to Gift yesterday, is the appropriate path."

Arianna studied her for a moment. "So you would interpret any Vision to point me in a peaceful direction."

"I do not believe Vision can be interpreted," Xihu said. "I believe it can be compared and perhaps the pieces will fall together."

Arianna's eyes narrowed. It wasn't quite with disapproval. It was as if her quick and agile mind were assessing all that she heard. Then she swept a hand toward the dais. "This is not a comfortable place for a real conversation. Let us go somewhere where we can both sit down."

Xihu followed Arianna behind the dais. Arianna took her through a small door to a room that had upholstered furniture and a fireplace with a warm fire burning in it. The room smelled of wood smoke and seemed extremely homey, but Xihu found the entire transition disturbing. She knew that Arianna had had guards listening in the audience chamber. Now that Xihu had passed some sort of test— what kind she wasn't sure—apparently, Arianna didn't want them to hear anything.

Arianna took a seat near the fire. She stretched out her legs and crossed them at the ankle. Then she pulled another chair close and bid Xihu to sit as well.

Xihu did. The fire warmed her legs. She hadn't realized how chilled she had become during the walk over.

"I suppose Lyndred told you that she believes I am Blind," Arianna said. "You probably think I need a Shaman to give me Sight."

Xihu froze. There would be no lying here. "Lyndred said that, yes."

"So you have come here as a response to my summons not because you are interested in serving me, but because you want to see if you can tell whether or not I'm Blind."

"I came because you said you needed a Shaman."

"Did you expect it to be a permanent Shaman?"

"Is it?" Xihu asked.

Arianna's small smile returned. "You're young, but you are well trained. Is it true that you belong to that small sect of Shaman who defied Kerde?"

Kerde was the leader of Protectors Village, and she had once been Rugad's Shaman. There were several Shaman who did not believe Kerde's ways. One of them had been the Shaman assigned to Rugar, the Shaman who had eventually worked with Gift's Islander father, Nicholas.

"You are well informed," Xihu said, not certain if that would work to her advantage or not.

"I try to know what I can about people." Arianna rested her wrist on the arm of a chair. "What little I know of you suggests you might be untraditional. Are you?"

Xihu shrugged. "I am what I am."

"A traditional Shamanic answer. Let me ask you questions, then."

Xihu nodded. She had hoped for this. It would give her insight into Arianna.

"If you were to become my Shaman," Arianna said, "would you tell me every Vision that you had?"

"That's not required."

"But would you?"

"Would it be a condition?"

"Yes," Arianna said.

"Then, if I agreed to be your Shaman, I would abide by your conditions."

"My conditions would be to tell me all your Visions, to follow all instruction, to analyze Visions only when told to, and to disregard most of your training from the Eccrasian Mountains. Could you do that?" Arianna's eyes sparkled. She knew that most Shaman would not accept such conditions. Shaman liked to think of themselves as the most independent of the Fey.

"If I agreed to be your Shaman," Xihu said again, "I would abide by your conditions."

"Would you agree to be my Shaman knowing those conditions?" Arianna asked.

Xihu studied her. Arianna was sprawled in the chair,

completely at ease with herself. There was something about her expression that suggested a hardness—not an evil, exactly, nor a love of cruelty. Just a tendency to use it if it became absolutely necessary—and a suggestion, however slight, that someday it would.

"Well?" Arianna asked.

This time, Xihu almost smiled. So, the Black Queen of the Fey was impatient.

"Would I be your Shaman knowing those conditions?" Xihu said. "No."

Arianna tilted her head back. "You disappoint me. I thought you did not follow all the Shamanic traditions."

"I don't," Xihu said. "If I did, I would be proud to serve the Black Family in any capacity."

"That's not my experience with Shaman."

"Your father's Shaman was not typical."

Something flitted through Arianna's eyes. It seemed like surprise. What other Shaman would she be thinking of? There had been none on Blue Isle since Arianna became Black Queen.

"Then what makes your choice?" Arianna asked.

"I will not be the only source of Vision to a Blind Leader."

"You believe I'm Blind?"

"You've given me no cause to believe otherwise."

Arianna stared at her, blue eyes so pale and cold that they looked sharp. "I do not have to defend myself to a Shaman."

"Of course you don't," Xihu said. "But you asked my reasons. I've told you."

"Lyndred is a power-mad girl," Arianna said. "She wants the Throne so she is trying to pit my brother against me, have him throw me off the Throne. And while we struggle against the Blood, she seizes power."

"I think that's a likely possibility."

Most people would have softened when she agreed with them. Arianna did not. In fact, her gaze got even sharper.

"But I also watched you yesterday with Gift," Xihu said. "You treated him too harshly."

"Did I? He came here for the Throne."

"He came here for you."

"Perhaps he believes that. Perhaps he has you believing that. But anyone who has touched the Black Throne is in service to it."

"Gift rejected the Throne."

"Did you see it?"

"I Saw the Seeking Light from the Throne. It was released when he let go."

Arianna looked away. "If I prove to you that I am not Blind, will you serve me?"

Xihu had hoped Arianna would not ask that question. "How would you do that? Tell me your most recent Vision."

Arianna held out her hand. She folded it into a fist. Then she slowly unclenched it. In the center of her palm, a tiny Shadowlands rose. It was barely the size of a stone, but it was clearly a Shadowlands. Yet Arianna did not release it as most would do. She also did not make it grow.

Xihu stared at it. She felt as if there were something wrong with it. Perhaps it was Arianna's willingness to prove her Sight, even when she claimed she would not defend herself against the charges.

"So," Arianna said. "Would you be at my side, following my orders and answering my questions?"

Something about this woman struck Xihu as unnatural. Arianna had said nothing when Xihu mentioned the Seeking Light, but logically she wouldn't. Xihu would have been startled at a confession.

"Why is this so difficult to answer?" Arianna asked.

"Because," Xihu said. "I love your brother and trust him. I do not like you."

Arianna closed her fist, crushing the Shadowlands. She stood rapidly and turned her back, but not before Xihu saw the complete fury on her face.

"Liking should not enter into it," Arianna said. "Your training said you must serve the Black Family."

"It's that training you ask me to deny." Xihu spoke as calmly as she could.

Arianna was silent for a moment. She lowered her head as if in thought. "So I did." She turned. "You are an amazing woman. You have proven, with a single sentence, to be the kind of Shaman I want."

The heat from the fire prickled against Xihu's side. The room was almost too hot.

"And yet," Arianna said, "your professed love of Gift shows me that I can never trust you. How very sad."

She sighed and circled the chair, flouncing into it like a young man who hadn't learned manners.

"Since you will be going back to my brother, and since you will probably accompany him to Leut, which means we will never see each other again, would you do me one favor?"

"How can I deny the Black Queen?" Xihu said, not answering the question. She would wait for the favor.

"Give me a ruling."

"On what?"

Arianna sat up. The image of youth was suddenly gone. In her eyes was an ancient wisdom, a cunning that startled Xihu with its ferocity. "Golems," she said. "Golems and loose souls."

Xihu stiffened. "I have little practical experience with them."

"Most people who lived off Blue Isle have little practical experience with them. I am asking something in theory."

"I will tell you my understanding of the theory," Xihu said. "I cannot guarantee that my understanding is correct."

"Such a proper Shamanic hedge. For one who defies tradition, you fall back on it often."

Xihu waited.

Arianna sighed, as if she were disappointed that her jab had not found its mark. "Is a person, freed from his body, subject to Blood against Blood?"

Xihu felt her palms grow damp. She didn't want to think about the implications of that question. "What do you mean?"

"Let me use an example," Arianna said. "My brother Gift left part of himself in a bit of stone, a Golem."

"Your brother Sebastian."

"The Golem lived for eighteen years, and then his Link to Gift was severed, making them separate creatures. For the sake of argument, if I were to destroy the Golem and its soul, would I, as Gift's blood relative, commit Blood against Blood?"

Xihu had to work to control her expression.

Arianna smiled. "I've shocked you."

"It seems an odd thing to need a ruling on," Xihu said.

Arianna straightened in her chair. "A light crossed Blue Isle threaded with black. Ever since that, Sebastian has acted strange. But I think something has happened to him and I do not feel safe around him—and I was afraid for what would happen if things had gotten out of control. I could ask the question in reverse. If he manages to kill me, is that Blood against Blood?"

Odd that she mentioned the Search Light in this context. Was it possible that the light had caused problems within a Golem? Perhaps. Had this been what turned Arianna dark and made her distrust Gift? Because his Golem had tried to harm her?

"So," Arianna said. "You're going to be traditional again and not answer."

Xihu shook her head. "I'm considering. There is nothing in the history of the Fey that helps me here."

Arianna folded her hands over her stomach and leaned back. She would have seemed like someone who was in no hurry if it weren't for the tautness of her body. There was something in the question that was extremely important to her. She tried to hide it, but Xihu could see it in her posture.

"I have not met Gift's Golem," Xihu said slowly. "I know that their Links are shut off, so there is no way to reach Gift through the Golem. This leads me to believe that the Golem is a separate entity with its own personality and thoughts. But its body is stone. It has no blood. So the question you are actually asking me is, What causes the Blood against Blood? The actual physical death of a person's body? Or the destruction of the soul?"

Arianna sat up, looking interested.

"I do not know the answer to that," Xihu said, "but I am inclined to believe that the death of the body is the important thing. Souls can be trapped in Fey lamps. They can change form and become Mysteries. There are many who believe that the Powers are ancient souls as well. I am not even sure the soul passes away. For example, if a Black Family member murders you, your soul will probably live on as a Mystery. But the Blood against Blood will happen as well. That leads me to believe the body is extremely important."

Xihu felt a trembling inside herself. She hated this question and she was certain she was causing a problem with her honest answer. "But then there are the historical concerns."

"Which are?" Arianna leaned forward.

"There is a story that Rugad's great-grandfather created a Golem for himself, and when his body died, had the Golem run the Empire until his grandson—the only one who was competent—was old enough to rule. That Black King was already dead, yet part of him lived on in the Golem. So, if someone had destroyed that Golem's *body,* would it be murder? And if that someone who destroyed the Golem was a member of the Black Family, would it bring on Blood against Blood? After all, the original possessor of the soul was dead."

Arianna nodded. Her eyes were extremely bright.

"But," Xihu said, "there are many who believe that the Black King had put his entire personality, his entire being, into that Golem through a Link, so that what died wasn't the man, only the man's body. In that case, would the destruction of the Golem's body decades later be murder? Would it cause Blood against Blood? I do not know."

Arianna was frowning.

Xihu had to hold her hands tightly together to keep them from trembling. "As to Gift's Golem, this case is even stranger. Gift lives separately from his Golem. They haven't seen each other in years. They have had different lives. The

Golem is regarded by his family as a person. Does that make a difference? What if it isn't the destruction of the body or the soul that creates the Blood against Blood, but the intent of the killer? If the killer has set out to destroy a *person*, then Blood will happen. If the killer wants to ruin a walking stone statue, then no Blood will happen."

"This must be a conscious attitude?" Arianna asked.

"I think it must be the unconscious one. So even if someone tried to delude herself into thinking that Gift's Golem is just stone, it will not work. She must truly believe it. If she was raised—as you were—to believe the Golem is her brother, then Blood against Blood will occur."

Arianna grunted and leaned back. "Let me alter the question slightly. What if the Golem trapped me outside my own body, in a Link perhaps, and took over the body for himself? If I destroy the Golem and not the body is that Blood against Blood?"

"If you destroy the stone, so that the Golem has nowhere to go if banished from your body?" Xihu asked, trying to clarify.

Arianna shook her head. "If I destroy the being—the personality—that has taken over my body, is that Blood against Blood?"

Xihu put a hand to her forehead. Her fingers shook and she no longer cared that Arianna saw her nervousness. "Has this happened? Is this why you do not want him here any longer?"

"He tried once," Arianna said.

There was bitterness in her tone. Bitterness and that sense, not so much that she was lying, but that the truth she told was not what she intended Xihu to understand.

Xihu stood. "If your brother Gift attacked you with a knife, and you killed him in self-defense, that would still be Blood against Blood."

"I know that," Arianna said irritably.

"So," Xihu said, unperturbed by the interruption, "if you were to destroy the body of someone who had taken over your body by crossing a Link, you would bring on the Blood."

Arianna let out a small sigh. Xihu looked at her, but could not read her expression.

"However, if you shatter a Golem without touching its personality, it can—with the proper magic—reassemble. So you can destroy the stone visage without creating the Blood because the Golem isn't really dead."

Arianna rubbed her chin with her right hand. Her fingers stopped and traced the edge of her birthmark as if it were unfamiliar to her.

"So if you destroy the stone body and banish the soul from yours," Xihu concluded, "you haven't killed it and there will be no Blood against Blood."

Arianna froze. And then she smiled. It was a cold, nasty smile. "You are better than I thought," she said. "You are a tremendous Shaman. Are you sure you will not serve me?"

Xihu's skin was still flushed, but she felt a chill run through her. She had done something, changed something, with her answer. "You said you could not trust me."

"I've had advisors I couldn't trust before."

Xihu touched the back of the chair. An advisor to the Black Queen. Staying in this strange place for as long as she had to. Living near someone she didn't trust, someone she actually feared. Leaving Gift alone.

"You are so silent when you think," Arianna said.

Xihu didn't acknowledge her. Shaman served as advisors to the Black Family, but there was one other purpose, one they never told anyone outside the Shamanic ranks. Shaman kept an eye on the Black Family. When Kerde returned to Protectors Village, she had failed in two ways: she had failed her service to the Black Family and she had failed in her service to the Shaman. There hadn't been a Shaman in close contact with a Black Ruler in nearly a hundred years.

"You are actually considering this, despite your love for my brother." Arianna sounded both pleased and surprised.

The Shaman who guarded the Black Ruler had an obligation to make certain the ruler remained on track. If the ruler did not, the Shaman was to contact the other Shaman and find a solution. Kerde had done that, but the Shaman had agreed there was no solution.

Xihu had a sense this Black Queen needed watching. But Xihu had no idea whether or not she could do anything, should extreme action be needed.

She took a deep breath and faced Arianna. Arianna had her head tilted up. She was smiling. Her features had softened. She looked intrigued.

"I will serve you," Xihu said, "if you do not banish Gift."

"No. I will not bargain for your services. You will work for me on my terms or not at all." Arianna pushed herself out of her chair. "Let's forget that last interchange. I will think of it as a reflection of your love for Gift, and you will think of it as a sign of our future relationship. Gift will be on his own, as he should be. You already heard my reasons for that, and I believe you understand them. If you can serve as *my* Shaman only, not the Black Family's; if you can think in terms of the Empire and not in terms of Gift, you are welcome to stay."

Xihu knew where her duties lay. If she had a choice, a real choice, she would stay with Gift. But he needed her less. Something was wrong here, something she might be able to correct if she stayed.

"I'll have to let Gift know my decision," she said softly.

"Of course," Arianna said. "I expected no less."

CHAPTER TWENTY-THREE

*B*RIDGE HAD NEVER felt like a supplicant in his life. He had always had a place to go, a job to do. Even when he had come to Blue Isle, he felt as if he were in charge of something—maybe not as important as the Empire, but a leader, nonetheless. Now he stood beside Lyndred at the base of the ramp and stared at Gift's ship.

Over Bridge's shoulder he carried some of his possessions. The rest were being stored by the loyal members of his crew. His ship had been confiscated by Arianna, and his crew dismissed. If things worked the way he hoped, he might get them work on Gift's vessel.

Bridge had never expected to be thrown out of the palace. He had thought that Arianna might send him back to his position in Nye. He'd never expected to lose that position completely.

Perhaps he should have. Lyndred had told him that Arianna had brought an Assassin into the North Tower while Lyndred was there. The message was clear: Arianna could find a way to destroy them if she wanted to. That she hadn't was evidence that she still thought them useful somehow.

"I'm going, Daddy," Lyndred said. "You can do what you want, but I think we're better off on the ship."

He stared at the masts. There were more than he was used to. "I think we should just leave Blue Isle and go back home."

He had never referred to Nye as home before, but he guessed it was the closest thing he'd ever had. He hated the place, but he felt safer there. And his daughter would be safer too.

"What can we do on Nye?" Lyndred asked. "At least here we might have a chance."

"A chance for what, honey?" He had his hand on the rope railing. The deck of the ship looked very far away. "A chance to overthrow a Black Queen we don't like? A chance to be banished just like Gift? What sort of chance do you see?"

"I think Gift might find a way to force her to step down."

"And what if he does? Are you hoping that something will happen to him? Are you hoping that you'll be able to step into his place?"

Lyndred gave him a withering look. "I'm worried about the Empire."

"So am I."

She ignored him, starting up the ramp instead. It shook beneath her weight. She didn't look back, and the implication was clear. He could do what he wanted. *She* was going onto this ship.

He sighed and followed her.

A Nyeian met them on the deck. Bridge thought it odd that Nyeian sailors would be on a Tashil ship. Then he remembered the Co clothing of the woman Gift had introduced as his guide. This was a diverse crew, filled with people from all over the Empire. In some ways, Lyndred was right. Gift knew more about the Empire than Arianna ever could. Gift, at least, had traveled across the length and breadth of it, and understood there were a hundred different cultures, coexisting uneasily under Fey rule.

"I have no instructions to allow you aboard," the Nyeian was saying to Lyndred.

"You don't need instructions," she said. "I'm the Black Heir's cousin. I should be—"

Bridge put a hand on her arm. She had never dealt with Nyeians who weren't used to following her orders. "I'm sorry. My daughter can be rude. Would you please let Gift know that we're here? I'm his uncle Bridge and this is my daughter, Lyndred."

The Nyeian glared at her before nodding to Bridge. Then the Nyeian snapped his fingers, and another Nyeian hurried to his side.

"See that these people don't get on board," the first Nyeian said. "I'll be right back."

He headed to the deckhouse. The second Nyeian stood in front of them, arms crossed. He was muscular, and it wouldn't take much for him to toss both Bridge and Lyndred into the river.

"Why did you do that?" Lyndred whispered. "I can handle it."

Bridge just looked at her. After a moment, she looked away.

A movement on deck caught his eye. A Gull Rider, sitting on the railing, peered at them. The Rider looked familiar. Bridge squinted, saw the tiny Fey face on the torso on the Rider's back, and realized he was looking at Ace. Was that the reason Lyndred wanted to come here? Because she hadn't given up on her Gull Rider?

He hoped it was more than that.

Lyndred didn't see Ace. But Ace realized that Bridge was looking at him. Ace took a small running start and flew off the ship.

The Nyeian returned. "You can come aboard."

He opened the small gate built into the deck—another Tashil feature—and Lyndred walked through it like she was the Black Queen. As Bridge walked through, he thanked the man.

Gift was watching from the door to the deckhouse. His face was drawn, his eyes rimmed with shadows. He looked thinner than he had two days before.

"I didn't expect to see you again," he said to Lyndred.

"We've been thrown out." She sounded proud. Bridge looked at her. She wanted to impress her cousin.

"I don't believe you." Gift's arms were crossed and he leaned against the wooden housing. His posture said that he didn't want anything to do with them.

"It's true," Bridge said. "Arianna knew Lyndred had visited you."

"Of course she did. It's the perfect setup. She warns me that I'm being watched, then she sends Lyndred here to talk with me, then she pretends to throw Lyndred out, so that you can come here, and find out what our plans are."

"Arianna banished you," Lyndred said. "I think she knows what your plans are."

"My daughter has a point. Unless Arianna is worried about something else, something I don't understand, then she should have no real interest in what you're doing."

Gift sighed and leaned his head back against the wood. He seemed very tired. For a moment he said nothing. Then he brought his head down again. "What do you want?"

Bridge turned to his daughter. This had been her idea. She had to speak for them.

She looked at him and raised a shoulder. He knew the gesture. *You tell him, Daddy.* Only Bridge wasn't going to say anything.

Gift stared at her. He was very still. Bridge had the sense that Gift would wait until one of them spoke. It had to be the Shamanic training. Most Fey didn't have that kind of patience.

"Um," Lyndred started, then glanced at her father again. "We were hoping—"

Bridge cleared his throat.

She stopped, licked her lips, and started again. "I was hoping we could go with you."

"Why would you want to do that?" Gift asked. "Have you been banished as well?"

"Kind of," Lyndred said.

She was still trying to impress him. Bridge had no patience for it. "We've been ordered to leave Blue Isle. We can go anywhere we want in the Empire, but we'll never have any status. Arianna wants us as far from her and as power-less as possible."

"Without forcing you to leave the Empire."

"I would see it as a compliment to you," Bridge said. "We're an annoyance. You're a threat."

"Oh, I'm supremely honored. I can't think of a higher honor I'd rather have her bestow." Gift pushed off the wall he'd been leaning on, and stood up straight. "Take your ship and go back to Nye. No one will bother you there."

"I don't think it's that simple," Bridge said.

"Oh? Afraid you might have to work with the people you mistreated all these years?"

"My father didn't mistreat anyone," Lyndred said. "If you'd come to Nye, you would have known that."

Gift studied her as if he hadn't expected her to come to anyone's defense. "I'm not in the position to take on two additional mouths to feed. I am not sure what I'm going to do with my own crew."

"You'll need us," Lyndred said.

"Oh?" Gift raised his eyebrows. "You can sail a ship?"

"No," she said. "But I've—we've—been with Arianna a long time. I might know some things you don't."

"You seem to assume that I'm going head-to-head with my sister."

Bridge noticed that Gift didn't deny it while at the same time making it sound improbable.

"I think you'd be foolish not to. She's Blind. Besides, as your friend said, you might try to get her to leave without resorting to violence." Lyndred sounded enthusiastic. For the first time in his memory, Bridge was embarrassed for his daughter.

Gift shook his head. "This isn't natural. No one should be talking about a Black Queen this way."

"Then maybe you should see it as a sign—" Lyndred started, but Bridge grabbed her arm.

"Shut up," he said.

She did. He never spoke to her that way.

"I'm sorry, Gift," he said. "My daughter has been strug-gling with Arianna for the past six months. Arianna thought

she could rely on Lyndred's Vision. Lyndred has gotten it
into her head that Arianna is Blind. It's created quite a conflict."

"And now you want me to take you in, conflict and all."
Gift didn't sound too eager.

"No," Bridge said. "My daughter hoped you would. She
believes in you, although she's not showing it well. Frankly,
I'm not sure why. Your options are limited and any path
you take is dangerous."

"I know that." Gift ran a hand through his dark hair. He
looked amazingly like Arianna, but his face was softer, and
his blue eyes lacked the cruel edge that made Arianna seem
so formidable. "What do you think of my sister?"

"She wasn't what I expected," Bridge said.

Gift let his hand drop. His gaze was on Bridge now, and
it was intense. "What did you expect?"

"Someone who was more compassionate. Someone who
had a commitment to peace. I expected her to be more like
my sister, Jewel, only without the warrior's stance. And I
thought she'd act more like a Shifter—emotional, a bit mercurial on the surface, strong and solid underneath."

If anything, Gift's eyes grew bluer. He stared at Bridge.
"You just described my sister."

Bridge shook his head. "No I didn't. Your sister is nothing like that. She stands like a warrior. She calls peace a rest
between battles. She is harsh and has no compassion at all."

"I know," Gift said. "But what you expected, the
woman you thought you were going to meet, that is my sister, Arianna."

"They say she went through quite a change just before
we got here," Bridge said.

Gift glanced over Bridge's shoulder. Without turning,
Bridge knew where he was looking. The palace. There was
no longing in his face, only a sadness, as if Arianna had
died. "What do you think happened to her?"

"She says she finally came to her senses and understood
what ruling was all about." Bridge shrugged. "I have to admit, one of the reasons I came here was because I disagreed
with her policies. In Galinas, bands of young warrior Fey

roam in the countryside. They're hard to control when there's no war. Our people aren't meant for peace."

"So you agree with her new policies." The intensity left Gift's eyes.

"No," Bridge said, and even Lyndred looked at him. "I thought perhaps she hadn't considered the effect of peace on the warrior class. It's not that they're bored by lack of fighting, it's that they're born to fight. It's in their blood and not to provide it means their magic tortures them. I wanted her to find a solution for that. I thought maybe going on to Leut might be good, but I wasn't sure. I was willing to talk with her."

Gift's face was impassive. He was watching Bridge closely.

"But when I got here, she wanted nothing to do with family. She didn't want to see anyone, and she only admitted us into the palace when she found out that Lyndred had Vision."

"So you hold to the Blind theory?" Gift asked.

Bridge sighed. He had been thinking about that a great deal and come to no conclusions. "I'm not sure. She's savvy, and she's clearly had Visions before. My father went for years without a Vision. Perhaps that's what's happening to her, and she isn't ready for it."

Gift nodded. It seemed he'd thought of those things as well.

"No," Lyndred said. "She's Blind. I know it."

Gift didn't even glance at her. "Have you ever experienced a personality change like this before?"

"I didn't know it was a change until you arrived. Up until that point, I thought the rumors I'd heard about her were wrong."

"But you interviewed the servants," Gift said. "You tried to find out what had happened."

Bridge shrugged. "It's my method."

"Arianna is worried about me, about the Blood, and I'm worried about the same thing," Gift said. "I could use an older and wiser counsel."

Lyndred glanced at her father. Bridge tried to ignore the

feeling growing inside his chest. No one had ever considered him important before.

"You've been around Rugad when he was Black King. Your father was being groomed to be Black King and so was your sister, my mother," Gift said. "You've seen a lot more of the traditional Fey world than I have. You probably know more."

"I doubt that," Bridge said.

Gift tilted his head. He had the look of them—the ones who had the talent, the heritage, and the charisma to be ruler of the Fey. "In all these years, you've done nothing to take the Black Throne for yourself. Why?"

At last, the question. Bridge wouldn't have stayed if Gift hadn't asked it. Arianna had not asked it, which, Bridge suddenly realized, was strange given her paranoia.

"I have a small Vision," Bridge said. "It was clear from the time I was a young man that I would never compare to my sister."

"But it was my understanding that my mother didn't come into her Vision until she came to Blue Isle."

"She was taller than me," Bridge said, hoping to end the conversation there.

Lyndred was watching him as if she hadn't thought of these things either.

"She could have come into a different kind of magic." Gift was smart, just like the others. Smart and compassionate. Jewel had had compassion.

Bridge smiled. "My sister was always a half step better at everything than the rest of us were. She was more vibrant, more alive, and she commanded a loyalty even when we were children. The more I've watched this family, the more I realize that the best rulers command that loyalty, at least when they are young."

"When they are young?" Gift repeated. He missed nothing.

"I think my grandfather commanded that loyalty for the first twenty years or more of his reign as Black King. Those warriors who were with him from the beginning would do anything for him. I think the years of rule and the harshness he used wore that charisma away, and in the later years he had to use force and intimidation instead of warmth."

"So did your father," Gift said.

Bridge started. He had forgotten that Gift had known his father. Gift had been a young boy when Rugar died here on Blue Isle. "I'm surprised you remember him."

"He stole me from my parents and would have raised me himself if he could," Gift said. "Fortunately, he died before he had too great an effect."

Bridge stared at Gift. Was the difference between Gift and Arianna that slight? That one had been raised— however briefly—by a potential Black King and the other had been raised by an Islander? "Perhaps he had a positive effect."

"I doubt it." Gift glanced at Lyndred.

She looked fascinated by this conversation. Had Bridge never explained to her the twists and turns of the family? Probably not. He had tried hard not to think about his sister or his father or his grandfather. He only dealt with his brothers in very small doses.

"So," Gift said, "you're not ambitious for yourself. But what about your daughter?"

Bridge stiffened. This was the key question, and how he answered it determined his relationship with Gift. Strange that, after a few moments with this young man, he felt almost as eager as Lyndred to join this ship.

"That's not a fair question," Lyndred said. "I'm an adult. I make my own choices—"

"Of course I'm ambitious for her," Bridge said, deliberately interrupting her. She stopped and caught her breath. Gift's blue eyes focused on him, drawing him in. "I would be lying to you if I said I wasn't."

Gift remained still. Bridge found he envied it. Lyndred was shifting her position. She was slightly out of Gift's line of sight, and she was shaking her head, as if she didn't want Bridge to continue.

But he decided that this man deserved his honesty. If Gift couldn't accept what Bridge had to say, then they would go on their way. If he did, though, they might be able to come up with a solution to a problem they both only vaguely understood.

"I thought, when I was in Nye, that Arianna was taking the Fey down the wrong path. I knew you had gone to become a Shaman—and I believed that was what you were going to do. And I thought, after fifteen years, that maybe Arianna had tired of ruling the Empire. She had never left Blue Isle. She didn't really know the lands she was in charge of. Some of her programs worked, but others were sowing seeds for great disasters, disasters I wasn't sure she'd understand."

Gift still hadn't moved. Bridge had his complete attention and it felt almost overwhelming.

"At worst, I thought she'd want my advice. At best, I thought she would appreciate knowing there was someone else in the family who could take over the Black Throne and serve in the proper manner."

"Worst, best," Gift said. "You were hoping for something in between."

"I was hoping that, with a little discussion, Arianna would step down and Lyndred would take her place." There. He had been completely honest. And now Gift could toss him off the ship.

"Daddy," Lyndred said, sounding shocked.

"You thought Arianna was a reasonable and logical ruler," Gift said. "You thought appealing to that logic and reason would gain your daughter the Black Throne."

"Yes."

"And when you came, you found—what?"

"A cold, demanding woman who was obsessed with keeping the Throne."

Gift nodded. "A cold, demanding, powerful woman. You waited for your chance and saw it when I came."

"No!" Lyndred said.

"I'd be lying if I said I have lost my ambition for my daughter. But as you can tell, she's not emotionally ready for any kind of responsibility."

"Daddy!"

Gift looked at Lyndred for the first time. "You're probably the only candidate for the Throne outside of my immediate family. You would need some training, but you would do all right."

She bit her lower lip and for the first time said nothing. Bridge smiled.

"If we ally with each other," Gift said, "we only make Arianna more paranoid."

"No," Lyndred said. This time she sounded calmer. "She expects it."

"That worries me too," Gift said.

"Perhaps it's a sign of her Vision returning," Bridge said.

"I hope so," Gift said. "If I turn you away, what will you do?"

"Attempt to go back to Nye, I suppose," Bridge said.

Gift made a small noise in the back of his throat. Lyndred was watching him too closely. Bridge felt that same urge to keep an eye on him, to trust whatever he decided.

"It took me half a year to get here," Gift said. "And if I listen to Arianna—"

Bridge found that *if* interesting.

"—I will be unreachable in Leut. If you return to Galinas and something happens, then it will take months for the news to reach you."

"She won't let us stay on Blue Isle," Lyndred said.

"How will she stop us?" Gift asked.

Bridge stared at him. Gift met his gaze. There was challenge in Gift's eyes.

"How long have you been thinking of this?" Bridge asked.

"I don't much like the idea, but I'm not willing to leave my home so soon. Arianna gave me two weeks. I'm going to use that time." Gift clasped his hands behind his back. The gesture was like Arianna's, only on Gift it seemed relaxed, without any military training behind it.

Lyndred was watching them both, her dark eyes bright with excitement. She could feel Gift relenting, just as Bridge could.

"If you're going to stay with us," Gift said, "you'll have to be willing to do whatever I ask, and to take the same risks I do. If I find out that either of you has gone to Arianna, I'll throw your possessions off the ship, and bar you from ever having contact with me or my people again. Is that clear?"

"That's not a very harsh punishment," Lyndred said.

Gift raised an eyebrow. "It depends on where I find out that you had contact with Arianna. If it's in the middle of the Cardidas beside the Eyes of Roca, it's a very harsh punishment."

"Oh," Lyndred said.

Bridge stifled a smile. His daughter would learn a lot from her cousin. She just might not like the lessons.

"Make your choice now, because by tomorrow morning, I'm sure I'll regret this."

"We'll stay," Bridge said. "I think this is an alliance that will be good for all of us."

Gift shook his head. "I hope you're right."

CHAPTER TWENTY-FOUR

*M*ATT HAD BEEN too tired to think himself a prisoner. He had slept for most of the first day—awakened only to bathe, eat, and put on fresh Fey clothing—and then had slept through to the following morning. Only then did he realize that he had been in the same room for two days. He wasn't locked in, but he wasn't really free either. If he left, he would lose his opportunity to see Rugad.

The Black Queen. He had to think of the man who had taken over Arianna as the Black Queen. A single slip and he would be forced to give up all the information he knew.

It wasn't until after dinner that the Black Queen was ready to see him. The pages made him leave his possessions behind, and then they led him outside the palace. They brought him back inside through another door, and led him through a maze of corridors until he entered a room where a fire blazed. It was a narrow room with tapestries on the window that showed scenes from Islander life. He recognized the history and the patterns in the furniture as well. This was all Islander heritage, even though everyone he had seen in the palace had been Fey.

The two chairs before the fire were hand-embroidered into a repeating pattern. His mother had once made her living doing needlework for the palace. She had said that the work was designed not to be distinctive, and the patterns were never signed. He would have no way of telling if she had done any of the work in this room.

But the needlework represented her, and it almost felt as if she were in the room. He felt a stab of homesickness so profound it nearly doubled him over. He knew what his father would have thought of this mission. He had no idea what his mother would think.

Now, faced with needlework that might have been hers, he was sorry she had learned about this mission from his brother. Alex had probably misrepresented the whole thing. If Alex had even bothered to tell her.

Matt's stomach clenched. The food he had eaten, good and unfamiliar, sat inside him like a lump. Now was not the time to be thinking of his family. Now was the time to prepare himself. He was about to meet the most evil Fey who ever lived. At least, that's what his father used to say about Rugad. Coulter even seemed to believe it was true. And he wanted Matt to stop him.

A door opened on the side. It startled Matt. He nearly knocked over the candle screen he'd been looking at, but he caught it with his right hand.

"An interest in embroidery. How unusual." That was Arianna's voice. It sounded exactly like the stone woman he knew in Constant, but it was not her inflection. This woman spoke Islander as if Fey were her native tongue.

Matt swallowed, then turned. He stood as straight as he could.

The woman across from him looked something like the Arianna he had met and something like Sebastian. Only this one had blue eyes, and a prominent birthmark on her chin. She wasn't beautiful, although she might once have been. There was a harshness in her face that lent it a stark quality, that made it almost seem bleak.

Matt bowed.

"Stand up, boy." The Black Queen sounded both disgusted

and amused. "You're in Fey territory now. We don't believe in false ceremony."

"S-sorry," Matt said as he straightened. His palms were clammy and his heart was racing. He had never been this nervous in his entire life.

The Black Queen was tall and thin, dressed in clothes similar to the ones the Fey Domestics had given him: a strange leather vest and pants. Her hair was braided down her back. She was the most unfeminine woman he had ever seen.

"I understand you're an Enchanter."

"Yes."

"Prove it."

He extended his hand, and formed a ball of fire in the middle of it.

The Black Queen looked at it and frowned. "Is that the best you can do?"

"Of course not," he said. "But we're inside."

"Such caution. Is that the way they train Islander Enchanters? To be cautious?"

She was trying to provoke him. He was tempted to set up a wall of flame between them or to smash the door behind him. Instead, he extinguished the fire, then scooped his right hand as if he were gathering air and lifted. Slowly.

The Black Queen rose off the ground. She didn't move and didn't panic like many others would have done. She watched him, seemingly amused.

From outside he heard a bang, and then the door opened. Several Fey guards poured into the room.

"Stay at your posts!" the Black Queen snapped. She hadn't even turned to look at them, but she had wanted Matt to know that they were there.

The guards backed out. Matt held her up. His arm was growing tired, but he wasn't going to let the tiredness defeat him.

"All right," she said after a moment. "You've proven your point. You can put me down."

He eased his hand down and she stepped forward as if

she descended from a platform. She was obviously familiar with this kind of magic.

"Impressive," she said. "You're strong and talented."

"Thank you." He let his hand drop to his side.

"But you are an Islander, by the look of you."

"Yes, ma'am."

"An Islander, willing to serve a Fey Queen?"

"I understood that you were Queen of Blue Isle too."

She smiled, but it didn't reach those blue eyes. "It's a minor title."

He took a deep breath. "I don't think so."

"Presumptuous." She came closer. "I like that. Tell me, why did you come here?"

"I heard that you were in need of an Enchanter."

"I sent that call out months ago. I got no response."

"That's because there are only a few of us on the Isle."

"A few?" She seemed interested. "How do you know?"

"I sense the others," he said. "I've met a few of them. The strongest ones are still children."

"And under the sway of Coulter?"

Matt felt cold. "Yes. His school."

"You went there?"

Matt shook his head. This was the only outright lie they agreed he would tell. "My father was Matthias."

"And this is supposed to mean something to me?"

The disinterest in her tone stunned him. He hadn't been prepared for her not to know who Matthias was. Arianna had said that Rugad would have her memories. "Matthias. The Fifty-first Rocaan. He nearly killed you when he killed your mother."

She tilted her head, studying him. Her expression hadn't changed, and he suddenly realized that she had known. She had been testing him. "You consider attempted murder a recommendation?"

"No," Matt said. "I meant to explain why I never went to Coulter's school even though we were in the same city. My father forbade it."

All true, so far as it went.

"And what does your father think of you serving a Fey?"

"My father is dead," Matt said.

"Recently?"

"Yes." Matt was under instructions not to give a date if he could avoid it.

"So you're here to poison me in your father's memory?"

"No!" Matt couldn't believe she was saying this. "I don't think of you as Fey. You're the Roca's blood. I wouldn't do anything to harm you."

"You see it as your duty to serve the Queen of Blue Isle?"

"Yes."

"Even though she's surrounded by Fey?"

"Yes."

"And is half Fey herself?"

"Yes."

"Your father hated the Fey, as I remember."

"He hated magic too, even though he had some," Matt said. "I'm not my father."

"Then why did you mention him?"

"You'd find out sooner or later."

She smiled and this time the look went to her eyes. It softened her face and almost made her seem like the Arianna he knew.

"You're a bright young man," she said. "But the request for an Enchanter came from my Fey background. It is a Fey magic requirement, not an Islander one."

"Until the Fey came, we didn't realize we had Enchanters among us," Matt said.

"Oh, yes you did," the Black Queen said. "You killed them."

Matt shuddered. How could she—he—go from warm to cold so very fast? "Things have changed."

"Not really," she said. "Fey and Islanders still mistrust each other. No one has forgotten we were at war fifteen short years ago."

"That's my whole life," Matt said.

Her smile was small. "And I'm sure a boy raised by the former Rocaan would be completely unbiased in his response to the Fey. Quite a dilemma, isn't it? You can't tell me of any contact with Fey and you use your father as an excuse to justify your lack of contact with Coulter, the only source of magic knowledge in Constant. Yet you appear here, a full-fledged Enchanter. Enchanters are born, but the spells you have used are trained spells. Who helped you?"

"I spied." He was lying again. He hadn't expected this.

"On Coulter and his little school?"

"Yes."

"But you said all the Enchanters were young there. So you haven't been spying for long. Yet your skills are quite developed. In fact, you have the skill level of an Enchanter who has been doing the work for at least five years."

She pegged it correctly. He had been sneaking to Coulter for at least that long.

The Black Queen crossed her arms. "I have quite a dilemma. I am in need of an Enchanter, but I want a Fey Enchanter. One I can trust."

"You're part Islander."

"And you are pure Islander. Your father was the keeper of secrets that could kill the Fey. In fact, my father struggled to keep your father away from Gift and myself, for fear that your father's religious magic would kill us."

"I'm not my father," Matt said again.

"If you were, I wouldn't have let you in here." She studied him. "It's a measure of my trust that I even asked you to demonstrate your powers for me."

"You can check me out," he said. "I'll even let you cross my Links. You'll see that I'm sincere."

When he mentioned Links, she raised her head slightly. He could feel how her gaze measured him. He wished he could control the way his heart was pounding inside his chest. He wanted her to take advantage of this. It would solve everyone's problems, and quickly.

"What an intriguing thought," she said. "If I had another Visionary on my staff whom I trusted, I would do exactly that. But you'll have to understand why I'm refusing. It would be a tremendous risk for me."

Matt bit his lower lip to keep it from trembling. "I hadn't thought of it that way."

"I'm sure you hadn't." She didn't sound at all sincere. "It's a sign of your youth. And that's my other problem. You're an Islander, you're young, and you come from a part of the country where there is simply too much rebellion. I need an Enchanter, but I'm not that desperate. I can wait."

Coulter had thought she was going to be that desperate. Coulter was convinced that Rugad didn't want to rule without an Enchanter. Matt hadn't expected Coulter to be wrong.

"You can train me," Matt said. "I am young and I am an Islander and I can't help where I'm from, but you could train me into being exactly the kind of Enchanter you want."

She studied him for a moment. "That's a possibility."

She walked over to him. He got a vague sense of two people staring at him—the woman he saw and the man he knew to be controlling her. How could he see Rugad? Was it the way his magic worked? Or was it simply his imagination, providing what he already knew was there?

She stopped in front of him. He understood what was different. The eyes looked like the eyes in a mask. They didn't quite belong with the face.

"All right," she said. "I have some things to settle. I'm not ready to train an Enchanter. I was hoping for one who was fully developed, older and Fey. But it looks as though I'll have to have you."

Matt's heart leapt at the same moment as fear gripped him.

"Come back to me in a year," she said. "By then my affairs should be in order and I'll be ready for you."

He had been so nervous he almost missed what she said. "A year?"

"Yes."

"That's a long time."

"In your short life, perhaps. Are you unwilling to wait?"

"No, no," he said. "I'll wait. You want me here, right? At the palace?"

"I don't care what you do as long as you come back here a year from now."

"I'm willing to start right away," he said.

She frowned at him. "Are you going to argue with me, boy? This is more of an opportunity for you than it is for me."

"No," he said. "I'm not going to argue."

"Then it's settled. I'll see you at this time next year."

She turned and walked out of the room. He stared after her, and then his knees buckled. He caught himself on one of the upholstered chairs.

He had succeeded, and he had failed at the very same time. They hadn't planned for this. They had thought he would be able to stay close.

He should have come in here with his knapsack. He should have brought the dolls and when she asked him to test his magic, he should have used the Islander spell. But he wouldn't have had time. Those guards would have been inside long before he was finished.

And now he had to leave. This was their big chance and he had blown it. They couldn't wait a year.

He didn't know what to do.

CHAPTER TWENTY-FIVE

*D*ARKNESS WAS FALLING as Dash pulled the carriage into a turnout. Coulter had decreed that they camp near the carriage, slightly off the main roads.

Arianna liked the breaks from the bump and jostle of the carriage. She hadn't ridden in one since she took a Golem's form. The stone was rigid, and each jolt made her worry that she would crack. She couldn't rest while they moved, and rest was becoming very important.

The moment the carriage stopped, Con was out the side door. He and Dash had established themselves as the ones who would set up their small camp. Coulter was left with the responsibility of helping Arianna. He didn't seem to mind.

She did. She hated to have help getting into and out of the carriage, and she hated not being allowed to lay out her own sleeping blankets. She wanted to cook one of the meals, even though she hadn't cooked over a fire since she had been in the mountains with her father fifteen years ago. She wanted the ability to do things for herself again.

As soon as she could, she'd go to the other side of the road, where the bank sloped down to the Cardidas and work on her Shifting. If that worked, at least she would gain control of something.

Coulter got out of the carriage before she did, and then waited at the bottom of the step for her. She lumbered to her feet, grabbed the door frame and eased herself out.

"How much farther do we have to go?" she asked as she took Coulter's hand. He helped her keep her balance as she took the steps to the ground. As she moved away from the carriage, she could hear the burble of the river.

"Two more days."

"It didn't take this long to get from Jahn to Constant six months ago," Arianna said.

"Then we traveled all the time." Coulter pulled her close and put his arm around her. "We didn't stop except to change horses and drivers. Remember?"

She didn't remember entirely. Then Rugad had her body and she had to live inside a space in Coulter's mind. She had been frightened then—for her future and herself.

She wasn't frightened anymore. Just determined.

She slipped her arm around his back. She could feel his solid muscles. After a moment, his body heat warmed her stone skin.

"Do you need help practicing your Shifting tonight?" he asked softly.

If he hadn't had a firm grip on her, she would have pulled away in surprise.

"No need to start, Ari," he said. "I watched you the night before we left. That's what you were trying to do, isn't it?"

She nodded.

"I might be able to help you."

"How?"

"I'll show you. First, let me tell the others we'll join them after a while." He let her go, then grinned. "They'll think the worst of us."

"I wish the worst were possible," she said.

His grin faded. "It probably is."

She shook her head. "I wouldn't be able to feel anything. And I'd be so cold."

"You're never cold, Ari," Coulter said. He slipped around the carriage and went to Dash and Con.

Never cold. She was always cold these days. Cold and dead, except inside. She cautiously made her way down the slope, finally sitting and easing herself down the bank to the edge of the water.

She wasn't sure why she wanted to be here. Mostly because she didn't want anyone else to see her fail at something that had once been as natural as breathing. It felt odd to let Coulter watch her, but Coulter knew everything about her, and it didn't seem to change his mind.

The Cardidas was darker than the land, like a black ribbon dividing the ground. There was no moon, at least not yet, and down here the daylight was completely gone. The air smelled cool and damp, the ground was probably wet, but she wouldn't be able to tell until she stood and wiped the dirt off herself.

After a moment, she heard footsteps on the grass behind her. A thin light illuminated the area around her. Coulter sat beside her. He was using his index finger for light. It burned softly, a glow of fire around the digit, circling it but not consuming it. She took her hand in his, careful not to touch the flame. That was the difference between their magics. His finger still existed as a finger. If she succeeded in Shifting, her finger would become a flame.

"Let's try some sympathetic magic." He extended his burning finger. "Touch your index finger to mine and absorb the flame."

"Will it burn me?" she asked.

"I've never seen Sebastian burn. Only crack."

She smiled. Coulter's face looked ruddy in this light. He was so handsome. She longed to touch him, not finger to finger but as a lover would. Instead she extended her index finger and touched the tip to his. The flame still surrounded his finger.

"Now," he said, "imagine the flame crossing over to your finger."

"It doesn't work that way."

"I know," he said. "Humor me."

She stared at their fingertips. His fire was cool and white, a source of light but not heat. Fires weren't just light. They were heat and passion and risk, all rolled together. They were barely at the edge of control, like a wild animal that someone had insufficiently tamed. She imagined the tip of her finger bursting into flame. But nothing happened.

"It's not working," she said.

"Keep trying." He sounded so patient.

She could imagine it. She even knew how the Shift should feel. But that place inside her mind, the place that controlled the Shifting, wasn't there.

It was in her body, in Jahn. Under Rugad's control.

She pulled her finger away from Coulter's. "I can't."

"Ari—"

She got to her feet. "It was stupid to try."

"It's not stupid, Ari." She recognized the tone as the one Coulter used with his students. "Try again."

"No. I could feel the Shift this time, Coulter. The mechanism isn't here. I can't do it, not in this—thing."

He stood too. "Right now, that's your body. It should be able to Shift."

"Well, it can't. It can't run either, and it can't walk very well, and it doesn't even need to eat. Why should I expect it to Shift?"

She walked down the embankment, careful not to slip. She felt Coulter watching her, making sure she was all right. But he was wise enough to leave her alone now.

The river burbled past her. One contingency plan gone. It was a vain hope to think this body could Shift, but it had been her best hope. Now she had to rely on everyone else.

She wasn't sure if she could do that.

CHAPTER TWENTY-SIX

MATT CARRIED HIS knapsack out of the palace. The Fey let him keep his new clothing. They had apparently burned the others. He was being escorted by four Fey soldiers as if he were some kind of threat. If he wanted to, he could snap a finger and light them all on fire. Or toss them against a wall. He could hold them in place with the force of his hand.

Surely the Black Queen knew that, so this was for show. Or perhaps it was an acknowledgment of his power, and a hope that he would acknowledge hers. Maybe she really believed he would come back within a year.

They had brought his knapsack to him, so it was a good thing he hadn't hidden the dolls in the room. Not that they were of much use to him now. He had failed.

Coulter and Arianna were coming to Jahn—they might already be in Jahn—and they were relying on Matt. What were they going to do now?

He had to hide his panic. He didn't want the guards to know how upset he was. He had to act as if he were honored, and that was hard enough with the panic gripping his stomach.

He was truly on his own.

The guards had led him into a great hall. One of its walls were covered with swords. He had heard of this room. His father had told stories of banquets held here, of ceremonies, and how Arianna's mother had lain in state here because her father had not wanted her in the Tabernacle as befitted a Queen of Blue Isle. And how Matt's father had not objected: he had seen the Fey Queen as a disgrace to all that the Isle had been.

The floor-to-ceiling windows looked black. Apparently, darkness had fallen and he hadn't even known it. Several torches hung in this main room, their light catching the swords. Matt looked at them. Several of the swords were made of varin. His father had told him that as well. They had survived the earliest battles for the Roca and had been placed on the wall in safekeeping. Other swords from other, lesser battles had also been placed on the walls, and the varin swords had gotten lost.

Con had found one during his fight with some Fey. He had told Matt that story shortly before Matt left. Con had been Matt's age then, and Con had told him the story to give him courage.

God will provide, Con had said.

Matt could only hope that Con was right.

The soldiers didn't even seem to notice where Matt was looking. He could use his magic to bring one of the varin swords to his hand. He could slice these soldiers apart, then run back to that room and slice the Black Queen in half. Rugad would die in Arianna's body.

But Matt didn't know if Arianna would live without her body. Even if she did, he didn't think she would be very happy with him. She hated the body she was in and she made that clear.

The soldiers had reached a double door. They pulled it open and held it for Matt. He walked through, leaving temptation behind him.

He was on a path that curved around the palace. To his right, the Infantry trained. He could hear their swords clashing. He was amazed that Rugad let them train at night. What was the point? Was he planning nighttime raids? Matt didn't know enough about Fey military policy to know if that was one of their tactics.

The soldiers led him around the palace to a gate he hadn't seen before.

"I had a horse," he said.

"The Black Queen said nothing about a horse," one of the soldiers said.

"But I came on a horse."

"Then you'll have to negotiate its return in the morning. Our orders are to escort you off palace grounds."

It wasn't his horse. It was Coulter's horse. He couldn't face losing the horse as well. "Please. Let me have my horse. There's a woman named Zayna. She's the one who sponsored me here. She'd know."

"You may see her in the morning," the soldier said. "Leave us now."

Matt stood in front of the open gate. He thought about the horse, the swords, the woman inside who wasn't a woman at all. He still had the glass dolls in his knapsack. Maybe he could use the horse as an excuse to come here again. He could attack the Black Queen at the right moment, after he was sure Arianna and Coulter were here.

"All right." He shrugged the knapsack over one shoulder and walked through the gate. He kept his head up as he stepped onto the cobblestone street.

The night was cold and the air had a dampness to it that made him even colder. All of the buildings had torches burning near their doors. The city was abnormally light.

Behind him, the gate closed. In spite of himself, he turned to look at it. He was shut out and he had nowhere to go.

Con had said he would take Arianna and Coulter into the tunnels below the city. There were dozens of ways to get to them, Con had said, but the easiest was through the ruined Tabernacle. At least Matt knew where that was. He would go there.

He wasn't sure what side of the palace he had exited on. He turned until he saw the bridge. It was lit as well. The torches on it reflected in the water below. Across that bridge was the Tabernacle and a place to sleep. At least he had been fed well in the palace, and he still had food left in his knapsack. Not much, but enough to survive on for a few days.

He would have to take this day by day, moment by moment.

He had to walk past the palace wall to get to the wide cobblestone street. It was wider than the others and better lit. Lamps hung from poles spaced four buildings apart. This was a wealthy area, apparently, and someone believed the extra light would keep it safe.

The extra light made him uncomfortable. He walked closer to the buildings than he normally would have. He didn't want to be seen—an Islander failure, tossed out of the palace before he had a chance to complete his mission. The Tabernacle seemed so far away. His father had taken this walk too, after fighting with the Islander King. After choosing to defend the Isle against the Fey instead of co-operating with Nicholas.

Matt hadn't thought this much about his father in months. He wasn't sure if it was the city that made him feel this way or his own failings. Or perhaps, for the first time, he felt as if he had gone up against an evil Fey, just like his father believed them to be.

Suddenly someone grabbed him, put a hand over his mouth, wrapped another around his chest and dragged him backward. He struggled, but the hands held him tightly. They pulled him into an alley darker than the road. A thin trail of light from the main street looked like salvation.

Whoever held him was larger and stronger. Matt was going to have to—

The hand holding his mouth let go and formed the symbol for silence. The symbol he and Wisdom had come up with.

He turned. Wisdom stood behind him. Wisdom's face was dirty, his hair—usually so beautifully braided—was tangled and matted. He looked even thinner than he had before. He put a finger to his lips and pointed toward the street.

Matt looked. Two Fey were walking in the direction that he had walked. They had no faces—or it seemed as if they had no faces. Coulter had told him about those Fey. They were Spies.

They're following me? he signed.

Wisdom nodded. He took Matt's hand and led him through the alley to the narrow street on the other side. This one wasn't as well lit. They crossed it and went into another alley.

Wisdom led him to a small house. It was dark. He went to the east side of the house, and felt along its foundation. Then he grabbed something and started to pull.

Matt watched for a moment, feeling as if this were a horrible nightmare. Wisdom glanced over his shoulder, his face eloquent. He wanted help.

Matt reached down and found that Wisdom was pulling on a handle. Matt grabbed it too, and together they tugged. A large door opened toward them, knocking them back. The hinges squealed, and Matt looked around.

No Fey, at least that he could see.

Wisdom pointed toward the opening.

"What's down there?" Matt whispered.

Wisdom pointed again.

"You first," Matt said.

Wisdom made the sign for *all right*. Then he pointed to another handle on the inside of the door. He wanted Matt to pull it closed after them.

Matt nodded. Wisdom crawled inside the hole, his feet making solid thunks against a wooden stair. He disappeared into the darkness. Matt hesitated, then shrugged. He had had only vague plans, and they included going under the city. He had a hunch that was where Wisdom was taking him as well.

Matt got into the hole and grabbed the door's handle. He climbed down, then pulled the door closed on top of him.

He couldn't see anything. He felt slightly dizzy. He put

his hands on the steps he had touched, and went down, tapping the next step with his foot before leaning on it. He couldn't even hear Wisdom's breathing. Matt's heart was pounding so hard that he was afraid it would knock a hole in his chest.

But he went down, and he counted the stairs as he went so that he would know how far he had to climb if he were going to reach the door again. He didn't hear anyone above him either, and he didn't hear that squeal of hinges as the door opened.

They weren't being followed, at least.

Why had the Black Queen sent those Spies after him? Had she known that he was lying? Or was that common procedure with anyone who wanted to be Enchanter to the Black Queen? Who did they think he would have led them to?

Matt shuddered. It didn't matter what they thought. He would have led them to Coulter and Arianna.

A hundred steps down, his foot hit stone. He felt a hand on his arm and he felt the hand make the sign for safe. He raised his left hand and used an old spell that Coulter had taught him. A lightstick formed in his hand and illuminated the small space.

Cobwebs covered everything. Dirt hung in ropes around them. The walls, mostly made of stone, were crumbling, and piles of dirt covered the floor. The stairs he had just climbed down were rotted. It was amazing that they had held his weight and Wisdom's.

Now he understood how Wisdom had gotten so filthy. He had been hiding in the tunnels.

"You followed me," Matt said.

Wisdom nodded. He signed, *Too dangerous to see alone*.

Their invented language had its weaknesses. Matt wished again that Wisdom would have let him repair his tongue. "Who is too dangerous? Rugad?"

Wisdom nodded.

"You knew I would fail?"

Wisdom shook his head. *Impossible*.

"My failing?"

The mission.

Matt let out a small sigh. "They're following me to see who I lead them to, right?"

Wisdom nodded.

"I was planning to go back tomorrow to get the horse and to see if I can use the dolls."

We do it my way, Wisdom signed. *We use the tunnels.*

"I'm not sure the magic will work through walls," Matt said. "Not with someone already in a body. We might get a random soul."

I will help you. We will see him together.

"I thought you were afraid of him," Matt said.

I owe him. Wisdom touched his mouth. For the maiming, Matt realized.

"You could let me help you. The Domestics would have helped you too." It was an old argument, but it was one they had never settled.

Wisdom shook his head.

"It would make things easier, especially now," Matt said.

Wisdom sighed. He glanced up the stairs and then leaned against the wall. He signed, *Patience,* which was his way of saying he had a long explanation.

"All right," Matt said.

Wisdom touched his mouth and shook his head. *You are the first true friend I've ever had. The first one who will do what I ask because you think it's right, not because I have Charmed you.*

"Well, we're friends now," Matt said. "You can talk."

No. This mission must be your choice. If I have my Charm, I might make you do what I want.

"I'll be all right," Matt said.

Wisdom took him by the arms. It was his way of telling Matt that he wasn't listening.

"All right," Matt said. "Try me again."

Wisdom let go of him, took a deep breath, and signed, *If you do what I ask you may die. We may die. It must be your choice.*

"Would we destroy Rugad?"

Wisdom nodded.

"Then it's my choice," Matt said. "Let me give you your voice back."

Wisdom looked at him.

"We're friends for good, and if you can talk, you might be able to help us more. Will you let me do that?"

It is a waste of magic.

"No," Matt said. "If we're going to take risks, we use all of our strengths. I could have used some Charm this afternoon."

Wisdom smiled. *How long would it take?*

"I don't know. I've never done anything like it before." Matt stared at him. "But I'm willing to try."

We do this, Wisdom signed, *only if you agree to follow my plan before you finish fixing me.*

"I don't even know what your plan is."

Wisdom nodded. *You must trust me.*

"I do," Matt said. "And I'm grateful for your help."

Wisdom sighed, straightened his shoulders, and then opened his mouth. Matt stuck the lightstick in the wall and prepared to use a spell he had only read about in books.

CHAPTER TWENTY-SEVEN

SOMEWHERE DOWN THIS river were the Eyes of Roca, the Cliffs of Blood, and the Roca's Cave. Gift had once walked from Jahn to the cave. It had taken what seemed like forever, and he had gone across land. He had no idea how long it would take by ship.

He wondered if Arianna would have him followed if he went east down the Cardidas instead of west. He supposed she would. Bridge had used the word *paranoid* to describe her. It seemed accurate.

Gift gripped the ship's wooden rail and leaned into the breeze. The air was cold and damp even though the sky was clear. The lights of Jahn prevented him from seeing all but the brightest stars. The stars had become familiar to him in the months he'd spent at sea. Losing them to the artificial light felt like losing old friends.

He heard a creaking behind him, and he turned. In the thin light from the shore, he saw a tall form behind him. The light reflected off the shock of white hair.

Xihu. She had been gone all day, summoned by Arianna. So much had changed just in the last few hours. He didn't know how he'd tell Xihu about Lyndred and Bridge. He doubted Xihu would approve. He wasn't sure he did, but he felt safer having them here. Lyndred struck him as an impulsive girl who wasn't used to thinking on a global scale. Her father was more sensible and, if Gift decided to trust him, might be the resource that Gift needed to help understand the rules of the Fey.

"Good to see you back," Gift said.

Xihu came up beside him and put her hands on the rails as well. "Staring at the future?"

"Thinking," he said. "I sent most of the Nyeians into the city to get us supplies. Everyone else is belowdecks. Unless you saw someone else, we're alone up here."

"And free to talk."

He nodded. She probably couldn't see that in this light, but he didn't care. They knew each other well enough to understand each other's silences.

"What did Arianna want?" Gift asked.

"What you had once hoped for."

"She wants you as Shaman?"

"Yes." Xihu did not sound pleased. "Arianna needs a pet Visionary."

"So she is Blind?"

"She made a Shadowlands for me to prove she wasn't."

Gift started. He had so accepted Lyndred's view, even while denying it, that the idea that Arianna could make a Shadowlands struck him as absurd. "It was a proper Shadowlands?"

"It was small and we didn't go inside it, but it looked like a proper Shadowlands. Maybe her Vision has diminished. Or maybe she's just tired of ruling with only herself for counsel."

"If that were true, she would have accepted my offer."

Xihu sighed. "You have to stop assuming that you know this woman. She is not the one you remember."

"I'm trying to accept that." The breeze shifted direction and blew a strand of hair across his face. He brushed it away. "Are you going to serve her?"

"Yes," Xihu said.

Gift's fingers tightened on the railing. When he left the Eccrasian Mountains with Xihu, he had told himself that she would become Arianna's Shaman. But somehow, after Arianna's transformation, he had thought that Xihu would turn the post down.

"She needs me more than you do," Xihu said.

"She's the Black Queen," Gift said. "Of course she does."

"I tried to get her to change her mind about banishing you."

Gift held his breath.

"She said no."

Of course she did. She was getting everything she wanted. She was taking away all that he had bit by bit.

"I almost decided not to serve her then," Xihu said. "But I realized I might be of more use to the Empire at her side."

"You certainly will. You can't do much for the Fey from Leut." He hadn't meant that to come out as sharply or as bitterly as it had. But the words were there now.

Xihu put her hand on top of his. Her palm was dry and callused, the skin almost scratchy. "I told her I care for you and I didn't like her."

"She must have wondered why you wanted to serve her, then." Gift was feeling betrayed and he wasn't sure why. This had been his idea from the beginning. Even this morning, when she had been summoned, he had told her to go and asked her to serve his family. He had thought it best that someone keep an eye on Arianna.

"She asked me questions," Xihu said. "I answered them. And then she asked me if I wanted to serve her."

"Questions?" Gift asked.

"Hypothetical situations," Xihu said.

He wasn't going to ask her what those situations were. He didn't have the right to know. Information between a Shaman and another Visionary was confidential.

"She knew I was coming back here," Xihu said. "I think she wanted you to know what I asked."

Gift shook his head. "It's none of my business."

"It might be," Xihu said. "It might have been a veiled threat."

Her fingers curled around his. The gesture was no longer soothing. It was designed to keep him at her side. How well she knew him. He would have walked away so that he couldn't hear what he wasn't supposed to.

Here he was following the rules of his people and Arianna was flouting them. Everything had turned upside down.

"She wanted to know if it would be considered Blood against Blood if she destroyed a Golem and its soul."

He stiffened. "She wants to kill Sebastian?"

"She used him as the example."

A coldness deeper than any he had felt in his life filled him. "Arianna loves Sebastian."

"She could barely call him by name. She mostly called him the Golem."

Gift pulled his hand from Xihu's. "She can't be my sister. She can't. Arianna loved Sebastian more than anyone, even our father. She always wanted Sebastian beside her."

"If she's not your sister, then who is she?"

"I've been trying to figure that out. Another Shifter, maybe."

"I suppose that could be possible," Xihu said. "But sometimes, Gift, the Black Throne corrupts those who sit in it. Your sister has been Black Queen for fifteen years."

"She's never touched the Throne."

"But that doesn't mean it hasn't touched her."

He was silent. The wind blew his hair in his face again. "Why would she want to kill Sebastian?"

"She feels he betrayed her. At least that's what she said."

"What do you believe?"

"She asked about Links. She said she knew that yours and Sebastian's were closed, so she knew that harming Sebastian wouldn't harm you. But it seemed to be a sideways question, as if there were an undercurrent I wasn't getting. You're not bound to Sebastian, are you?"

"I don't know. I'm not sure how the magic works in creating a Golem. All I know is that he has been a part of me my whole life, and if I could figure out how to reestablish our Link, I would."

"You didn't close it?"

"No." Gift would have told her the story, but he wasn't sure how much he could trust her anymore. "Did you tell her it was all right to kill Sebastian?"

"I told her that I believed destroying a Golem did not cause Blood against Blood. I also told her I wasn't sure of this, that I am not an expert on Golems and I know no one who is."

"You think that will stop her?"

"I think I might be able to stop her. I hope that she'll seek my counsel enough to listen to it, to stop her craziest schemes."

That sounded like the Xihu he knew. He walked back to the rail and took her hand, holding it lightly in his. "I know we planned to do this, but you don't have to serve her if you don't want to."

"There hasn't been a Shaman to the Black ruler in nearly a hundred years," Xihu said. "Some of the changes in the Empire were caused by the lack of a Shaman. I hope to remedy that."

"Nice answer. But you still don't have to if you don't want to."

"My wants don't figure into this, Gift. I have to serve where I am most needed."

"She needs you more than I do." He worked to make sure that didn't sound like a question.

"She needs more than I can provide," Xihu said, "but I am what she has at the moment."

"And me? I'm sane and going to Leut, so I'll be all right?"

"No," Xihu said. "You are a sensible man, but you have to be careful as well. I just can't be in two places at once."

She took his other hand in her own. They were standing at the bow like lovers, holding each other's hands in the moonlight. She hated this as much as he did. After all, she was going to a palace she had never seen before, to serve a woman she didn't like. The bitterness he felt left him.

"I'm sorry," he said. "You surprised me. I thought you'd stay here."

"I would," she said. "But I sense a real need there."

He nodded.

"You must listen to me now," she said. "I will tell you two things and you have to hear the first before I tell you the second."

She sounded serious. She hadn't spoken to him like a Shaman much during their trip. Mostly, she had spoken to him as a friend.

"You must trust your own heart," Xihu said. "You must believe in yourself. You are the only one who has ever rejected the Black Throne. That was prophesied. You are the center of what's to come, and that's usually a good thing. You must use the rules as guidelines only. If you stray outside of them, make sure it is for the right reason."

"How will I know what that is, Xihu?"

"If you do it for malice or greed or anger, you are wrong. Listen to yourself, Gift. You have an innate sense of right and wrong, the most developed sense of justice I have ever felt among our people. I think it comes from your Islander heritage. It is certainly not Fey."

He smiled and then, knowing that she couldn't see the smile, squeezed her hands. She squeezed back.

"This next is the hardest." She had lowered her voice. "I was hoping that Skya would tell you this, but she is not going to. I think she is afraid of it."

"Of what?" Gift asked.

"She wants nothing to do with the Black Family. She has told you of her father, right?"

"The Visionary who got himself killed and nearly destroyed a country." Gift didn't even try to keep the disgust out of his voice. "Yes, she told me."

"You must realize this is a powerful heritage. It sowed terrible doubt inside her, and made her the outsider that she has become." Obviously the two of them had spoken of this. Gift wondered why Skya had waited so long to tell him.

"When she finally told me, I understood."

"Then did she tell you her father's last Vision?"

"No," Gift said.

"The day her father sent her to Nye, he told her of the

Vision he'd had concerning her. He said she would one day carry the heart of the Empire within her."

Gift gripped Xihu's hands harder. He might have been hurting her, but he couldn't make himself let go. "You know what that means, don't you?"

"I do now, yes." Xihu sounded calm, but she didn't want to tell him. He could feel it. It was as if she were betraying confidences tonight—Arianna's to whom Xihu felt no loyalty, and now Skya to whom, it seemed, Xihu felt much loyalty. Or was she simply afraid of Gift's reaction?

Gift waited. He knew Skya wouldn't tell him whatever this was. She had had a chance when she told him about her parents, and she hadn't said anything.

"She's pregnant, Gift," Xihu said. "She's carrying your child."

He let go of Xihu's hands. He turned away from her so that she wouldn't have a chance to see the expression on his face, even in this darkness. His first thought wasn't of Skya or the child, but of himself, standing in a Vision, holding a newborn and crying.

"Gift?" Xihu said. "You must listen to me, Gift."

His mother had wanted this. She had said the child was the most important thing. His mother had known. She had given up her freedom for children, children that would unite the Islanders and the Fey. She had given up her life to have Arianna.

Look where that had gotten them.

"Gift." Xihu put a hand on his shoulder. "You know what this means?"

"We have an Heir." Gift felt numb. Why hadn't Skya told him? She knew he loved her. Maybe that was what she was afraid of.

"Yes," Xihu said. "You have an Heir. And you must take care of this child. It has to be the most important thing to you. Your child will inherit the Throne even if you do not."

"No." Gift shook his head. He didn't want a child of his—any child—to be mixed up in this crazy political life. "Arianna will have children."

"Arianna will never let anyone close enough to her. Gift, this is the Empire's only chance. You must have this child."

"I'm not in charge of the child. I didn't even know it existed until a moment ago." If he had, would he have done anything differently? Maybe he would have heeded his mother's warnings. Maybe he wouldn't have seen Arianna.

But that wasn't true. The child was conceived on this trip. He would have come to Blue Isle, and he would have seen his sister. He would just have been more protective of Skya.

"I'm sorry to tell you this way," Xihu said. "But I had to. I won't say anything to Arianna or to the rest of your family, but you must take care of Skya. Because if she dies and it's at the hand of a family member, that's Blood against Blood."

"I just invited Lyndred and Bridge to stay aboard this ship."

"Perhaps you want to rethink that."

Gift shook his head. "I don't know what to think any longer. The child changes everything."

"Does it? I think, in some ways, it gives us hope."

"Hope?" He turned to her. She looked old and sad.

"Before, it was you or your sister who held the future of the Fey. Now it is your child. Perhaps that was why everyone saw you as the center. Because of this child."

"And what if it isn't Visionary? What if it doesn't have the qualities a member of the Black Family needs?"

"You're the strongest Visionary in your family. Skya's a Warder with a Visionary parent. If this child is not a Visionary, then the magic has gone wrong."

That didn't reassure him. Part of him wanted the child to be simple, ordinary. An Islander without magic. A person who had no responsibilities to the Empire or the world.

"All right, then." He needed to talk with Skya. He needed time to think about the way everything had changed. "Thank you for telling me."

Xihu touched his face, her fingertips brushing the line of his jaw. "I'm going to be continuing my work for the Black

Family," she said. "It is your family that holds my loyalty, Gift. Remember that."

He nodded, and then pulled her into a hug. She held him tightly. He buried his face in her shoulder. She smelled faintly of cinnamon. He would miss her. Now more than ever.

It would be the first time in years that he had lived without a Shaman nearby. He felt as if he were losing a lifeline.

He felt as if he were losing a friend.

VISIONS

[Two Days Later]

CHAPTER TWENTY-EIGHT

*T*HE CARRIAGE BOUNCED down the last of the mountain road, hit a rut, and toppled Arianna into Coulter. He grunted and helped her right herself. She had tried not to fall into anyone, knowing that this body weighed so much more than most, but Dash was probably as excited as she was. They were on the outskirts of Jahn.

They were coming home.

She glanced at Con, sitting in the seat opposite. He was staring out the window, his face tight. He loved it here too. Together they had planned to restore the Tabernacle, make it safe for Islanders and Fey to worship together. Then Rugad had reappeared, and that dream had disappeared.

The road abruptly switched from dirt to cobblestone and the horses slowed down. Coulter took Arianna's hand. "I'll make sure no one sees you, but be careful."

He had already told her that a dozen times. He didn't want her looking out the windows, and when they stopped the carriage, he didn't want her to get out until he told her to.

Dash was going to buy some supplies before they crossed

the bridge and went into the Tabernacle. They also had to find a place to keep the carriage and horses. Coulter didn't want the horses too far from them, but Arianna felt they had no choice. Rugad was smart and anything out of the ordinary, particularly around the Tabernacle, would catch his attention.

Arianna squeezed Coulter's hand and peered out the window. She recognized the buildings; they were whitewashed, which indicated that they were at the very outskirts of the city. These were the dwellings of old Islanders, those who had been adults before the Fey onslaught. She had thought them strange and unyielding, uncomfortable with change. Now she was relieved to see them.

"This would probably be a good place to get supplies," she said.

"I was thinking we'd wait until we got farther in," Coulter said.

"No. There will be Fey farther in. They could be working for Rugad. I suspect attitudes have changed in the few short months I've been gone. It would be better for you three Islanders to stop here than farther into the city."

"Good point," Con said. "I never really thought this community had its uses before."

Arianna smiled at him. He smiled back then leaned out the window, and shouted the plan to Dash.

Coulter frowned at her. "We'll be drawing attention to ourselves too early."

"We won't draw any attention here," she said. "That's what I'm trying to tell you."

He stared at her, then he sighed and shook his head.

Con leaned back into the carriage.

"Did he hear you?" Arianna asked.

"He'll stop at the first place that looks promising," Con said.

"At least tell me," Coulter said, "that you'll stay in the carriage when we stop."

"I will," she said. "And so will Con. He's well-known in Jahn."

The road rose and turned, making the carriage sway from side to side. Outside, Arianna heard the clip of other horses, some conversation in properly accented Islander. The neighborhood looked wonderful. The smell of the Cardidas mixed with horse manure and too many bodies too tightly packed wafted through the open window and she inhaled deeply.

She had actually missed it.

The carriage eased to a stop. Arianna glanced out her window, saw several merchant buildings near the edge of the road. These were still whitewashed and had old signs. Coulter opened the door and stepped out. He and Dash went to one of the stores, and disappeared inside.

"It's not as changed as I thought it would be," Con said.

"There hasn't been enough time," Arianna said. "Another six months and we won't recognize the place."

"Do you think Matt's in the palace?"

"I hope so."

"Coulter seems more and more reluctant." Con glanced out the window. This was the first chance they'd had to speak alone since the trip began. "Is he having second thoughts?"

"He would rather hide in Constant than come back to Jahn. He would be happy if he and I lived out our lives there."

Con studied her. "That seems harsh."

"From him or from me?"

"From you. He loves you."

"I know that. But he doesn't know what it means to stand up for himself."

"Where would he have learned it? He told me how he grew up, unwanted by the Fey, then raised by an Islander who wasn't his real father, who died because Coulter made a mistake."

"That's what he doesn't understand," Arianna said. "Coulter made no mistake. Adrian would have died anyway."

"This disturbs you," Con said.

Arianna nodded. She kept an eye on the shop that Coulter and Dash had gone into. She didn't want to be caught in the middle of this conversation.

"When it comes time," she said, "I'm not sure if Coulter will be able to do everything he's supposed to."

"I'm sure he's learned by now."

"No." Arianna saw the shop door open, but no one came out. "He's spent all this time reviewing his failure. He hasn't considered all the things he did right."

"Was that a lot?"

She glanced at Con. He really didn't know. "Coulter saved my life twice. He's saved Gift's life once that I know of, and probably more than that. Even his mistake was an understandable one. I don't know why he flogs himself about it."

"Because it left him alone." Con spoke softly.

Arianna frowned. No wonder Con understood. He was alone, and had been as long as Arianna had known him. All he had had was his religion, and that had been destroyed when he was a very young man.

"I guess it did," Arianna said. "But it was by his choice."

The door was still open. Dash carried some sacks out, but Coulter remained inside.

Coulter could have come to her. She always expected him to. Instead he had waited fifteen years, and had only come because he knew she was in trouble.

He saw that as a failure too. If Coulter had been successful, Rugad would not be running Arianna's body right now. Rugad—and all shades of him—would be dead.

Finally Coulter came out. He, too, was carrying sacks. Dash went back for more. Already Coulter had provided a lot for this trip. The carriage, the horses, the coin. He had done more than most would have, and she had been thinking it hadn't been enough.

Perhaps he wasn't the only one focusing on his failures.

Dash emerged from the building carrying more sacks. He went to the back of the carriage where Coulter was already working. Arianna knew what they were doing; they were tying the sacks in place, making sure they were ready for whatever came.

Con was playing with the small silver sword around his neck. It was a symbol of the position he had once held in Rocaanism. He'd been Aud, which had been normal for a boy of his age. Fifteen years later, he still thought of himself as an Aud. If Rocaanism had survived Rugad's attacks, Con would probably have been in its upper echelons by now.

Coulter opened the door to the carriage and crawled inside. He nearly bumped his head on the top of the frame. Dash walked past the window, and the carriage shook as he climbed to his post. Arianna heard Dash cluck at the horses, and then everything jarred forward as they drove away.

Coulter looked paler than usual.

"What is it?" Arianna asked.

"Gift is here."

"In Jahn?" She had thought he might be on the Isle, but she hadn't expected him to be here. "Is he at the palace? Is he all right?"

"He's been to the palace and there are rumors of some sort of rift between him and"—Coulter glanced at her—"the Queen."

Arianna let out a small sigh.

"The Islanders don't know what that means, but the Fey are really worried about it. The Islanders in that store were saying that it was probably good the Queen kicked Gift out, since he's so Fey."

Arianna started every time Coulter referred to Rugad as the Queen. But he was reporting what he heard, and that would have been how the Islanders spoke. "Has Gift changed?"

"I don't know," Coulter said. "But there seems to be a dislike of him I haven't noticed before. And it seems deeply rooted in what they call his 'Feyness.' Dash pointed out that you—the Queen—were part Fey too, but they said that since you were raised by your father, you aren't nearly as Fey as Gift. They seemed to think Gift was here to destroy all the Islanders and make Blue Isle a Fey homeland."

"Where would they have gotten that idea?" Con asked. "Gift is a gentle man. He would never do such a thing."

Arianna folded her hands in her lap. "From Rugad."

"That's my guess," Coulter said.

"So where's Gift?" Arianna asked.

"He's on a ship in Jahn harbor. He's under orders to leave Blue Isle—and the Fey Empire—in little more than a week."

Was Rugad afraid of him? Had Gift seen through him? "He's been banished?"

"So far as I can tell," Coulter said. "This is all rumor."

"How did you get them to tell you so much?" Con asked.

"I didn't," Coulter said. "Dash did. He said he'd been out of the city for a month and wanted news."

"Amazing." Con shook his head slightly.

"I don't understand. If Rugad wanted to get rid of Gift, why not order him off the Isle immediately? Why give him a week?"

Coulter glanced at her. "Obviously, he's planning something."

"Gift should know that. He's smart enough."

"Maybe he's trying to figure out what."

"Maybe." Arianna felt cold. She rubbed her arms to warm herself and then realized that this body couldn't be cold. The chill had come from within. "I don't like this, Coulter."

"I didn't think you would."

"We have to see Gift."

"I know."

"If I were Rugad, I'd have Gift's every movement watched. So you and I can't just go up there."

"Rugad could recognize all of us," Coulter said.

"Except Dash," Con said.

"He was with us when we rescued Arianna."

"But Rugad didn't see him," Con said.

"Rugad won't be watching Gift's ship," Arianna said. "He has too many other people for that."

"He'll have them watch for anything unusual," Coulter said.

Arianna nodded. "I would be considered unusual, but neither of you would. Nor would Dash."

"Except that we're all Islanders," Coulter said.

"How would someone describe this to Rugad?" She leaned forward, excitement filling her. This was better news than she had thought. "Three blond Islander males went to Gift's ship."

"A lot of the Fey around the palace saw me," Coulter said. "They might recognize me."

"Two, then. All we have to do is let Gift know we're here." He would be able to help her. Gift was very creative. Together, the two of them could defeat Rugad. She knew it.

"He may not know that the woman he saw wasn't you," Coulter said.

"But he'll know that I wasn't acting like myself," she said.

"He'll believe me." Con spoke softly. "He was very grateful to me for all I've done for Sebastian."

"You're right. He will." She hadn't felt this good in months. "We'll go to the place where Con was going to hide us. Then we'll send Con and Dash to Gift to arrange a meeting."

"If he's being watched, someone will follow him," Coulter said.

She let out a long breath of air. "I wish I could Shift properly."

Coulter bit his lower lip. "Maybe I could shield you, or make you appear to be a fourth blond Islander."

She grinned. "I have never been a blond Islander."

"But for a very short time," he said, "I could make someone think you were."

"I still think we should hide the carriage," Con said.

"Yes," Arianna said. "You and Dash do that. Coulter and I will meet you at the base of the bridge on the Tabernacle side. Four blond Islanders to visit Gift. I trust you know where the ship is?"

She directed that last to Coulter.

"I have a vague idea," he said.

It would be vague. Coulter wasn't really native to Jahn. Neither was Dash.

"We'll find it," she said.

Coulter took her hand. "Your mood has shifted. What do you think Gift can do for us?"

"I don't know," she said. "But we were a good team once. We'll be a good team again."

CHAPTER TWENTY-NINE

WISDOM HAD AN uncanny sense of time. Matt still thought it was the middle of the night when Wisdom woke him up. But Wisdom assured him, still using sign, that it was morning.

Time had gone by so quickly. Matt had spelled Wisdom the first night, and then rested to restore his magic the second. Matt had tried two different spells, both of them powerful, before he found one that worked. The problem was not so much that Wisdom couldn't talk, but that Rugad had cut out his tongue.

The spell Matt had first tried was one to restore a voice, which wasn't quite necessary. The second didn't work at all, and the third was a growth spell. Matt had to touch the stump of Wisdom's tongue and start it growing. He also had to end the spell before the tongue became too big to carry inside the mouth.

Wisdom had played with the tongue, touched it, rolled it like a child, but he hadn't spoken with it. He still preferred sign. It was as if he were afraid of his own magic.

When Wisdom had awakened him this morning, Matt

had to do another lightstick. He watch Wisdom as he signed the plan to go to the palace.

"How do you know this place so well?" Matt asked.

Wisdom had simply smiled. He had been roaming Blue Isle for fifteen years, and during most of those years he had been homeless and begging. Matt sensed that Wisdom's six-month stay at the school had been his longest anywhere. And now, Matt knew, Wisdom had stayed because of him.

They ate a silent breakfast from the supplies in Matt's sack. Matt felt for the hidden space in the back, reassuring himself that the dolls were still there. He wasn't done yet. He just wasn't going to do this the way that Coulter had planned.

He knew they were in Jahn. He had felt across his Link for Coulter, and found him close. That was good. The quicker he acted, the better.

Wisdom seemed impatient to go. He finished eating long before Matt did. While Matt finished and carefully repacked the knapsack, Wisdom crouched beside him, rocking on the balls of his feet and watching as if each movement slowed them down.

Then Matt stood, slung the sack over his shoulder, and Wisdom grinned. He took the lightstick and headed down a corridor filled with more cobwebs than the passage they had slept in.

During the night Wisdom had somehow cleaned himself up. His braids were fresh. No strands of hair stood out from them. He had managed to scrub his face and he had gotten the dirt off his clothes.

Matt was the one feeling grimy and nervous. He didn't know exactly what they were going to do and that unsettled him. The Words said nothing about the range of the dolls, and it had no advice on whether or not a person had to be in the same room. Matt was going to have to err on the side of caution. He would make sure he was in the same place as the Black Queen when he tried to catch Rugad's soul in the doll.

The corridor twisted and turned. He couldn't see that far ahead so each corner was a surprise. He had a sense that they were heading north, but he really couldn't tell. Wisdom wasn't saying. He was just walking, head up, as if he knew where he was going.

Suddenly the corridor opened up. They were in a newer section. The stone was clean and the floor was covered with only one layer of dust. There were no cobwebs. Someone came down here regularly.

Wisdom held out a hand, blocking Matt's entry. Matt waited, his heart pounding. Wisdom looked both ways, as if he were going to cross a particularly busy street, then ventured into the wider corridor. He put a finger to his mouth and beckoned Matt forward.

The corridor turned slightly and then opened even wider. As Matt walked past, he started. There were iron bars on his left side. Beyond them were cells. They looked old, but they had fresh straw in them. They had been used, and recently.

He shuddered.

Wisdom came to a fork in the corridor and took the left. It was dirtier than the right. He went to the end of it. There seemed to be no place to go. He pushed on a stone and it creaked open.

The sound echoed in the confined space. Wisdom gave Matt a nervous glance. If someone heard, then they would have to find a place to hide. He didn't want to end up in one of those cells.

The stone had opened a door barely big enough for Matt to walk through upright. Wisdom signaled for another lightstick. Matt made it and handed it to him.

This corridor was narrow and filled with dirt and cobwebs. It was so filthy that Matt could barely see where they were going. Clearly, no one had used this place in a long time.

He wondered how Wisdom had known about it and then he remembered: Wisdom had once been Rugad's assistant. When Rugad had first taken over the palace years ago, Wisdom had been assigned to find out everything about it. Apparently, he had traced all these passages then and no one had been here since.

Wisdom took a few steps, then pulled Matt forward. This corridor forked too, and to the right was an extremely narrow passage. Stone stairs disappeared into the darkness. Matt had the sense that those stairs were part of another staircase, separated from them by the thick wall. It was almost as if someone had planned this passageway when this section of the palace was built.

They started up the stairs. Wisdom went first, knocking down most of the stringy cobwebs as he went. Dust swirled around the lightsticks. Matt and Wisdom climbed for a long time, and the farther up they went, the narrower the passage got. At the three-hundredth step, Matt found himself pressed between the walls, sometimes struggling to get his knapsack through the opening. He grunted once and Wisdom glared at him. Apparently they were in an area where they could be overheard.

Matt had lost count by the time they reached the top step. It opened onto a small platform. Two different corridors branched off. Both corridors seemed to end about a hundred feet away.

Wisdom signed, *Prepare your dolls.*

Matt crouched in the small, dirty space and opened his knapsack. He removed the first doll, his hands shaking.

The Words instructed that he remove the doll's head and put two drops of the Roca's blood inside to attract a free soul. He removed the head and cradled it on his legs so that it wouldn't clang against the stone floor. Then he removed one of the vials of blood. He put the two drops in and then added just a little more in case he needed extra help.

Carefully, he set the vial down, and put the head back on the doll. He replaced the doll in the knapsack. He followed the same procedure with the other doll.

When he was finished, he put the vial back inside. Then he nodded to Wisdom.

All right, Wisdom signed. *Here's what we will do.*

He paused for a moment, as if he couldn't figure out how to communicate this next part to Matt. Then Wisdom closed his eyes and shook his head. He sighed, opened his eyes, and bit his upper lip. "These," he whispered, "are listening booths."

Matt started. He hadn't heard Wisdom speak, not even since their experiment. It was like hearing a cat talk. But Wisdom wasn't paying attention to Matt's reaction. Instead, he was looking over his shoulder at the dead-end corridors.

"They haven't been used for a long time." Wisdom spoke Islander with a strong Nye accent. He almost seemed like a different person when he spoke. It wasn't because of the Charm. He didn't seem to be using it. It was just that when Matt imagined Wisdom's voice, this wasn't the way he had thought of it.

"I will wait in this one, and you will wait in that one. There is a secret door in each. When we hear voices, we'll use the secret doors. You'll let me go first. Rugad will recognize me. And he will talk to me. That's when you come out."

"I think it would be best to touch him with the doll," Matt said.

"If that's so," Wisdom whispered, "then you must sneak up behind him. That may not be easy. Just remember that your mission is to get him. Everything else is secondary."

Matt nodded. Wisdom spoke like the soldier he had been.

"I think you should take only one doll," Wisdom whispered.

"What if it doesn't work the first time?" Matt asked.

"Then use your magic to pull the other to you."

Matt nodded.

Wisdom stared at him for a moment, as if he were going to say more. Instead, he squeezed Matt's shoulder. "Good luck," he said.

CHAPTER THIRTY

$\mathcal{T}$HE ACTIVITY AROUND the *Tashka* was frenetic. Lyndred hadn't realized it took this much work to prepare for a voyage. Gift had sent the Nyeians to get provisions, and they would return in large groups, carrying bags and boxes and barrels to be stowed in the hold. The Domestics were getting supplies from some of the Fey areas of Jahn. They didn't arrive with as many boxes or bags, but they carried other items that didn't seem to match—jars, seeds, scraps of wool.

Lyndred was sitting on deck, her feet up. She felt useless. She had offered to help a dozen times and no one had taken her up on it. Her father had brought some chairs on deck, and some of that special lemon drink that Skya favored. It was a Pitakan drink that was both sour and sweet. The Domestics approved of it because they said it prevented scurvy. Lyndred was developing a taste for it as well.

Gift was below, talking with Skya. They'd been having serious discussions for the last two days. At one point, Lyndred had heard Gift yell at Skya—something about family and honor and love. Her own father had gone gray and started to talk as loudly as he could, as if he were embarrassed to hear other people's arguments. Lyndred wasn't. She wanted to hear it all and had been unable to.

A movement at the end of the ramp caught her eye. Two Islanders, short blond men, stopped and waited for two others. One of the Islanders wore a hooded cloak and was taller than the rest. They conversed for a moment, and then they started up the ramp. They were walking very slowly.

She stood. No one else seemed to notice. The Nyeians were busy with their duties. Her father was looking the other way.

"Daddy," she said. "Look."

He turned and his eyes widened. "I'll get Gift," he said, and rose swiftly, disappearing belowdecks before she could stop him.

The Islanders were almost up the ramp now. She didn't think they should come on deck. She went toward the small gate and guarded it, as the Nyeian had done that night she had first arrived.

The Islanders were coming up two by two, the tall one in the back. One of the men up front was not much older than she was. The other had a thin face for an Islander and sharp blue eyes. His blond hair curled and he wore a sword around his neck.

He was one of the handsomest Islanders she had ever seen, and he looked vaguely familiar. And then she realized where she had seen him before.

In her Vision. He was the blond man from her Vision. The one who would give her a child that would break her heart.

Involuntarily, she clasped her hands over her chest. Her eyes filled with tears, and she looked behind her for someone, anyone, who could help her.

She was alone on this section of the ship.

"Excuse me," the Islander—her Islander—said in heavily accented Fey. "We're looking for Gift."

She turned back to him. She wanted to scream at him. She wanted to tell him to go away. But she couldn't speak at all.

"He's not expecting us, but he will see us," said the blond man in the back row. "My name is Coulter. I—"

"Coulter?" She felt overwhelmed. She hadn't expected to see her blond man and Coulter too. "You're not supposed to be here."

"You know who I am?"

"No." She wasn't thinking straight. She had never seen a Vision come to life before. The man didn't seem to notice her. Men always noticed her. What was wrong with him?

Coulter was looking at her with something like alarm. "Why did you say I shouldn't be here?"

She didn't want to answer him. "I—um, you'll have to wait. My father went for Gift."

The Islander in the hood hadn't moved. Even though it was sunny, Lyndred couldn't see that Islander's face. It made her think of the Assassin, which made her even more nervous than she already was.

"He's coming, Lynnie." Her father had come up behind her. He put an arm behind her back and she leaned into it.

"Who sent you?" her father asked the Islanders.

"We came on our own behalf," Coulter said. "We—"

And then he stopped and looked past them. Lyndred turned too. Gift was walking toward them. His eyes widened when he saw them and he shouted, "Coulter!"

There was joy in his voice. Lyndred had never heard him sound joyful before.

"Let them in!" Gift shouted. "Let them in!"

Lyndred pulled the gate open. Coulter hurried past the other two, and Gift hugged him. They were laughing and pounding on each other's backs. The two Islanders who had been up front eased past Lyndred onto the deck, but the fourth Islander made his way slowly, almost as if he were injured.

Once he was inside, Lyndred closed the gate behind them. Gift and Coulter were still laughing and talking together, unable to complete sentences in their happiness to see each other. Then Gift reached out a hand and said, "Con! I barely recognized you. You don't look like a boy anymore."

"I wasn't a boy then," Lyndred's Islander said as he went to Gift. He started to take the hand, but Gift pulled him close. The Islander looked happy and relieved at the same time.

Finally, Gift freed himself from both men and walked toward the tall Islander. Lyndred moved out of their way.

"Sebastian!" Gift said as he approached. "I've missed you."

Lyndred looked with interest at the hooded person. She had assumed she was looking at an Islander because the others were Islanders. She had never seen the famous Golem. She found she was actually curious about him.

Gift raised his hands and pushed back the hood. It fell back to reveal a face very similar to Gift's, only carved of stone. Lyndred had expected the resemblance, so she didn't look at the face too closely, focusing instead on the realistic-seeming hair and the grayness of the skin.

"What is this?" he asked, turning toward Coulter.

Lyndred continued to look at the Golem. She realized then that while the features were like Gift's, they were a female version.

"She's not a what," Coulter said.

The other two Islanders hadn't moved. They were watching the exchange carefully.

"I'm a who," the Golem said.

Lyndred swallowed. The Golem spoke with Arianna's voice.

"Ari?" Gift ran his fingers along her cheek. "Arianna?"

The Golem nodded.

The happiness that had filled Gift's features was gone. He grabbed Coulter by the chin and examined his eyes, then did the same with Con and the other Islander, looking for Doppelgängers, wondering if he had been tricked.

Apparently, Gift was satisfied with what he saw because he let them go. "All right," he said softly. "Someone tell me what this is all about."

CHAPTER THIRTY-ONE

THE SKIN WAS familiar—smooth stone, shaped like his own. The eyes were familiar too—gray instead of blue, the gray of a stormy sea. But the features were Arianna's except there was no birthmark on the chin. Gift didn't know what that meant. He wasn't sure what anything meant anymore.

"Tell me," he said again.

"Perhaps we should speak in private." Coulter was looking at Lyndred and Bridge.

"I don't know how it will matter," Gift said. "They've already seen this. They'll have questions. We may as well answer them."

"Well, I'm not fond of speaking before strangers." The creature before him—a Golem, he was sure of it—sounded like Arianna. "Who are these people?"

"My cousin Lyndred and my uncle Bridge," Gift said.

"I don't understand how they fit in," the Golem said.

"It doesn't matter," Bridge said. "We'll leave, Gift, if you want us to."

Lyndred was chewing on her lower lip. She had come

farther than Gift expected. Two days ago, she would have yelled at her father for offering to take them away. Now she seemed to understand the need to leave. If there was a need. They already saw the creature, heard Gift call her Arianna. They probably had heard of the connection with Coulter while they were in the palace.

"Stay," Gift said. "You're privy to almost everything else."

Almost everything. Unless they had overheard some of his fighting with Skya, they didn't know she was pregnant. He wanted to keep that to himself. He didn't want Skya to become a target.

He glanced around the deck. It was clear. The Nyeians who had been working above were on the starboard side. They wouldn't be able to hear the conversation.

"Now tell me."

"I'm your sister," the Golem said.

"If you're Arianna, who did I see in the palace?"

"Rugad." Coulter had come to the Golem's side and put his arm around her.

"Don't do this," Gift said. "Rugad's been dead for fifteen years. I saw his body."

Out of the corner of his eye, he noticed Bridge stiffen at the mention of Rugad. Lyndred was just looking confused.

Coulter took a deep breath. "Remember when Rugad crossed your Link into your mind?"

"And you threw him out and closed all my Links," Gift said.

"Well, he did the same to Ari, remember? Only she fought him for hours and it took a lot more effort to get him out."

"I remember." Gift had been in the Roca's Cave when his father had brought Arianna in, unconscious and nearly dead. Coulter had saved her that day, just as he had saved Gift when Rugad had invaded his mind.

"After everyone left her mind, Arianna found an infant. She thought it was Sebastian—remember, we thought he might have died the first time he shattered—so she cradled it and took it inside herself."

"It was Rugad?" Gift looked at the Golem. She was watching him with wide gray eyes, as if trying to read his mood.

"The infant," Coulter said, "had all of Rugad's memories and his personality up to that moment."

"It was only a month or so before he died," the Golem said.

"And six months ago, when that black light crossed the Isle, it awakened the growing Rugad inside Arianna's mind."

Gift started. When he had touched the Throne.

"If it had happened ten years later," the Golem said, "as it was planned, he would have taken me over and no one would have ever known."

"As it was," Coulter said, "she was able to fight him. I helped."

"We almost had him," the Golem said.

"And then he trapped Arianna and me inside one of my Links, and shut her out of her own body. We decided to escape at that point, and try again later. That's what we're doing here."

"How did you escape?" Gift asked.

"She stayed inside my mind for a while," Coulter said. "And then, with Sebastian's help, we built a Golem."

Gift leaned against the railing of the ship. So that was what his mother had meant when she had said that Arianna had been taken over by darkness. Why his mother hadn't been certain if he had been touched by the same darkness. If Rugad had left something in Gift's brain, then perhaps seeing Arianna would have triggered it.

He had even mentioned it to the false Arianna and she had said he would be all right. Apparently, Coulter had gotten Rugad out of Gift's brain quickly enough.

"I've heard of this," Bridge said. "Not in this case, but in our family."

Everyone turned to him. Gift looked up slowly. He felt as if he were underwater. Part of his mind was reviewing everything he knew, everything he had Seen, everything he had heard.

"Rugark, Rugad's grandfather, had a Golem," Bridge said. "It was rumored that when Rugark died, he put all of his knowledge into that Golem so the Golem could rule instead of Rugark's son. The Golem disappeared when Rugad came of age. Apparently Rugark believed his son unworthy of the Black Throne and had taken precautions to save the Empire."

"You think that's what this was?" Lyndred asked. "Saving the Empire?"

"I think Rugad knew that Arianna and Gift were untrained in our ways. I think it was a precaution." Bridge looked at Gift. "If it's true."

It was true. It had to be. He pushed off the side of the deck and walked away from the group. All of the Visions he'd had when he touched the Black Throne were finally making sense.

—His long-dead great-grandfather alive as if he had never died, sitting on the throne in Blue Isle, smiling at him—

—And his sister was standing before the Black Throne, looking at it with such longing that it frightened him. He wanted to warn her, to tell her to stand back, but he almost didn't recognize her or the look on her face. He took a step toward her—

—His sister, her face gone as if someone had drawn it and then wiped it away, calling his name—

—His sister, screaming—

—Arianna wrapped her hands around her skull. She was screaming—

—His great-grandfather said, "You will never defeat me. I know more about Fey magic than you ever will."

Then there were the Visions of the Shaman in Protectors Village, seeing a man with coal-black hair being given the Throne by Arianna. They saw his great-grandfather kill a man with no tongue. They saw him touch the ground in Leut. They saw him threaten Protectors Village. But they hadn't been sure it was Rugad, because they all thought Rugad was dead.

And then there was the clearest thing of all, the Warning

sent by the Powers to Madot: *The hand that holds the Scepter will hold it no more and the man behind the Throne will reveal himself in all his glory.*

The man behind the Throne had been Rugad. The hand holding the scepter was Arianna's, and she lost it to Rugad, just as the Visions said she would.

His mother had tried to warn him. She had said that Arianna was infected with dark magic, magic triggered by the Searchlight from the Black Throne. The Searchlight, she had said, sought dark magic or Black Blood to fulfill the Throne's mandate. It wanted the Triangle and then the world.

But Arianna wouldn't have gone for the Triangle of Might any more than Gift would have. She had been a peaceful Queen. And Gift had rejected the Throne. So the Search Light had awakened Rugad inside Arianna's mind.

It all made sense now. No wonder his mother hadn't wanted him to come here. If that woman in the palace had Rugad's mind and memories and cunning, he would find a way to get rid of Gift.

You must be vigilant, his mother had said. *You must do all you can to avoid the Blood against Blood.*

Now he knew why she had said that to him. He couldn't just go after Rugad. Rugad was inside Arianna's body. Rugad had Black Blood. And Gift had sent his own Shaman away. To be with Rugad. Who had been asking questions about Golems. He hadn't been asking about Sebastian. He had been asking about Arianna.

Gift turned. They were all watching him: Coulter, looking the same as ever; Con, who had grown up; the Islander he didn't know; Lyndred, whose eyes were wide; Bridge, who seemed uncertain; and Arianna. His sister. His fluid, graceful sister, who was being forced to live in a house of stone.

The Nyeians had left their posts and had gathered around as well. They must have seen him from a distance, seen that something was wrong and come to protect him.

"You can go back to work," he said. "Leave us here."

They nodded, and went back to the other side of the

deck. He was shaking, but he no longer felt paralyzed. He had been reluctant to move against Arianna. It got easier, knowing that the person he had seen was Rugad.

What Gift had to do—what they all had to do—was find a way to get rid of him without causing the Blood.

"It is me, Gift," Arianna whispered.

He walked across the deck and took her in his arms. The stone was cool, like Sebastian's skin was cool, but that only made it feel familiar. She bent her head and placed it on his shoulder.

"I'm sorry," he said softly so that no one else could hear. "I knew something was wrong. I just didn't know what. I thought it was you and I thought you hated me, Ari. I was having trouble figuring out why."

"I'd never hate you, Gift."

"I should have known." He rocked her. "I had a feeling something was wrong. It was what brought me home. But I didn't know what it was. And when I got here, I was so confused."

She raised her head. "It wasn't something we knew about. How could you have figured it out?"

"The Visions." He was speaking louder now, conscious of the others watching him. "I had Seen so much of this, but it hadn't made sense until now. I kept Seeing Rugad and I kept Seeing you being hurt. I even went to all the Shaman in Protectors Village. They didn't understand the Visions any more than I did. In fact, they said that I looked like Rugad, so the Visions could have been about me."

"You do look like him." Coulter stepped closer.

Gift shook his head.

"You do. We do, I guess." Arianna nodded toward Bridge. "Coulter and I Saw the part of Rugad that grew inside my head. He was young, and he was handsome then. He had lost the looks as he grew older."

"In the end, we wear the face we deserve," Bridge said.

Arianna frowned. She seemed uncertain about him. Gift was becoming more and more certain all the time.

"Did you See Rugad?" Gift asked.

"No," Bridge said, "but my Vision is limited. Though I

must say that Arianna—I mean the woman in the palace— reminded me of Rugad and I told her so once. She seemed pleased."

"She was pleased," Lyndred said. "She said she was using Rugad as a model."

"I would never have used Rugad as a model." Arianna sounded shocked. "What is he doing?"

"He's continuing where he left off," Gift said. "And I sent Xihu to him. She said he was asking questions about Golems. We thought he was asking about Sebastian, but he was asking how to get rid of you without starting the Blood."

"Rugad will come at us sideways," Bridge said. "That's his method. He'll find a way to get rid of you, Arianna, and you, Gift, without touching you. That's how he got rid of my father."

"Xihu said she would do what's best for the Black Family, but she's thinking that the person in the palace is Arianna." Gift ran a hand through his hair. "I'm so relieved that it's not."

"Maybe you can send a message to her," Lyndred said.

Gift shook his head. "Contact from me would be very suspicious. Xihu knows something is wrong."

"None of us can go to the palace," Bridge said. "We'll have to find another way."

Gift looked over at Coulter, suddenly realizing he was missing a piece of information. "How did you know I'd be here?"

"We didn't until we came to Jahn. We have our own plan for getting Arianna's body back."

"We can use more ideas, though," Arianna said. "I want to make sure this works."

"You've taken a long time to fight him," Bridge said. "You should have fought earlier. Six months gave him time to consolidate his power."

Arianna shot a look at Coulter. Coulter looked down. No one spoke.

"Well, that explains one thing," Lyndred said. "It explains

why he's Blind. He doesn't have his own body, and I'll bet he can't use yours."

"He can Shift mine," Arianna said. "But he was trying to keep me alive and trapped so that he could use my Vision."

"He has Vision," Gift said. "Xihu saw him make a Shadowlands. It was one of the reasons she decided to go to the palace."

"He doesn't have Vision, Gift," Arianna said. "I know this for a fact. He'll never get it. It was one of the things that caused him great distress."

"Then how would he make a Shadowlands?"

"What did she say about it?" Arianna asked.

"Only that it was small and didn't look all that impressive."

"If you were trying to convince someone of your Vision," Bridge said, "would you make a large Shadowlands?"

"A Shadowlands from the outside is just a box," Arianna said. "If I could still Shift, I could create one at the tip of my finger or in the palm of my hand."

Gift let out a small sigh. Of course. He hadn't thought about that. Neither had Xihu. Why would they? It was conflicting magic. "He's got a lot of tricks. I had a Vision in which he told me he knew more about magic than I ever would."

"Have you ever had changing Visions?" Bridge asked. "The kind where it seems as though there could be a hundred different versions of the same event?"

"Yes," Gift said. He saw Lyndred nod too.

"All those Visions rest upon one moment. When that moment goes away, so do most of the Visions. Only one of them comes true."

Gift waited. Arianna was watching Bridge carefully.

"You are one of those focal points," Bridge said, "and from what I can tell, you're the focal point around which the future of our people is going to be decided."

"But Arianna is the one everything is happening to," Gift said.

"Everything *has* happened to," Arianna said. "I can't be a center, Gift. My magic is gone. My power is gone too. No one would accept me as Black Queen—and certainly no Islander would accept this. They'll continue to see Rugad as the leader as long as he wears my skin. If the center is one of us, of course it has to be you."

He stared at all of them. "I can't just charge the palace."

"Of course not," Bridge said. "Rugad will be more subtle than that. So will we."

The use of "we" caught Gift's attention. Bridge was speaking with complete sincerity. He was willing to fight with them.

Lyndred smiled.

"All right," Gift said. "You need to tell me exactly what's going on. I want the history and I want your plan, and I want to know how you developed this Golem for Arianna."

He was speaking to Coulter, but it was Lyndred who caught his attention. Her smile had faded.

"Can I say something?" she asked. "I mean, I know I'm not considered part of this yet, but I was the one who spent the most time with Arianna. I mean, with Rugad."

Arianna turned her head toward Lyndred. The movement was slow, but the look was sharp. It seemed as if Arianna was reevaluating her opinion of Lyndred.

"Go ahead," Gift said.

"I told you about the archers, and how Arianna—I mean Rugad—implied that she was the one who set up the Islanders to attack you."

"You were attacked?" Arianna asked.

Gift held up his hand. "I'll tell you later."

Lyndred glanced from Gift to Arianna and back again. Then her gaze met Coulter's. "Well, the last time I saw Ar—Rugad, he already knew that I had come to see you. But he let me see something anyway and I thought it was just directed at me, but now I've met Coulter and I'm not sure."

Bridge leaned his head back as if in recognition. Obviously, Lyndred had shared this with him.

"Is this why you told me I shouldn't be here?" Coulter asked.

"Tell me what Rugad did." Gift tried to keep his voice calm, but he had trouble. Lyndred irritated him and he wasn't sure why.

"He brought in an Assassin."

"An Islander?" Arianna asked.

Lyndred shook her head. "A Fey Assassin."

"I thought they were myth," Gift said. He'd mentioned them once to Skya, and she had given him such a furious look that he hadn't asked again.

"I thought so too," Lyndred said, "but this person wasn't a myth and Daddy says that Rugad has used Assassins before."

"It should have been clear to me who we were dealing with right then and there," Bridge said. "There was no way you could have known about Assassins, Arianna."

"Anyway," Lyndred said, "he gave the Assassin an assignment and I knew he was doing something subtle, but I didn't know what it was. I still don't. All I thought was that it was a warning and that I should be careful now that I wouldn't be beside Ari—Rugad anymore."

"It had something to do with me?" Coulter asked.

She nodded. Gift was watching her closely. He found that when she spoke of the palace, he believed her completely.

"Rugad sent the Assassin to the Cliffs of Blood to kill you," Lyndred said. "Why would he do that?"

Arianna had taken Coulter's arm. Coulter's gaze met Gift's. Their gazes held for a long moment. Coulter understood, just as Gift did.

"He's brilliant," Coulter said. "How can we fight anyone that brilliant?"

"We did it before," Arianna said.

"And obviously we didn't win," Coulter said.

"Would someone tell me what's going on?" Lyndred raised her voice plaintively. She was young. That was part of the irritation. And she had been badly spoiled. How could a man as sensible as Bridge spoil his child like that?

Gift let out a small breath. He was thinking about his cousin because he didn't want to think about the implications of what he had just heard. He was glad he learned it now, not a few hours ago, when he thought that the woman in the palace was his sister.

"Coulter and I are Bound," Gift said. "It's a Life Binding. You kill him, and you kill me."

Lyndred's face paled. "Wouldn't that bring on the Blood? I mean, Rugad had to know that, right? So really he'd be killing you."

"He could claim an accident," Bridge said. "It's the way my grandfather worked. He did something similar with my father. My grandfather had had a Vision of my father's death here, and still he sent him. Should that have brought on the Blood? I would have thought so. The Powers, apparently, did not."

"That's why he said three weeks," Lyndred said.

"What?" Gift asked.

"He said to try to kill Coulter after three weeks. If he couldn't, that was all right, but waiting for three weeks was perfect."

Gift nodded. Somehow this made him calmer. He had fought Rugad before. He was familiar with the man's mind. Even this order made sense. "I would have been on the sea in three weeks. No one who knew about the Binding would have made the connection."

"You would have just died," Coulter said.

Gift looked at him again. "Like you."

"That means we have an additional problem." Bridge looked even more upset than his daughter did.

"The Assassin," Gift said. "We'll be able to deal with him."

"He expects Coulter to be near the Cliffs of Blood," Lyndred said.

Bridge shook his head. "You don't understand. Assassins never give up. And to my knowledge, Assassins rarely fail."

CHAPTER THIRTY-TWO

$\mathcal{M}$ ATT STOOD IN the listening booth. In his right hand, he clutched one of the dolls. He had been standing there for a long time—he had no idea how long—and a moment ago, he had heard a door close.

He had pushed himself closer to the back wall. Earlier he and Wisdom had opened the secret door wide enough for him to slide through. The door's hinges creaked, and Matt didn't want to make a lot of noise when he entered the room.

They didn't open Wisdom's door. Wisdom said he wanted to make noise. When he entered, he wanted to be noticed.

Matt glanced toward Wisdom, but couldn't see past the platform. They had doused the lightsticks long ago.

There was shuffling inside the room. Matt peered through the small crack of light he got from the open door, and saw what he had seen every other time: part of a stone column, a chair, and in the distance, a bit of blue sky through one of the floor-to-ceiling windows. He had a feeling they were in one of the towers, but he wasn't sure which one. They had climbed too high to be in that great hall with all the swords. He hadn't gotten a complete look at the palace, but that seemed to be the only other place that had windows which covered an entire wall.

The outside door opened and then closed, as if someone had entered the room.

"Good." It was the Black Queen. "We have a lot to discuss."

"You wanted me to discuss troop readiness, Arianna," said a male voice that Matt didn't recognize. "The Infantry is hopeless. I can't believe you've let them deteriorate this far."

"You're insubordinate," she replied, but the words were spoken with affection. "I'm mending my ways."

"But not fast enough. I wish you had taken on this task years ago. Maybe then we'd be ready to sail to Leut by spring. As it stands, if you take these troops to Leut, you'll make the Fey into a laughingstock."

"Are you telling me this is impossible, DiPalmet?"

"I dislike the word *impossible*," DiPalmet said. "How about *extremely unlikely*?"

The Black Queen laughed, and a chill ran down Matt's spine. "You are good, and you anticipated my objection before I could even utter it. I don't like extremely unlikely either, but I am willing to listen to that. Tell me, then, when do you think it is likely?"

"I think you should send for some of the older troops from Galinas. Most of Rugad's elite forces were killed fifteen years ago, but the older troops, the ones left behind to keep the peace, are good as well. Most of what I have to work with now are second-rate soldiers who were either left behind to keep track of Jahn while Rugad fought his battles and whom you decided to keep alive for some reason, or the descendents of the handful of Rugar's soldiers who had somehow managed to survive the Destruction of the Failures years ago. Not a promising bunch."

"You fit into that category," the Black Queen said. "You're one of the few I let roam free on Blue Isle."

"I'm a Charmer, not a military leader. And I'm sure there are better Charmers in Nye."

The words sounded charming enough to Matt. Smooth and political and exactly the right thing to say.

"I'm sure there are." The Black Queen was silent. Then Matt heard footsteps, and his eyes caught movement before he actually realized what that movement was. The Black Queen had walked to the windows. He could barely see her, silhouetted between the column and the window itself. She was looking out the windows as if she saw something there.

"If I send to Nye," she said, "I'd have to wait a year to get those soldiers ready. Minimum."

"Are we in a great hurry?" DiPalmet asked. "We've waited fifteen years."

"I would like to act as soon as possible. Fifteen years was too long, don't you agree?"

There was a grating sound from the other side of the room. Even though Matt knew what it was, he felt his body stiffen.

"What was that?" the Black Queen asked.

"It was me." Wisdom's Charmer voice was deep and musical. It seemed warm, even though Matt knew it wasn't supposed to sound that way.

"By the Powers," the Black Queen said. "What hole did you crawl out of?"

"Probably one that wasn't buried as deep as the one you crawled out of, Rugad."

"Rugad?" DiPalmet said. "What's this? Have you gone crazy, Wisdom? Have your years of exile warped your mind this badly?"

"Get help, DiPalmet," the Black Queen said.

"I'm not crazy, DiPalmet," Wisdom said, "and I'm not dead. And you were right. There are better Charmers than you on Nye. There are better Charmers than you in the room."

"DiPalmet, I gave you an order," the Black Queen said.

"I can't leave you with him," DiPalmet said.

"You can't help me with him either. Now get me some guards."

"Yes, ma'am."

Matt saw a blur as DiPalmet left the room. This was his chance. He slid through his own door and it didn't screech, even though he expected it to.

"I thought you lost your tongue," the Black Queen said. She had turned so that her left side was facing Matt. She was looking toward the other side of the room.

"Don't play games with me, Rugad. I know who you are and I know how you got there."

"Then you'll remember what I said." The Black Queen took a step away from Matt.

He was breathing shallowly. He held the doll in a death grip.

"You said I'd be punished." Wisdom's tone was mocking. "I don't think you're in a position to punish anyone."

"I have my power back," the Black Queen said.

"All but your Vision."

Matt moved toward the column. His shoes didn't make any sound on the stone floor.

"What do you want from me?" the Black Queen asked.

He could see Wisdom now. Wisdom did look crazy. Cobwebs hung off him, and his face was streaked with dirt. His scars were visible in the bright light, and his braids surrounded him like a blanket.

"I want you to get a taste of how I've lived the last fifteen years," Wisdom said.

Matt eased the head off the doll.

"If you can speak, you didn't live the way I wanted you to."

Matt clasped the neck in his right hand.

"My tongue came back recently. It was a gift from a friend."

Matt ran forward and shoved the doll against the Black Queen's hip. She turned and stared at him for a moment, then looked down.

Wisdom stayed rooted in place. There were footsteps on the stairs.

For a moment, the Black Queen seemed to separate into two beings. Her body started to crumble. Matt saw a shape made of smoke rise from her eyes. The shape looked like a young man, with a handsome Fey face and eyes the color of night. The shape stretched, and drifted toward the jar.

The footsteps sounded closer.

Then the shape pulled up, as if something grabbed it. It rose, and the face peered into Matt's. Matt took a startled step backward, and the shape absorbed into the Black Queen's body.

The Black Queen's hand caught Matt's.

"I thought you were too old to play with toys." With her other hand, the Black Queen yanked the doll from Matt. She flung it toward the window. It hit the ancient glass and shattered. "That's an old magic, Matthias's son, and it only works against loose souls."

The Black Queen held Matt's wrist and pulled him closer.

"I am not a loose soul. I own part of this body. It's mine. I was raised here, and I cannot be pried loose by Islander tricks."

Her eyes were darker when the shade was inside her. Her voice was deeper too.

"I know what you are," Matt said.

"That really doesn't matter," the Black Queen said, "because you're not going to live long enough to do any more damage."

The Black Queen's face was only inches from his own. With a twist of his finger, Matt could hurt her. He could even kill her, but what would that do to Arianna? He didn't know, and he didn't dare find out.

Wisdom grabbed the Black Queen's shoulders, trying to pull her away.

The door burst open and guards rushed in. All of them were Fey. DiPalmet was yelling, but Wisdom turned toward them.

"*Stop!*" he yelled in Fey and to Matt's surprise, they did.

"Keep going!" DiPalmet said. "Get him!"

"They won't." The Black Queen's voice was dry. "He was always the best Charmer I knew."

"*You will not harm Matt or myself, ever,*" Wisdom said to the guards. Then in a normal tone, he said, "Come on, Matt."

Matt shook himself free of the Black Queen. It was unexpectedly easy. Wisdom stepped away, and grabbed his arm as the Queen reached inside her boot.

"You're supposed to take them prisoner!" DiPalmet yelled.

Wisdom pulled Matt forward. The guards parted. Wisdom's grip was hard. Matt turned—he was going to say that the passage would be quicker—when Wisdom made a gurgling sound. He arched his back and his eyes widened with surprise.

Blood gushed from his mouth, and he fell to his knees. The Black Queen bent with him, her knife still in his back.

Now the guards started to move forward as if the spell broke with Wisdom's death. And Wisdom was dead. His eyes were glazed and he was losing too much blood.

The guards rushed toward him. Matt looked at the Black Queen, who smiled at him. She let go of the knife and Wisdom fell forward. Matt was all alone here, and he had to get out.

The first of the guards was just reaching for him when he ran his hands along his length and made it seem as if he had burst into flame. They screamed and stepped backward. He flung a fireball at them, not caring who it hit.

"You!" DiPalmet yelled. "You stop!"

But his Charm didn't seem to work on Matt. Or maybe the wall of flame protected him. He ran for the passageway, but someone was already guarding it. He used the levitation spell, lifting and flinging the guard aside. Then he dove through the door, not bothering to pull it closed.

He flung frantic fireballs behind him. He was probably setting the entire palace on fire, but he didn't care. He ran down the stairs. The fire around him lit the cobwebs and flame skittered across them, lighting the staircase all the way down.

He wondered if he would run out of air, then realized that he didn't have to. He made a clear bubble of air around his face so that he could breathe.

Matt wasn't sure exactly how to get out of here, but he would find the way. Once he was at the dungeons, he would be fine.

He could hear screaming behind him, and then shouting. Then he heard a door creak open just above him. He flung another fireball up the stairs and continued running, sometimes tripping over his own feet, sometimes missing a step, but always managing to catch himself.

He had no idea where he was. He wished he hadn't listened to Wisdom's plan, but done it on his own. Not that it would have made the spell work. The dolls didn't work at all, and Coulter had to know that. They all had to know that.

But if Matt had come alone, Wisdom would still be alive.

Matt reached the bottom step and turned toward the corridor, the clean corridor. A door was open on the side, the side he and Wisdom hadn't gone down, and the entire corridor was lit, not with flames from the cobwebs, but from torches and Fey lamps.

Foot Soldiers, Beast Riders, a dozen guards, cut off all his escape routes. He knew a hundred spells, but none that would get him out efficiently, none that would keep him from being hurt.

He intensified the flames around him, and then saw what was through that open door.

The Hall with all the swords.

"Varin swords, varin swords," he muttered. "I need a varin sword." And then he recited a summoning spell.

Some of the Foot Soldiers were coming toward him, not caring that he was surrounded by flames. They had a crazy look in their eyes. He'd heard from his father that Foot Soldiers didn't care about themselves. All they cared about was the kill.

Matt backed against the wall. Wasn't his summons working? He didn't know what else to do.

One of the Foot Soldiers slashed at him with an open

hand. The nails at the end of his fingers were long and so sharp that they cut the skin on Matt's arm, flaying it right off. He screamed.

Matt had to let Coulter know, even if he didn't make it out. He opened his Link and let the information fly.

Chapter Thirty-Three

*E*ACH REVELATION MADE Gift look older and stronger and fiercer. Once Coulter would have put a hand on his old friend's shoulder to comfort him, or maybe to apologize for yet again placing him in a position that neither of them wanted.

But something about this new Gift prevented that. It was as if the soft and gentle edges of the Gift he had known had been worn away, and the Gift he saw now was a honed version, rather like steel after it had been forged.

Gift wasn't just the center. He was their only hope.

Arianna had her hand on Coulter's arm. The cousin—Lyndred?—kept shooting frightened glances at Con, although why anyone would be frightened of Con was beyond Coulter. Dash looked alternately fascinated and confused. And Bridge reminded Coulter of Adrian—conscious of the fact that he lacked the power of the others, but content that his knowledge could be of use.

"I don't believe anyone is infallible," Coulter said. "The idea that Assassins never fail had to be something that someone told you to scare you."

"Perhaps," Bridge said. "But—"

His voice vanished and in its place was a long drawn-out scream of terror. Coulter put his hands over his ears. The pain was excruciating. He fell to his knees, tears running down his cheeks.

The hands over his ears weren't helping. The scream continued, louder and louder, deafening everything. Gift was crouched beside him. Arianna slowly got down, but Coulter didn't want to see any of them. He couldn't think. All he could do was try to make this stop.

And then he realized that there were words buried in the sound. Words he understood in a voice he recognized.

It didn't work, Coulter. It didn't work. He's not a loose soul. He's grown in there. You have to do something else. There's stuff in the Secrets that might work, but you have to read the Words, understand it.

Coulter could see Arianna's lips move. She was saying his name. Her hands were on his wrists. Gift was talking to someone—Bridge?—asking for help. And the cousin was running toward the stairs, as if she were getting someone.

They're surrounding me and they're trying to kill me and I'm barely holding them off and I don't know how to get out of here and they're cutting off my skin and I've got a fireshield, but I don't know what else to do. I'm trying to do a summons, but it's not working.

It was Matt, contacting him through the Link. Somehow knowing that made Coulter calmer.

Maybe I'm running out of magic. Maybe I—

You're not running out of magic, Coulter sent through the Link, using all the power he had. *You're panicking. You have to think. Make a physical barrier so that they can't touch you. Then hurt them if you have to, but get out of there. Where are you?*

The palace, I'm at the palace. I don't know where. In one of the tunnels, but oh, God, oh, God, here they come. Oh—

Keep the Link open, Matt. Let me know exactly where you are.

But there was no response. Gift was still talking to him and Arianna held him in a death grip. Coulter closed his eyes. In his mind, he saw himself and the open Link to Matt, the one that he had decided to risk when they sent the boy to Rugad.

Coulter walked to the edge of the Link and saw nothing. He heard vague shouting and a scream from far away. He wasn't sure if he should travel the Link and enter Matt's mind to help him, or if he should let the boy save himself.

Matt had the power. He just had to use it.

You can do this, Coulter sent.

There were hands on his face, cool hands, and a soft, unfamiliar female voice that dragged him away from the Link.

No, he said, but he didn't know if he thought it or said it aloud.

His eyes opened and he found himself looking at the most beautiful Fey woman he had ever seen. She had dark eyes that were exotic even by Fey standards, swept upward at an angle that perfectly matched her eyebrows and sharp cheekbones.

"There." She took her hands away from his temples and looked over her shoulder at Gift. She was speaking Fey. "I brought him back for you."

"Who in God's name are you?" Coulter snapped in the same language. "Don't you know what you just did? You've left Matt alone there. He may not survive without me."

He cursed, and closed his eyes, but he couldn't reach the Link.

"I'm sorry," the woman said. "Gift said you needed help so I—"

"I can't reconnect." Coulter opened his eyes. "Help me reconnect."

"I didn't break your Link," the woman said. "I simply made your presence stronger here than there. I don't have a lot of power. It won't last for more than a few minutes."

"That's a few minutes too many."

"What is it?" Arianna asked.

"Matt's in trouble, and he was asking for my help."

"Where is he?" Dash asked.

"The palace somewhere."

"Then go to him," the woman said.

Coulter got to his feet. He was slightly dizzy and his ears were ringing. "It sounded as if he were facing an army. I'm going to need some help."

"We'll go," Gift said.

"You can't!" Lyndred said.

He turned on her. "Try and stop me."

"She's right—" Arianna started.

"We don't have time for debate." Gift pointed at Con and Dash. "You and you come with me. Skya, get Ace to bring some Gull Riders, and Bridge, have the Foot Soldiers catch up when they can."

"If you go to the palace with a force like that, you'll be risking the Blood," Arianna said.

"And maybe Rugad's in enough turmoil that this is the moment we've been waiting for." Gift put a hand behind Coulter's back. "Can you run, my friend?"

"Like the wind," Coulter said, hurrying forward to prove it. "Like the almighty wind."

Chapter Thirty-Four

*C*OULTER'S VOICE INSIDE his mind calmed him. Matt remembered the exact words for the summoning spell. Before he recited it, though, he intensified the fire around him. A Foot Soldier who had been shoving his hand into the flames screamed and backed away, his skin on fire.

Matt winced. He didn't want to hurt them, but they were crowding him now, their eyes reflecting the flames. The panic he had been feeling moments before rose again and before it completely overtook him, he recited the summoning spell. He had said it wrong before.

He begged the Powers for a varin sword. Anything to get him out of here. He tossed a fireball into the swarm of Foot Soldiers and it exploded when it hit the floor, making more of them scream, but not stopping the ones who were getting close to him.

They weren't reaching inside the flames anymore, but he knew that they were going to. They seemed to be waiting for him to make a mistake, to do something that would give them an opening.

There were footsteps on the stairs above him. He was

boxed in. He was about to scream for Coulter again when a sword floated in from the Great Hall.

The sword was ancient and nicked, not at all like the swords he had seen in the Roca's Cave or in the Vault. It floated toward him, and instead of going around some of the Fey, it went through them, cutting their skin. They screamed and backed off. One of them reached for the sword and lost a finger. He looked at Matt in surprise.

Matt was just as surprised. He'd heard about this, but had never seen it. The sword reached him, then reversed itself so that he could grab it by the rotting leather hilt. He had to douse his own flames to do it, and the Foot Soldiers rushed forward.

He swung the sword and screams echoed around him. This sword didn't cut. It sliced through things as easily as butter. Hands had fallen beside him, Foot Soldiers falling back, clutching bleeding arms. Blood was spurting, mixing with the fire that was burning on the floor.

Infantry were coming down the stairs, their faces smeared with soot, eyes red rimmed. Matt took a wild swing at them too.

"Stay back!" he shouted.

But they hadn't seen the damage so they didn't. He didn't want to cut anyone anymore—he'd seen enough blood—so he formed another fireball and threw it up the stairs, hoping that the Infantry would be smart enough to stay away.

Then he covered himself in flames again, waved the sword, and ran for the passage that led to the Great Hall. It was the quickest way out of the palace.

There were Beast Riders in the hall—most of them Dog Riders—and real dogs snarling and yapping, and more Infantry, and a few Domestics looking terrified.

The Dog Riders came toward him and he was screaming, swinging that sword. They rose on their hind legs, jaws open, teeth foul with saliva and foam. He connected with necks and dog heads and paws and it hardly took any effort at all. He heard yelling and whining and moaning behind him and the floor was slippery with blood.

He ran across the hall toward the door. Two Infantry started toward him and he threw a fireball at one of them, waved his sword at the other, then careened through the door itself.

The courtyard was full—Bear Riders, Horse Riders, Hawk Riders, swooping down at him. A full Infantry unit was coming from the barracks. More Foot Soldiers at the gate.

Helpmehelpmehelpmehelpme! he sent to Coulter, but he got nothing in return.

They were coming closer, and some of them had spells. He thought he saw a dark shape moving across the ground—a Dream Rider. If it covered his face, he would not be able to think, not be able to do anything at all.

He dropped the sword and raised his arms. Foot Soldiers ran toward him. He could hear the growling of Bear Riders.

"Lightning," he whispered in Islander.

Thunder boomed overhead. Storm clouds formed and the sky grew dark. A Foot Soldier grabbed him by the waist and yanked him forward, but Matt kept his arms up.

The air was charged. His hair rose on the back of his neck.

Lightning rippled across the sky. Everyone looked up except the Foot Soldier who had Matt. Matt couldn't shake him off. He couldn't do another spell, and to have this Soldier touching him when the lightning hit might hurt him as well.

Matt leaned toward the sword.

The lightning moved slower than real lightning, creeping down the sky. Everything was green.

Matt reached the sword as the Foot Soldier stripped skin from Matt's right side. He was bleeding. He could feel the sticky wetness inside his shirt.

The green light made the Fey look gray and sickly.

Matt picked up the sword as the lightning forked, and slashed the Foot Soldier, cutting off both arms. The Soldier screamed and fell back, and Matt dropped the sword. He clutched his side and started to run.

The lightning was striking in sections. The air filled with screams, and the acrid stench of burned flesh. Matt jumped over bodies as he ran toward the gate.

He wasn't sure he was going to make it. The lightning wouldn't hurt him—he was the originator of the spell—but he was losing so much blood. He'd lost track of all the places he'd been hurt.

There was another boom of thunder and the lightning started again. He remembered, suddenly, what Coulter had told him. The lightning would continue until the opponents were dead or until he made it stop.

Matt staggered out of the gate onto the cobblestone street. Islanders were crouched under building overhangs and beneath signs. Many were inside. Some were clutching children.

He hadn't been specific in his spell. Some of them might die. He glanced over his shoulder. No Fey were following him.

He raised his arms, the pain intense, the pull against his damaged skin so harsh that he nearly blacked out.

"Lightning," he whispered in Islander, "Stop."

The electricity instantly left the air. The clouds parted, the sun returned, and he let his arms drop.

He staggered forward, not sure where he was going to go, what he was going to do. His legs buckled beneath him, and he collapsed on the cobblestone. He was cold. He'd heard that was what happened to people who lost a lot of blood.

He hoped Coulter had heard him. He hoped they would figure out a way to stop Rugad. But he wasn't sure they would.

Chapter Thirty-Five

*T*HE SKY TURNED black and thunder echoed all over Jahn. Coulter, running along the wide cobblestone street toward the palace, stopped and looked up.

Lightning. Slow lightning, rippling across the sky before it attacked. This was a spell he had made up. There was no counterpart for it in a Fey Enchanter's magic. There was nothing else that replicated it, not even Weather Sprite magic. He had taught Matt to use this spell only when nothing else could be done.

Gift stopped and looked at the sky. "This looks familiar."

He had been with Coulter the only time Coulter had used the spell.

"I told him it was for emergencies."

"Does the boy listen?" Gift asked.

"Yes."

"Then we'd better hurry."

Dash and Con caught up with them, breathing hard. "What are we looking at?" Con asked.

"Magic." Coulter looked behind them. The Foot Soldiers Gift had ordered were running across the bridge. The sky was filled with Gull Riders.

Coulter felt cold and it had nothing to do with the change in the weather. "All the Fey need to leave. Get them down, and get them hidden."

"Why?" Gift asked.

"Because I don't know how specific Matt's spell was. This magic may attack all Fey."

"Then we have to get you safe," Con said to Gift.

"I'm half Islander," he snapped. "I'll be all right."

"Con's right," Coulter said.

"There's nowhere for me to go except forward," Gift said. "Tell those Gull Riders to get out of the sky. Have the Foot Soldiers find cover. Tell them to come out when the lightning goes away."

"I'm not going to leave you—" Con started.

"Go!"

Coulter wasn't used to this decisiveness from Gift. But he appreciated it.

The air had an electric feel to it. The hair rose on the back of Coulter's neck. Everything had a greenish glow. Maybe he was wrong. Maybe Matt, in his panic, had cast the spell to include everyone but him.

Coulter raised his arms, and created an invisible barrier above himself and Gift.

Lightning rained down around them, forking and splitting and exploding behind the palace walls. Flames rose and so did smoke. In the distance Coulter could hear screams.

He knew what the smell would be. He remembered how awful the destruction was. What a horrible spell he had created. And then he had taught it to Matt.

Matt? Matty? Are you all right?

There was no answer through the Link. He cursed the woman whom Gift had gotten to help him.

Gift tapped his arm and they started forward again. They were running side by side now, Dash following like a puppy. The sky was getting darker.

Coulter didn't like the look of this.

Thunder sounded one more time, and the lightning forked. In the strange greenish light, he could see Islanders huddling against buildings, stretched flat against the ground. Some of them were staring at Gift with open hatred, as if this were his fault.

And then the lightning stopped. The greenish color left, and the air lost its charge.

"Ahead!" Gift shouted.

A blood-covered boy staggered out of the palace gate and fell to his knees. Fires burned behind him, and smoke rose from the North Tower.

Matt had done a lot of damage.

Coulter sprinted ahead of Gift. Matt sprawled on the cobblestone. His entire right side was stripped bare of skin. He had no skin on his left forearm and he was bleeding from a dozen places. His face was so pale that it looked ghostly. If it weren't for the rise and fall of his chest, Coulter would have thought Matt dead.

Coulter chanted a spell to place a protection over the wounds, and then another to stop the blood from leaking out. Then he eased Matt into a sitting position and cradled him, putting his hand over Matt's heart.

Matt's skin was cold, but his eyelids flickered. He was alive, but barely.

Coulter would have to give him some of his own strength. He closed his eyes, and willed the strength to travel from his own body, through his hand, and into Matt's.

"What the—?"

Coulter opened his eyes. Gift was crouching beside him, looking shocked.

"Is this Matthias?" Gift asked.

Coulter could have answered honestly and scared Gift even more, but he didn't. He no longer had the strength for it.

"Dash," Coulter said, his voice a harsh rasp. "Is anyone coming out of the palace?"

"Not yet," Dash said. He was breathing hard.

"Coulter," Gift said. "Is this Matthias?"

"It's his son," Coulter said, his voice breaking. "He's a good boy, Gift. He's not like his father."

Gift crouched and put a hand on Matt's forehead. "We have to get him help."

"I'm trying," Coulter said.

"You try too much and you'll kill yourself." Gift slipped his arms under Matt's body. "I have Healers on the ship. They can do something."

He hoisted Matt up. Coulter kept his hand on Matt's heart. They started back toward the ship, not running, but hurrying as best they could. Dash guarded their backs. Above them, a phalanx of Gull Riders appeared, apparently deciding to venture out now that the sky was clear.

Islanders emerged from their hiding places, watching the procession go by. How strange it must look to them: the Black Heir and three Islanders, one seriously injured, hurrying down Jahn's busiest thoroughfare.

Then Gift stopped and raised his head. He turned toward the palace. "Look," he whispered.

Coulter turned. Smoke still rose from the North Tower. But from windows in South Tower, he saw a movement. For a moment, he thought it was Arianna, but the fear that coursed through him told him it was not.

"He's watching us," Coulter said. "I told you not to come."

"He knew I'd be involved," Gift said. "He's been planning for this."

Then he started forward again, loping, cradling Matt's head as they ran. Coulter could barely keep up with them. The skin on his back crawled as if he could actually feel Rugad's gaze.

And Matt's skin grew colder each step of the way.

CHAPTER THIRTY-SIX

THE DIZZINESS WAS gone, but he didn't feel quite like himself. He felt frail, and his body echoed with pain.

"He's waking up," a woman said in Fey.

Matt opened his eyes or tried to. His vision was bleary and his lashes stuck together. He raised his right arm to wipe the sleep from his eyes, and nearly yelped in agony.

A cool hand touched his shoulder. "It's easier if you stay still."

That was Coulter's voice. Matt blinked several times and managed to open his eyes properly. A Fey woman he didn't recognize took a cloth and wiped his face, cleaning his eyes for him.

"Thank you," he said, but it came out as a whisper.

He was in a bed, blankets tucked around him. The room was small. It was filled with people: Coulter, Dash, Con, Arianna, and a blue-eyed Fey man he'd never seen before. The Fey woman was older and unfamiliar, but she had a softness to her that Matt had seen in Coulter's Domestics.

"Where am I?" he whispered.

"On my ship." The unknown man spoke. He looked familiar. "My name is Gift. I understand you're Matthias's son."

Gift. Arianna's brother. He looked like her, only his skin was a light brown instead of gray and his eyes the color of a clear sky.

"You didn't like my father," Matt whispered.

"I don't know many people who did," he said.

"Gift." Arianna had caution in her voice.

He ignored her. "But your father helped mine save us from Rugad once upon a time. We owe him a lot for that."

"It didn't work," Matt whispered.

"It worked for a while." Gift had a warm, reassuring voice. His eyes were warm too. "I understand you fought Rugad alone today."

"I wasn't alone." Matt glanced at Coulter. He wondered how angry Coulter was. "Wisdom was there."

"I know," Coulter said. "We found out he was following you. I didn't think he would do any harm."

"Did he?" Arianna asked. She had never liked Wisdom.

"He's dead." Matt closed his eyes. He could see Wisdom arching his back, mouth gushing blood.

Coulter's cool hand moved from his shoulder to his forehead. "What happened?"

"He may not be able to tell you yet," the Fey woman said. "You should let him rest."

"We may not have time for rest," Gift said. Funny how Matt could already recognize his voice. "Rugad knows he's here. And he probably knows where he's from. So we need to know the next step."

Matt willed himself to open his eyes. It took more effort than it normally did.

Everyone was still looking at him. Arianna's eyes held concern. Gift had a crease in the middle of his forehead. Coulter looked the most worried. He hadn't moved from Matt's side.

Matt tried to move up so that he was sitting, but the pain shuddered through him again. His left arm felt heavy.

"Don't move," the Fey woman said. "You're covered with healing stone."

He looked down at himself. A solid gray material had been painted over him where the Foot Soldier had touched him. His arm was hidden by the same material.

"You nearly died," Coulter said. "Chandra saved you."

"I repaired you," the Fey woman who was apparently Chandra said. "Gift and Coulter saved you."

"Just Coulter, actually," Gift said. "When I caught up to him, he'd already found you. He was keeping you alive by letting you share the beat of his own heart."

Matt looked up at him. Coulter's cheeks were flushed. Coulter had taught him that too—another emergency spell. It only worked if there was affection between the people involved.

Matt felt his heart surge—no one had really ever cared for him, not even his own family—and then it sank. "I failed."

"You damaged the palace," Gift said. "I wouldn't consider that a failure."

"Wisdom's dead, and all those Fey—" Matt's voice broke.

"You did what you had to do." Arianna put a hand on Coulter's shoulder, as if she were speaking to him as well as Matt. Her skin was the same color as the stone wrapped around Matt.

"Tell us what happened," Gift said again.

So Matt did. He told them about the first attempt and how Rugad had said that he could come back in a year. Then he told them how Wisdom had saved him from the Spies and taken him to the tunnels under the city.

After that, Matt found himself short of breath. Chandra gave him some water and something else, something that tasted good and made him feel refreshed.

"I don't think he should talk any more," she said.

"I want to," he whispered.

Coulter brushed the hair off his forehead. "You don't have to tell us in such detail."

"I want to," Matt repeated and then, before anyone could object, he continued.

He told them about restoring Wisdom's tongue and how Wisdom refused to talk and why. Then he told them Wisdom's plan, and how they went through the listening booths.

"You had the Soul Repositories from the Place of Power?" Gift asked.

"Yes," Matt said, and then he told them how Wisdom approached Rugad, and how wrong everything went from there. Tears streamed down his face as he talked about the fires and getting trapped and using the varin sword.

"I heard your voice," he said to Coulter. "You saved me."

"I did nothing like that. You saved yourself."

Chandra took Matt's good hand in her own. "Now can we let the boy rest?"

"I have just a few questions." Gift sat on the edge of the bed, on the wooden frame so that he didn't disturb the mattress. "Is that all right, Matt?"

"I don't know how I can help you. I failed so badly."

"Actually, you tried and the method didn't work. That's not a personal failure." Gift wasn't saying that to make him feel better.

"You came after me," Matt said. "Why?"

Coulter started to answer, but Gift held up his hand. He seemed to know the question was for him.

"You were Linked to Coulter. You needed help, and you were at the palace, trying to do something for Arianna. That's why."

So even though Gift hated Matt's father, Gift could help Matt. Matt's father wouldn't have done that.

Gift said, "Tell me why the Repository wouldn't work."

"I thought he was a loose soul," Matt said. "From everything I heard, he'd invaded Arianna."

"He did," Arianna said.

"He said he was born in that body, like he grew up there."

"I should have known that," Coulter said.

"He said the body was his."

Gift frowned. "But the body is Arianna's."

"He's right, though," Arianna said. "He did grow up in there. The baby, remember."

"And the person who invaded Arianna," Coulter said, "is the man who died fifteen years ago, not the child with all the memories that she carried in her mind."

"But that child is magic, right?" Gift was looking at Chandra.

"I don't know what else you would call it," Chandra said, "but I am no expert on these things. You need Xihu."

"Xihu is with Rugad." Gift sounded annoyed.

Matt was trying to focus on this, but he was beginning to get tired. He willed himself to stay awake.

"Is the magic part of her brain?" Gift said.

"I was in that part of Ari's brain," Coulter said. "He had an actual room in her mind."

"And he was threaded through everything," Arianna said, "like he belonged there."

"That's why the Repository didn't work," Gift said. "You had the wrong tool."

"There's another one we can use?" Coulter asked.

Arianna's eyes lit up. Matt had never seen her look so alive. "Of course there is. Oh, Gift, I wish I had seen that sooner."

"Would someone tell me?" Coulter asked.

Matt eased out a small breath. He saw the section of the Words as if it were written before him. He understood too. "The Lights of Midday."

Gift grinned at him. "That's right."

"Those globes?" Coulter asked.

"Yes. Remember when Dad and Adrian picked them up in the Roca's Cave and Ari and I screamed?"

"That was why we had to hide you away from everything during the battles, because you were afraid that light would . . . burn away your magic." Coulter said those last four words very slowly, as if he suddenly understood as well.

"You absorbed the Words," Coulter said to Matt. "Can you make some globes?"

Matt nodded. His head felt very heavy.

"What would it take?" Coulter asked.

"Sand." Matt's voice was a rasp. "From the beaches beneath the Slides of Death. Someone to make glass with it. And inside a lining of water from the fountain in the Roca's Cave. Just before you close the globe you put it in, and let it sit for a month before—"

"We don't have a month," Gift said.

"I'm sorry," Matt whispered. It all felt like his fault again.

"No need to be sorry." Gift sounded oddly elated. "I think we need to make a detour. We have to go to the Place of Power. There are still some globes in there, right, Coulter?"

"No," he said. "They've all been used."

"There are some more in the Vault," Matt whispered.

"Rugad may want me to leave Blue Isle, but I'm going to do the opposite." Gift grinned. "I'm going to the heart of Blue Isle's power."

"Won't he try to stop you?" Con asked.

"He might," Gift said. "We'll have to be prepared."

"And the Assassin?" Arianna said.

Matt raised his head. No one had told him about an Assassin.

Coulter eased him back down. "By now, the Assassin's probably learned that I was headed for Jahn. We didn't exactly make it a secret. We'll just go back and keep an eye open."

"Assassins are impossible to see," Chandra said.

"I don't believe that anything's impossible," Coulter said.

"Neither does Rugad," Matt whispered and fainted.

THE ASSASSIN

[Two Days Later]

CHAPTER THIRTY-SEVEN

DAWN. THE SUN had risen over the Cardidas, turning the water its familiar rust-red. The sky was red too, and orange and pink. Sunrises were tremendous on Blue Isle. Xihu hadn't seen the like anywhere, and she had always thought them beautiful in the Eccrasian Mountains.

But she wasn't enjoying this one. Her eyes stung from the acrid smell of smoke that still lingered in the air. She hadn't slept in two days, and she had used most of her reserves.

She stood just outside the gate. The Islanders and Fey were waking up, beginning to fill the streets, going about their business. Most didn't realize how serious the damage to the palace and its Fey occupants had been.

Arianna had wanted it that way.

The Healing Wing of the Domicile was full, and they had had to expand into the Infantry barracks and the closed wings of the palace—anywhere they could make a clean bed. Xihu had never seen so many wounded.

Most were badly burned. She didn't have Healing talents, even though hers was a Domestic magic, but she did have small abilities. She had used all of them, and then more. She had helped mix potions to ease pain, she had applied salves. For two days, she had comforted the dying. She couldn't believe that this kind of carnage had been caused by one man. One young man, some had said. Little more than a boy.

She hadn't seen him. When she asked Arianna what had happened, Arianna had given her a measuring look. For a moment, it almost seemed as if Arianna believed that Xihu was involved. But Xihu couldn't have been involved in something like that. It would have stolen her magic.

Apparently, Arianna realized that, for she said, "It was a disgruntled Islander. The son of the former Rocaan—you know, the one who murdered my mother. He was an Enchanter, and so is his son. The boy wanted to burn the palace the way the Fey once burned the Tabernacle. And he wanted to kill me as he said his father should have done thirty years ago."

It sounded right, and the handful of Fey who had met the old Rocaan said the boy looked just like him. But the story had a stilted quality that lacked the fury Xihu would have expected.

And then there was the dead Fey in the North Tower, the Charmer that Arianna had killed in self-defense. Xihu had helped remove the body—there weren't enough Red Caps nearby to do the work. Arianna had to send for them from other parts of the Isle—and Xihu had seen things she hadn't understood.

No one knew why the dead Charmer traveled with the Rocaan's Islander son. No one knew why a boy who claimed to hate the Fey had a Fey assistant.

Nothing made any sense. And last night, Xihu had heard the rumor that Gift, along with two Islanders, had carried the boy to his ship.

Xihu couldn't ask Gift. The night of the fires, Gift left Jahn. His ship had sailed inland, and Xihu had heard that Arianna was furious about this. She believed that Gift was going to the Islander Place of Power.

Xihu let out a sigh. She was thinking horrible thoughts

and some of them were because of her exhaustion. She had stepped outside the gate because she wanted a reminder that life went on without the horrible stench of burning flesh, the cries of people too injured for help.

Some of the Infantry—the ones that were uninjured—had been enlisted to end lives that couldn't be saved, people who were in too much pain to continue. She couldn't do that, nor could any of the other Domestics, no matter how much they wanted to. Sometimes she wondered if too many of the injured were being kept alive. Their wounds looked too serious to recover from. But she wasn't a Healer, and the Healers kept reassuring her that most of the Fey who lived through the first few hours would survive.

Standing outside the palace didn't give her the satisfaction she wanted. Watching the locals begin their day made her very uncomfortable. Arianna hadn't been honest with them. She had told them that during the freak storm the palace had been struck by lightning. Those who had seen the injured Islander Enchanter had been told that he was hurt during the resulting crisis.

The Fey seemed to know all, though, and there were rumblings about retaliation. Xihu clutched her hands together. Part of her felt sympathy with that—the boy had done so much damage. But Gift's presence made her wary. She should have known if Gift had planned to send an Islander in. The fact that Gift arrived at the last moment made her wonder if something had changed since she left the ship.

There was no way to know. With the ship gone, Xihu was committed to her course. She liked Arianna even less after this attack—Arianna's calm response and all the lies angered Xihu, although not as much as Arianna's reaction to the injured. She wanted to know how many would be back at their posts and how quickly. She was more concerned with the damage to the Fey forces than she was with the individuals involved.

Xihu sighed. Kerde had once said that the biggest curse of the Black Family was their inability to understand that they ruled an empire of *people*, not of things. Xihu had never seen that in Gift. Even when he had been making hard decisions, like asking Rudolfo to impersonate him on the ship, he had known that he was risking a life. Perhaps that sympathy disappeared with time. Perhaps some members of the Black Family had never been born with it. Perhaps that was why Gift used to say Arianna was more suited to rule than he was.

Xihu turned and walked back through the gate. She hadn't really examined the damage much, being more concerned with saving lives, but it struck her now.

The stable had burned to the ground. The horses were dead—most burned or put to death afterward. All of the hay and supplies that had been sitting outside were now charred ruins. There were scorch marks on the cobblestones.

The fire had consumed most of the North Tower. One side of it—the side with the staircase—had crumbled inward and the Domestics who specialized in building structures had declared it unsafe. The rest of the palace was unharmed. Apparently, there had been a lot of damage from the hidden passageways—smoke threading throughout the entire building—but none of it was serious.

Arianna had put a cleanup crew on the main part of the palace to scrub the scorches off the stone and to get rid of the smoke smell. And she had chosen a team to rebuild the North Tower. She had seemed more irritated that one of her favorite places was gone than she was about the wounded scattered around the grounds.

Xihu ran a hand through her coarse white hair. She headed back toward the Domicile, when someone called her name. DiPalmet hurried toward her. His thin face was pinched. Ever since the confrontation with the Islander, DiPalmet had had a look of someone who had been forced to understand something about himself that he didn't like.

"Arianna wants to see you," DiPalmet said.

"I have duties in the Domicile," Xihu said.

"I know." DiPalmet glanced in that direction. He had actually been in the Domicile a few times and had used his Charm to convince the desperately injured that they had enough strength to survive. Sometimes, the Healers said, that was all it took.

But sometimes it wasn't.

"I'll go for you," DiPalmet said. "Arianna says this is important."

And they certainly wouldn't want to anger the Black Queen, would they? Xihu didn't say that, but she felt it. "Did she say what she wanted?"

"Only that she has a few questions you would know the answers to."

More hypotheticals. Hypotheticals which Xihu was beginning to realize weren't hypothetical at all.

"I have a few questions too." DiPalmet put his hands behind his back, a movement that reminded her of Arianna. But his expression was nothing like the Black Queen's. It was worried.

DiPalmet had always kept to himself. He had never come to Xihu before, at least not on his own accord. And he usually covered his voice with the Charm that so irritated any good Visionary. That Charm was gone now.

"What are they?" Xihu asked.

DiPalmet looked from side to side, then glanced behind him. When he seemed satisfied that no one could overhear, he said, "Arianna wants to send a force to Constant. That's where she said this unrest came from."

Retaliation was a typical response for a Black Ruler. Xihu waited.

"But Gift sailed in that direction. We've had Spies watching his ship. They say he took that Islander Enchanter aboard, and now they're heading toward the Cliffs of Blood."

Xihu didn't move. "What, exactly, does Arianna want to do?"

"She wants to send in troops and burn the city of Constant which she said houses the Islander religion and is the source of most unrest. She wants to kill all the people in the area."

"A sweep-and-burn," Xihu said. "I haven't heard of one of those in decades."

"Actually," DiPalmet said, "Rugad did one after an uprising in the center of Blue Isle fifteen years ago. Arianna says she's modeling this response on that one."

"But she has another goal in mind," Xihu said.

"She says we get two added benefits: we destroy their religion completely and we get the Place of Power."

"She rules Blue Isle. I don't see why she has to destroy to get what she's in charge of."

"She believes the rebels hold the Place of Power as well as control the religion. Our Spies confirm part of that. They say the man who came to Arianna almost a year ago about rebuilding the Tabernacle was on Gift's boat before it sailed. And, they say, the other Islander Enchanter who tried to help the Golem Sebastian kill Arianna six months ago was on the ship as well. That Enchanter was placed in charge of the Place of Power by Gift fifteen years ago."

Xihu didn't like any of this. "What's your question?"

"I've heard rumors that Visionaries have Seen the Blood. Is that true?" DiPalmet's usually golden voice shook.

Xihu saw no point in lying to him. "Yes."

"If Arianna sends a fleet and a force and tells them to sweep-and-destroy in the region where Gift is, and they kill Gift, will that cause the Blood?"

Now they were in a tricky area. Xihu rubbed her hands along her arms. "Does Arianna know that Gift is going in that direction?"

"Yes," DiPalmet said. "I told her myself."

Xihu looked at the palace, at its destroyed North Tower. Somehow, she got the sense that Arianna wasn't out to kill Islanders for revenge. There was something else going on. Something greater.

Apparently DiPalmet felt that way too.

Xihu shook her head. "There are so many factors. If Arianna warns the troops to stay away from Gift, it'll be fine. But then again, she could say she assumed they already knew not to attack the Black Family."

"Do you think she is trying to kill him?"

Xihu looked at DiPalmet. "Would you be talking to me otherwise?"

"What the Black Family does is its business."

"Then why ask me at all?"

"Because I think this was the first volley in a battle that will lead to the Blood, and it frightens me."

"It frightens me too," Xihu said. She had no words of comfort for him, nothing she could say that would make this any better.

"Will you talk with Arianna?"

"And convince her not to retaliate?" Xihu smiled. They both knew that was impossible.

"Perhaps mention the problem with Gift," DiPalmet said. "For my peace of mind."

He didn't want to be the one to give the order that would cause the Blood. Xihu nodded. She understood that. "I'll see what I can do."

She picked up the skirts on her robe and walked across the filthy cobblestone to the kitchen door. Here the smell of smoke was still strong and slightly sour. She turned back toward DiPalmet. "You'll go to the Domicile for me?"

"I'm on my way now," he said.

She thanked him and went inside the kitchen, stopping near the ovens. The bakers were making bread, and over the stench of smoke, she could smell the yeast.

In truth, she was relieved to get away from the Domicile for a while, especially after that conversation with DiPalmet. If DiPalmet was right, those poor souls in the Healing wards were only the first in a long protracted war, a war Xihu had once hoped to avoid.

Now the best she could do was counsel a ruthless ruler on ways to avoid the Blood.

CHAPTER THIRTY-EIGHT

*T*HE CLIFFS OF Blood rose around him, their red stone a reminder of the Eccrasian Mountains, the jagged peaks a skyline unlike any other he had ever seen. Gift stood on the deck of the *Tashka* and felt his discomfort grow.

From the Cliffs ahead, he could feel the pull of the Place of Power. When he'd first felt it, fifteen years ago, he hadn't known what it was. Now he did.

He looked up at one of the mountainsides and saw a dark spot, an obvious opening in the stone. He knew, from long experience, that what seemed obvious to him wasn't visible to many others. Lyndred and Coulter would be able to see it, and maybe Bridge. Skya, with her Warder's abilities, might be able to see it too.

Everyone else saw only mountain.

The breeze was cool here, and felt good. The trip up the Cardidas had been easy and successful. His new captain had worried that the river would become shallow somewhere in the center of the Isle, and it hadn't. The ship had fared well, and they had arrived faster than Gift expected. Which was good, because if they could get the Lights of

Midday and then return to Jahn quickly, he might still be able to catch Rugad off guard from Matt's attack.

Gift had heard, from some of Bridge's people who joined the ship at the last moment, that the North Tower of the palace had been destroyed and a lot of Infantry were injured. Rugad would be conjuring a revenge plan, but it had to be elaborate. He probably knew that Arianna and Gift were involved, and so he had to be careful to prevent the Blood.

Gift was wondering if their own plan would cause the Blood. He wished Xihu were here to consult. The Lights of Midday attacked the magic in the brain, burning it away. But in this case, the magic was Rugad. It would leave Arianna's body alone, but Rugad would be gone. All of Rugad. But Rugad was a construct, not a person. Gift hoped that would make all the difference.

Still, he was taking Skya's advice. He was facing the Visions instead of running from them.

Skya. He had been arguing with her ever since he confronted her about the pregnancy. Her reason for not telling him was that she was unsure whether she wanted to have the child. She had even spoken to the Healer about getting rid of it. The Healer had stopped her, saying that if Gift were its father, there would be problems. The Healer made her check with Xihu. Xihu believed getting rid of the child was like killing a member of the Black Family.

Skya wasn't sure. She was waiting until she had a chance to meet with some of the Island's Healers to see if they would help her. But she never got a chance to get off the ship. Then Gift found out. He wanted to marry her and have the child. She said she wanted neither.

I don't want to be bound to you in any way, she had said over and over.

Finally he had said to her, *You are. Now.*

Since then, they hadn't spoken.

But Skya was the smallest of his problems today. He also had to try to talk with Arianna one more time. She said she understood the implications of this path that they were going to take against Rugad, but Gift wasn't convinced.

He heard a creak on the deck behind him. Coulter came up beside him.

"They don't change, do they?" he said, looking at the mountains.

"They've been here a lot longer than we have." Gift sighed. "Sometimes it feels as if I never left this place."

"It's gone through a lot of changes since you were here." Gift smiled. "So have I."

Coulter put a hand on Gift's back. "Chandra doesn't want Matt taken off the ship."

"I thought you had a good team of Healers at the school."

"I do," Coulter said. "And his mother is one of the best Healers in Constant, although she doesn't call her abilities by that name."

"What's Chandra's hesitation?"

"I think she's worried about him leaving her care. Sometimes magic is specific to its user, you know."

"Do you have any Healers to spare from the school?"

"Yes."

Gift nodded. "Bring Matt up and tell Chandra she can come with him. I'll take care of the rest."

Coulter headed belowdecks. Gift watched him go. This would be the difficult part. He went to the Sailors and asked them to lower one of the small boats. Then he had a Nyeian get Bridge and Dash.

While he waited, he watched the Sailors load the boat with a few provisions, some Tashil floating cushions—guaranteed, or so he had heard, to keep a swimmer afloat until someone could rescue him—and oars.

Gift glanced at the sun. It still hadn't risen above the mountains. He had some time, then.

Bridge came to the deck first, looking sleepy, followed by Dash.

"I'm going to need you both today," Gift said. "You're going to Constant. The Sailors will help you get in the boat. Dash, have you ever rowed before?"

"No," he said.

"I have," Bridge said.

"I'm afraid I'll have to ask you to row today. Are you in good enough condition?"

Bridge grinned. "One thing I learned from my father is to make sure you're always in shape to run."

Gift smiled. He remembered how Bridge's father, his grandfather, used to say that to him. "Good, then. The Sailors will help you into the boat. Leave room for Matt."

A Sailor helped Bridge to the side of the ship and then threw over the rope ladder. Bridge climbed down it like a pro. Dash was the one who balked.

"I can't swim," he said to Gift.

Gift didn't have time for these kinds of worries. "I need you in Constant. You're going to have to go by boat. Have one of the Sailors explain the flotation cushions to you."

The Sailor who was beside him rolled her eyes. But she started to explain how the cushions worked to Dash, and her voice was surprisingly compassionate.

Coulter backed out of the deckhouse, giving instructions. Gift approached and watched. Matt was on a litter being carried by two Nyeians. He hadn't been heavy when Gift carried him back from the palace and he looked even lighter now. Matt had used most of his energy talking to them two days ago. He was improving, Chandra said, but not quickly and not as much as she would like.

Gift had wanted him walking by now. He wanted Matt to help them get into the Vault. Chandra had told him that was impossible.

She followed the litter up the stairs.

"We're going to have to get him to the boat," Gift said. "Is that going to be possible?"

"I can levitate him down," Coulter said.

"Can you do it from up here?" Gift asked.

"Sure."

"Chandra, you're going with him," Gift said.

"Good. I don't think he should be alone, not for anything." She looked at him. "I'm not sure moving him is the best thing."

"When we're done here, we're going to take this ship back to Jahn, and I fully expect to be in the middle of a battle by the time we get to the city. It's better that he be with friends and family."

"Coulter and Arianna are his family. Wisdom was too. His mother and brother want nothing to do with him."

Gift was silent. He hadn't thought about how Matt's actions—maybe even his magic—would have been seen as a betrayal by his family. His father had been strongly anti-Fey, and antimagic, despite his own powers. Perhaps the rest of the family was too.

"Then, for a short time," Gift said, "you'll have to be his family. I need Coulter and Arianna."

Chandra frowned. "I can't convince you to wait?"

Gift shook his head. "I no longer have the time."

She sighed. She apparently understood much of what was going on and didn't seem to approve. "Then," she said, "I wish you the best of luck."

"Thank you."

She walked to the deck. He followed. Coulter was leaning over it, his face red, his hands outstretched. He was lowering the litter all by himself, using only his magic, keeping its ends level and its movement slow.

It had nearly reached the boat when Gift approached. Dash and Bridge reached up and took the ends of the litter, holding it gently as Coulter lowered it to the bottom of the boat.

The boat was long and wide in the center. Still, it would be a tight squeeze with four adults and one injured boy.

Coulter started to climb over the rail.

"Wait," Gift said. "Let Chandra go first."

She gave Gift a funny look, then climbed over and made her way down the rope ladder.

Gift waited until she was near the bottom before he said to Coulter, "I want you to stay on the ship."

"Why?"

"Because of that Assassin."

"He won't get me," Coulter said. "I'll be cautious."

"It's both of our lives you'd be risking."

"I could say the same about you."

Gift shook his head. "I've been thinking about this. The

Assassin wouldn't dare kill me. He's promised not to kill Black Family. Besides, he's Fey. He knows the strictures. He's after you."

Coulter looked down at the boat. "I know Constant better."

"Dash knows Constant."

"How are you going to get to the Vault?"

"The same way you would, I suppose."

"But Matt's brother, Alex, who guards the Vault, hates Fey as much as his father did. That would be like me facing the Assassin."

"Not quite," Gift said. "I'm only half Fey. The other half gives me every right to go into that Vault."

Coulter wasn't looking at him. "Have you told Ari?"

"No."

"She won't like it."

"She's one of the reasons I'm doing this," Gift said.

Coulter looked over his shoulder. The gesture was appealing and rather young. Coulter obviously still loved Gift's sister, and they hadn't acted on it in all these years. "You aren't playing fair."

"I'm not playing," Gift said. "My sister and I both need you. There is a good chance you'll die if you get off this ship. As long as this ship is in the middle of this river, and the Assassin is on the shore, you're safe if you can stay out of sight. The moment you put your foot on the ground, you're a doomed man."

Coulter turned back toward the water. "Constant isn't the town you remember."

"Good," Gift said. "I remember a rather bleak place."

Coulter leaned over the railing again. "I don't like this."

"I know," Gift said. "But you have to accept it."

"Do me a favor, then."

As he spoke, Gift knew he had won the battle. "What?"

"Take a Gull Rider or two. Make sure someone guards you from above."

It was a good idea, and one he should have thought of. "All right. Send Ace with us, will you?"

He grabbed the rope ladder, and swung himself over. He

hung onto it for a moment and looked at Coulter. "I made a lot of mistakes, Coulter. I didn't realize how good a friend you were. And I left you here, alone, doing the job I should have done. It's time I take responsibility for things. Maybe past time."

Coulter leaned toward him. "Be safe, Gift."

Gift grinned. "I plan to."

CHAPTER THIRTY-NINE

$\mathcal{A}$RIANNA HAD SET up a temporary post in the South
Tower. It looked a lot like the North Tower had—columns
and floor-to-ceiling windows, tables and wooden chairs
scattered about—but it wasn't quite the same. The South
Tower's views were partially blocked by both the North and
West Towers. Xihu hadn't realized until she walked into
this room that the North Tower had been slightly taller than
the others.

This tower was in one of the older parts of the palace,
and its staircase was crumbling. Xihu had had to keep one
hand on the wall as she came up, and she was careful to step
on the outside of the stone stairs so that she would miss the
cracked centers.

At least this wing didn't smell of smoke. The scent had
gotten into everything. She could still smell it on herself. She
was beginning to wonder if it would ever go away.

Arianna stood at the south windows, which provided the
only clear view of the city. Xihu hadn't seen Arianna much
after the disaster. She hadn't realized that the Black Queen

had hacked off her hair like a soldier's—so short it barely covered her ears.

She still wore her soldier's clothing—the jerkin and breeches—only now she no longer hid her military bearing. She wore a sword on her right hip, a knife on her left. But unlike her defenders, she was uninjured from her meeting with the Islander Enchanter.

"When I summon you, I expect you to report promptly."

Xihu sighed. From this vantage, Arianna had probably seen her talking with DiPalmet in the courtyard. "DiPalmet had questions only I could answer."

Arianna turned. Her face seemed harsher than it had just a few days ago, as if this attack had hardened her resolve. "What kind of questions could a Charmer have?"

Technically, Xihu didn't have to answer that question and they both knew it. But Xihu wanted to answer it. It allowed her to discuss some of her concerns. "He wanted to know if he's responsible if the Blood comes because he carried out your orders."

Arianna smiled slightly. "What did you tell him?"

"I didn't know." Xihu crossed her arms. "You know that Gift has gone east. You are also planning to send troops there. Are you going to instruct them to leave him alone?"

"Would it ease your mind if I did?" Arianna asked.

That was too easy. "Yes."

"Then I will. I will remind my troops that any attack on Gift is an attack on the Black Family and therefore an attack on me. Was there anything else my Charmer wanted you to do for him?"

Xihu bristled as she supposed Arianna wanted her to. They both knew that a Charmer's magic didn't work on a Visionary, but the implication was still irritating. "No."

"Good." Arianna walked toward the nearest chair and kicked it toward Xihu. "Then we'll discuss what's really important. Sit."

Xihu grabbed the back of the chair and pulled it close. She sat down and immediately wished she hadn't. Her exhaustion caught up with her and made her woozy. She willed herself to ignore it. Her mental abilities had to be at full when she spoke to Arianna.

Arianna brought over another chair, and then, before sitting, went to a table toward the back. She picked up a smoke-stained knapsack and brought it toward them.

She sat down and put the knapsack on her lap. Then she reached inside, and removed a glass doll.

"Have you seen this before?" she asked.

It seemed like an important question. Xihu shook her head.

"The Islander Enchanter brought it. He also brought some vials of blood." Arianna took one out. "I saw these years ago in the Islander Place of Power. They're called Soul Repositories. They capture loose souls and trap them, rather like Fey lamps."

"The souls in Fey lamps weren't loose when they were taken."

"I know," Arianna said. "That's why we have Lamplighters, to facilitate the transition. But Islanders weren't as sophisticated with their magic. They put a few drops of their former leader's blood in the base of the doll and the loose soul would have to investigate. It worked then, and I saw it work when I was younger."

Xihu looked at the doll. It was very old, the glass flawed. Its head wasn't attached, but could come off like the top of a jar.

"He brought one into the room with him," Arianna said. "I think he didn't understand how these worked and thought he could capture me."

"I heard that Gift rescued him," Xihu said. "Surely, if you knew how these dolls worked, Gift would too."

Arianna raised her eyes to Xihu's. There was a flatness to Arianna's expression. "Who told you that Gift rescued the boy?"

"Several people," Xihu said. "None saw it directly."

"I had heard nothing about Gift." Arianna spoke so calmly that Xihu was convinced she was lying. If Arianna really hadn't known about Gift, she would have been very angry. "Perhaps the boy thought to do this on his own. After all, these dolls come from his father's religious magic."

"Aren't you afraid to hold it, then?" Xihu had heard that some of the Islander religious magic could kill with a touch.

"No," Arianna said.

She held it out to Xihu. Xihu took it. The glass was smoother than she expected and cool against her skin.

"Souls inside a Golem are loose souls," Arianna said. "These things capture loose souls."

Xihu ran a finger over the doll's delicately formed face. "You want to use one against Sebastian."

"I want to capture the soul inside, and destroy the Golem. However, when we had our discussion the day you decided to join me, I forgot to ask you how to destroy the stone body."

"Golems are not my specialty. I've told you that before."

"But you know something of them."

"I know they shatter," she said. "But usually what causes that comes from inside, not the outside. I would assume that whatever shatters regular stone from the outside would shatter them as well."

"It takes a lot of power to destroy stone," Arianna said.

"An Enchanter would have it," Xihu said.

"It seems we have no Enchanters," Arianna said. "At least none that would work with us. Our enemies have two."

Our enemies. Xihu sighed and extended the doll to Arianna. "You don't have to destroy the stone," Xihu said, feeling as though she were betraying a confidence and not knowing why. "If you capture the loose soul, the Golem is as useless as this doll is right now."

Arianna smiled. The smile was surprisingly warm. "I am too linear sometimes. I had forgotten how good it is to have another thinker, one who specializes in other methods of thought."

"I take it there is a way to release the soul from these dolls."

Arianna nodded.

"Then I would make sure, if you want the soul to remain captured, that no one knows how to get it free."

"That'll happen as soon as my troops level Constant. You see, Xihu, I'm not sending anyone to destroy my brother. I'm getting rid of the Islander religion. That's what made the boy attack me. And that's what will harm us, if we let it."

"I don't believe in that kind of retaliation," Xihu said.

"You don't have to." Arianna spoke softly. "But I have learned that it's the only thing that works."

CHAPTER FORTY

*T*HERE WAS A boat dock near Coulter's school. Dash directed them to it. Gift was relieved that they had arrived. Rowing hadn't bothered him, but Matt's continual soft moans had. Each time the boat shifted slightly, Matt made a sound of pain. Chandra tried to ease him, but the things she did didn't seem to work.

The boy would get better. Chandra had convinced Gift of that. But he had long months of healing ahead of him, months during which pain would be his constant companion.

They tied the boat to the dock, and had to struggle to remove Matt from the bottom. Gift left the bags he had brought for the Lights of Midday in the boat. He would have to return for them. For once, Gift wished that Coulter had been with them or Matt had been conscious enough to help. They probably hurt the boy unnecessarily, banging him around like a sack of meal.

In contrast, carrying him up the slope and along the river path until they reached the school was easy.

The school surprised Gift. He had expected a building

like the Tabernacle or the palace, something spectacular. Instead, Coulter had cobbled together several homes into a maze. There was a dirt area out front that looked like a Pitakan playground, but which was, Dash said, a place for the students to practice their skills.

When they had the school in sight, Gift sent Dash ahead to get Healers and helpers to bring Matt inside. Gift and Bridge struggled with the litter, trying to make sure that Matt was comfortable.

Then a swarm of people left the side door of the school. Seger ran ahead of the crowd. Gift would have recognized her anywhere. She had been Rugad's Healer, and had saved Sebastian's life. She had stayed on with Arianna and had helped Coulter spirit her away from the palace.

When Seger reached Gift, she smiled at him. "You look good."

"So do you."

She held up her hands. "Let me take your burden. I'm used to carrying these things."

Other Healers had surrounded the litter. Gift was startled at how many of them there were at the school. He and Bridge crouched so that they were able to pass off the litter at an equal height to everyone around them, so that Matt wouldn't get bumped again.

The group carried the litter away, leaving Gift and Bridge standing outside.

Gift studied the others. Most of them were young, and most had tan skin, which suggested a mixed heritage. Some had upswept features while others had rounded cheeks and blue eyes. There were young Islanders in the mix, and one or two pure Fey.

Coulter had never told him how diverse this group was, only that most of them had been dumped here by their parents. Most of the parents had been Islanders who hadn't known how to deal with their magical offspring. Some were the results of mixed relationships between Islanders and Fey, and neither side wanted to raise the child. In some ways, Coulter had become a surrogate parent to a number of children.

Gift smiled at them and continued forward. He wanted to make sure Matt was settled before he went to his next stop, and he wanted to see Sebastian.

"So," a voice said from beside him. "The Black Heir joins us from his lofty perch on the Eccrasian Mountains."

Gift looked down. Scavenger was standing beside him. He looked no older than he had fifteen years ago. "Scavenger. I never thought I'd be glad to see you."

Scavenger looked up. "You gonna let your Gull Rider join us?"

"He's on the lookout. There's an Assassin after Coulter."

"Coulter?" Scavenger frowned. "Who would—?" And then his mouth dropped open. "Rugad wouldn't."

Gift shrugged. "He already has. It might avoid the Blood."

"It probably would. There's an argument to be made that someone should break the Binding between you and Coulter so that you wouldn't have to die."

"Coulter says that's not possible."

Scavenger snorted. "You always believe everything Coulter says. You're a grown man and you still don't realize that boy likes being you, even in a small way."

"He's not a boy, Scavenger."

"He didn't want to leave here, you know," Scavenger said. "He liked having your sister all to himself."

"He's been doing well. It's Matt we're worried about. He went up against Rugad alone and lost."

"If he'd lost," Scavenger said, "he'd be dead. Which, I assume, is what happened to Wisdom."

Gift nodded. He let Scavenger lead him across the dirt yard. Scavenger looked over his shoulder at Bridge.

"You're not Rugar," Scavenger said, "and you're too young to be Rugad in the flesh. I assume you're one of Jewel's brothers."

Behind Gift, Bridge chuckled. "And you must be the famous Red Cap who knows more about magic than the rest of us."

"That's my Uncle Bridge," Gift said.

"You'd better be trustworthy," Scavenger said. "I have a lot invested in this side of your family."

Bridge smiled. "I'm not very fond of my grandfather."

"No one is, but be warned. I'm not afraid of any Fey."

"Scavenger," Gift warned.

Scavenger shrugged and let them into a warm kitchen. A cistern sat on one side, ovens on the other. In the middle was a large table that seemed to double as a food preparation area. Two young Islanders, a girl and a boy, were chopping vegetables. As Gift came in, the two of them stopped. The girl curtsied and the boy bowed.

"Your Highness," they said in unison.

Gift started. He had forgotten Islander ways. "It's all right," he said. "Stand up."

They did, but he could see a wariness on their faces, a nervousness at being in his presence. He wondered if Arianna had had to deal with this while she lived here.

At that moment, the kitchen door opened and Sebastian walked in. Leen was behind him. She grinned at Gift, but waited for Sebastian to reach Gift first.

Sebastian still moved slowly, but he looked different. His gray skin had no cracks in it. The smoothness made him look younger. When he saw Gift, he smiled. Gift hurried to his brother and hugged him. His skin was smooth and cool, as it had always been.

Gift had missed him more than he cared to admit.

"I . . . did . . . not . . . ex-pect . . . you," Sebastian said. "It . . . is . . . good . . . to . . . see . . . you."

Gift smiled. "And you."

Then Sebastian gave Dash a worried look. "Where . . . is . . . Ari?"

"On my ship," Gift said. "She's safe. She's with Coulter."

"Ship?" Sebastian asked.

"It's a long story, and one I don't have time for, I'm afraid. I have a lot to do here today, and then I hope to go back to Jahn."

"The . . . plan . . . did . . . not . . . work." Sebastian sounded sad.

"No," Gift said. "But it was a good plan, and it gave us ideas on how to get rid of Rugad the right way. Only Matt got badly hurt."

Sebastian nodded. Up once, down once. Such a familiar gesture. Gift was amazed at how little his brother had changed. "I . . . was . . . a-fraid . . . of . . . that."

Gift put his hands on Sebastian's shoulder. "I will come see you when this is all over."

"I . . . can-not . . . come . . . with . . . you?"

"No. I need you here. There's a Fey Assassin after Coulter."

"Why?" Sebastian asked.

"I'll explain it later," Scavenger said.

"I need you to make sure that this Assassin stays away from the school," Gift said. "Coulter's pretty angry because I didn't let him come with me today."

Sebastian smiled—his slow beautiful smile. "He . . . would . . . be. I . . . will . . . make . . . sure . . . no . . . one . . . harms . . . Coul-ter . . . or . . . the . . . school."

"I'll make sure of it too." Leen stepped aside and Gift reached for her, pulling her close. She looked different—stronger and older. Gift could see how she had become Coulter's second in command.

"Thank you," Gift said, knowing he could trust her. "Let me make sure Matt's settled before I go."

"I don't know why you're in such a hurry," Leen said as she led Gift through a large dining room with several scratched and well-used tables. "One night won't make a difference."

"It might make all the difference," Gift said. "Matt caught Rugad by surprise. It'll take him some time to recover. I don't want to give him that time."

Behind Gift, Scavenger grunted. Sebastian, who had been following, said, "Did . . . any . . . one . . . else . . . get . . . hurt?"

"Several Fey died," Gift said softly.

Sebastian didn't ask any more questions.

Leen led Gift into a corridor. It twisted and turned, and it became clear that this was where the buildings joined. The corridor's patterns made no sense otherwise. Finally they ended up in a Domestic area.

Gift slipped in, followed by the rest of his group. Empty beds sat side by side, healing blankets were folded against the wall, and bottles of potions, wellness liquids, and herbs were scattered on a nearby table.

Matt was on a bed toward the far end of the room, covered with a healing blanket to his waist. The stone material that Chandra had used to bind his wounds was peeled back, and Gift saw mottled flesh and swelling.

The boy was still very ill.

Several Healers and Domestics stood around him. Seger looked up at him and smiled. "Gift."

He walked toward her, hugging her with one arm. "Take good care of this boy. He almost saved all of us by himself."

"It looks as if he's lucky to be alive."

"He's going to need more than we can give him," one of the other Healers said. "We'll need the Islander woman."

"No!" Matt's voice was soft.

Seger went to his side, and put a comforting hand on him. "She'll want to know, anyway."

A tear formed in the corner of Matt's eye. "I don't want her."

"You'll need her if you're going to heal well," the other Healer said. "Such wounds became her expertise in the war."

"What are we talking about?" Gift asked.

"The Islander woman that they're referring to," Seger said, "is Matt's mother."

"What can she do?" he asked.

"Let these wounds heal," Seger said. "All we can do is repair the skin with the same clay as Golems are made of. It's not the best solution, as you can see. He'll lose range of motion, and he might still succumb to an infection that so many victims of Foot Soldiers get. We don't have good remedies against our own magic."

Matt was watching the whole interchange. The tear had fallen from his eye, staining the pillow.

"I was going to take you to her anyway," Dash said from

the back of the room. "She's one of the keepers of the Vault."

"No," Matt said again. "I have to take you to the Vault."

"You're in no condition to go anywhere," Seger said.

"You can't go to the Vault," Scavenger said to Gift. "It's got all the holy secrets. Holy water, everything. Matt's brother is as crazy as Matthias was. He'll never let you in there."

"He's going to let me in there," Gift said.

"Not without me," Matt said.

"I'm sorry." Gift crouched beside Matt. "I'm going."

Matt's skin was so pale that he looked translucent. "You need me, even if Alex isn't there. You won't know what to get."

Gift smiled gently. "I've seen the Lights of Midday before."

"Get . . . them . . . from . . . the . . . Ro-ca's . . . Cave," Sebastian said.

"There aren't enough," Gift said. "Coulter and Dad used most of them there. We need as many as we can get, and we don't have time to make them."

"You'll need to focus the beam." Matt's voice was raspy.

Gift frowned. "From the Lights?"

Matt nodded. "Otherwise you'll have to lure Rugad outside. Then you'd send a wide beam of light and everyone nearby with Fey magic will be affected."

Gift leaned on his heels. He was embarrassed to realize he hadn't thought of that at all. Matt was right. The light flowed out like a wide flat beam and destroyed anything in its path. That was how it hit Gift and Arianna the first time.

"So what else do I get?" Gift asked.

"Diamonds to cut through walls," Matt said. Seger put her hand on his forehead. She gave Gift a warning look. "Emeralds to narrow the beam. And the black stones, the heartstones, to choose the target."

"All right," Seger said. "That's enough."

"How do I use the stones?" Gift asked.

"Line them up horizontally. Diamond first, then a hand-span away, the emerald, and another hand-span, the heart-stone." Matt grabbed Gift with his good hand and squeezed. "Whoever holds the heartstone must think of the target and only that target. Or it will not work."

"Will I need anything else?"

Matt's eyelids fluttered. "I hope not," he whispered. "I truly hope not."

CHAPTER FORTY-ONE

*L*YNDRED STOOD ON deck with her back to those disturbing mountains. Ever since the ship had come close to this part of the river, she had been drawn to the mountains. Now that they had anchored not far from the place Coulter called the Roca's Cave, the drive to go there had been even stronger.

This was as close as she had ever been to a Place of Power, and she found its effect disturbing. The fact that Coulter said everyone with Vision and strong magic had similar feelings didn't help her at all. So she looked at the city of Constant instead.

Constant looked like a dreary place. Even though the sun had risen above the mountain peaks, sunlight still hadn't touched the valley floor. The stone houses were shrouded in shadow.

She had no idea how anyone could live here, let alone love the place. It looked dank and gloomy and wretchedly poor to her.

Or maybe it was just her mood.

She had awakened to find that her father, Gift, Dash, and

Ace had taken Matt off the ship. Gift had forbidden Coulter and Arianna to go. Coulter was angry about it although he claimed to understand. Lyndred didn't. Gift trusted her father enough to take him on this mission, but there was no reason to leave Lyndred behind. She was a full Visionary, more talented than her father, and she was stronger. Her father hadn't used his warrior's muscles in years. She would have been a good asset, but Gift hadn't even thought of waking her.

Soft footsteps echoed behind her, but she didn't move. She didn't want to talk to anyone.

"Lyndred?"

Her heart leaped and her hands dug deeper into the rail. She had to will herself not to turn around. Con was behind her. "I'm waiting for my father," she said in her coldest tone.

"I'm sorry to interrupt." He leaned against the rail so that he could see her face. Which meant that she had to look at his, the face from her Vision.

"I just wanted to know what I have done to offend you," Con said. "I'd like to make it up to you if I could."

He spoke Fey gently, and it was not a gentle language. His accent negated the harsher syllables, making the words pretty.

She didn't know how to talk to him. "You didn't do anything."

"Then perhaps we can start again. I've enjoyed a good friendship with your cousins. I'd like to get to know you better."

"You're one of the religious Islanders, aren't you?"

"I was a second son, given to the Tabernacle when I was a child. I became an Aud. But Rugad came, burned the Tabernacle, and nearly destroyed the religion." His smile was sad. "There really hasn't been a place for me since."

Her heart turned. She understood that kind of sadness, although she wasn't sure why. "I heard that you religious Islanders are dangerous."

"If I were dangerous, would Gift and Arianna have brought me with them?" He had her, but she said nothing.

"What is it, Lyndred? You can't really hide from me on a ship this size."

The water glistened below them. Here the Cardidas was the color of fresh blood. Was this what she had Seen that day? Or had she really Seen blood on the water?

"I've Seen you in my Visions," she said. "You broke my heart."

"*I* did?" He sounded shocked.

"You give me a child I don't want," she whispered. "So please, stay away from me."

"A child?" He looked startled as if the possibility of children had never occurred to him. "Our child?"

She didn't have a direct answer for him. The Vision had been clear that the child was hers. Whether or not he fathered it wasn't clear, only that he would "give" the child to her.

He looked beyond her, as if he were staring at the Place of Power. "I've seen too much magic to deny this. I understand the truth of Visions. I also know that they can be changed."

She leaned on her elbows.

"You and I," Con said, "we're so different that I can't imagine—"

"You find me attractive, don't you?" she said in a flat voice. "That's why you're worried that I won't speak to you."

He glanced at her quickly, then looked away. "I find you intriguing. Not anything like your cousins."

He wasn't hiding his feelings from her. If anything, his attempt at a denial made his interest in her clear.

"Well," she said in that same flat voice. "I find you attractive too. It terrifies me. I thought Vision was something that allowed a Visionary to avoid what's going to happen."

"You think we're fated."

"I hope not." She pushed away from the rail. "To me, it feels as though you've already broken my heart and I've only known you for two days. This is the first time I've really spoken to you. I'm sure the pain I feel from the

Vision is only an echo of the pain I will feel. I'd like to avoid that."

He nodded. "I feel I should apologize for something I haven't done yet."

He was a gentle soul. That made things even harder. "I wish it were that easy," she said, and walked away.

CHAPTER FORTY-TWO

SOMEHOW GIFT EXPECTED Matthias, the man who had murdered his mother, to have lived in a great home. Gift was surprised when Dash led him to a stone cottage that was the same as the other cottages around it. Only this one had the feeling of neglect.

The bushes out front hadn't been trimmed in years. Flowering plants still had the dead brown remains of last summer's blooms. The wooden door was shredded with time and weather.

Standing on the threshold, Dash behind him and Bridge on the steps, Gift felt ashamed of how he had initially thought of Matt. Gift had assumed he would be as bad as his father. Matt had been shuttled to Coulter because his parents hadn't known how to deal with him.

Gift knocked on the scarred wooden door. He waited, listening, hoping to hear some movement inside. There was nothing. He knocked again, and this time, he heard the scrape of a chair move, and a female voice say in Islander, " 'Twill be just a moment."

He recognized the accent from the Kenniland Marshes, so he was surprised when the door opened and he saw a statuesque redheaded woman with care lines that ran down her face. Red hair was common here. And she was tall, like Matthias had been.

Before Gift could say anything, she gasped, then bowed. "Highness."

He was surprised she recognized him. She hadn't looked that aware of anything. The air from inside was stale, her clothing needed washing, and her hair fell in stringy waves down her back.

"Stand," he said.

She did and moved out of his way to let him in. Dash followed and so did Bridge. She said nothing.

The front room was clean, but the furniture was meager. The kitchen was spotless, with a single loaf of bread resting in the middle of the table. The bedroom down the narrow hallway had an unmade bed and clothing scattered along the floor.

She stood behind a wooden highback chair and stared at him as if he were a figment of her imagination. Her face was puffy. It was clear she had once been a great beauty, but the beauty had been destroyed by a grief so deep it had etched itself on her face.

"I understand that you're a healer." He lowered his voice, made it gentle. He hadn't planned to do that. He had planned to browbeat the woman until she came to her son. But now, he saw that she was broken too. Just in a different way.

"Na like Fey Healers." Her eyes were wide, wary. She didn't know what he wanted and she seemed frightened by that.

"What do you do?"

"I make potions. Salves. Ta help with simpler wounds."

"I understand you did a lot during the attack on Constant."

" 'Twas different. We dinna see injuries like that ana more."

"But you found a way to treat them?"

Understanding filled her face. "Some. The ones like burns."

The loss of skin was something like a burn. He lowered his voice even further. "Do you have a son named Matt?"

She glanced at the kitchen, then at him, as if Matt had something to do with that room. "I do. What's he done?"

There was censure in the words. Poor Matt. No wonder he had sacrificed so much. He was desperate for affection.

"Matt nearly died defending my sister and me," Gift said.

She put a hand to her mouth as if she could take back the words, and then closed her eyes.

"The Fey Healers say that we need your help to make him well. Matt doesn't want you to come. I think he doesn't want to risk that you *won't* come."

Her eyes flew open. They were filled with tears. "I'll come."

She went into the kitchen, picking up a basket along the way. In the kitchen, she started filling the basket with bottles and herbs. Her fingers moved quickly, as if part of her had started to panic.

Gift said, "I also need to ask you how to get into the Vault."

She froze. " 'Tis na wise for ye ta do that, Highness."

"It's important," Gift said.

"Me son Alex, he dinna like Fey. He is na gonna take kindly—" She shook her head as if she didn't know exactly what to do.

"I'm not just any Fey, ma'am. You know that."

"I do. But Alex, he be his da's son. 'Tis dangerous for ye."

"Does he have the same powers as Matt?"

She shook her head. "He sees things."

"He has Vision?"

"He dinna like ta talk about it." She grabbed more supplies. "Where's Matty?"

"The school," Gift said. "I understand you have reservations about going there, but I don't think taking him from there—"

"No. I been ta the school afore. 'Twas me husband that dinna like it." She laid a cloth over the basket then turned. "Ye won't be going with me, then."

"No," Gift said. "I have to go to the Vault."

She put her hand on the door. "Ye must think me a disgrace. Mayhap I am."

She looked at Gift sideways and in that subtle gesture, he saw Matt. He had thought Matt favored his father, but apparently he took after both parents.

"I lost meself when Matthias died. Alex, he took care a me like I done Matthias. And Matty, he got lost in it all. Alex and him split about the school, about magic, about the Fey. I dinna have the strength ta fight it." She straightened. "I do love me son. I jus thought, when he went ta Coulter, he went somewhere safe."

Then she let herself out, leaving Gift to contemplate her rebuke in silence.

CHAPTER FORTY-THREE

*A*RIANNA WANTED A fleet of ships and a squadron of troops, so DiPalmet was down by the docks, investigating the ships that had not been converted to trade ships. Most of the military vessels had, and if they were still seaworthy, most of them were on the Infrin, getting supplies from Galinas or Etanien or some other exotic place. Even Bridge's ships were gone on a trade mission with Nye.

The ships DiPalmet had left were mostly rotted sculls from Islander voyages and two from Rugad's invasion force. Those were in bad shape as well, untouched mostly because of their military configuration. Having such a ship approach Nye would make some worry that an attack was beginning again.

DiPalmet sat on the edge of the dock and tucked his legs against his chest. The Cardidas flowed beneath the dock like wet rust, and the sun, even though it was out, cast no heat. He was damp and cold and unwilling to go back to the palace.

There would be no fleet. There were a few ships at best. And then there was the problem of the troops.

He had enough trained Infantry to form the basis of a solid fighting force. And there were some Beast Riders, a few Bird Riders, and some Foot Soldiers. But certainly not enough to make the kind of force that could lay waste to an entire region.

He had checked and double-checked his figures. He had sent notices to outlying areas, asking for more troops—although that would do no good. The notices went out the day before, and no one would be able to get to Jahn on time, except maybe a few Bird Riders.

It would be his thankless task to tell Arianna that if she wanted troops, she might have to add an Islander force to the mix. After all, until her change of heart six months ago, she did have a fairly strong Islander fighting force.

DiPalmet might even know where to find the man who had served as her captain of the guard. A man named Luke. He now had a farm just south of Jahn. DiPalmet wondered if Luke would help Arianna. She had demanded Luke leave the palace shortly after her illness. He had seemed relieved to go.

But he was a good military man and a good tactician. DiPalmet had seen Luke's plans for an Island defense when Arianna had asked for one, years ago, and it had been sound.

The question was, Would an Islander be willing to torch part of his homeland in retaliation for an attack on the palace? DiPalmet didn't know. But he felt as if getting help from outside would be the only way to carry out Arianna's plans.

CHAPTER FORTY-FOUR

*E*VEN THOUGH MATT'S mother had not told Gift where the Vault was, he had little trouble finding it. Dash knew that the access to the Vault was in the Meeting Hall, and where the Meeting Hall was. After a stop at the boat for the bags, they went to the Hall.

It was in better shape than Matt's home. The Hall was clean, with new furniture. Someone had left a lamp and flint near the door. Gift lit that, then went through the open door to the tunnel.

The stairs were wood and smelled new. When the three men reached the tunnels, Gift shuddered. The tunnels reminded him of the ones under Jahn. They had the same feel: the damp stone, the rotted wood, the dripping water.

Gift had to be calm and aware. He was taking a large risk. He didn't even know how many Lights of Midday were here. If there were only a few, then he would be doing all this for nothing.

Gift felt a powerful urge to hurry along the corridor. At some point, they had entered the mountain itself. He could feel the Place of Power, pulling him toward its center, farther up the mountainside.

The walls were now one piece, carved from the mountain by hand—or by nature itself—just like the Black Palace in the Eccrasian Mountains. Only this place was a pulsating red.

Gift had no idea how far he had gone when Bridge gasped behind him. Gift whirled, expecting a miniature Matthias waving his arms like an Enchanter and sending balls of fire down the corridor. Instead, the three of them were alone.

"What?" Gift asked. He sounded testy. He was feeling testy.

"The stone," Bridge said. "It's bleeding."

Gift brought the torch closer. The stone wasn't bleeding. Water ran down its side from some fissure in the wall.

"We're inside the mountain now," Gift said. "The stone is red. That's why this part of the Eyes of Roca are called the Cliffs of Blood. That's also why the Cardidas looks so dark."

And then he froze, remembering something he had forgotten in all his years away from the Isle.

He and young Matt were related. Just like his father and Matthias had been related. His father speculated that their common ancestor had been the Roca. Matt had descended from the second son; Gift from the first. If Gift killed Matt's brother, that too might bring the Blood against Blood.

"What?" Dash asked.

Gift handed Bridge the torch. "If Matt's brother decides to attack, I can't touch him. We're related. Distantly, but it might be enough to bring on the Blood."

"Isn't it a bit late to tell us that?" Bridge asked.

"I just remembered it. But I'm related to him through my Islander side, so you and Dash can defend me all you want."

"But does this young man know he can't kill you?"

Gift shook his head.

"Wonderful," Bridge said. "We walk into the heart of a

magic that murdered more Fey than anything else, and now you tell us that you can't fight if you have to."

"I don't expect to have to," Gift said. "But you'd better lead, just in case."

Dash took the torch from Bridge. "I'll lead," Dash said. "I'm not related to anyone. I hope."

He walked down the corridor, and Gift followed, Bridge at his side. Bridge's jaw was set, and in these shadows, he looked vaguely like his father, Rugar. Gift had never seen Bridge angry before. He hadn't realized how deep the resemblance went until now.

"We're in the Place of Power," Bridge said softly, not loud enough for Dash to hear. He sounded surprised.

"Yes," Gift said.

"But the main section is above us," Bridge said.

Gift looked at him, startled. He had thought that Bridge's Vision was minimal. "You can feel it that strongly?"

Bridge nodded. "This is like the Eccrasian Mountains."

"You were there?"

"Before your mother was born," Bridge said.

Ahead of them, Dash stopped. He held the torch out and in the small circle of light that it created, Gift could see a large door. It had been carved out of a single block of stone, but it was gray.

"I think this must be it," Dash said.

A wooden bar, stout enough to lock anything inside, sat beside the door. It was so thick that no sound could have seeped through it. But Matt's brother might have been listening as they came through the corridor.

Bridge reached around Dash and pulled the door open. It screeched as it went back.

So much for a silent arrival.

Gift felt the hairs on the back of his neck lift. He turned around.

His mother, Jewel, was standing behind him. She looked as young as Lyndred, and Gift could see that there were indeed differences. His mother's features were sharper, her eyes darker. She slipped her arm through his.

"Don't worry," she said softly as if Bridge and Dash could hear her. "I'll protect you."

Gift let out a small breath. He hadn't realized how nervous he had been. His mother's presence reassured him. She wouldn't let any harm come to him—at least, if the Powers let her prevent it.

He slipped his hand over hers and patted it. He had missed her. Even though he had seen her in the Place of Power on the Eccrasian Mountains six months ago, he had still missed her.

Dash and Bridge had gone inside. Gift was only a moment behind them, although it felt like a year.

The room was large and warm, as if there were a fire burning inside it, but there was no fireplace. The room had a lot of furniture—couches, a bed, tables, chairs, and even a small area for preparing food. On the far wall was a small wooden door that Gift would have to crouch to get through. But he knew, without a doubt, that the things he wanted were through there.

He saw a movement through the corner of his eye. His mother stiffened. He wondered, suddenly, if her appearance was as altruistic as she made it sound. As a Mystery, she was able to appear to three people: the one she loved the most—that had been his father; anyone she chose—that had been Gift; and the one she hated the most—that had been Matthias, Matt's father. Matthias was dead, but did that mean she could now go after his children?

Gift wished he had asked her.

The scraping of a chair against a stone floor brought him back. He turned toward the movement and saw—Matt. Only Matt was healthy and angry, blue eyes flashing.

No one had told Gift that Matt's brother Alex was his twin.

"Fey are not welcome here." Alex sounded different from Matt. His words were sharp, pointed.

Gift slipped his arm from his mother's grasp and walked toward Alex. They were almost of a height. But Alex looked as if he hadn't reached his full growth yet. He wore the black robes of the Rocaanist religion. He had tied a bright red sash around his waist, and a silver filigree sword around his neck.

Gift hadn't seen the trappings of the religion in years. He had been raised to fear them, even though it was the religion of his father. He felt that fear now and shoved it aside. This time, the religion would help him.

"My name is Gift," he said in his warmest voice. "I'm Nicholas's son."

"The Betrayer King," Alex said.

Behind him, Gift heard his mother gasp. Bridge had moved to his side and Dash stood close enough to reach him if he had to.

"My father and yours saved the Isle."

"And then put your half-breed sister on the throne, turning us all into a Fey wasteland."

Gift hadn't expected the surge of fury that ran through him. Alex's blue eyes glittered. Gift had a sense that Alex wasn't entirely sane. But how could that be? Matt was the Enchanter. The mother had said that this boy, Alex, had Vision. Visionaries didn't go insane. Enchanters did, when they were very old. But Matthias had not been a young man when Gift saw him. Had he gone crazy then, and passed along his insanity to this son?

"You're not welcome here," Alex said again.

"I have as much right to be here as you do," Gift said. "Maybe even more of a right. I'm a direct descendant of the Roca."

"So am I," Alex said. "My father said so."

"My lineage says so," Gift said. "There has been an unbroken line from the Roca to me. It's documented. I am a child of the firstborn son."

"The firstborn has no place in the religion," Alex said.

"Except as the secular head of it." Gift straightened and put his hands behind his back.

Gift's mother stepped beside him, brushing against his right side. "He's just like his father."

But Alex did not look at her, and Gift took that to mean he did not see her. So, she could not target Alex after all.

"I need to see the Vault," Gift said.

"This is it," Alex said. "You've seen it. Now go."

"I need to see the interior."

"No. It's part of the religion. You are not."

"Tell Bridge to strangle him, and let's be done with this," Gift's mother said. "There's no way you can explain to this fool what you need."

She was right. Gift turned and walked for the wooden door. Alex ran after him. He saw Dash put out a hand and hold Alex back.

"No!" Alex yelled. "You can't go in there."

"Don't listen," Gift's mother said.

"Gift," Bridge said. "Maybe I should go first."

Gift reached the small door. He glanced over his shoulder. Alex had slipped beyond Dash and was running toward Gift. Gift turned and grabbed Alex. He was surprisingly strong.

"You can't go in," Alex said. "You can't."

"I will," Gift said. "If you try to stop me, you'll hurt us both."

He handed Alex to Bridge, who held him tightly. Jewel stood beside them as if she were guarding them.

Gift wiped his hands on his breeches, took a deep breath, and pressed down on the door handle.

The little door swung open, and a wave of heat hit him. Wetness trickled down his face, and he had a brief flash of memory—the way that Islander holy water killed, by melting. He brushed at the wetness, and realized it was sweat. His own sweat.

Gift had seen the world from a Fey perspective too long. It was time to acknowledge his other half. His Islander half.

"Please," Alex said again. "It's a sacred place for my religion. You can't go in there."

"I lived in the Roca's Cave," Gift said. "It, too, is a sacred place."

"But you don't believe."

"I believe in the magic that exists in these mountains." Gift used the same gentle tone he had used with this boy's mother. "I have need of this magic now, to save the Isle."

"For the Fey." Alex spat.

Gift shook his head. "For all of us."

"You lie," Alex said. "You're just trying to destroy what's left of our religion."

"I need the Lights of Midday. Read your Words. It'll tell you that the Lights destroy some kinds of magic. That's what I'm going to use them for, just like the Roca intended."

"You can't take things from here." Alex was struggling hard now. "No one has taken things from here since the Roca lived here a thousand years ago."

Gift's mother had been right; there was no reasoning with this boy. Gift bent and stepped through the door.

He looked up into a world of light.

The room was white, even though it, too, had been carved out of the mountain. It was the exact opposite of the room with the Black Throne in it half a world away. The ceiling and walls were white, and the floor was white as well.

The Throne Room in the Eccrasian Mountains had been empty. This room was cluttered with so many things that Gift couldn't take them all in at once.

The air was warmer than it had been in the room behind him, but not stale. He could feel a pull ahead of him and he looked in that direction. Corridors branched off this room leading into the mountain. One of them led directly to the Roca's Cave.

It would be so simple to walk through that corridor, to go into the Cave itself, and contact the Shaman in the Eccrasian Mountain. If he told them about Rugad, would they help him form the Triangle?

He glanced over his shoulder. His mother was not with him. She wasn't in the room outside either. It was as if she were afraid of this place.

Perhaps she had good reason to be. There were things in here that were also in the Roca's Cave: tapestries covering the white walls, drums that seemed to be made of skin, Soul Repositories like the one that had held her once. There were also vials of holy water and vials of the Roca's blood. A table was set up, just like the one in the cave, for a ceremony that Gift knew nothing about.

But he didn't see the Lights of Midday.

Ahead of him was a stone altar and on it a loose pile of papers that could only be the famous Words, the basis of the Rocaanists' religion. He would go nowhere near that.

He looked at the freestanding shelves, at the vials of holy water, and between them, the swords, and he felt a deep disappointment. Had he wasted half a day? Did he have to go to the cave after all and take the few remaining Lights? Or should he get Matt to instruct people at the school on how to make more?

That would take time, time he didn't have. Rugad would have figured out a way to get revenge by now. If Gift gave Rugad too much time, they would all lose. Rugad had years of experience. The only thing he lacked at this point was his Vision and his vast armies.

With time, the second part could be changed.

Then Gift looked up. Dozens, maybe hundreds, of globes hung from the ceiling. For a moment, he thought they were the source of light in the room. Then he realized that they were simply reflecting light back.

The Lights of Midday. He had found them. But he had no idea how to get them down. He couldn't touch them. They might hurt him. He leaned back through the door. "Dash, bring the bags. I'll need your help."

Dash glanced at Bridge, who was still holding Alex. The boy had stopped struggling. His head was down, and Gift recognized the posture from Matt. Alex felt defeated. Gift wondered if that would haunt them all someday.

Dash stuck the torch in a torch holder, and came in through the door. He gasped when he saw the room. "It's holy," he said.

Gift glanced at him. He hadn't realized that Dash had been raised a Rocaanist. He seemed too young. "I doubt I can touch them. You'll need to get them down."

"Too bad the boy won't help. It would make things easier." Dash glanced at Gift. "You can hold the bags, can't you?"

"I think so." Gift crossed the floor toward the globes. As he did, jewels lit up beneath his feet: first a ruby, then an emerald, a sapphire and a diamond. He could have sworn they hadn't been there before.

Dash let out a small breath. Gift moved off the jewels, but they flared forward, as if he had ignited them, pointing the way toward the stone altar.

"It wants you at the altar," Dash said.

"It's not going to get me there." Gift felt cold despite the warmth of the room. He had touched the Black Throne, and that had started this mess. He wasn't going to touch its equivalent in this white room, in this holiest of places for the Islanders.

Gift beckoned Dash to follow him. Dash did. He also avoided the jewels, stopping below the globes as Gift had.

The globes hung just above Gift's head. It would be a stretch for Dash to reach them, but he would be able to. He handed Gift the bags.

"Don't touch the globes themselves, or you'll Blind me," Gift said. "Use your knife to cut the strings they hang from, and hold them by the strings only."

Dash went pale. "I can't do this."

"You have to," Gift said. "I can't ask my uncle and that boy won't. If I accidentally brush one of those things, I have no idea what will happen. If you do, it'll send out a brief light and it'll hurt, but I should be able to survive that. I did when my father discovered the properties of these things."

Dash didn't look reassured. He handed Gift the bags. Gift held the first as far away from himself as he could. He held it open, wrapping the bag's material around his hands to protect them.

Dash removed his knife from his belt, then reached up, easing his fingers between the globes, and touched the string. Gift held his breath, worried that there would be some trick to the string as well, but there wasn't. Dash gripped the string tightly with one hand, and then, above his fist, he cut the string.

The globe bounced once, but didn't touch him. Gently, Dash used the string to lower the globe into the bag that Gift held open.

They glanced at each other. He could see his own relief matched in Dash's eyes.

Together, they removed the rest of the globes. Gift counted. There were seventy-five here. Some other strings hung nearby, old and rotted and empty. A long time ago, someone had taken twenty-five others. He wondered what the reason had been.

The bags were scattered all over the floor. There were more than he, Dash, and Bridge could carry in one trip. They would have to take Alex out of here, and then come back for the bags.

It would take the rest of the afternoon.

Gift sighed. He had hoped this would be easy, but like everything else in battles against Rugad, it was not.

CHAPTER FORTY-FIVE

ARIANNA WATCHED CON. He was staring over the edge of the rail into the river. She sat in a deck chair that Coulter had found for her. Neither Lyndred nor Con had seen her during their argument, and Con still seemed unaware of her presence. She had sat there quietly since Coulter had awakened her, shortly after Gift left.

Arianna knew why Gift had gone, but she hoped he had thought through the mission. He wouldn't be able to carry those Lights, and she wasn't sure Dash could handle all that Gift expected of him.

The sun had reached its midday height and the river was orange-red. On the shore, some of the Islanders were fishing, and others moved back and forth from the stone quarry that had hollowed out one of the mountains.

When Arianna had been a young girl, trapped in the Roca's Cave and watching the activity below, she had thought this a horrible place. Coulter had shown her how it had its own beauty—a stark, harsh beauty, but a beauty nonetheless.

She would miss it, but she would be happy to return home. The palace had burned and she hadn't even been able to see the destruction. From her view off the ship, all she had seen was smoke. Matt didn't really know what had been harmed, but from his story, she could guess—the North Tower, the Great Hall, and the old residences. Her childhood rooms, perhaps.

It saddened her, but she didn't blame Matt. She blamed Rugad.

Arianna leaned back in the chair. It felt odd not defending herself. She had to wait here, like a traditional Islander woman of her father's generation, for the men to return.

She was not a woman accustomed to waiting. The Shaman—the one who had befriended her father—would have said that waiting was a lesson Arianna needed to learn.

She didn't enjoy learning it this way.

The air was chill. Normally, she would have been wrapped in a blanket, but she didn't need one. This stone skin of hers seemed impervious to discomfort. She had been out here for hours now, watching for Gift or Dash or Bridge, watching the skies for Ace. She even scouted the shore, wondering if she could see the Assassin lurking. But she saw nothing. The most interesting thing before her had been Lyndred and Con, and that show had broken up some time before.

Arianna tilted her head back. Since she couldn't be active, she had decided that planning was one of the few things she could offer. Rugad knew they had left Jahn by ship and that they were going toward the Cliffs of Blood. He would be watching the river. He would be expecting them to return the same way.

He would also be watching the roads. What they needed to do was return by sky. Years ago, Arianna had seen a contraption that allowed a person to be carried by Hawk Riders. She wanted to talk with Skya about it, and see if Skya knew how to make such a carrier, but the woman was proving elusive. When she wasn't yelling at Gift, she was hiding in her room. Arianna had no idea what Gift saw in her beyond her stunning beauty. She certainly wasn't social, and she didn't seem to be all that nice.

Still, she had a Warder's magic, and Warders knew things that most other Fey did not. Arianna would find a way to talk with her before the end of the day. Because, if they could build a few of those contraptions—and if they had enough strong Bird Riders—Arianna, Gift, and Coulter could fly back to Jahn. They could send the ship back as a decoy, so if Rugad sent anyone down the river, the force would find the ship. And by the time the ship returned to Jahn, the attack against Rugad would be over.

Arianna scooted her chair back and everything slid. For a moment she thought the ship was tilting, and then she realized it was her. The chair held her as she leaned backward—

—she was walking in burned-out ruins, ruins of a much beloved and very familiar place. Ruins so great that she wasn't sure she would ever be able to repair it. Her heart twisted, and she knew that nothing would ever be the same again. She—

—reached for Coulter's face. He caught her hand, laughing. She couldn't remember when she had last seen him laugh. It was a nice sound. It—

—made up for all the blood, flowing like a river, away from her.

—Something glinted in the trees and Ace flew over her like an avenging spirit. She wanted to fly too.

—Then she saw herself, handing a symbolic scepter to a man with dark hair. A Fey man with hair that ran to his collar. A man who, from the back, looked like Gift. Or Bridge. Or Rugad—

Her chair had tipped over backward. She was lying on her back, her legs and feet still bent over the seat of the chair as if she were sitting up. No one had noticed. Con still stood at the railing, staring at the shore. None of the Sailors were on deck.

She hadn't been out long, then.

Then she realized that she was stuck in this awkward position. She thought of calling for help, but couldn't quite take the embarrassment of it. So she pulled herself backward by her elbows until her legs straightened and her feet hit the chair. Then she rolled over and stood up.

As she brushed herself off, Con turned. Slowly, she picked up the chair. By the time she had finished, he was at her side.

"Are you all right?" he asked.

She glanced over Con's shoulder at the shore. The Visions had left her feeling hollow. "I wish this were over."

"It will be," he said. "And soon."

She nodded, but his words didn't comfort her. The last time they had defeated Rugad at a great price. She had no doubt that, if they won this time, the price attached to this victory would be one none of them wanted to pay.

CHAPTER FORTY-SIX

*Y*OU WANT TO send for *Luke*?" Arianna said. "Luke, the captain of the guards, the man I sent from here in disgrace?"

DiPalmet winced. He was standing in Arianna's private chamber. She was finishing her midday meal.

"I'm sorry," he said. "All I remember was that Luke seemed like a good man."

"Seemed like?" Arianna shoved away a plate of cold beef and bread, and picked up a goblet filled with water. "He hovered in my bedroom while I was unconscious, which was not something a guard generally did. And when I came to, he treated me strangely. I didn't do more to him because I could prove nothing, but I know a lot. He has ties to the group on the Cliffs of Blood. His adopted brother is the one who runs the school. He also was close to Sebastian. Luke and his little soldiers are not an option."

DiPalmet nodded and wished desperately that his Charm worked on a Visionary. He hated having to make arguments without the benefit of his magic. "I thought to bring in Luke because we don't have a lot of trained Fey soldiers.

You concentrated for fifteen years on disbanding the army and using Islanders as guards. Then you suddenly expect us to have a force ready to level an area of the country. It isn't going to work."

He was a bit more strident than he had planned to be, but Arianna had attacked him for what he considered to be a good idea. He hadn't known some of what she had said about Luke, but Luke had never seemed like a man who made rash decisions. If Luke were actually allied with the group from the Cliffs of Blood, he would be there. That he remained on his little plot of land said much about his commitment to Arianna.

He was probably as confused by her changes as DiPalmet was.

Arianna was staring at DiPalmet as if he had suddenly become a Beast Rider. "What do you mean?"

DiPalmet had reached the limits of his patience. "If we want a true military force we have to recruit from other parts of the Isle, and most of those folks will be too old to fight. No one has fought a battle here in fifteen years. If we really want trained troops, we should send for the border patrols from the countries in Galinas. At least they kept up with their drills for all these years."

Arianna set the goblet down, slowly and deliberately. "I don't really care if the troops are well trained. Didn't I tell you that? They aren't going to be fighting a trained group of soldiers. This is a rape-and-pillage mission. Wasn't I clear about that?"

"You said it was a slash-and-burn." DiPalmet clasped his hands behind his back.

"A slash-and-burn is not about soldiers who follow orders. The best slash-and-burns happen when soldiers do not follow orders. Am I being clear now?"

"Yes, ma'am." DiPalmet cleared his throat. "But there is a problem."

"You are full of problems today." She crossed her arms. "What's this one?"

"The last time the Fey sent troops into that area—"

"Fifteen years ago," she said, as if that were important.

"—we lost a battle that we should have won. The Black King showed up to direct the troops himself, and the Islanders slaughtered him."

She closed her eyes. Her face was flushed. Then she shook her head. When she opened her eyes again, they shone with anger.

"Fifteen years ago," she said, "the Fey and Islanders were at war. Now we have a band of renegades who need to be put in their place. All it will take is the destruction of their little piece of the Isle. Do I need to find someone else to set this up?"

Rugad would have done it himself, DiPalmet almost said, but bit back the retort. When his own anger eased, he would regret talking to the Black Queen like that.

"No, you don't need to send anyone else. I'll take care of this. But be aware that no matter how many people we send to the Cliffs of Blood, most of them will have to go by foot. We don't have a lot of ships and the ones we do have aren't in very good shape."

"This Isle was conquered by only a handful of ships. We don't need a fleet."

"I thought you said a fleet."

Arianna's mouth narrowed. "I asked for what I wanted. You can't provide that, so I'll take what I can get."

He hadn't seen her this angry. It gave her a power that she didn't normally have.

"The key to this mission is that it happen immediately. It's the middle of the afternoon. I want troops marching by dawn. I want the ships launched at first light. Is that clear?"

"Yes."

"Good. The faster we put down this uprising, the better everything will be."

DiPalmet nodded, but he didn't agree. He had a hunch the crazed Islander's attack on the palace had been simply the first volley in what could be a prolonged war.

He sighed. He had rather enjoyed the peace. He would miss it.

$\mathcal{B}$RIDGE LEANED INTO the oars. He put his entire body into rowing. His hands were sore, but he didn't mind. The afternoon was beautiful, the river strangely enticing. Gift was rowing furiously too, and Dash sat between them, keeping an eye on the bags. The bags bulged with the globes. Bridge had been warned not to touch them and twice he'd had to shout for Dash to keep a bag away from him.

Bridge wasn't really afraid of them, but he figured caution was important.

They were lucky they had taken such a large boat. Bridge had expected the globes to be small, but they were twice the size he had thought they would be. A small bag of jewels sat near him. Dash had plucked those as well, and not just the ones that Matt had described. He had thrown in a few others just in case.

Bridge was surprised at his own elation. He felt useful and powerful for the first time in his life. And getting rid of Rugad seemed like the right thing to do. Finally, he wouldn't have that old man watching his every movement, following his every step.

The ship floated near the northern end of the river, not far from the edge of the Cliffs of Blood. He could feel the Place of Power beckoning him, but he could ignore it. If he never saw the place, that would be all right with him. He didn't need to see it. He had seen enough in this life, in this world.

He wondered what would happen when Arianna regained her throne. Would she remember how much Bridge and Lyndred had helped? Or would Gift tell her about Lyndred's statement—how badly she wanted the Black Throne? Would the mistrust between the generations continue?

Bridge hoped not. He was doing everything he could to prevent it. The future lay with Jewel's branch of the Black Family. Even though he had ambitions for his own daughter, this trip had shown him how much she needed to learn.

He glanced over his shoulder. The ship was closer. He could see Lyndred standing by the rail, Con a few feet away from her. Coulter was by the gate, and Arianna was near the bow. Skya stood apart as she had from the moment Bridge met her.

"I knew he wouldn't listen," Gift said softly.

"Who?"

"Coulter. I asked him to stay out of sight."

"I think he's there to greet us," Bridge said. "I saw him come up from belowdecks."

"Still," Gift said, and rowed even faster.

Gift's mood didn't bother Bridge. He was still pleased with the way the day had gone. When the boy Alex looked upon Gift with such hatred, Bridge had thought the entire plan would come apart, but it hadn't. Despite the boy's strength, Bridge had been able to hold him. And once Gift had argued that he had the Roca's blood flowing through his veins as well, the boy stopped struggling quite as hard. When the jewels lit up on the floor, the boy had let out a small moan and turned away.

It had been a victory that Bridge hadn't entirely understood.

Ace flew above them in a search pattern. He'd fly to one side of the river, and then the other, combing it, making it clear that he was on guard. A few of the other Gull Riders left the ship as the boat got close, searching as well.

"Almost there," Dash said.

Bridge looked over his shoulder again. The ship was very close. He called to Gift to draw up his oars. Gift looked over his shoulder, much in the way that Bridge had, then grinned. He apparently was pleased by the mission as well.

Gift's oars came out of the water and rested inside the boat. Water dripped down the inside of the boat's frame. Bridge aimed the boat toward the side of the ship, then brought his own oars up.

Behind him, he heard the rope ladder slap against the side of the ship. The boat glided into place, and he grabbed one of the rings on the ship's side. Dash grabbed another.

From above, Sailors sent down ropes. Gift grabbed one and tied it to the stern of the boat. Bridge took the other and tied it to the bow. That would hold it while they got out. Then the Sailors could worry about pulling up the boat and its precious cargo.

"Rope ladder," Bridge said. "You'd think after this successful excursion they'd have something fancier for us."

"If you're worried about it, old man," Gift said with a smile, "you can wait down here with the globes and I'll have the Sailors pull you up."

Bridge grinned. "I've climbed more rope ladders than you've ever seen, boy."

"I really don't want to spend the night in the boat," Gift said. "If you can't go up quickly, you should let me go first."

"Learning how to be patient is good for someone like you." Bridge grabbed the sides of the rope ladder and carefully, so that he wouldn't disturb the boat, pulled himself to a standing position. "Watch and learn."

"Just make sure you reach the top before nightfall," Gift said.

Bridge's grin grew. He liked this nephew of his.

Scaling the ladder went quicker than Bridge had thought it was going to. Perhaps it was the teasing. Perhaps it was the energy he had gotten from the successful mission. Either way, as he looked up and saw his daughter's worried face hanging over the ship's side, he let go with one hand and waved at her.

"We did it," he shouted. "We have them."

A small cheer went up from the deck. Even Lyndred smiled. Coulter bent over the side as well, holding the ladder steady. As Bridge got near the top, he took Coulter's outstretched arm and let him support Bridge on the last part of the climb.

As he crested the rail, he saw something flash on the mountainside. At first he thought it was the Place of Power, then he looked up. That was a darkness.

A flash. It came again. He shuddered. He had seen a flash once before, when one of his men had died.

By an Assassin's hand.

Without thinking, he let go of the other side of the ladder and grabbed Coulter's head, shoving him down on the deck. Bridge shouted, "Assassin!," as an arrow caught the sun.

Coulter's grip on his arm pulled him forward, across the railing, but Bridge couldn't find a handhold. He lost his balance and slipped against the side of the ship. He flailed for a moment, shoved his feet as far inside the ladder as he could, but it wasn't far enough.

He slid down the side of the ship, grabbing for anything he could reach. His feet got tangled in the ladder, and threw him backward. His feet broke free, and he fell, his daughter's scream trailing down the side of the ship with him. There was nothing to grab onto, nothing to break his fall.

He kicked the side of the ship so that he wouldn't hit the boat, then he made himself turn in midair. He would try to go in the water feet first.

That was the only way he would survive.

Chapter Forty-Eight

*B*RIDGE HIT THE side of the boat with a thud so terrible that Gift wasn't sure how anyone would survive it. The boat rocked horribly; Dash grabbed the globes and hung on in case the boat overturned. Gift leaned over the edge and saw that Bridge had gone deep underwater. He could see the trail of bubbles, but not Bridge himself.

He had no idea if Bridge was conscious.

Gift dove off the side. The water was so cold it took his breath away. He followed the bubbles down. The sunlight didn't penetrate very deep, and the water became murky quickly. He couldn't see his hand in front of his face. His own chest was becoming tight with the urge to breathe, but he knew if he didn't find Bridge this time, he wouldn't find him at all.

As he swam he made big sweeping motions with his hands. He was about to give up when his fingers brushed fabric.

His lungs were straining now. He wasn't sure he'd have enough strength to resurface. Still, he reached down, caught the fabric, and found his uncle's arms. Gift pulled his uncle against him. Then Gift wrapped one arm around Bridge's chest and held him close as he dragged him up.

Bridge was clearly unconscious.

Spots were dancing in front of Gift's eyes and he had a horrible feeling he was turned around in the water, that he didn't know up from down. He couldn't see the sunlight at the top. He couldn't see anything in this murky brownness.

So he let a single air bubble out of his mouth. The bubble brushed against his face as it floated what seemed to Gift to be sideways, but which he knew had to be toward the surface.

He followed the bubble, his legs kicking hard. His chest hurt, and he was having trouble keeping his grip on Bridge. Gift had no idea how far away the surface was, only that he was their only hope to find it.

His breath would have to last until he did.

His lungs were straining, fighting for air. It was all he could do to keep his mouth closed, to not take a breath. The movement was nearly involuntary. He had to concentrate on not breathing, and on kicking his feet, and on holding Bridge close.

He had seen this. How stupid had he been? He had seen this, dying beside the boat. Only he had thought it had been on the way to Leut. He hadn't recognized the waters of the Cardidas, dark and murky. He had thought he was in an ocean, but who would be in an ocean in a boat? And this sinking feeling wasn't an undertow. It was his uncle's weight, making Gift struggle.

It had been a Vision of his own death. His and Bridge's.

He wasn't going to make it. His lungs were burning. He didn't realize he had gone so deep.

Then he noticed that the water was lighter. He was actually seeing particles in the water, a thin ray of red through the brown. Sunlight. He was nearly to the top.

Gift gave one last mighty kick and broke the surface, gasping and struggling for air. He rolled immediately on his back so that he pulled Bridge's head out of the water. His uncle was a dead weight. Gift had no idea if Bridge was even alive.

The boat was beside him, and the ship beyond that. Gift didn't see any concerned faces, though. He thought he heard screams and shouts.

Only Dash looked at him, peering over the side of the boat as if he hadn't thought he would ever see anyone again.

Gift swam close to him. "Throw me one of those flotation cushions," he said. Or at least he tried to say it between gasps and mouthfuls of river water.

Dash looked surprised and then chagrined, as if he hadn't thought of it. He reached behind him and tossed a cushion. It landed beside Gift with a splash. With his free hand, he caught it and held it against himself.

It would float, but he wasn't sure how long. Still, it made him feel as though he were expending a little less effort.

He kicked even closer to the boat. "You're going to have pull Bridge over the side. Be careful not to capsize the boat."

"Or fall in." Dash's eyes were wide. Gift remembered then that Dash had said he couldn't swim.

"If you stay braced, you won't fall. Just make sure he doesn't land on those globes."

Dash nodded. He extended his hands.

Gift positioned himself under Bridge and pushed him forward. The weight of Bridge's body made Gift sink, but he was able to hold Bridge up.

Dash's hands brushed against his and grasped the wet fabric of Bridge's shirt. Gift came up for air. Then he went down again, pushing on Bridge's torso and back, until he felt Bridge's body move away from him.

When Gift surfaced he saw that most of Bridge's body was in the boat. Dash had his own body between Bridge and the boat's bottom. Gift grabbed Bridge's right leg and put it inside the boat, then did the same with the left.

The left leg bent at an odd angle. Apparently, that had been what hit the boat.

Dash slid him against the bow, away from the globes.

Gift rolled on his back again. Somewhere in the struggle, he had lost his flotation cushion. He was having trouble catching his breath. He hadn't expected this kind of exertion.

Above him, he saw Bridge's face, pressed against the side of the boat, saw an oar hovering above him, saw a Gull Rider flying toward the shore.

Dash was extending the oar. Gift had floated away from the boat. Dash looked terrified.

Gift made himself breathe, then he swam toward the boat as carefully as he could. He narrowly missed getting hit by the oar. He grabbed it, and let Dash pull him forward.

Then Gift climbed into the boat, careful not to trip on his unconscious uncle.

The air was frigid. He glanced up. No one was watching from the ship. He thought he heard someone yell, but he couldn't be sure.

He had no idea what had happened. Dash moved more of the globes away, and Gift ran a hand over his uncle's forehead. His skin was clammy. Gift turned him on his side, pounded his back, and river water came out of Bridge's mouth.

Bridge coughed, then his eyelids fluttered. He started to speak, coughed some more, and then spat out water and weeds.

"Don't try to talk," Gift said.

Bridge ran a hand over his mouth. He said, "Assassin."

Gift looked up, but he couldn't see anything. And he knew that, from here, there was nothing he could do.

Chapter Forty-Nine

At first, everything looked strange to Ace. Bridge shoving Coulter down, then losing his balance and falling off the side of the ship, people on deck screaming, Gift diving into the river. It happened small and far away, and for a moment, Ace couldn't quite comprehend it.

He swooped low to help Gift and, as he went down, he saw an arrow sticking out of the railing at the place where Coulter had been. It couldn't have been fired from the ship; it had to have come from a long distance.

Ace flew back up and as he did, Coulter started to stand. Another arrow hit the railing. Coulter fell to the deck, and crawled toward the deckhouse.

Ace flew past the ship, higher than he had gone before. He saw another arrow. It came out of a clump of bushes on the side of one of the mountains, but he couldn't see who released it.

He called to the other Gull Riders, then flew for that clump of bushes, staying high as if he were going to fly over it. A fourth arrow released, and he thought he heard a scream.

The audacity of the shooter stunned him. He had clearly stalked his prey all afternoon, waiting until no one paid attention, then shot at Coulter. If Bridge hadn't seen something, and acted quickly, Coulter would be dead.

The bushes looked empty until Ace was directly overhead. Then he saw the shape of a man, gray like the stark branches, hidden within the clump. The man was hard to see but his bow and arrows weren't.

The Assassin.

Ace felt anger flare through him. With his hand, he signaled the other Gull Riders, but they weren't as close as he was. He dove, beak outstretched, for the back of the Assassin's neck.

Ace hit it with such force that he almost cried out in pain. His beak sunk into the soft flesh, ripping and shredding at blood vessels, hoping to find the artery.

The Assassin didn't scream. He flailed at Ace with his free hand and then dropped his bow so that he could reach Ace better. Ace flapped his wings and dug his talons into the Assassin's shoulder. A flinch of pain ran through the man, but he still didn't cry out.

The other Riders were above him now, diving toward him. Ace pulled out his beak to smash it into the neck again when the Assassin's hands closed on him. Ace pecked at the webbing between the fingers, but he couldn't get the Assassin's hands to move. They squeezed, then yanked, pulling him off. Hunks of bloody skin came out with his talons.

The other Gull Riders were flocking around them now, but the Assassin didn't even seem to notice. He brought Ace forward and Ace saw the man's face. There were no features at all, like a Spy without a mask.

Ace flapped and struggled, but the Assassin didn't let him go. With a simple twist of his hand, he snapped Ace's Gull's neck. All of the strength left his Gull's body, and he couldn't shift back to Fey form.

He looked up into those empty eyes, praying for one of his companions to poke them out, but no one came close. They all seemed shocked by the way the Assassin was holding Ace.

Ace wanted to shout to them, but he couldn't. He was rapidly losing all of his strength.

The Assassin's hand covered Ace's head, and he tried to push it off. And as the fingers gripped his tiny, thin neck, he knew he wouldn't be able to fight this one.

That didn't stop him. He struggled until the end.

CHAPTER FIFTY

*C*OULTER CRAWLED TO the side of the deckhouse. The arrows seemed to have stopped. Lyndred, Arianna, Skya, and Con were on their bellies. One of the female Sailors was screaming, and there was blood on the deck.

Those arrows hadn't come from the ship.

A moment ago he had seen Ace fly past as though he were pursuing something. The other Gull Riders had gone as well. Coulter leaned around the deckhouse, saw the Riders' white shapes inside a clump of bushes against the nearby mountainside.

The Assassin had gotten extremely close.

Then a bloody form rose in the air, and the Gulls followed it, following their nature, as gulls did.

The Assassin knew how to fight Fey. Of course. That was his purpose, not to fight others, but to fight Fey. Riders could be defeated by appealing to their animal natures.

Coulter removed his shirt and used it to cover his blond hair. It wouldn't fool the Assassin for long—not with the sun shining on his pale skin—but it would buy him precious time.

He crawled to the other railing, careful to stay low, and when he rose up, he saw the Gulls fighting over the body of one of their members. The Fey on the Gulls' backs were hitting their Gull bodies, trying to make them obey, but the Gulls saw food and they were reacting instinctively.

There were feathers on the bushes.

He would only get one chance at this.

"Lightning," he whispered, and he aimed it at that single spot.

Above him, the sky darkened, and thunder boomed. With a squawk, the birds broke apart, and the Riders seemed to regain control. Coulter wanted to warn them away but couldn't. They started to dive again, reassuring him, letting him know that his target was still there.

Lightning rippled across the sky. He would kill his own Gull Riders if they weren't smart enough to move, if they didn't remember the stories that Matt had told.

But if they moved, they would warn the Assassin.

The sky had turned an odd green. The lightning gathered, and then stabbed the ground.

Feathers rose and some of the Riders flew away. Not as many as Coulter would have liked.

The bushes caught fire, and in it, he thought he saw a man's torso engulfed in flame.

Coulter let out a small sigh. That had been too close.

THE BLOOD

[Two Days Later]

CHAPTER FIFTY-ONE

THE DAY WAS cold and misty, with a bit of fog. A perfect sailing day. Grantley stood on the deck of his ship, and looked across the bow at the ship flanking his. They were both old vessels, in poor condition, but he was able to get them seaworthy, and for that the Black Queen had made him Captain of this mission.

Captain. He liked the sound of that.

He studied his crew. The Sailors stared at the water as if it were giving up secrets. The handful of Nyeians aboard were older, used to working in an ancient boat. None of them seemed interested in the mountains, but the soldiers were. He had Foot Soldiers and Beast Riders, a few Red Caps, and a hold full of Infantry. He had to give them all small duties to keep their nervousness from showing.

He had to work at keeping his from showing too. Until two days ago, he had been the captain of a trading vessel who had successfully fought off Leutian pirates twice, and managed to bring home some of their cargo. He had lived through horrible battles, watched men die in a myriad of different ways, and hadn't lost a single crew member.

That story—true as it was—hadn't impressed the Black Queen. She had only snorted when she heard it, looked at him with her strange pale eyes, and said, "He'll do."

Her assistant, DiPalmet, however, thought it a good recommendation. DiPalmet was the one who looked at Grantley's ship and decided it was too small. DiPalmet was the one who told Grantley that if he could fix the two warships and find a crew for both, he could lead the mission.

Grantley was supposed to listen to the minor Visionary on board if she had a Vision to report. Otherwise, he was to get his ships to Constant and begin leveling the area. Slash-and-burn, the Black Queen had called it. Mass destruction, DiPalmet had said with a bit of embarrassment.

Grantley could do that.

Then as he was leaving, the Shaman the Black Queen had found pulled him aside. "You watch whom you attack. The Black Heir, his family, and friends are there. You make sure you don't touch any of them."

He had agreed, of course. Who wouldn't?

"He went there by ship," she said. "You know his ship?"

Grantley nodded again. He had seen the Tashil ship and he had envied it for its speed and grace in the water. "I won't touch him."

"Make sure you don't."

Even now, two days later, the conversation still disturbed him.

He glanced at the rising mountains around him. In all his travels to Blue Isle—and in his thirty years there had been plenty—he had never gone down this part of the Cardidas. His Sailors told him that it was straightforward, a simple river with no tricks, but he was cautious anyway. He'd seen too many traders lose ships by misjudging a river's power.

He wished he could talk to Targil. She commanded the ship beside his and was a trader as well. She had been his recommendation to command the other ship, but he was wondering now at the choice. The ship had kept level with his all the way from Jahn. It was almost as if Targil were sending him a message, as if she wanted everyone to know that she was his equal even though he had been given this command.

He hadn't expected her jealousy or her recklessness. Since she didn't own the ship or have any responsibility for its cargo, it seemed as if she had license to try things she wouldn't normally attempt. She had sped through the narrows out of Jahn. And now he couldn't shake her.

Her crew seemed out of control as well. He heard shouts and laughter, and thought he saw drinking. He had told her that the mission was an important one, and she had laughed.

"Don't you see what they're doing?" she said. "They don't want control. They want destruction. You don't hire captains like us if you want things to go as planned."

He disagreed. He saw this as a chance at a career he'd never had, a career he would have wanted if his folks hadn't pushed him and his Charm toward domestic service. He hadn't been suited to that, so he had bought a ship and learned how to use his Charm in trade. It had been a profitable business, one he would go back to when this was all over.

If Targil didn't ruin it for him.

She didn't have Charm or Vision. Her magic when it had come had been something more Domestic, something she didn't like to discuss. She had turned her back on it all and had become one of the better traders, although not as good as Grantley.

He would talk to her when they docked. He would make certain she didn't do something she would regret later. She had said no one would report what they did, but she was wrong. There were troops a day or so behind them now—Infantry, more Beast Riders—all ready to aid in the battle that Grantley and Targil were to start.

The Islanders wouldn't know what happened until their city was leveled and their countryside burned.

"Ship ahead!" one of the Sailors called.

Grantley frowned. He had been told there was little traffic on the Cardidas. Because of the mountains, the river didn't go through many towns. Most of the ship trade went west of Jahn, not east.

He couldn't see anything in the fog. "Where?"

"You can't see it yet," the Sailor said. "I've been checking with some of the Ze. They say there's a ship coming in our direction."

The Ze were sea creatures that also swam in the Cardidas River. The younger Ze grew up in the river, and then swam to the ocean when they were full grown. The Sailors considered them a boon because the Ze were smart and easy to communicate with. Most creatures of the deep, according to Sailors, were either not very bright or not very communicative.

"How far away is it?"

"The Ze don't measure distance like we do," the Sailor said. "I'd say it's around the bend."

Grantley snapped his fingers at one of the Nyeians who had served with him on several trade ships. The Nyeian didn't even have to ask what Grantley wanted. She brought him his precious Tashil magnifier, a long tube with glass that somehow made far away things look big. He had paid a fortune for it, and had never regretted it. The magnifier had been the thing that had saved him during his meeting with the pirates.

He took the magnifier from her and put it to his right eye, closing his left. Through the fog, he could barely make out large rocks jutting into the river on both sides. Then a slight bend. Beyond it, he thought he saw the shape of a ship.

"What should we do?" the Sailor asked.

"We wait," Grantley said, still looking through the magnifier. "Send word to Targil to wait for my signal before doing anything."

"Yes, sir," the Nyeian said. She disappeared.

As Grantley's ship drew closer to the jutting rocks, he could see around the bend better. There was a ship behind it, quite a distance away. They had half the morning before they ran into it.

"Should I send for the Beast Riders and the Infantry?"

The Sailor sounded enthusiastic. All of them seemed a little too eager for the battle ahead.

Grantley squinted. Yes. That was the *Tashka*. His hands were clammy. Imagine if he had attacked it. What would have happened to him if he killed the Black Heir to the Throne?

He shuddered.

"Should I get them?" the Sailor asked again.

"No," Grantley said. "Find me another Nyeian. We have to let Targil know that she must leave that ship alone."

"Why?" the Sailor asked. "It's clearly coming from Constant."

Grantley lowered his magnifier. "It's the Black Heir's ship."

The Sailor went gray. "Oh," he said, understanding now what he was suggesting. "I'll get the message to Targil myself."

"Good." Grantley brought the magnifier back up to his eye.

Thank the Powers that the Shaman had warned him.

He hated to think what would have happened if he had attacked without knowing who was on that ship.

CHAPTER FIFTY-TWO

GIFT HATED THE fog. It made the air colder and damper than usual. Even though he was wrapped in a Domestic spelled cloak, he still felt the wetness on his face.

He stood on deck because he couldn't stand going below. Bridge was down there in great pain. One of the Domestics, a lesser Healer than Chandra, was tending his leg. Gift had wanted Bridge to get off the ship and wait at the school, but he had refused.

I'm the only one on this ship with military experience, he said. *That might count for something.*

Gift had to admit that was true. Without Bridge, both he and Coulter would be dead now. If Bridge hadn't acted quickly, then Coulter would have been shot and, by rights, Gift as well.

How quickly, how neatly, things turned.

The Assassin was dead, burned beyond recognition. The area around him had been blackened and charred by the lightning strike. When Gift had visited it, the area still tingled with power. He had left as quickly as he could.

Late that night, after Bridge had had some rest, Gift had

spoken to him. They both agreed that the moment in the water was probably the Vision Gift and others had been seeing. The fact that they had argued, playfully, about who would climb the ladder made the difference between Gift living and Gift dying, hence the moment's importance.

After that conversation, Gift had no way to convince Bridge to leave the ship.

Gift had lost the same argument with Skya. He wanted her to stay in Constant, out of the reach of the Black King. She had given Gift a withering look and had said, *See? This is what I mean. You and I are no longer equals. I am a woman to be protected, carrier of something more important than myself.*

He had denied that, but as he left, he wondered if he had been wrong. He was thinking on a larger scale than Skya. She was trying to maintain her individuality. He was trying to maintain an Empire.

Now he had her working on a way to hold the jewels without touching them. She had hated that as well— *Warder's work,* she had said—but she was doing it.

Gift used the edge of his sleeve to wipe the moisture off his face. Rugad, through Lyndred, had warned them on purpose of that Assassin, probably to appease the Powers. But Bridge was right; it was luck that Coulter had survived. Luck, and Bridge's experience. Someday Gift would have to ask Bridge what his past contacts with Assassins had been.

He sighed. It wasn't the weather that had him in this foul mood. It was the loss of Ace, his best and most trusted Gull Rider. Several other Riders had been injured, and they had opted to stay at the school where Chandra could treat them.

But Ace was dead. Gift had seen his broken body, still in its Gull form, both his Gull neck and his Fey neck hanging at odd angles. He looked smaller somehow, as if the force of his personality had made him all that he was.

Gift would miss him, but Gift wasn't taking his death as hard as Lyndred.

She had looked at Ace's broken body, put a hand to

her mouth and said nothing, but her eyes got hollow. When she knew that her father would be all right, she left his side and disappeared into her cabin. She hadn't been out since.

Arianna was the only one who seemed unaffected. She had a grim determination that kept them all focused on the task at hand. She was the one who got the Gull Riders to stay at the school. She was the one who agreed that Bridge should stay. And she was the one who actually had the makings of a plan for their return.

She had wanted Gift, Coulter, and herself to fly back on those contraptions that Rugad had used. Skya had known how to make them. But with the death of Ace and the loss of the Gull Riders, there weren't enough Bird Riders to handle the contraptions, even if someone had been able to make them.

The group had to go back by ship.

Arianna was extremely worried about this. She felt that Rugad would be watching for them, preparing for them. They needed to find a way to survive.

It was difficult to fight from a ship and they didn't have a lot of weapons. She and Gift agreed that they'd hold the Lights of Midday until they got back to Jahn. They had no bows and arrows, very few things that could be used to attack from the water.

Only Beast Riders and Coulter.

Gift wasn't sure if Coulter would use his powers to attack Fey again, as he had done so many years ago. Arianna had said that she would work on him. Gift didn't know if she had been successful.

One of the Nyeians touched Gift on the shoulder, startling him out of his reverie. "Ilipe would like to speak to you."

Gift didn't like the sound of that. Ilipe was his best Navigator. Gift walked to the wheel. Ilipe was handling it himself. He didn't even look at Gift. He stared straight ahead, as if he could see through the fog.

"There's word of other ships." Ilipe's voice was hollow, as if he were speaking in a large cave. Perhaps he was. He was getting information from four different Sailors, and he was steering the ship.

"From what?" Gift had learned to ask long ago. Some creatures in the deep didn't see all that well and couldn't be trusted. Some inexperienced Sailors used them anyway.

There was a momentary pause before Ilipe said, "The Ze."

The Ze could be trusted. "Where is it?"

Again the pause. Information took time to travel along these Links. "The ships are ahead of us. Not far. But I cannot be exact."

"I don't suppose a Ze would know whose ships they are."

"The Ze say ships are rare here." Ilipe still stared straight forward. Apparently he had already asked that question himself.

Gift stiffened. Why would Rugad send ships? Was he going to risk attacking Gift directly? Or did he assume that the Assassin had succeeded and Gift was dead? "How many ships?"

"Two." Ilipe's mouth remained open for a moment as if he had forgotten to shut it. "They are covered with barnacles and have much rot. The Ze think they are not very seaworthy."

In one of their conversations, Arianna had said that Rugad would have to work hard to find an army to send forth. That had apparently been true of his navy as well.

"They travel side by side. The Ze think that is dangerous."

The Ze were quite opinionated. Gift almost smiled. "What else have the Ze observed?"

Ilipe paused. "Two things. First, the ships carry a lot of weight. Second, the Ze are also helping them navigate the river."

Gift let out a small breath of air. So the ships knew about his presence as well. He peered into the fog. They were too far away to see, but close enough that the Ze were working with all sets of Sailors. In this strange fog, he might not know that the ships were near him until they were right on top of him.

He stopped a nearby Nyeian. "Get my sister, a Bird Rider, and Coulter. Make it quick."

The Nyeian nodded and hurried belowdecks. Arianna wouldn't arrive quickly—that wasn't in her power at the moment—but Coulter would.

The Bird Rider came up first. It was Beak, an extremely experienced Gull Rider, the only one of the group that attacked the Assassin who had managed to keep her Gull self under control. She was delicate, her black hair feathered like most Riders, her large nose strange on her tiny face.

"There are ships ahead," Gift said. "Let me know how far away they are and what kind of force they have, if any."

She nodded, then Shifted to her Gull form as she flew away. Her clothing littered the deck like leaves on a windy day.

"What's happening?" Coulter came out of the fog like an apparition.

Gift told him.

Coulter looked very serious. He peered into the fog. The Nyeian came up, with Arianna not far behind. The fog was good cloak right now, but it wouldn't last. Gift turned to the Nyeian one last time. "Get me a Weather Sprite and Skya."

The Nyeian nodded.

By the time they had finished the discussion, Coulter had told Arianna about the ships.

Arianna's expression hadn't changed. She had looked concerned when she had come up and she looked concerned now. Gift still wasn't used to the immobility of her face. The old Arianna would have had a reaction, however slight, to the news.

"I can't believe any Fey would attack knowing that Gift is on this ship," Coulter said.

"Maybe they don't know," Arianna said.

"When Beak gets back, we'll send her out again," Coulter said. "We'll tell them that this is the Black Heir's ship. They have to know that Gift is on Blue Isle."

Gift nodded. "That might work."

"Of course it will work," Arianna said. "Any Fey who

knows about the Black Heir will tremble at killing him. But that doesn't solve the real problem."

"It solves *our* problem," Coulter said.

She turned. "Does it?"

"Of course it does. They'll let us pass. Won't they?" He asked this last of Gift.

"Most Fey would," Gift said, remembering his reception all through Galinas and Vion.

"So we'll get to Jahn and we'll be able to face Rugad," Arianna said. "At what cost?"

Gift felt cold, and knew that the chill wasn't coming from the fog.

Skya joined them. She walked past Gift and stopped beside Coulter, as if he had become an ally. Coulter saw Gift's glance and gave a minute shrug, as if to say he hadn't chosen that position. Her dark eyes met Gift's. He wasn't ready to update her. When had she stopped being his partner? When had he replaced her with Arianna and Coulter?

When he had found out about the child. When he had realized that she hadn't been honest with him.

He turned away. "What are you talking about?" he asked Arianna. "What do you mean, cost?"

"Rugad isn't going to send two ships to attack us."

Skya's eyes widened. She caught on fast.

"He's sending them on another mission. If they kill us, fine. It'll seem accidental, at least to those who count."

"The Powers," Skya whispered.

"That's right." Arianna's words were clipped.

"So what's the mission?" Coulter was pale.

Gift was shaking. He knew exactly what the mission was. He had lived through a similar one fifteen years ago.

"He's going to burn the countryside. He's sending them to destroy Constant." Gift kept his voice as level as he could.

Coulter shook his head as if he couldn't believe it. "They didn't do anything."

"He knew you were hiding Arianna there, didn't he?" Gift asked. "He knew about the school."

"He knew that Matt came from there," Arianna said. "He knew that Matt was Matthias's son. Matt told him."

"Then we have to go back," Coulter said. "He won't do this with just two ships. There'll be more troops. We have to help."

"We help here." Skya's voice was soft. Gift met her gaze. She looked away from him. "That's what you're discussing, right? Two ships coming here. Now."

"Yes," Arianna said.

"Then we destroy the ships and we continue forward."

"And if those ships destroy us, Rugad wins," Coulter said. "He wins the Empire without causing the Blood."

"What do you suggest?" Skya's voice held deep sarcasm. "That you shield this ship from view? That we make it as hard to see as that Assassin back there and sneak into Jahn?"

Gift looked at her. "That might be a plan."

She glared at him. The anger that she had been rigidly controlling flared out of her eyes, only to be dampened as if it had never been.

"Coulter's right," Arianna said. "Two ships can't destroy Constant. There's too much magic there and Rugad knows it. He has to have a larger force."

"We can use the Riders to find out what that is," Gift said.

"We can't engage those ships," Coulter said. "Not with you and me and Arianna and Skya on board. We can't. We'd risk too much."

"We'd need a good strategy," Arianna said to Gift as if Coulter hadn't spoken. "We'd have to attack them without warning."

He nodded. "Surprise always works."

"What about those globes?" Skya asked.

"No," Arianna said. "They're for Rugad."

"We might not get to Rugad," Skya said.

The Nyeian approached, a Weather Sprite behind him. This was one of the older Weather Sprites, one of the ones who had come with Bridge. Gift did not know her name. Her face was leathery and tough from too much time outdoors. Her features were almost hidden by her wrinkles. Like Gift, she wore a Domestic spelled cape. She looked lost inside hers, as if the years of her magic took away some of her mass.

Gift held up a hand to her, signaling her to wait until they were done.

"We will not use the globes," Arianna said.

"We don't have many weapons here." Skya looked at Gift. "This is not a military ship."

"Do you think Rugad is on one of those ships?" Coulter asked.

"No," Gift said. "I'd be surprised if Rugad ever came back to the Cliffs of Blood."

"That's a hunch," Skya said.

"If you had seen how he died here, you would understand why he would never, ever get close to the Place of Power again."

"Gift's right," Arianna said.

"But this is not close to the Place of Power," Coulter said. "Maybe he meant to meet us here."

"He sent an Assassin," Gift said. "He's not taking a risk on his own these days."

Beak emerged from the fog. She landed on the deck and immediately shifted into her Fey form. Even though she was naked, she didn't seem to be cold.

"We have perhaps an hour," she said. "I'm not good at measuring the speed at which ships travel."

Gift nodded. He turned to the Weather Sprite. "Can you clear the fog all at once, so that we have a direct view of that ship?"

"With help," she said.

"Do you have enough Sprites?"

She nodded.

"Good," he said. "Get them and prepare them. You'll do it on my order."

She spun and headed back into the fog.

"I hope this means you have a plan," Arianna said.

Gift shot a look at her, hoping she understood. She

blinked, a long close of the eye, as if the message were received, and then she sighed softly. She did understand. The plan took Coulter.

"It doesn't matter how many weapons they have or what kind of Fey are on board that ship," Gift said. "The Fey developed their fighting style because Enchanters were rare."

"No," Coulter said.

"Two fireballs," Gift said, "landing in the middle of the ships. The Ze say those ships are old and poorly kept. They'll ignite."

"In this weather?" Skya snapped.

Gift turned. He was angry at her too. "Then you think of a spell that will work for him. You're the one trained as a Spell Warder. It's your job. We have the best weapon of all here. Help us use it. Find us a way to destroy those ships."

"I am not a weapon," Coulter said.

"You're all we've got." Gift sounded harsh even to his own ears. But he had to be harsh. Coulter had let them down once before. Arianna had said that Coulter hadn't wanted to go back to Jahn, even when it became clear that he had to. Gift couldn't let him fail now.

"We can think of something else," Coulter said. "Skya's right. The globes—"

"Could hurt every Fey on this ship." Arianna sounded just as harsh as Gift. "Gift's right, Coulter."

"Think of it as a way to redeem yourself," Gift said.

"Redeem myself?" Coulter asked. "By killing people?"

"If you don't," Gift said, "we'll die. Just like Adrian did."

Arianna sucked in a breath. Coulter looked even paler than he had before. "That's not fair," he said.

"I'm not trying to be fair. I'm trying to save lives. Why is it when things get difficult you can never see that?"

Skya wiped water off her face. She shook her head slightly, and then said, "I might be able to manage a fireball. A small one. I have enough magic to do it."

"One won't do us any good," Gift said. "We have to attack both ships."

"Maybe that and one of the globes—"

"No," Arianna said. "You don't know how those globes work. I do. If they're used wrong, they'll hit everyone who is within range. On all the ships."

"Then I don't know what to do," Skya said.

Gift was watching Coulter. He was peering through the fog again, as if he could see the other ships.

"I'll do it," Coulter whispered.

CHAPTER FIFTY-THREE

GRANTLEY USED HIS magnifier to check the progress of the *Tashka*. The fog was thick and he continually had to wipe off the lens. Still, he could see a group of figures on the deck, but he couldn't see who they were.

To his surprise, Targil had understood the reasons Grantley had decided not to attack. She had supported him completely. She had even wondered if they should do something as they passed—some kind of uniform bow or shout in recognition of the Black Heir.

Grantley had decided against that. If they sped by quietly, the Black Heir wouldn't even have to know what the ships were doing. Somehow, Grantley had a feeling the Black Heir did not know about the pending attack.

Grantley brought his magnifier down. He would stand at attention on the deck and watch as the ships passed. It would probably be the closest Grantley would get to the Black Heir.

Then, miraculously, the fog cleared. Above, a cloudless sky appeared and the winter-thin sunlight was almost blinding.

He could see the *Tashka* clearly. It was newer than his ships by decades. Faster and stronger. He was glad he wasn't meeting it on the high seas. He probably wouldn't have survived the encounter.

The fog crowded the edge of the river as if it were being held back by a wall. Was this a Sprite spell? He glanced at Targil's ship. There were no Sprites on her deck. She was there with her Sailors, looking surprised at the sudden clarity.

A blond man stepped forward on the deck of the *Tashka*. He looked almost ill, his pale skin pasty even from this distance. There were Fey behind him, but Grantley couldn't see them as clearly.

The blond man lifted his right arm over his head. Then he flung his hand forward as if he were throwing a ball.

Which he was.

A huge ball of fire landed on the deck of Targil's ship. Screams echoed from the Nyeians, but the Fey were grabbing sails and blankets and coats, trying to smother the fire out, but the flames were spreading as if there were more than wet, rotted wood fueling it.

"Get assistance!" Grantley shouted. "Bird Riders. Wisps! Make the Wisps hurry!"

Nyeians were running belowdecks, his own people were coming above. Targil was shouting and some of her people were abandoning ship. Inky black smoke was rising.

The blond man had his head bowed as if he were gathering strength.

"Hurry!" Grantley shouted.

One of the Wisps found him. She was stick-thin, her long wings pressed against her back in fear.

"Go to the Infantry," Grantley said. "Tell them that the *Tashka*, which was supposed to have the Black Heir on it, is actually an attack ship. Tell them to—"

The blond man moved. He was raising his arm again.

"Tell them to attack," Grantley said. "No holds barred."

There wouldn't be time to talk to another Wisp.

"Then," Grantley said, speaking as fast as he could, "after you've delivered that message, go to the Black Queen and tell her that it looks as if her brother is leading an attack force. Tell her to prepare to take him prisoner. Warn her."

A ball of fire was heading toward his deck. It looked larger than the one that went for Targil's, but he couldn't tell the exact size. He just knew that it meant he wouldn't survive.

"*Go!*" he said.

The Wisp rose in the air as the fireball hit behind him. He heard it smash into the deck as if the ball had weight and substance. Fire spread like water through the wood.

He glanced at Targil's ship. It was a smoking hull, cracked and sinking. There were Fey in the water swimming toward shore.

"Abandon ship!" Grantley shouted. "Abandon ship!"

The Nyeians were the first to jump. The fire was growing, the flames as high as his emergency boats. There was fire licking at his coat. Only the Domestic spell was keeping it off—and that wouldn't last long.

The fog was closing around them again, making the smoke thick. He kept shouting at his crew to abandon ship, but between the smoke and the fog, he couldn't tell if anyone was obeying. Then he heard faint splashes and knew that some were.

A hundred Fey would go down. They were belowdecks. They wouldn't get out in time.

He ran to the railing. He couldn't see Targil's ship anymore. He couldn't see the *Tashka*. All he knew was that fire had moved to the side of the ship, eating the wood like locusts attacked plants.

There were screams all around him, hideous screams made more powerful by the fog. He knew his duty as a soldier. It was to stay with the ship. But he had only been a soldier for a few hours. He couldn't stomach dying.

He gripped the now-burning railing and plunged over the side, falling deep into the icy water of the Cardidas. There were people splashing around him, and flaming bits of wood falling into the water.

If he swam carefully, he would get to shore. If he was careful, he wouldn't drown. He kicked hard and started forward, wood hitting the water around him and hissing as the flames went out. His hands would hit bodies, bits of the ships, occasionally someone live who grabbed at him.

He would shake them off. They had to survive on their own, just as he did.

Survive to tell what the Black Heir had done to his own people.

CHAPTER FIFTY-FOUR

*T*HE SMELL OF smoke mixed with the damp. The screams, the sounds of flames, the bodies splashing into the water all sent chills through Gift. He glanced at Arianna who was staring at the fog as if she could see through it. The fog was brownish-yellow now because of the reflected flames and the smoke. She had never ordered an attack before, but she had spent years knowing she might have to.

Gift went to the rail and took the slippery wood between his fingers. He could see water below, churning and foaming, filled with debris. The ships were on the port side now. The *Tashka* was passing them.

Con came up beside him. Gift hadn't even realized Con was on deck. "Some of those people in the water are alive. Shouldn't we rescue them?"

Gift had been trying not to think of that. "We can't."

"But now that they are no longer a force, they aren't our enemies."

"I wish it were that simple," Gift said.

"You think there might be another Assassin among them?"

A long wail pierced the air, rising above the other screams like a signal. Someone was in great pain.

"I don't know," Gift said. "I can't risk my sister, my uncle, my cousin, or my child to find out."

Con frowned at him, and Gift realized that no one besides him, Skya, and Xihu knew about the child. That had changed now.

"I think I'll go below, then," Con said. "There are prayers that need to be said."

Gift didn't contradict him, but he wondered how a man who had slain Fey himself could think himself worthy of asking a god—any god—to save other lives. Gift's beliefs were more Fey than not. He had seen a Mystery, so he believed in the Powers, but in the Powers as once-living Fey who were just as capricious dead as they had been alive.

They didn't seem to care for the morality of things. Sometimes, he thought they were more interested in the entertainment. Well, he hoped they'd gotten their enjoyment from this afternoon's festivities. He hadn't.

The screaming was growing fainter and the debris in the water had lessened. He was watching the foam on the surface. It was red.

There was blood on the water.

Gift beckoned to Coulter, but apparently Coulter didn't notice. Instead, Arianna came to his side. Gift pointed down. "Do you think that was what the Vision meant?"

She stared for a long moment. The blood was like a slick on the surface, leaving a stain on the side of the ship. How had that happened? Most of the injuries should have been from burns, not from open wounds.

"I don't see anything, Gift," she said.

He pointed. "See? The blood on the water."

"The water's no different than it's always been," she said. "Most of the debris from the ships is gone."

Her voice was curiously flat as if she had worn out all of her emotions.

Maybe he had too. He could see blood, though, a thick layer of it over the water's surface.

"How come I can see it?" he whispered. "How come I can see it and still talk to you?"

"A Warning, maybe," Arianna said. "Half a Vision."

He closed his eyes. It wasn't over yet.

CHAPTER FIFTY-FIVE

ARIANNA STARED AT the water, the charred bits of wood floating in it, the clothing. The occasional body. Gift had closed his eyes as if he were in pain.

She didn't see blood. Just destruction.

And it was only beginning. They both knew that. Gift had gotten them this far. She would get them the rest of the way.

She left his side before he opened his eyes.

The deck was quiet. Coulter still stood where he had been when he released the last fireball. She knew he hated doing these things, but they had no choice. This time, she wasn't going to comfort him. He had to learn how to fight on his own.

The Sprites were gone, and Con had gone below after he had spoken to Gift. Skya leaned against the deckhouse and Lyndred was slumped beside her, head buried in her knees. That meant no one had told Bridge what was going on. He was probably curious. But that wasn't Arianna's job right now either.

She went up to the first Nyeian she saw. "Find Beak for me."

He nodded and disappeared into the fog. She tilted her head into the moisture-laden air. It was rather nice to stand in the cold and damp and to be as warm as she would have been inside a palace. Maybe she was getting used to this form after all.

Within moments, Beak stood in front of her. Beak had put on pants and a cloak that beaded with moisture. Her feathered hair was beaded too. Apparently, she had been on the deck watching everything instead of below like so many others.

"Good," Arianna said. "I need to send you on another mission. You're not too tired?"

Beak's thin smile was nearly hidden by her nose. "It doesn't matter how tired I am. I'll do what you need."

Arianna nodded. She believed that of Beak. "I want you to get another Bird Rider—one you trust as much as yourself— and fly west. I'm convinced you'll find either more ships or some ground troops or both. When you do, I want you to return to us. Report their position and stay."

"All right."

"Then the other Rider should continue until he sees more. If that means he goes all the way to Jahn, so be it. I want to know what surprises Rugad has in store for us."

"Jahn and back?" Beak asked.

"Yes," Arianna said.

"You'll need a strong Rider, then." She took a deep breath. "We don't have many left."

Arianna gazed into the fog. She hadn't really discussed the Assassin's killings. She didn't want to focus on the losses. Not yet.

"Do you have anyone who will work for us?"

"One," Beak said. "He's young. It's better if I go to Jahn. I'll be able to see things he won't."

Arianna didn't like it, but she had to accept it. "His name?"

"Lesley."

Arianna winced. Young enough to be born after the Nye campaigns and named in the Nyeian tradition.

"He's a Sparrow Rider." Beak offered that last as if she were worried about Arianna's response.

Arianna made a sound of disgust. "No more Gull Riders?"

"A few," Beak said, "but none who would serve you as well as Lesley."

Arianna sighed. She trusted Beak. "All right. But have him return as soon as you see what lies ahead. I want to know how big a force there is, and where they seem to be going. I do *not* want you to talk with them. Is that clear?"

"Very."

"Good," Arianna said. "Tell Lesley I expect to see him shortly. I wish you the best flight of your life."

Beak smiled. "I have a hunch it will be the most interesting."

She left. Arianna watched the fog swallow her. Then she looked across the deck. Gift was still peering into the waters below. Coulter had joined him. That was good. They would talk to each other. They needed to. They were very similar in ways that she didn't have time to think about.

Lyndred had disappeared, but Skya was still leaning against the deckhouse. She was watching Gift, a look of contemplation and sadness on her face.

Arianna walked toward her. Skya noticed her long before she arrived, and watched her progress across the deck. They hadn't spoken to each other much. Skya's chin rose slightly as Arianna stopped in front of her.

"How skilled a Warder are you?" Arianna asked.

Skya shrugged.

"I am not asking these questions out of curiosity," Arianna snapped. She didn't have time for moods and everyone's seemed to have changed once they caught the scent of smoke on the wind.

"I have been a guide for a long time," Skya said. "My Warding days are long past."

"Yet you helped Coulter with a spell that made the fireballs catch wet wood, and you also were able to protect him when Matt shouted through their Link."

"I still have some of my skills."

Arianna bit back anger. But she made herself remain calm as she said, "Can you work with the Domestics to create cloaks that will shield the wearer from view?"

"Like Spies?"

"A Spy's magic shields him from view," Arianna said. "I want to have the cloak do that."

Skya frowned and bit her lower lip. "I'm not used to doing Domestic spells."

"Why didn't you tell my brother that, then, when he asked you to devise something that will allow the light to pass through the jewels he collected?"

"He told you that?" Skya sounded surprised.

"He asked me for my advice." Arianna crossed her arms. "I'm the one who said the Domestics might be able to come up with something."

"They weren't willing to," Skya said. "They thought it a weapon."

"It's a tool," Arianna said.

"I know. I told them that." Skya straightened to her full height. She was as tall as Arianna. She hadn't noticed that before. So, Skya did have a powerful magic. She just hated to use it. "They're making it now."

"Good," Arianna said. "Now I want the cloaks."

"What for?"

"You don't have any reason to know."

"If I'm developing the system, I do."

"You're developing the cloaks to save my life and my brother's. Is that enough for you?"

Skya lowered her head. Then she nodded, still not meeting Arianna's gaze. "I can devise the spell that you want. The Domestics can do it. How many cloaks do you need?"

"At least five," Arianna said.

"Five?" Skya raised her head. "We don't have the time or materials for that."

"Then use existing cloaks. But have them done in a day. Can you do that and finish the tool that Gift wanted?"

Skya nodded.

"Good. Then get to it."

Skya didn't move, but she smiled at Arianna slowly. "You're just like him, you know."

"Gift?"

Skya nodded.

"I suppose you hate me for that."

"No." Skya's voice was soft. "I like you more than I want to. And that's my problem."

Skya slipped away then, leaving Arianna to stare after her. That was an apology of sorts. One Arianna didn't exactly understand, but one she was glad she had.

She needed the team to work together, without a lot of debate. She had a hunch these next few days would be the crucial ones.

She wanted to make sure everything went right.

CHAPTER FIFTY-SIX

XIHU SAT ON the steps leading up to the South Tower. Her robe was tangled around her feet, and she was leaning uncomfortably against the stone wall. Her right cheek felt scraped.

She'd had a Vision, the first one since the attack on the palace. It was a single Vision too, and it seemed very quick. She remembered slipping as it started and came to herself as her head smacked against the wall. In the space of an eye-blink, then, her Vision had happened.

She pulled herself up, feeling her muscles complain. Nothing was broken, but she would be bruised. She wanted to go back to her rooms and rest, but she knew that wouldn't be wise. She had promised Arianna that she would share the Visions. That was the main reason Xihu had agreed to come to the palace. This Vision hadn't been that different from some of the others, but its timing might be significant.

Xihu smoothed her hair, used her sleeve to wipe the blood off her cheek, and climbed the stairs. Her legs were tired. She had already climbed these stairs twice, mostly to reiterate answers she had already given. Arianna wanted to make certain she understood everything Xihu was telling her, so she asked the same questions in different ways.

By the last dozen steps, Xihu was using the thin wooden railing to pull herself up. When she reached the top, she knocked on the door. A moment later, DiPalmet opened it. He looked surprised and concerned when he saw her face.

"What happened?" he asked. "You just left."

She ignored him and stepped inside. Arianna was seated at a table, looking over papers that obviously had something to do with the Isle. The Fey rarely committed anything to the page.

Arianna did not raise her head, but continued to scrawl on the paper before her. "What is it now?"

"You had said you wanted to hear Visions." Xihu sounded as tired as she felt. DiPalmet brought her a chair, but she shook her head. If she sat down, she might have trouble getting up. She didn't want Arianna to know how sore she was.

"Yes, I did." Arianna finally set her pen down. When she saw Xihu, her eyes widened ever so slightly. "So, you were treated to one as you left me?"

"One," Xihu said. "A brief one."

Arianna shoved the papers aside and folded her hands on the table. "DiPalmet, take these to the tiresome traders who are waiting in the audience chamber."

"They wanted to get the papers from you," he said.

"I rule here. They don't get to order me around." Her voice was flat, her gaze still on Xihu.

DiPalmet took the papers and hurried away. He gave Xihu a curious glance as he went. Arianna waited until the door clicked shut before she said, "What was this Vision?"

"It was a sudden change in location," Xihu said. "So quick that I remember losing my balance at the beginning of the Vision and seeing the steps again as I hit my face against the wall."

Arianna moved her head slightly. They both knew Visions like that were unusual.

"I was looking at the Cardidas," Xihu said. "Smell was the strongest part of this Vision. It was the smell of dampness like the kind after a sudden rain or of fog. And that was mixed with the faint stench of smoke."

"Are you sure that wasn't in the air here?" Arianna asked. "You smelled it and confused it with your Vision?"

Xihu shook her head. "The smells were different. Here the scent is already old and fading. There it was fresh. It smelled like woodsmoke mixed with charred flesh."

"All right," Arianna said.

"The Cardidas was flowing in front of me. The top layer of the water was moving slower than the rest of the river. It was blood."

"You've Seen that before."

"Yes." Xihu wasn't sure why she was feeling as if she had to defend her Visions. "But timing is often important. I don't know what you were doing up here, but perhaps—"

"I was signing documents that some traders below needed to open a route to Leut. Apparently, the Leutians are even more enamored of documentation than the Islanders or the Nyeians. Such a waste of time."

"You don't think that caused it?" Xihu asked.

"We can't rule it out. But I suspect someone else did something that caused this Vision. Had you thought of that?"

Xihu licked her lower lip. She was getting a headache. "Have you Seen this as well?"

"No." Arianna's answer was curt.

"Perhaps it would be best if you told me what you've Seen as well. Going on my Vision alone is not going to work—"

"For whom? For you? I have no trouble with this system."

"Of course." Xihu smiled slightly.

"Is that all?"

Xihu's head was pounding. "Are you expecting a battle on the Cardidas?"

"You know the plan. Constant is on the Cardidas. That's probably what you were seeing. The ships should be arriving shortly. I'm sure they'll begin my campaign."

"That doesn't feel right. It was like a Warning. I wouldn't get a Warning for that, would I?"

"I would hope not." Then Arianna sighed. "Where were you in the Vision? Here?"

"I don't know." That disturbed Xihu as much as the Vision had.

"Were you on the water or off it?"

"I don't know," Xihu said.

"Then we do not deviate from our path." Arianna stood and walked to the window. Xihu was beginning to see that as a sign of dismissal. "Now, get some rest. You look ill and I'm sure I'll need your services in the next few days."

Xihu nodded. The pain and the exhaustion were showing. She was careful not to limp as she walked to the door, because she knew that Arianna could see her reflection in the window.

Xihu closed the door as she started down the stairs. Arianna had a point. Xihu did need her sleep. She would catch a few hours before going back to the Domicile. She was getting so tired that she was beginning to mistrust her own judgment. Yet there was something about the Vision, something that had come in that flash that she couldn't put her finger on. Something that identified the place and the time.

Maybe when she woke up, she would know. But she wouldn't count on it. All she could count on was that she had more work than she had ever had in her life. There were still so many injured, and too many had died, more than she wanted to think about. It wasn't the fault of the Healers. The wounds were just too severe.

All those deaths. Xihu shuddered. She had a feeling there would be more.

CHAPTER FIFTY-SEVEN

LYNDRED LEANED AGAINST the door to the cabin the Domestics used as a makeshift hospital. Her father was in the biggest bed, the one they had used for Matt. He had slept through the entire battle, through all the screams, and the stench of burning, and the hissing splashes as large flaming objects fell into the water.

She had never experienced anything like it. She had watched and listened, terrified. She had been terrified since she saw the bloody feathers rising in the air, before the Gull Riders chased after Ace's body, two days before.

Ace. She rubbed her eyes with her thumb and forefinger. She could still see him, his body beautiful as it flew toward that Assassin. If she closed her eyes, she could see his naked form when he had Shifted in front of her the first time. She could even see the way his hair feathered down his back, the dark smoothness of his skin, the strangeness of his Gull Rider's hands.

But she couldn't see his face.

This was the feeling from her Vision. It had been compounded in that moment when her father had fallen off the ship and disappeared beneath the water. All she had done was scream. Gift had dived in after him. Gift had saved him.

She hadn't done a thing.

She stared at her father. His skin was gray. His face looked older than ever. The Healers said the pain was bad, even though he would recover. The rocking of the ship aggravated the injury. He would be in pain for the entire trip, but he had insisted on coming because he believed that Gift needed him, that Arianna needed him. So far, they hadn't. But they needed Lyndred even less.

If her father was awake, she would ask him how she could be useful, how she could make decisions because they were right, not just right for her. But to wake him up now to answer her questions was something the old, selfish Lyndred would have done. Now she understood that was wrong. Still, she could have used his strong arm around her, his comforting voice telling her that even though she had cared for Ace, a Gull Rider wasn't for her.

She squeezed her eyes shut as if she could squeeze out the thought. She and Ace hadn't really talked since she had come on the ship. She had tried to avoid him, and he had seemed angry at her. Now she'd never talk with him again.

She wiped at her eyes, then opened them. Her father still slept. This wasn't his problem anyway. It was hers. And no matter what advice he would give her, no matter what comfort he held, he couldn't change who she was.

She pushed off the wall and walked through the narrow corridor toward her cabin. As she walked, she heard a voice droning in Islander. The words were soft and she couldn't make them out.

She followed the sound of the voice and saw that the door was partially open. Con was inside, on his knees, holding his filigree necklace in his hands. He was facing the porthole, but his eyes were closed. He seemed to be reciting something. She couldn't catch all the words. Something about protection and guarding souls and receiving help from the Roca, bringing his words to God's ear.

Then he bowed his head, touched the sword to his lips, and stood. He saw her and his face softened.

"Lynnie," he said, using her father's nickname for her. The gentleness in his voice made her eyes fill with tears.

"I didn't mean to listen," she said in Fey. "I was passing and I heard your voice and—"

"It's all right." He didn't move. He knew that she didn't want to get close to him and was respecting that. "I meant for my words to be overheard."

"By me?" she asked.

"By God."

She flushed. She didn't believe in God. She didn't believe in anything. "How do you know He's listening?"

"By faith." Then he smiled. "But I'm sure you've heard that before. It doesn't really help, does it?"

She never had heard that before, but she didn't want to break the mood by saying so. "What helps, then?"

"It's different for all of us. Your people believe in Powers and Mysteries. Mine believe in the Roca and God."

"Are they the same?"

"If I knew, I'd be a lot wiser than I am." He put the necklace on, and then tucked it under his shirt. "Where were you going when you were passing by?"

"I was going to my room. There isn't much for me to do."

His eyes were a deeper blue than Gift's, and his skin was rosier. He was thinner than he had been when she first saw him, and that had only been a few days ago. The stress showed on him too, just in different ways.

"How are you doing with the loss of Ace?" Con asked the question so quietly she barely heard him. If he knew about Ace, did everyone else? Probably. It had been impossible to hide when she had gotten the news.

"I'm fine," she said, but her voice shook. "I've been through death before. My mother's dead."

But it wasn't the same. She had been a little girl when her mother died, and it had been a long time before she understood that her mother wasn't coming back. By then, she had gotten used to being without her mother. Her father had done his best to shield her, and life went on.

Now her father was injured and she wasn't sure how she

had felt about Ace—she was afraid that she had loved him and not really acknowledged it—and suddenly he was dead.

"Ace was a good man," Con said.

She nodded. There was a lump in her throat.

"He died defending us."

"I know."

"He said he was initially on your ship," Con said. "He said your father sent him away."

"He volunteered to find Gift."

"Because he knew better than to get too close to a member of the Black Family. He said he wasn't worthy of you."

"That's a lie!" She put a hand over her mouth, then made herself lower it. "I didn't mean you lied."

"I know."

"When did you talk to Ace?"

Con shrugged. "A few times here and there. He kept an eye on you."

And she had watched him, although whenever he looked, she had made sure she looked away.

"I'm sorry," she said, "that I was so mean to you."

For the first time, a bit of color touched his cheeks. "That's all right. You're worried about the Vision."

"Not anymore." She came inside the room. The distance between them wasn't great at all. "I think you're a nice man."

He put up his hands as if to hold her away from him. "Don't, Lyndred."

"Don't what?"

His cheeks were flaming red now. "Don't flirt with me."

"If it's because of the Vision, I've decided that I can't let my feelings go," she said. "I did that with Ace and he's dead. But I can tell you I find you attractive."

Con nodded, but backed away. "I know. But I also know that you use sex to keep people from getting close to you."

She froze. She felt a hollow anger, more of a pain, as if he had slapped her and she had deserved it. "How do you know that?"

The flush had traveled from his cheeks to his neck and

into his shirt. "I watch too. I don't want to be another man in your life, Lynnie. I—" His voice broke. "I was supposed to be an Aud."

That stopped her. "I thought you were an Aud."

"Once. But the religion is truly gone. We don't understand it anymore. All we knew was wrong. Maybe even— all the rules."

"But you were just praying," she said.

"I believe God is still there," he said. "And I believe God sent me to you. To be your friend."

"Friend." She would rather have put her body against his, felt his warmth, taken comfort where she could find it. "Friend?"

"Isn't that all right?"

"It's fine," she said, and she could hear the echo of the words she had used earlier to describe how she felt about Ace's death. "I can always use friends."

"Lynnie—"

"Lyndred," she said. "Please. Only my father calls me Lynnie."

And then she left the room, closing the door behind her. She hurried down the corridor to her own cabin and went inside.

Too much was changing too fast. For eighteen years, she had lived the same life. Now she didn't know anything anymore.

She didn't even know what she needed to do for herself.

CHAPTER FIFTY-EIGHT

*I*T WAS NEARLY dark when Lesley returned. The fog was thinning, but still cold. Arianna watched as Gift pulled his cloak closer. Coulter had moved from his spot. He looked wan and tired. Using that much magic always took a toll on him.

Lesley was so tiny that he looked like a small hunk of coal hurtling through the air. When he landed on the deck, his sparrow's wings folded against his back, and then he Shifted. Coulter had a cloak for him and handed it to him without a word.

Lesley nodded his thanks, wrapped himself up, and looked at Arianna. "Infantry, Foot Soldiers, and Beast Riders. A lot of them. I couldn't count them all. They're marching in a long column and they're heading east."

"Just like the ships," she said.

He nodded. "It took me half the day to find them and half the day to return. I didn't stop at all. I can't give you exact distances, but I'm guessing we'll meet with them sometime tomorrow."

Arianna let out a small breath. An entire unit or more.

"He's going to destroy Constant," Gift said. "You know it."

She did know it. She just didn't want to admit it. "What kind of weaponry do they have?" she asked Lesley. "Can they attack us?"

"Probably not. I didn't see many quivers among them."

"What kind of Beast Riders were with them?" Gift asked.

"Mostly larger animals. They're traveling at a quick pace, so they kept their animal forms. A lot of Bear Riders and Dog Riders. A handful of Bird Riders."

"Did they see you?" Arianna asked.

Lesley grinned. "That's one of the benefits of my small size. If they did, they didn't pay much attention."

"What about Beak?" she asked.

"Beak flew on the other side of the river just to be safe. She made sure I was headed back here, then she went on to Jahn. She was pretty worried about this military unit."

So was Arianna, but she wasn't going to admit that to Lesley. She put a hand on his shoulder and squeezed. "Thank you. You did excellent work. Go belowdecks, get some food and rest. I suspect we'll all be quite busy tomorrow."

He nodded and left, trailing the cloak behind him.

"We need a plan," Gift said.

Arianna had been thinking of this all day. "We're going to have the Weather Sprites shroud us in fog. I want complete silence as we go past that Infantry. They won't think anything of it, if we don't give ourselves away."

Coulter's mouth opened. He looked shocked. "What are you thinking? We have to stop that unit. They're going straight for Constant. If they kill everyone, then Rugad will own the Place of Power."

"He already owns the Place of Power," she said. "He would have attacked sooner, but he didn't realize we were a threat before."

"Arianna," Coulter said. "There are people in Constant that we care about. Leen, Scavenger, Sebastian. Not to mention Matt. You can't leave them to this fate."

She sighed. "I know. But we only have a few resources to deal with an army of this size. One of those resources is you. The other is Skya, whose abilities are limited because of her Warder's magic. You're exhausted, and Skya's working on more important projects."

"What's more important than saving lives?" Coulter snapped.

"It'll take the army at least two more days to reach Constant. Then they'll have to set up, because the Fey like to attack at dawn. So nothing will happen for three days."

Gift was watching her closely. Coulter's face was slowly turning red. He was getting very angry.

"By the time they're ready to attack, we'll already have defeated Rugad. Then we can call them off."

"And what if we aren't successful?" Coulter snapped. "We just leave our friends to an ugly death?"

She looked at him. "We send Lesley to them tomorrow morning, after he's rested. Beak assures me that he's trustworthy, and I think he's proven that today. Leen and Scavenger know how to fight the Fey. They also know how to use some of the tools in the Place of Power. They should be able to rally a defense."

Coulter took a deep breath, as if he were suppressing anger.

"Coulter," Gift said softly, "look at it this way. If we use your strength to destroy this army, then we lose the fight to Rugad, and he'll just go after Constant again. Only the next time, he'll be even more vicious than he was before."

"I'm trying to save as many lives as possible," Arianna said. "This seems like the best solution."

Coulter walked to the railing. He stared ahead as if he could see through the fog and the dark, as if that army was so close that he could hear them.

Gift put his hand on Arianna's arm. "It's a good plan. I trust you have one for Jahn as well?"

"Part of one. I was hoping that we wouldn't have to face any ground troops."

Coulter walked back to them. The heightened coloring had left his cheeks and he was as pale as he had been before.

"When you send Lesley, tell him to talk to Matt. Even though Matt won't be healed, he'll have to fight. It's the only way everyone will survive. And Matt will have to enlist the help of Alex."

"The boy in the Vault?" Gift asked.

"It might be easier than any of you think. If Alex uses all the power at his disposal, Rugad's army won't stand a chance."

"As long as he doesn't attack our friends who happen to be Fey at the same time," Gift said.

"Matt's aware of that problem," Coulter said.

"I'll warn Lesley all the same," Arianna said.

Coulter nodded. "You were right, Ari. This is the only way it's going to work."

"I know," she said.

CHAPTER FIFTY-NINE

*D*iPALMET FOUND HIMSELF in the South Tower, his stomach churning. He had gotten up a half hour before dawn. He had eaten a hurried breakfast, spoken to the Domestics who were working the kitchen, and then received word that Arianna wanted to see him. Usually, their first meeting wasn't until mid-morning, but ever since the attack that first meeting kept getting earlier and earlier.

He wasn't enjoying the orders he was receiving either.

"Are you listening?" Arianna snapped.

He hadn't been. He had been wishing he were somewhere else, even though he could see the dawn through the east windows. It was one of Blue Isle's most spectacular dawns—the golds and pinks mingling against a faint blue sky. Maybe if he were alone, he would enjoy it. Maybe if he weren't thinking about troop counts and ship orders and—

"DiPalmet?" Arianna was standing with her back to that splendid sunrise. She had moved the tables and chairs out of the way as if she found them a nuisance. He wondered how much time she spent up here.

"I'm sorry," he said. "I haven't had any root tea this morning."

She sighed. "You are my assistant. That means you should be ready whenever I summon you."

I'm here, aren't I? he wanted to say, but he didn't. He knew better. "I'll endeavor to improve."

"Do we need to start again?" she asked.

"No," he said. "You want me to send for troops from Galinas, along with fifteen ships—"

"For the first trip," she said. "I'll order more in the future."

"And you would like to reassemble these military companies." He listed the dozen companies she mentioned. She was very well informed about Fey history, but sometimes she seemed vague about the present.

"So you were paying attention," she said. "You just looked as if you weren't listening."

He shrugged. Listening was a talent of his. Sometimes he heard more than he wanted to, even when he wasn't trying.

"Arianna," he said.

She smiled. "Whenever you use that tone, you're going to reprimand me."

"I was just wondering if you—I mean, most of those companies haven't been assembled since the Nye campaign. The original armies will be elderly. We're going to have to tap progeny, or find someone to re-create them."

She stared at him for a long moment. He watched her eyes go from dark blue to light and back to dark. He wondered what caused that, then decided he didn't want to know.

"The companies are legendary," she said. "If we can find the original Leaders, we'll be doing well. We'll have those Leaders reform the companies with the best soldiers they can find, soldiers of all types, and then send those companies here."

"There are units that have been fighting border skirmishes all through the Empire." DiPalmet knew that because he had checked with some of the Fey who had come over with Bridge. "Perhaps these units should also be in the first wave."

"And then who will protect our borders?" she asked.

"Theoretically, our borders should be sound."

"You just told me there were skirmishes."

"It's just if you plan to conquer Leut," he said, "you should have the best possible troop complement. I'm not an expert, of course, but it would seem to me that to go in with strength is the right way."

"I suppose it would seem that way to you." She crossed her arms. "But I'm not sending the troops immediately. I will make sure they are properly trained."

That seemed like another reprimand. "Of course."

"And I will be the one commanding them." Her eyes twinkled when she said that. She raised her chin slightly, as if she expected him to decry the wisdom of that idea.

"I expected as much," he lied. She had no military experience. She was more foolish than he thought.

"You expected it, but you don't like it."

He shrugged. "My opinion is nothing."

Her smile broadened. "At least on matters like this."

There was a knock on the door, and then, without Arianna's response, the door opened. A Domestic leaned her head inside. "I'm sorry, but there's a Wisp here. She says she's from a ship you sent toward Constant. I thought it sounded important."

Arianna glanced at DiPalmet. He wasn't sure, but he had a hunch she was as surprised at this news as he was.

"It is important," Arianna said. "Send her in."

The Domestic stood aside. The Wisp entered. She looked delicate, like all Wisps, and her wings were tattered at the edges. She had flown hard.

She bowed her head when she saw Arianna. No one was certain anymore which customs to follow, Fey or Islander, so they used a combination of both.

"Your news?" Arianna asked.

The Wisp raised her head. Her skin was gray with fatigue but her eyes were still bright. "Early yesterday, our ships

came upon the Black Heir's ship, the *Tashka*. It attacked us
without warning, using fireballs and Weather Sprite magic.
We expected to sail past so we were undefended. Our ships
sank rapidly. I have no idea how many died. Grantley sent
me to inform the Infantry and to let you know. He said that
you should understand the Black Heir is on a rampage, and
you should act accordingly."

DiPalmet's already unsettled stomach turned again. This
was the Blood everyone had been talking about. It had finally arrived.

"Was the Black Heir on the ship?" Arianna seemed
calm.

"I don't know," the Wisp said. "We assume so. It is his
ship, after all."

"No one saw him?"

"It was foggy until the fireballs launched." The Wisp's
wings trembled as if the memory disturbed her.

The whole concept disturbed DiPalmet. Why would the
Black Heir attack defenseless ships?

"Who launched the fireballs?" Arianna asked in that
same dispassionate voice.

"I don't know," the Wisp said.

"You didn't see it?"

"I did," she said. "It was an Islander. I don't know
who."

Arianna's expression flattened. DiPalmet was beginning
to realize that showed a repressed anger. "How old?"

The Wisp shrugged.

"A boy?"

"No," the Wisp said. "A man full grown. I can't judge
their ages better than that."

"You don't have to." Arianna turned to DiPalmet.
"Have you ever seen my brother's friend Coulter?"

"I haven't," DiPalmet said, but he'd heard stories. He'd
even heard the rumor that Arianna and Coulter had been in
love. Judging by the coldness in her tone, that was not true.

"It sounds as if my brother went to Constant to get
Coulter. There's more going on here than we thought, Di-
Palmet."

DiPalmet already had that sense.

Arianna turned her attention back to the Wisp. "You warned the Infantry?"

"I did," the Wisp said. "But they're really not prepared to fight a ship. They'll do what they can."

"You warned them that the Black Heir might be on board?"

"Grantley told me to let them know that the Black Heir had gone crazy and was on the attack. He didn't want them to show the Heir reverence."

"They have to show him some," DiPalmet said. "They don't want to kill a member of the Black Family."

The Wisp's wings were vibrating. "He didn't tell me to clarify that."

"Let's hope they already know that," Arianna said without conviction. "You've done what you can. I appreciate the report. Go to the Infantry barracks. One of my officers will debrief you."

The Wisp nodded crisply and then left.

Arianna watched her go. DiPalmet was swallowing hard, trying to force down the nervousness that was eating him alive.

"My brother insists on making things difficult," Arianna said without turning around.

"So it would seem," DiPalmet said.

"We're going to have to contain him before he can bring on the Blood."

DiPalmet waited.

Arianna turned. Her eyes were bright. Instead of being upset by this news, she seemed almost elated. "I doubt the Infantry will be able to stop him, not if he has an Enchanter on board. We'll have to prepare for him here."

"What do you want me to do?"

"Send the remaining troops to the waterfront. Let them all know that he's a renegade."

DiPalmet nodded.

"Have those without magic use bow and arrow. Use only Bird Riders to attack the ship. Let our people know that Gift should not be killed. He must be captured alive."

"If they use bow and arrow, there's no guarantee that he won't get hit before anyone storms the ship."

Arianna shrugged. "My brother is a smart man. He'll understand the dangers and protect himself accordingly."

"What if you're wrong?" DiPalmet asked.

"I am not ordering his death, DiPalmet," she said coldly. "I want to know why he believes that he can attack us without consequences. I also want to know if he is working alone."

"You know how dangerous this is?" DiPalmet asked.

That flash in her eyes was so full of fury that he almost took a step back. "It is my job to worry about such things. Not yours."

He nodded.

"Trust this, DiPalmet," she said. "I'm the one protecting the Empire. I won't do anything to harm it."

He wanted to trust it. But he was getting to the point where he wasn't sure he could trust anything anymore.

CHAPTER SIXTY

$\mathcal{A}$RIANNA TOOK SHALLOW breaths, trying not to make a sound. Sebastian had once shown her that, in this body, she could survive without breathing at all, but she hadn't been able to manage it. Seger said that Arianna expected to breathe, so she *had* to breathe. Now she wished she had learned the lesson.

The ship glided silently through the river. Fog enshrouded them so tightly that the air almost glowed. It was very cold. Only the people who needed to be were on deck: the Sailors, the Navigator, the Weather Sprites, Gift, Coulter, and Arianna. Everyone else had opted to ride out this part of the journey belowdecks. Gift had allowed them to do so; if they were above and made too much noise, the Fey army would know that a ship was passing.

There was no actual fog on the deck. Since the fog was a Weather Sprite creation, they could dictate where it went. It surrounded the boat, but did not permeate it. If Arianna hadn't known that the ship was moving, she wouldn't have believed it. Everything was eerie, as if they had stepped out of time somehow and were existing in a world where there was nothing except the ship and the grayness surrounding it.

A couple of the less competent Bird Riders had flown ahead and were holding position, promising to let the ship know when they had passed the army.

Arianna had also asked the Sailors if there were any water creatures that could surface and tell them the same things. The Sailors weren't sure, but they would ask. Their task was doubly difficult right now. They had to make sure the ship was following the correct river channel, and they had to make sure they did not make any sounds.

Instead of dampening sound, the fog seemed to make it worse. She had spent her entire time on deck listening to the laughter and camaraderie coming from the shore. The conversations held in Fey, the bawdiness, the smells of camp food were, in many ways, reassuring. It meant that the Infantry was not traveling night and day to get to Constant.

It meant that she still had some time.

The voices had faded a while back and so had some of the clanging. Still, she didn't believe in letting herself go too soon. She needed confirmation that they were past the army before she so much as moved.

Then she saw a Bird Rider land on deck, followed by another. The second Rider landed on Gift's shoulder, making him start. The Rider, another sparrow, leaned toward Gift and seemed to be speaking to him. He turned to the first Rider and said something so softly that Arianna couldn't hear him.

Slowly she made her way across the deck toward her brother. He was already walking in her direction, coming not to her, but to the Weather Sprites.

"The Riders say we've passed them," he said to the main Sprite as Arianna reached them. "Continue the fog for another hundred yards and then let us emerge from it. Can you keep the fog back there until dawn?"

"Of course," the Sprite said, sounding a bit offended that Gift had even asked.

"Good," Gift said.

"Are you sure the Riders are accurate?" Arianna asked.

Gift nodded. "These two may not have the abilities that Beak and Lesley do, but they are reliable."

She wished she had made the decision for herself, but she said nothing. It was impossible to have two leaders give orders and this was Gift's ship. She would let him take care of most of the decisions.

The ship emerged from the fog into a clear cold night. The sky was filled with stars and a pale sliver of a moon. The water looked black, and the mountains were mere shadows in the distance.

Arianna looked toward the shore, but saw nothing. She didn't expect to see much—it was too dark for that. But she heard nothing either. And if Rugad's army had been there, she would have heard someone—a sentry, a startled Infantry-man up to take a pee—call out that he'd seen a ship.

One more hurdle passed.

Then a Gull Rider burst out of the fog, and sprawled across the deck. Coulter stood over it as if he were afraid it came from the army, but Gift held his arm.

The Rider shifted into her Fey form, and suddenly Beak was standing before them. Gift removed his cloak and wrapped it around her. She smiled gratefully. Her face was pinched, her skin mottled red and gray. She seemed to have a chill or some kind of windburn. Feathers littered the deck.

Arianna had never seen a Gull Rider look so exhausted.

"Well?" Gift asked.

"Somehow Grantley sent warning that we were coming." Beak's voice was hoarse. Arianna had to step closer to hear the words. "What's left of the Infantry is being deployed at the shores of the Cardidas. The word is that this is a renegade ship. Some don't even believe you are on it, Gift."

Arianna glanced at him. He was frowning.

"The idea being circulated is that some rebels, half of them Islander and half of them Fey, are trying to destroy the peace. The attack on the palace was the first volley. The attack on the ships in the Cardidas was the second. The Black

Queen"—and then Beak bobbed her head toward Arianna—"beg pardon, ma'am, but that's how they're referring to Rugad—the Black Queen wants to stop this rebellion before it becomes a full-fledged war."

"So destroying Constant and sinking this ship will accomplish that?" Gift asked.

"The soldiers think so. I think it sounds like a tremendous excuse to get rid of you." Beak shivered. Her eyes had sunken into her face. "All of you."

"Rugad can't give orders to destroy this ship knowing who is on it," Arianna said. "No matter what the armies think."

"Rugad has ordered that the ship is to be captured, not sunk, and that prisoners should be taken. But the folks that were gathering on the shoreline when I left did not look like the kind who were organized enough to take prisoners."

"One of those famous accidents that Rugad is so good at," Gift said. "How are we going to get through this one? If Rugad is prepared for a ship, there'll be arrows."

Coulter shrugged. "I'll do what I can."

"We'll be in the middle of a city," Gift said. "You can't use some of your spells there."

"I wasn't thinking of those spells," Coulter said. "I made up a protection spell when I was a boy. It's like a shield around the entire body. I think I can put that around the ship."

Con came above deck, Lyndred beside him. They were staring at the sky as if they hadn't seen it in a long time. Then some Nyeians came above. Out of the corner of her eye, Arianna saw her brother look for Skya, but of course, she wasn't there.

"It's going to be a large force," Beak said.

"That presents more of a problem than I had anticipated."

Lyndred joined the group. "We're past the army, aren't we?"

"Yes," Gift said.

"Are we safe, then?" she asked.

"That's what we were just discussing," Coulter said.

Then, to Arianna's surprise, he briefed Lyndred. Lyndred nodded. She did look older than she had when she came on board. Her eyes used to twinkle. They hadn't twinkled since Ace died.

"Why can't we use the same fog to get past them?" she asked.

Gift looked at Arianna as if he expected her to have an answer.

"We can," she said, "until it comes time to dock. I had thought we'd be able to walk unencumbered through the streets. The warning Grantley sent prevents that now. I have no idea how we're going to get near the palace."

"Well, if Matt was right," Gift said, "we won't need to get near the palace to use the Lights of Midday as long as the jewels do focus the power of that magic."

"It's a city full of people," Arianna said. "I don't want to damage hundreds to destroy one."

"The only way we're going to find that out," Coulter said, "is when we use the globes. We can't test this before hand."

"And we have another problem," Arianna said. "Coulter severed his Link to my body. The moment the Lights of Midday have gotten rid of Rugad, I need to be back in my own body, and I'm not sure how to do that."

"Coulter," Gift said, "you could open my Links. Ari could travel through them."

"Not good," Coulter said. "What if we don't get rid of Rugad? Then he has access to both of you. I can't permit that."

"Arianna still has a Link to herself," Gift said.

"Not in the way that we're thinking of," Arianna said. "I'm pretty sure Rugad has closed off that route."

"Ari lived for a short time in my mind," Coulter said to Gift. "I could walk her into the palace and then when Rugad is gone, I could touch her body and see if she transfers."

Beak was swaying on her feet. Arianna put a hand on her shoulder, partly to support her and partly to get her attention. "Go below. Thank you for all you've done."

"I could help—"

"After you've rested," Arianna said.

The others were watching them silently, as if chagrined that they hadn't noticed how tired Beak was. Con put an arm around Beak's back and helped her to the deckhouse.

"That plan," Arianna said to Coulter, "is too risky. We need to figure out a way to get me back there, a way that will work."

"Well," Coulter said, "we're going to have trouble just docking and walking into the palace."

"Maybe not." Lyndred had been watching Con. When she turned to the group, she looked sad. "If we do this right, I should be able to get into the palace."

"Rugad knew you got on this ship," Gift said.

Lyndred nodded. "And he knows that I wanted to become Black Queen someday."

Arianna let out a small snort. "You told him?"

"Yes."

Arianna repressed a smile. That was something she might have done, before she and her father were forced to leave the palace, before she learned so much while fighting Rugad the first time.

"But he would know that I wouldn't fit in here, at least not well. We could let me off, cover me with blood, and I could tell him that my father is"—Lyndred's voice broke a little—"is dead, and that I just managed to escape when we came near shore, and that I've been walking. That I know things which would help him defeat you. He might let me in for that. I'll wager no one will stop me at the palace. I lived there for six months."

"So we get you there," Gift said. "The problem is getting Arianna there."

Lyndred didn't look at him. Instead, she turned to Arianna. "I'll take you inside my head, if you're willing."

"And if that works," Gift said as if Arianna couldn't speak for herself, "then how do you propose to get Ari back to her body?"

Lyndred raised her head defiantly. "I may have forged a small Link with the person I thought was the Black Queen."

"*May* isn't good enough," Gift said.

"I am a Visionary," she said. "I can probably help Ari find the right Link that will bring her back to herself."

"I don't like *probably* either."

"Do you have a better suggestion?" Lyndred snapped.

Arianna let out a small breath. It wasn't about their suggestions. It was about what she felt she could do. She had had Skya make the cloaks, but a Golem's gait would be obvious. She could travel inside Coulter, but then who would operate the Lights of Midday? She didn't want any Fey to touch them.

What it came down to was whether or not she could trust Lyndred. "Why would you do this?"

Lyndred's dark eyes met hers for a moment and then looked away. "Because I need to be useful."

"Not good enough," Gift said. "You just reminded us you wanted to be Black Queen. What better way to do it than to get rid of Ari inside your own mind, let Rugad's forces get rid of me, then take the Throne for yourself?"

Lyndred gasped. "I wouldn't do that!"

"I don't know that."

"My father is on this ship. Even if I wanted to harm you, I wouldn't want to lose him."

Her words echoed across the river. Arianna had seen the two of them together. She believed Lyndred. "First, tell me, honestly, why you want to do this."

To Arianna's surprise, Lyndred's eyes filled with tears. She blinked several times. When she started to speak, her voice was husky. "Ace. He told Gift not to trust me. And he was probably right. I watched him die, and I couldn't do anything. He believed in you all, enough to die for you. I've never done anything like that. I didn't even know people did, until Ace."

Arianna studied her. Coulter moved half a step forward. Gift crossed his arms.

"I thought being Black Queen was all about who was smartest, and who had the most Vision. I had the most Vision of anyone I knew. I thought it would be simple once you were in power. I didn't know how much courage it took and how much knowledge. I thought I could do it all, and now I know I'm just a baby compared to everyone else."

"You want to do this to prove you have courage?" Arianna asked. "You could die. If you make a mistake, we both could die."

Lyndred raised her gaze to Arianna's. "I'll have you with me to prevent me from making a mistake."

"If we're wrong about the Lights of Midday," Gift said, "then you and Arianna might lose your magic."

Lyndred paled. She obviously hadn't thought of that. "How else are you going to get her to the palace? Is there anyone left there that she has a Link to?"

Gift looked at Arianna. Arianna shook her head. She hadn't Linked with anyone while she was there.

"Then if you're willing to take the risk with me, I'm willing to take the risk with you." Lyndred looked directly at Arianna.

Arianna thought about it for a moment. "Lyndred and I—and maybe Con and Dash—can get off outside of Jahn and walk in. You sail in using the fog as we just did. But once we get into the palace, how will you know that we're close enough?"

"We need an open Link," Coulter said. "Someone can shout a message through it."

"Open mine and Ari's," Gift said.

"No," Coulter said. "We're taking too many risks with you as it is. Ari and I have a new Link, one we forged to get her to the Golem. That might work."

"And it might not," Gift said. "Let's go with established Links."

"If we go with established Links," Lyndred said, "then you should consider one more."

"What would that be?" Coulter asked.

"Mine with my father," Lyndred said.

"Have you ever traveled it?" Coulter asked.

"No," Lyndred said. "But it's there. Arianna can explain to me how to send a message through it."

Gift shook his head, an ever-so-small movement that Arianna wasn't sure if anyone else caught. But she did.

"I like the plan," Arianna said. "It has merit."

"It has too many risks," Gift said.

"You mean, I'm the risk," Lyndred said.

"Yes. You were the one who reminded me that Ace didn't trust you. He was infatuated with you. He might even have loved you. And if he couldn't trust you, why should I?"

"Then why does everyone else ask Skya for help?" Lyndred said. "You don't trust her, yet you love her."

Gift took a step backward, as if Lyndred had actually struck him. Arianna started to go to him, but Coulter caught her arm. His grasp was light, and she doubted Gift even saw it.

"There are some things that Skya can do well," Gift said, "and there are some things she refuses to do."

"Well," Lyndred said, "I may not be good with people, not in the way that Ace wanted me to be, but I'm smart and I'm one of the best Visionaries in the family. I can do this, and I won't betray anyone. I'm not that stupid."

"I don't think the Empire's future should be based on your test of courage," Gift said.

"Why not?" Lyndred asked. "Because you didn't have enough courage to take the Black Throne in the first place?"

"Enough," Arianna said. "Ultimately, this is my decision, and I think Lyndred offers us the best plan. We'll take the boat when we get close to Jahn. We'll disguise Lyndred so that she looks bruised and bloody, and then we'll find our way into Jahn."

"Ari—" Gift started, but she didn't let him finish.

"You'll stay here with Coulter. Coulter will be the one who'll use the Lights of Midday, and you'll direct them toward Rugad, after you get the signal from us. Then we'll see what happens. If we're lucky, this will work."

"And if we're not lucky?" Coulter asked.

Arianna stared at him.

"I think you know the answer to that," she said.

CHAPTER SIXTY-ONE

XIHU DIDN'T HEAR the plan until well after dawn. She had spent the night tending the injured from the last attack. Three more Infantry died, all of them young women who hadn't yet come into their magic. One of them had died sobbing for her mother. She had been little more than a baby, sent to war.

Xihu had gone outside after the last death and had taken in the sunrise. Then she had gone to the kitchen for a bit of food. There she had noticed there didn't seem to be the usual guards getting their breakfasts. She had commented on that to one of the cooks, who had told her about the attack on the river.

Gift, attacking ships? What had happened since she left him?

Xihu had tried to see Arianna, but Arianna had sent back a message that she was busy, and Xihu should try again later. So Xihu had no choice but to go to the Cardidas herself.

A cacophony of voices rose around her. The entire harbor was full of people. Soldiers of all types were gathered in units. Most of them were studying bows and arrows—apparently they had not seen that weapon before. The various Beast Riders were discussing ways to get to a ship in the harbor, and the Foot Soldiers had already commandeered the free boats. The warehouses were full of soldiers, many of whom leaned out the sides, and the shoreline itself was covered with Infantry.

She had no idea there were this many soldiers left in Jahn. She thought the force Arianna had sent to Constant contained most of the battle-ready. But she noticed that most of the Fey around her were extremely young. Some wore ill-fitting uniforms that had clearly belonged to someone else.

This army was assembled from leftovers. It was raw and untried, even more so than the one going to Constant.

A shiver ran down Xihu's back. Arianna was doing this on purpose. She knew that stray arrows could hit Gift. She was hoping this inept group of soldiers would find a way to kill her brother.

Xihu grabbed one of the Foot Soldiers as he hurried past. He glared at the hand on his arm before looking up and seeing that she was a Shaman.

He was so young that he still had skin problems. He hadn't reached his full height either. He must have just come into his magic.

"Tell me where your Leader is," she said.

"How am I supposed to know?" he asked and shook her off.

She stared after him. Hadn't they trained young people on Blue Isle to recognize their elders? Had everything fallen apart?

She stopped a young Infantry woman whose skin was too pale to be pure Fey and whose eyes had a touch of green to the brown. "Where's your Leader?" Xihu asked again.

The woman pointed toward the eastern edge of the river, and Xihu thanked her. Then Xihu got off the road and walked down an embankment leading to the water's edge.

The ground was soft and muddy after being trampled by so many feet. She hurried as quickly as her robes allowed her, catching snippets of conversation, most of which had to do with how to sink a Tashil ship.

A few of the Infantry had found slingshots and were discussing how to launch burning torches at the ship. Others were separating their units into those who could swim and those who couldn't.

No one spoke of taking prisoners.

Xihu hurried on.

The farther into the mass of people she went, the clearer it became that no one led this group. But the woman had pointed this way, and that meant she thought there was someone who could help Xihu.

She had walked past three warehouses before she stumbled on a group of older Fey. They had their heads together and they were talking softly. She recognized none of them.

"Do any of you lead these soldiers?" she asked.

No one turned. She repeated the question.

Finally, a man looked up. He appeared to be in his fifties, his skin craggy and his hair touched with gray. When he saw that Xihu was a Shaman, his eyes widened.

"What can we do for you?" he asked.

"I need to find whoever's in charge of this," she said.

"No one," he said. "Some of the units still have their commanders, but most went on the excursion a few days ago."

"You're not a Leader?" Xihu asked.

"I am, but I retired after the Blue Isle campaign." He patted his leg. "Nearly lost it in the Battle for Constant. The Healers fixed it, but I'm no longer capable of doing a forced march, even if I wanted to."

"So you're in charge, then."

"Not really." He swept a hand toward the five Fey behind him. "We were just discussing how we could prevent this ragtag group from becoming a mob."

"What's your name?" she asked.

"Nandar." One of the older naming systems. That surprised her.

"How was this group even assembled?"

"Voluntary. People from the palace were going door to

door asking, 'Would you like to serve in the Fey army tonight?'" He shook his head. "That's not how it was done in my day."

"Mine either," Xihu said.

"This new Black Queen doesn't seem to know what she's doing, does she?"

Xihu revised his age upward at least two decades. No one in his fifties would call a Black Queen who had been on the throne for fifteen years new unless he had lived a relatively long life.

"I think she knows better than most of us give her credit for."

"A mob isn't going to wage an effective operation."

"It is," Xihu said, "if your goal is the Black Heir."

He glanced at the river as if it had suddenly overflowed its banks.

"You saw it too, didn't you?" she said. "All that blood on the water. You saw it."

Nandar nodded. "I'm a minor Visionary, but I've been privileged to listen to the Powers once or twice. I've seen blood on this water since I was a little boy."

Then he was meant to be here. Xihu didn't like that.

"Do you really think she's trying to kill the Black Heir?" He ran a hand through his thick hair. "Does she know that he's on the ship?"

"It's his ship. She may say she doesn't know for sure, but I do. Where that ship is, Gift is." She didn't bother to tell this minor Visionary that if Gift wasn't on the ship, he was in Constant, where the other Infantry was headed.

"So if she claims she has an untrained army who got overzealous, there's no disproving her, right? The Powers'll let this go?"

"It's a gamble," Xihu said. "But it's probably a good one."

Nandar shook his head. "And I'll be a part of it."

"Not if you help me."

He looked at her. "How?"

"Inform these Fey that the Black Heir is on board. Tell them the penalty for killing a member of the Black Family."

"That might not stop some of the Foot Soldiers," he said. "They attack first and think later."

She knew that, and she had seen a lot of young Foot Soldiers who weren't battle trained. Most of them probably didn't know how to handle real blood lust yet. All they had learned was how to hold it back. When it was released, it would be very dangerous.

"Then you're going to have to take control of this mob," she said. "Make sure they understand the orders are to take the crew of the ship prisoner, not to sink it."

"I hadn't heard that order," he said.

"You're hearing it now."

"From a Shaman? You can't participate in military matters."

Her eyes narrowed. "I can participate in preventing Blood against Blood. Do you want to be a party to that?"

He shook his head.

"Then do as I say. Get this mob together."

Nandar scanned the area, and she could almost read his thoughts. He knew what an impossible task organizing these soldiers would be.

"What if it was supposed to be this way?" Nandar asked. "What if the Black Heir is supposed to die here?"

"Then he will die," Xihu said. "And maybe the rest of us will too."

CHAPTER SIXTY-TWO

*L*YNDRED SAT IN the center of the boat, the cool wood against her thighs, as she watched the *Tashka* disappear into its veil of fog. She felt her heart sink and wondered, for the first time, if she was up to this.

I hope so, Arianna said. *Because it's too late to change now.*

Lyndred started each time Arianna actually spoke. Lyndred hadn't experienced a Link, let alone had someone else inside her mind. It felt odd, as if her head had expanded slightly, as if it were a place she didn't really recognize.

Arianna had said that it was possible to block thoughts, but they weren't going to be together long enough for that to matter. So, for the next half-day, they would have to listen to each other.

Lyndred glanced at Con. He was at the stern of the boat, rowing for her, and Dash was at the bow. They were along for protection. When they got near the shore, they would don their cloaks and no one, not even Lyndred, would be able to see them. She would have to trust they were there.

Don't worry, Arianna said. *I'll help you through this.*

If Lyndred closed her eyes, she could actually see her cousin inside her mind. This Arianna was so different from the other two that Lyndred had met. Unlike the stone Arianna, this one had fluid movements. Unlike the Arianna that Rugad was pretending to be, this one had an innate grace. This Arianna was a beautiful woman and no one would have ever said that she looked cruel.

I've never done anything like this before. Lyndred had already learned that she didn't have to answer Arianna aloud to be heard.

I'm aware of that, Arianna said. *You'll have to listen to me if the time comes. Otherwise, just do as we instructed.*

Lyndred nodded, and then wondered if Arianna had sensed the movement.

Of course I do, Arianna said. *Now open your eyes. You're making me nervous.*

Lyndred opened her eyes. The morning was clear and calm and very cold. Precisely the kind of morning they didn't want, Gift had said as he helped her onto the ship. They had hoped for low clouds and a heavy rain, something that would discourage the troops waiting on Jahn's bank.

The northern shore wasn't that far. Lyndred could make out rocks and a muddy bank leading up to the road. That road went into Jahn. If no one helped them, they would be walking for two hours before they got to the palace. She hoped that they would find a way into the city proper that didn't require much walking.

Saving your strength? Arianna asked.

Lyndred started. She still wasn't used to having her most private thoughts overheard.

When Arianna had first entered Lyndred's mind, Lyndred had felt a strange relief. Then she had realized that the emotion she felt was not her own, but Arianna's. Arianna had said that she trusted Lyndred, but it wasn't until she heard Lyndred's thoughts and felt Lyndred's emotions that she actually understood why Lyndred was doing this.

Lyndred wondered how it had felt to be inside that stone body. It seemed strange to see it on the *Tashka,* empty, no soul inside it at all. The eyes were open, but they were all one color, like rest of the body.

Lyndred had looked until Arianna made her turn away.

"Not much farther," Con said.

Lyndred nodded. She reached for the small vial that Skya had given her. Skya, for all she professed to hate Warder's ways, had sent one of the Domestics to buy a small bag of supplies when they were in Constant—skin, bone, and blood, stored in a Warder's pouch. The Warder used those items to practice magic, or to enhance their magic.

Much as she had hated it, Skya had been using the bag to help her with the spells that everyone seemed to require of her. She had given Lyndred a vial of blood, not for magic, but for disguise.

Lyndred pulled off the stopper and winced at the smell. She shuddered at the idea of putting some of that blood on her skin.

Have Dash rip your clothing and put most of it on the fabric, if it bothers you that much, Arianna said.

Doesn't it bother you? Lyndred asked.

It's not my skin, Arianna said.

Lyndred took a deep breath, and stuck her finger in the vial. Then she started to put the blood on her face.

"No!" Con said. "That looks painted. Let me."

He put the oars up and let Dash propel the boat. Then Con took Lyndred's shirt and tore it down the sleeve. He poured some blood in the rip, sprinkled some on her pants, and then poured some more on his hand.

"What are you doing?" Lyndred asked

Con didn't answer her. Instead he flung the blood at her. It hit her full in the face. The stench was incredible. She gasped and shrieked and wiped at it with the back of her hand.

"Perfect," Con said, dipping his dirty hand in the water. "Now it looks as though you were near someone who bled all over you, and you tried to get rid of the blood. In an hour or so, that'll be dry, and you'll look just right."

She wasn't sure she liked his idea of just right, but she

didn't say so. Her skin crawled and she resisted the urge to stick her face in the water, and wash all the blood off.

"Better put on your cloak," Dash said from the front of the boat.

Con nodded and slipped his cloak on. Lyndred wouldn't have even known he was there except that the oars were back in the water. She saw the shadow of a figure at the stern, but only because she was looking for it. Otherwise she wouldn't have noticed at all.

She turned. Dash was putting on his cloak as well. He vanished too, leaving only a filmy shadow of himself as he continued rowing.

The boat scraped against rock.

"You're going to have to be the one to get out and pull us ashore," Con whispered. "Just in case anyone sees us."

"And we won't be able to give you verbal advice unless we're absolutely sure we're alone," Dash said. "You're just going to have to trust that we're beside you."

More faith. Apparently that was her lesson for this trip.

She got out of the boat, and shuddered as the icy water touched her legs. The river was waist deep here, deeper than she expected. Apparently, the boat had hit the rocks up front, not here in the center.

Her skin prickled, then went numb with the cold. Her breeches were so wet that they clung to her. She splashed forward, her boots slipping on the rocks, and she managed to keep one hand on the side of the boat as she walked to the front.

Then she took the pointed bow in her hands and tugged. The boat moved more easily than she expected, and she almost fell. She tugged again, digging her boots in the mud between some of the rocks, and the bottom scraped against rock.

The front part of the boat suddenly got lighter, and there was a splash in the water beside her. Then she felt hands brush hers. Dash had gotten out and was helping her.

There was another splash as Con got out. He sloshed toward the shore quickly, taking his first step in mud. She didn't see any of this, not really, just a shadowy figure, splashes, and a footprint.

Dash's hands stopped touching hers and the bottom of the boat slid back into the water. She glanced up. People were coming down the road.

She tugged the boat as hard as she could. She felt the weight of the boat in her back and arms, and she cursed herself for not doing much sword work while she was at the palace. She dragged the boat all the way to the mud, and secured it as best she could. It would probably get stolen, but they had all expected that. Gift had called it a small price to pay for this little ruse.

She staggered up the embankment, slipped again, and slid, landing sideways in the mud. It was cold and slimy and made her feel even worse.

Excellent, Arianna said. *The worse you look, the more believable your story.*

Well, she looked pretty awful. And she felt awful too. Weaker than she wanted to and more inexperienced than she had ever realized.

The people—a pair of Islanders—passed on the road above. They had glanced down once, seen that she was Fey, and continued as if her problems didn't matter to them.

She supposed they didn't.

They should, Arianna said, and Lyndred felt an alien fury. *I've worked hard to mix these communities together. How has Rugad managed to ruin that in less than a year?*

Lyndred didn't know, and at the moment, it was the least of her worries. She pulled herself out of the mud and onto the road. Then she wiped her filthy hands against her pants and stood.

She was already tired and thirsty. By the time she reached the palace, she'd be completely exhausted.

She'd have to be. Rugad would see through anything else.

CHAPTER SIXTY-THREE

*N*ANDAR HAD SPOKEN to the other Leaders, and they agreed that they had to make sure the battle plan was clear. They were spreading through the crowd of soldiers, trying to divide them into sections.

Nandar had already spoken to one group. Xihu had listened. He had tried to show them the importance of taking prisoners, but no one seemed to care. They felt that he had no right to change the orders of the Black Queen. Nandar had tried to explain that this was not a change of orders, but they weren't listening.

Xihu suspected this would happen all up and down the waterfront.

She had slipped away before Nandar had finished. What they needed was a Charmer, someone who could explain and sway. At first she thought of sending to the palace for DiPalmet, and then she realized that he might not even get the message. She would have to deliver it herself.

She was walking along the water's edge, past the first warehouse, listening to the heightened voices around her, the quarrels that were breaking out as the Leaders were trying to take control.

This wasn't any Fey army that Xihu recognized. This resembled the ragtag bands that had fought the Fey. The great Black Rulers would have been ashamed that their people had come to this. Even Xihu was. If this was a highly trained fighting force, they would listen to their Leaders. They wouldn't think that they knew best. They would be lusting for blood, but the lust would be under control.

Xihu lifted her robe above her boots and hurried a little faster. The quicker she brought DiPalmet here, the better off they would all be.

She felt a chill, suddenly, and smelled damp. The hair rose on the back of her neck. A change in the weather, only this one didn't feel natural.

Despite her hurry, she stopped and looked behind her. The first tendrils of a thick white fog were reaching toward her. The tendrils came from a fog bank that hovered near the mountains. The fog was just outside the harbor, and completely hid the river from view.

She felt bile rise in her throat, and she swallowed hard. That had to be the *Tashka*. Gift was coming in a cloud of fog. Had he been warned that there was an army here?

For a moment, she stood in place, feeling completely indecisive. The ship would be here quickly. Soon the army would be enveloped in fog.

Would they be smart enough to realize that the fog hid the ship they were planning to attack? Or would they think it a trick of the weather and disperse?

She hoped it would be the latter, but she couldn't guarantee it. Maybe the fog would buy her some time. Maybe it would allow her to get to the palace, find DiPalmet, and bring him back. Maybe he would be able to make his speech before these inexperienced soldiers began the mistake of their lives.

That was all she could hope for.

She clutched her robes in both hands and started to run, praying that she and DiPalmet would make it back before the fighting began.

CHAPTER SIXTY-FOUR

*G*IFT PACED THE deck. He felt trapped inside the bubble of fog. He wished he could see, and at the same time knew that seeing would compound his problems.

The Navigator said they were heading into the harbor. They had slowed down long before they had let Lyndred, Arianna, Dash, and Con off outside of Jahn. The ship would stop soon, and they would all find out if the army outside was fooled by the fog.

The Healers had brought Bridge on deck. He sat near the starboard side railing on a chair that kept his leg outstretched. He was so swaddled in blankets that Gift wondered how he could be comfortable.

Coulter had moved the bags of globes to the starboard side of the ship. He wasn't pacing. He was standing, hands threaded in front of him, as if keeping their power under control while waiting for the command.

Skya was getting the jewels from below. She had designed three wooden holders, like hand mirrors, only with the jewels in the center instead of glass. She had tied a string to each, measuring a hand's length. Bridge would hold the diamond and think of shattering walls. Skya would hold the emerald and think of narrowing the beam, and Gift would hold the heartstone and think only of Rugad.

Coulter had suggested using Nyeians, afraid that Gift's hand on the holder would cause the Blood, but Gift was willing to take the risk. He was gambling on a couple of things: that Skya was correct—the Visions were more manipulation than warning; that the Powers wouldn't see Rugad as a living being since Rugad was a construct, and, as a construct, wouldn't be part of the Blood.

If Gift was wrong, he was risking everything. But he wasn't tied to that construct by Blood. Besides, Coulter was holding the actual weapon, and the weapon was not going to be used to kill anyone—just to destroy an invasive magic. It was exactly this sort of hairsplitting that Rugad used all the time. Gift only hoped it would work for him.

As soon as Skya brought the jewels up, they would be ready. Now all they had to do was wait for Lyndred to send Bridge the signal.

Gift stopped beside Coulter, careful to stay clear of the globes.

"I was wondering," Coulter said. "Do we need to get rid of the fog to send out this light?"

"I don't think so," Gift said, "but the moment we do send out that light, we pinpoint our location."

"We're going to need a way to defend ourselves."

Gift shook his head. "I need you on those globes. There's no guarantee they'll work for anyone but an Islander."

"Then we should have kept Con and Dash here," Coulter said. "I might be more useful defending us."

"I don't think this will take very long. When we're through, you can drop the globe and defend us until Arianna gives the order to stop the fighting."

"If she can give that order," Coulter said.

Gift sighed. He wasn't going to listen to Coulter's pessimism. Not now.

Skya left the deckhouse and started across the deck toward them. Her pregnancy was beginning to show. Her stomach, normally flat, was rounded. Her breasts were fuller, and the extra weight she was starting to put on showed in her cheeks. He thought it made her even more beautiful, but she didn't. She wouldn't even share his cabin anymore, saying that she needed to separate her heart from his.

He had tried to talk with her the night before, but she wouldn't discuss their relationship. Not until this fight was over.

He wished she had stayed in Constant. Then, at least, he would have known she was safe. Instead, she was risking her life and the baby's life helping him get rid of Rugad.

She handed him his heartstone. The black gem winked as if it had a life of its own. He held the polished wood handle and shivered.

This was their only chance.

"I don't know Islander magic," Skya said, her hand brushing his. "But if it's anything like Fey magic, you'll need to take a mental precaution."

His grip on the handle tightened. "What kind of precaution?"

"Think only of Rugad. If you think of Arianna or of him taking over Arianna or of him looking like Arianna, you risk directing this beam at her."

"And, by association, Lyndred."

Skya nodded. "This is very dangerous magic we're tampering with."

"I know."

"Then be careful." Her dark eyes met his, and in them, he could see concern. But after only a moment, she broke the gaze and headed toward Bridge. Gift supposed she was giving him a similar speech.

The Navigator signaled him. They were inside the harbor and had dropped anchor. The Sprites were making the fog even thicker to protect all of them.

He could hear the rumble of voices, speaking Fey. There was an army out there, on the banks of the river, waiting to kill him. A Fey army.

He hoped his own people remembered to stay as quiet as they could. He hoped Coulter wouldn't panic. He hoped the jewels would work as Matt said they would.

He hoped many things.

Most of all, he hoped that the plan would work.

CHAPTER SIXTY-FIVE

*I*SLANDERS WERE KIND. Lyndred hadn't expected that, not in the middle of this crisis. But the only person who didn't avert his eyes and keep walking when he saw her stumbling, muddy and bloody, through the streets of Jahn, was an Islander farmer who had dropped off supplies on the east end of the city. He had pulled his wagon over, offered her a ride, and didn't say a word when she seemed to tilt his wagon more than her slight build suggested she might have.

He didn't blink when she told him she needed to go to the palace, although he did ask her if she wanted medical attention, saying his sister was good with herbs and poultices and she lived just south of Jahn. Lyndred had refused, but had thanked him. He had offered twice more before letting her out about three blocks from the palace.

"You'll have to walk the rest," he had said. "There's some military to-do going on up there that's tying up the streets."

The military to-do was the arrival of the ship. She knew that, even though the nice Islander didn't. She could see the fog through the buildings on her left, big rolling white clouds that seemed to fill the center of Jahn.

Arianna had been silent throughout the journey, for which Lyndred had been grateful. She was afraid she'd reply verbally to Arianna. Arianna respected that, and helped her by saying nothing at all.

But Lyndred could feel Arianna's growing nervousness. Or maybe it was Lyndred's own. Her stomach was jumping and she felt colder than she thought she would. The river water had dried in muddy crusts, making her clothing feel heavier than before.

Do you think Rugad would be at the river? Arianna asked.

Lyndred felt the nervousness increase. Now she knew it wasn't hers, but Arianna's. *No,* she thought. *I think he would want to stay as far away from the so-called mistake as he possibly could. That way, he could say it was a misunderstood order or something.*

I was thinking the same thing, Arianna said. But obviously, she had been worrying about the other plan.

If he is there, we'll find out at the palace, Lyndred thought. *Then we can go down there.*

All right.

Arianna remained silent after that. Lyndred staggered the last three blocks, weaving in case someone was watching her. When she reached the main road, she was stunned to find it empty.

They must already be at the river, Arianna thought.

It looked as though everyone were at the river. The storefronts were empty, the houses tightly closed up. There was no one on the streets at all. The Islander could have brought them here, and hadn't even known it.

Lyndred crossed the street, tripping purposely on a cobblestone, and catching herself before she fell. There were a dozen guards by the closed palace gate, and there were more on top of the wall. They were preparing for Gift in every way they could.

This isn't good, Arianna said.

Lyndred agreed, but she was going to finish this. The guards saw her at the same time, turning their heads in unison. She ran toward them, a broken, ragged run that she had seen a Nyeian prisoner use once. She didn't pick up her feet, but dragged them along as if they hurt.

She tripped again on the cobblestone and sprawled facedown. For a long moment, she lay on the cold stone, her heart pounding.

"Lyndred?" One of the guards had come forward, just as she had hoped. He crouched beside her and put a hand on her shoulder. "Lyndred?"

She moaned.

"Are you all right?"

She made herself look up. The guard was young, Infantry, and good-looking. She had winked at him a few times, and flirted with him once or twice. But she had never learned his name.

"I—need to see Arianna." Lyndred made herself speak huskily as if she hadn't used her voice in a long time.

"I can't let you do that." The guard looked distressed. "I have specific orders not to let you, your cousin, or your father inside."

"My father's dead," Lyndred whispered, the lie feeling strange, as if by telling it she might be jeopardizing her father's life.

A frown creased the guard's forehead. At least he was listening.

"What're you doing?" another guard shouted.

"Just a moment," the first guard said.

She pulled herself up and grabbed his arm. "Please let me see Arianna. I have to tell her what Gift has planned."

"Are you alone?" the guard asked.

She nodded.

He touched the blood on her face. "What happened to you?"

"I escaped," she said.

"But this is blood."

"My father's."

The guard put a hand beneath her arm and helped her

up. She stumbled against him, and he put his arm around her, pulling her tight. She let him carry most of her weight, and she limped a little with her left foot for good measure.

"What are you doing?" the second guard asked again.

"Send someone inside," the first guard said. "Tell Arianna that her cousin is here, claiming that Bridge is dead, and that she knows what Gift's plans are. Tell her that it looks real to us."

The second guard peered at Lyndred. He checked her eyes for gold flecks and her chin for a Shifter's mark. He was more efficient than the first guard. "I guess that it's not our decision. You'll have to wait here."

Lyndred didn't answer him. She let herself slip out of the first guard's grasp and down against the wall. She leaned on it as if she didn't have enough strength to hold herself upright. But she listened as the guards gave orders to another guard, instructing him on how to talk to the Black Queen, and then she heard footsteps hurry away.

If this doesn't work, Arianna said, *we'll try to go in through one of the tunnels.*

The first guard crouched beside her. "What can I get you?"

She shook her head.

"When was the last time you ate anything?"

"I don't remember," she said.

"Well, let me see what I can find."

He left her, and came back a moment later with some fresh bread and a mug full of chilled water. Lyndred took the mug first and drank as if she hadn't had any liquid in days. Then she wiped her mouth with the back of her hand, and noted that her skin came away filthy. She shuddered, and handed him the mug.

He took it. "Some food too?"

Her stomach was too knotted for food. "Maybe in a while."

Then she heard footsteps behind her, and the guard stood. Apparently, the messenger was back from Rugad. Lyndred couldn't overhear what was being said, but soon the guard returned.

"The Black Queen has agreed to see you.

The Black Queen, Arianna said snidely.

"Thank you," Lyndred said.

He helped her up. She leaned against him again. Then he led her through the doors that led into the Great Hall.

The palace smelled faintly of smoke. Several of the swords were down and the stone was charred near the door. Arianna seemed startled by the changes.

The guard didn't take Lyndred to the North Tower as she expected. Instead, they went to the South Tower. The smell of smoke was fainter here.

The fire damaged the North Tower, Arianna said. *Remember?*

Lyndred had forgotten. She hadn't paid a lot of attention to the details of Matt's story, thinking, at the time, that it had little to do with her.

She made sure she slipped once on the stone stairs. The guard caught her and held her even tighter as he helped her the rest of the way up. But she wasn't enjoying his touch the way she normally would. She wasn't sure if that was because of Arianna's influence or because of the loss of Ace. And fortunately for their peace of mind, Arianna had no comment about the change.

They reached the top of the stairs. The door was open. Lyndred could feel Arianna tense. Lyndred tried not to let that have an effect on her.

The guard called out that they had arrived, not the normal protocol at all, but he seemed to be afraid to let Lyndred go. Another voice, one Arianna didn't recognize but Lyndred did, echoed the announcement.

DiPalmet.

Who's that? Arianna asked.

Lyndred let her memories of DiPalmet answer the question. The guard helped her inside. She collapsed against him, trying not to look like a threat.

The South Tower had been set up like the North Tower: tables, chairs, the clean floor-to-ceiling windows. Lyndred got a sense of disgust and a brief memory—of being led away from the towers by the enemy—that didn't belong to her.

Then she concentrated on what was before her. A woman, her hair chopped off, her face hard and masculine, stood, legs apart, and hands clasped behind her back.

I don't look like that! Arianna said.

And she didn't. But Rugad in Arianna's body did.

"So," Rugad said. "You're back."

I am! Arianna said softly.

"I am," Lyndred echoed. Her heart was pounding.

"You look terrible," Rugad said.

"I—" She was having trouble concentrating on his words. "I—I've come a long way."

Send now, Arianna said.

Daddy! Lyndred screamed in her own mind. *We're here! Start! Start now!*

She felt the words circle out of her head and travel down a tunnel of light. She was dizzy and Rugad was looking at her strangely. The guard continued to hold her up.

But she had done it.

She was here.

And they could begin.

CHAPTER SIXTY-SIX

*T*HEY'RE IN," BRIDGE said.

Coulter felt the muscles in his shoulder tighten. He had been worried that they wouldn't make it and afraid that they would. Now they were in. If he wanted to save Arianna again, he had to act.

Skya sat on the ground in front of Bridge and held up her jewel. Gift sat in front of her and held up his. Bridge tied his string to Skya's jewel, and Skya tied hers to Gift's.

They were ready.

It was up to Coulter.

His palms were sweating. He remembered how it felt holding these globes before, how they turned warm in his hands, how they illuminated everything.

He remembered the screaming.

"Let's go, Coulter." Gift sounded calm, but they both knew he was not.

Coulter reached down and pulled open a bag. He picked up the first globe by its sides and immediately light flared from it. The light headed directly for Bridge, who moved the jewel closer to his head than Coulter would have wanted, almost like a protection.

The light missed Bridge, and hit the diamond. Bridge closed his eyes, as if in relief, and then the light traveled from the diamond to the emerald. Skya stared at it, mesmerized, as the light moved through the emerald to the heartstone.

Gift wasn't looking at Coulter or at the jewels. Instead, he was staring intently at the light beam which was now a hard, brilliant white instead of the greenish black he expected. It cut through the fog like a beacon in darkness, and Coulter heard voices rise from outside.

The ship had been discovered. They wouldn't have much time.

He glanced down at his hands. The light from the globe was so intense that he saw his bones through his skin. The globe was getting hot. Beads of sweat were running down his face already, and they had just started.

The light remained steady. He had no idea how much power was in one of these globes, nor did he know how much power they would need. Last time they had been trying to kill an army. This time, they were trying to burn a construct out of Arianna's brain.

He hoped it wouldn't take as much time.

At least the light wasn't hurting Gift or Skya or Bridge. There were no screams from outside, so it probably wasn't hurting that standing army either. Coulter just hoped the light was getting through walls, as it was supposed to, and reaching Rugad.

He uncovered another globe with his foot, bent over, and picked the globe up with one hand. Then he dropped the first globe while grabbing the second so that the light would be unbroken.

It wasn't quite. There was a small break, less than an instant, and he hoped it wasn't enough to cause a problem.

The dropped globe rolled toward Bridge. Coulter's breath caught. He hoped the globe wouldn't hit Bridge. Coulter had no idea what it would do to him.

Bridge didn't even seem to notice it rolling toward him. Coulter kept one hand on the globe he was using and waved the other hand at the rolling globe, pushing it away from all of the Fey gathered at the side of the ship.

He would have to be more careful next time. He would have to make sure no one even got close to being hit.

Coulter put both hands back on the second globe. The light was still flowing from it. He could feel that light like the heat from a fire, only mixed in with this feeling was a sense of great power.

He swallowed hard. This was fighting, but not fighting— rather like taking over someone from the inside.

The light was burning a hole through the fog. No matter how hard the Sprites tried to cover it, the hole still remained. Magic against magic. The strongest power always trumped.

He supposed it would be that way with Rugad. If Rugad's construct was more powerful than the Islander magic, he would win. He would have Arianna's body and the Black Throne forever.

A thunk caught his attention. An arrow wobbled in the railing of the ship, not far from Gift's face. Gift didn't seem to notice—he couldn't notice. He had to concentrate on Rugad.

Coulter couldn't do anything either. Most of his magic took his hands, and he didn't dare let go of the globes.

He screamed for one of the Sailors to find a way to protect Gift, Skya, and Bridge. The Sailor nodded and gestured toward another Sailor as he ran toward that side of the deck.

But Coulter knew that, no matter what they did, it wouldn't be enough. The light that was supposed to destroy Rugad was leading his soldiers right to the *Tashka*.

And Gift.

CHAPTER SIXTY-SEVEN

*Y*OU'VE COME A long way?" Arianna said scornfully. "Just how far is that?"

DiPalmet watched her. He knew that she and Lyndred had had a falling out, but he had expected more compassion from Arianna. It was obvious that Lyndred couldn't stand on her own. She was covered in dried blood. Her clothing was ripped and filthy, and she was visibly exhausted.

"Please," Lyndred said. "Daddy's dead."

"So you've said, but I see no evidence of that."

DiPalmet crossed his arms. Was Arianna afraid that Lyndred was a spy? Or going to try to hurt her? It was fairly obvious that Lyndred wasn't in any condition to hurt anyone.

"He died on the Cardidas. I had to get off the ship."

Something reflected off the fog outside. DiPalmet saw it, but he doubted anyone else did. Arianna had her back to the south windows, and Lyndred was looking directly at her. The fog looked as if it were being lit from within.

"So you're coming back here?"

"I thought you would want to know what he planned."

"How would you know if he hated you enough to kill your father and go after you?"

The light seemed to be getting closer. DiPalmet took a step forward, thinking perhaps that he should tell Arianna, but she gave him a warning look.

"I think he wanted me to tell you," Lyndred said softly.

She seemed vague and distracted, almost as if she were having trouble concentrating. Arianna seemed to notice that too.

"What are you doing here? Really?" Arianna asked.

The light rose up to the window and came through. It was a single straight beam that seemed to have the power of the wind behind it. DiPalmet had seen nothing like it before.

"Arianna!" he cried.

She turned and the light hit her square in the forehead. She made a slight squealing sound and staggered backward, trying to hold her hands in front of her face.

"Lyndred," she managed. "A Shadowlands! Put me in a Shadowlands!"

Her voice was shaking. She fell to her knees. The light seemed to bore right through her forehead. Her eyes were closed, but DiPalmet could see the shape of them through the lid. He could see her skull through her skin.

He shuddered. She was right. A Shadowlands would protect her from the light. "Help her," he said to Lyndred.

"No." Lyndred took a step forward. She glanced nervously at the light. It was directed toward Arianna, and no one else.

The guard touched her arm. "Help her," he said, as if he didn't understand the change in her.

"No," Lyndred said again.

"What are you doing to her?" DiPalmet asked.

"Nothing." Lyndred stopped beside Arianna and looked down at her. The light illuminated the filth on Lyndred's clothing.

Arianna had fallen to the floor. She was crawling away from the window. DiPalmet went to her side and grabbed her arms, pulling her where she needed to go. He felt the light. It was hot.

"Behind. The. Column." Each word seemed like an effort.

He dragged her behind the column, but the light went right through it.

"How do I protect her from this?" he asked.

"You don't," Lyndred said.

The guard put a hand on her shoulder. "Make this stop."

"I'm not doing it," she said. "Isn't that obvious?"

"Then why are you here?" DiPalmet asked.

"To help Arianna," Lyndred said.

"Then help her!" he snapped.

"It's not time yet," Lyndred said.

The air was filled with a slight burning smell.

"This is killing her," DiPalmet said.

"Not her," Lyndred said. "It's not killing Arianna."

DiPalmet was becoming desperate. Arianna was leaning against him, barely conscious now. "Yes it is."

"No," Lyndred said. "Arianna's fine. The light's not touching her. It's killing Rugad. And I'm supposed to watch until he's good and dead."

CHAPTER SIXTY-EIGHT

*G*IFT WAS CONCENTRATING on Rugad as he had once felt him, a presence within his own mind. He remembered how Rugad had seen himself, as an older man with a young face, a face that looked like Gift's except that it was dark—dark hair, dark eyes, dark skin. Much darker than he had ever been. Gift focused on that young image and that old person, and sent the light directly to it.

Bits of the light fell on his hands, burning him. He wondered if Skya felt the same thing. He hoped it wouldn't hurt her or the child within her. But he could say nothing. Do nothing. Not yet.

He was dimly aware of the activity around him. Sailors putting up canvas, wood, anything. Voices shouting, arrows hitting the deck around him. He couldn't move. He didn't dare move. He didn't dare break his concentration.

Again he focused on the image. Coulter had described it in the same way: the creature he had seen inside of Arianna's mind had been a young man with Rugad's soul. A young man who had looked startlingly like Gift, the young man Gift would have been if he had been born to two Fey parents.

He opened his eyes for a brief instant. The light continued to flow through the heartstone and into the swirling fog. He could imagine the light flowing over the entire city and going through the palace walls, finding Rugad, and piercing him, the way it had once pierced him on a hillside. Only now he might not have the defenses to deal with it.

Now it might kill him.

Gift closed his eyes again, and as he did, something struck him in the arm. Intense pain burned through him, and he felt the wooden handle slip through his fingers.

He was losing the heartstone.

He opened his eyes, and caught the stone with his other hand, not breaking the connection. The light continued to flow.

Then he looked at what was causing the pain.

An arrow stuck out of his right bicep, blood oozing around it.

The wound could have been worse, but he knew this was bad enough. He had to keep concentrating, had to keep directing all of his energy toward Rugad, no matter how long it took.

No matter how much this wound drained him.

He had to stay conscious. He had to stay aware.

And he couldn't do anything about the arrows that were hitting the deck around him. The best defense was holding this stone, making sure that Rugad died.

Even if it cost Gift his life.

CHAPTER SIXTY-NINE

*D*IPALMET HAD HIS arms wrapped around Arianna's body as if he could protect it from the light. The light flowed through the column and directly into the brain, destroying Rugad.

At least, Lyndred hoped it was destroying Rugad. There was no way to tell. Rugad wasn't speaking anymore, and the body wasn't moving.

We can't let it go on too long, Arianna said.

We can't stop it too soon, Lyndred thought. *We can't leave any of him in there.*

But how to know when he was really and truly gone? The eyes looked empty, but that could be an act. He could be waiting for Arianna to get back inside, and then do something to her there.

Let me see the face, Arianna said.

Lyndred stepped closer. The eyes were half open, their blue—once so intimidating—was bright, flaring from the light within. The skin was even lighter than it had been before. It was as if every part of that body were being invaded by the pure white light being sent from the ship.

"I don't know what you're doing," DiPalmet said, "but stop. She's dying."

It certainly looked that way.

We can't kill the body, Arianna said. Lyndred could feel her panic. *If we do, I'm lost.*

I know, Lyndred thought.

The panic grew worse. *Don't do this to me. Gift won't let you.*

I'm not, Lyndred thought. *I have to wait until the right moment.*

If she could recognize the right moment.

The guard stepped up behind her. "Do you want me to take her out of here?" he asked DiPalmet.

"I don't know," DiPalmet said. "Not if she stops this."

The eyes went from glassy to empty. The head turned to one side as if nothing held the muscles in place anymore. The arms drooped, then slid to the floor.

Nothing controlled the body. It was obvious now. Whatever had been inside was gone.

He's dead. Lyndred, he's dead!

If he's not, Lyndred thought, *can you kill him when you get inside?*

If he's not dead, he's got to be wounded, Arianna said. *I can always leave, and we can do this again.*

That sounded sensible to Lyndred. She took a deep breath.

Daddy! she thought with all the power that she had. *Daddy, make the light stop. We think he's dead!*

CHAPTER SEVENTY

STOP!" BRIDGE SHOUTED. "Stop! They think we've killed him."

"Think?" Coulter said, not willing to let go of the globe. There was a pile of burned-out globes at his feet. His right arm ached from the strain. "Shouldn't we wait until they know?"

"How can they know?" Bridge asked. "They can't until Arianna can go in!"

Coulter let go of the globe. It bounced off the others, then clanged on deck, and rolled toward the Fey at the end again. The sudden loss of light made him blink hard. He felt dizzy, as if something had been pulled from him.

The ship was rocking oddly, as if a wind had come up and created waves. More arrows hit the deck, and there was a muffled cry. He looked toward it. One of the Sprites fell backward.

The fog thinned.

"Coulter!" Skya shouted. "Gift's wounded."

How had he missed that? The ache he felt in his arm, the

exhaustion he was feeling, was that what Gift had been experiencing?

He hurried toward them. Skya had her arms around Gift. She was cradling him. There was fear in her eyes. For the first time, Coulter realized that Skya loved Gift. She just never showed it.

Gift's face was ashen, and his sleeve was covered with blood. "Did we do it?"

"We think so," Coulter said.

Arrows continued to clatter around them.

"We have to get somewhere safer than this," Bridge said.

A dripping wet Foot Soldier pulled himself up the side of the ship and over the railing. One of Rugad's soldiers. He reached for Skya and she kicked at him, her boots connecting with his stomach, as his long nails shredded her pants. Coulter grabbed him, and flung him back.

Suddenly more Foot Soldiers were on the railing. They must have swum from the shore toward the light.

"Get our soldiers from below!" Coulter shouted. "Get them now."

He flicked his fingers at each of the Foot Soldiers, using a magical push to send them backward into the river. That wouldn't hold them for long, but at least it wouldn't kill them. Or it wouldn't kill all of them.

Gift was saying something. The fog was becoming so thin that Coulter thought he could see the shore. The Sprites were still gathered in their circle, but the Foot Soldier he had pulled away from Skya was grabbing one of them, reaching for her head and—

Coulter sent a bolt of fire at him, and the Foot Soldier screamed. Then Coulter shoved him as well, and he toppled against the rail, alight, but without enough momentum to fall. One of the Sailors lifted the Foot Soldier's legs and toppled him overboard.

Arrows were falling in a wide pattern. They no longer had the hole in the fog to shoot at but they knew the general area.

Gift's lips were moving, but Coulter couldn't understand what he was saying.

"Move the ship!" Skya shouted. "He's saying that we must move the ship!"

Of course. Until Arianna got her body back and could give orders. Coulter turned toward the Navigator. "Get your Sailors in position. We've got to raise anchor now!"

The ship was rocking again. How many Foot Soldiers were out there?

Their own Foot Soldiers were coming up from below and rushing the railings, getting in the way of the Sailors. The entire deck was chaos.

It would be up to him. It was always up to him.

Coulter closed his eyes and swept the sides of the ship, severing any part of any Fey touching the outside of the ship below the deck level.

Screams surrounded them, followed by splashes.

He opened his eyes. Skya's gaze met his, troubled.

"Go!" Coulter said to the Navigator. "Go!"

CHAPTER SEVENTY-ONE

I'M GOING THROUGH *the Link,* Arianna said.

Lyndred wasn't sure how they would do that. She hadn't been certain on this point from the beginning.

Arianna's body was lying before them, the mouth slack, the head tilted back. DiPalmet was making a soft sound in his throat, almost like a keening.

The light had stopped only a moment before. The guard was kneeling beside the body, hands above it as if he didn't know what to do.

Touch me, Arianna said.

At first, Lyndred didn't understand what she was saying. Then Arianna sent her a picture. Lyndred nodded, and reached down, touching the body's hands.

They felt lifeless.

Hurry! Arianna said.

I'm touching her, Lyndred thought.

There should be a Link here. You said you had a Link!

I said I thought *I had a Link,* Lyndred answered defensively.

"What are you doing?" DiPalmet said to her.

"I'm trying to save her."

"How can you do that? You're a Visionary."

Find me the Link! Arianna said.

Lyndred closed her eyes, saw those few moments when Arianna—the person she had thought was Arianna—had looked at her with amusement or compassion. And a small door formed at the edge of Lyndred's mind.

Arianna—the real Arianna—ran for that door and pulled it open before Lyndred could stop her.

Then hands grabbed Lyndred's shoulder and yanked her back. "You can't touch her." It was the guard's voice. "You killed her."

Lyndred opened her eyes. Nothing had moved in the body in front of her. Nothing had changed.

"You saw me," Lyndred said. "I didn't send that light. It's not within my powers. You know that. You both know that."

"Then what were you trying to do?" DiPalmet said.

"I'm trying to Link with her," Lyndred said.

The body still hadn't moved, and Arianna wasn't talking to her inside her own mind. Had Arianna vanished, then? Lyndred couldn't tell.

Had Arianna gone through the wrong Link?

Lyndred couldn't tell that either.

"What would Linking with her do?" DiPalmet asked.

"It would save her. You have to let me go!"

"How did you know this would happen?" the guard asked.

"You know how," Lyndred snapped. "I told you. I told you I knew what Gift was going to do to her."

They both recoiled as if she had struck them.

"Now let me help her before she dies!"

DiPalmet studied her. "What were you saying about Rugad?"

"I don't have time to explain," Lyndred said. "Either help me or get out of my way."

DiPalmet moved. "I'm sorry."

"Save it," Lyndred said. "You'll be more than sorry if something happens to her because of your stupidity."

Then she took Arianna's hand back in her own. The hand was actually clammy. And it still felt lifeless. Lyndred wondered if there would be a heartbeat. She didn't want to try to find one.

She closed her eyes again.

Arianna? she thought. *Are you still here?*

Arianna was gone and the door was still open. Lyndred was alone in her own mind. She walked up to the Link door and looked through it.

And saw nothing except light.

CHAPTER SEVENTY-TWO

*A*RIANNA STEPPED INTO her own mind and closed the door behind her.

It was dark inside her brain and it smelled faintly of burned flesh. Black ropes, crisped and burned to nearly nothing, hung around her, and on all sides, she saw blasted areas where walls had once been.

Rugad. He had been threaded all through her.

She touched one of the destroyed walls. Behind some of the blackness was pink flesh. Hers.

It was as if she were in a house in which all the contents had burned, even the tapestries on the walls, but the walls remained. Damaged, but they were there.

Still, she moved slowly. She knew that this part of his construct was gone, but she wasn't sure if the rest was left. She followed the burned-out trail deeper into herself, down to the core.

Years ago, she had taken a small baby into that core, and built a room for him so that he could grow. She was afraid to go there, afraid to see what he had done.

The deeper she went inside herself, the more she could

feel him. There was residue of pain here. The stench of burning flesh grew worse, and the ropy blackness had a viscous quality that felt like blood.

Had they, in saving her, destroyed her body? Was she, except for this essential part of herself, dead? Would she have to live forever inside that Golem's body, unable to be the woman she had once been? She wouldn't be able to tell until she reached that center, and reintegrated with herself.

If she could.

She closed her eyes and sent herself to the very center of herself. Then she opened her eyes, and saw the room where she had once lived.

It had been torn apart. All her secret things, her dreams and wishes and memories, had been thrown in a corner. She couldn't tell what Rugad had done to the rest of the room because the inner wall had exploded outward.

She stepped over the rubble and looked inside. The inner room was the one she had made for the baby. It was the one that had become Rugad's. It was now a large crater, as if a giant fireball had been tossed inside it.

There was nothing left of Rugad. Nothing at all.

There was barely anything left of her.

She would have to rebuild everything, reorder everything, repair all parts of herself. And she wasn't sure where she could start.

Arianna?

The voice was faint, so faint she could barely hear it, yet it sounded like someone shouting. Rugad? Please, no, it couldn't be Rugad.

Arianna, are you still alive? Please answer me, Arianna.

It was Lyndred.

I'm fine, Arianna sent.

No you're not. I think your body is dying.

In this kind of shape, with all of these problems, that was possible. She was going to have to reintegrate herself without repairing anything.

Or she was going to have to let this body die.

Arianna? Arianna, please hurry.

She stared at the destruction, the ropy bloody mess, then

she walked over to the corner where Rugad had tossed everything that belonged to her. She picked up a painting of Coulter—not as he really looked, but as he saw himself, a tall Fey with blond hair and blue eyes. She ran her finger across the surface, tracing the brushstrokes. He was beautiful either way.

Then she set the painting aside and found the portrait of her father. His beloved, lost face, smiling at her as he often had when he approved of her.

Arianna?

She missed him so much. She missed his advice and counsel. And if she left this body, she might not have this portrait. She might lose some of her memories.

She would lose even more of herself.

Please hurry.

Then she looked at the ruined walls. But it would be so painful. She wasn't sure she was ready for this kind of pain. But it was the only choice. Best to get it over with.

She slipped her hand into the wall behind the memories, and then she slid back into herself.

Her brain hurt. Her body ached. Her lungs were on fire. She hadn't had a breath in a long time. She took in a mouthful of air, and then opened her eyes.

Lyndred was looking down on her. The girl was a fright, dried blood matting her hair, mud all over her face. DiPalmet was behind her, looking terrified, and the guard was behind him, seeming overwhelmed.

"Arianna?" Lyndred asked. "Are you all right?"

No, she wanted to say. She had never been in this kind of pain in her life. It hurt to think, and the logical connections, the way she used to get from one part of her brain to another, weren't working right.

Still, she had to find the way to control everything. If only she were able to fight the pain.

"Arianna?"

"Bring in the army." Her voice was a whisper. The words were in Islander, but they were drawn out. Her tongue was having difficulty moving; her lips were not working properly. "Call off the attack on Gift."

"But Arianna—" DiPalmet started.

"Now!" She tried to yell, but she spoke no louder than she had originally.

"Yes, ma'am." He stood.

"Get me a Healer," she said.

"Yes, ma'am."

"And when my brother comes here, let him and Coulter in to see me." Each word was an effort.

"But Arianna, he tried to kill you."

She made herself look at Lyndred, praying Lyndred would understand what she was trying to do. "Was it Gift who held that light?"

"Of course not," Lyndred said. "You—"

"See?" Arianna said to DiPalmet. "Let him up here. This family can't fight each other. We don't dare fight."

He stared at her for a long moment, and then he turned around and left.

"See that he does what I asked," she said to Lyndred.

"Yes, I will." Lyndred squeezed her hand. "I'm so glad . . ."

But Arianna missed the rest of it. She closed her eyes and let the pain take her away.

CHAPTER SEVENTY-THREE

*T*HE *TASHKA* WAS gone, taking the fog with it. The fighting had stopped long before the order to cease had come via a Wisp, who told Xihu, Nandar, and the other Leaders. The little war was over, as strangely as it had begun.

Xihu stood at the water's edge. She knew that something momentous had happened here, something she hadn't understood. The Wisp had no answers except to say that Arianna had called off the fight and wanted to see her brother. Xihu had asked if Arianna planned to kill Gift herself, and the Wisp had given her a strange look.

She's too weak, the Wisp had said. *She might have died.*

So the light was an attack against her, but what kind of attack? And how had it changed her mind?

Xihu was sure she would find out when she went back to the palace. All that mattered was that war had been averted. The Blood against Blood had stopped.

The sun was out, thin and cold. She had never been so happy to see the sun in her entire life. The fog had been thick and unnatural. It had hidden the fighting from view, in some ways making the hideous even uglier by keeping it out of sight.

But the remains of it were in front of her, the arrows on the surface, the bodies floating on the water, the charred bits of flesh on the crest of a wave.

And then she focused on the Cardidas. It was red. It was always red. But not like this.

There was blood floating on top of it. A slick of blood, still fresh, from all the shattered bodies, all the destroyed lives. The blood frothed as tiny waves created by the wind beat their way toward shore.

This was Gift's Open Vision. This was the blood she had seen, flowing beneath everything.

She stared at the blood, and thought of all the sacrifices, and was glad that things hadn't been worse.

THE BLACK KING

[One Week Later]

CHAPTER SEVENTY-FOUR

*C*OULTER HAD TO help Arianna into the Roca's Cave. She hadn't been inside the cave in fifteen years, not since the day she had become Black Queen.

The cave looked different than she remembered. It was smaller, the red floor still startling, even though she knew how the change had happened. The cave was warmer than she remembered too, and the white ceiling even brighter.

The entire cave smelled of fresh water. She had forgotten that too, along with the soothing sound of the burbling fountain below.

"Are you all right?" Coulter asked.

He wanted to know if she was comfortable being inside the cave. She didn't answer him. Being comfortable or not wasn't relevant. What really mattered was that she was here, and that they were going to try.

There had been so much to do after they took the palace back. So many dead and wounded, so many lives shattered. Gift had lost a lot of blood, but it became clear very fast that he would live.

Arianna wanted the Healers to concentrate on the injured Fey, but they focused on her first. She couldn't stop them.

They said that no magic would heal the damage the Lights of Midday had caused inside of her brain. Rugad had woven his personality all through her, like a black thread in the middle of an all-white skein. In order to remove the black thread, the Lights had had to destroy the skein.

Now she had no magic of her own—except Vision, which was somehow tied to her and not to her body. Her ability to Shift was gone, but so were some of her nonmagical abilities, like her ability to walk. She would have to relearn everything, like a baby.

It was only her own determination, the Healers told her, that had enabled her to speak, that same determination that had allowed her to speak rapidly as a Golem instead of slowly the way Sebastian did.

Gift had suggested that she assume her Golem's body again at least until they figured out a way to repair this one. She had rejected that idea. Much as she hated the way this body had been injured, she still preferred it to skin of stone. She could feel Coulter's strong arm against her back—the pressure of it, the texture of his skin against the fabric of her gown, the heat from his body beside hers.

When he kissed her—and he had kissed her when he found her alive and in her own body again—she could taste him. She liked the feeling of air in her lungs and the way her heartbeat felt within her chest. All of the sensations of being alive belonged to this body, not the Golem's body. If she ever had to return to that, she would see it as a defeat.

She suspected she could repair her mind, bit by tiny bit, with years of concentrated work. But that would mean neglecting her duties as a ruler, and she couldn't do that. She had to try something else.

"Do you still want to do this?" Coulter asked. "It's a great risk."

She knew that. The magic in this cave was Islander magic, and hers was—had been—Fey. The magic in here could kill her.

That had been the risk from the beginning.

"I'm half Islander," she said with more conviction than she felt. "This should work."

Coulter took a deep breath. "I'll be willing to help you. I'll be at your side from now on. I'll help you with all you need to do in Jahn so that you can continue your rule—"

"No," she said.

He stared at her. She could see the hurt behind his eyes. What she wanted to tell him was that taking the least risky way was usually his method, not hers. She didn't want to depend on his magic. Even though her Vision remained, everything else was gone. She didn't want to live that way unless she had no other choice.

Here, she had a choice.

The Words, at least according to Matt, said that anyone who drank from the fountain became like God. Gift said that the Place of Power in the Eccrasian Mountains also had a spring running through it. Fey history said that the Fey had no magic until they went into the Place of Power.

It might have been as simple as taking a drink.

It might have been more complicated than that.

She was going to find out.

Coulter's grip around her tightened. "Holy water kills Fey," he said. "If you swallow this—"

"I know the risk," she said.

"But Arianna, is this risk worth your life?"

She frowned. She could live in a broken body, repair it bit by bit, and perhaps never get it all back. She would still have her abilities to think, and she would have the feeling of sunlight against her skin, the smell of roses in the summer, the sound of birds in the garden at night. But she wouldn't have all of herself.

"I don't look at it that way," she said. "I need to try everything I can to return to myself. I owe it to myself."

"Ari—"

She leaned her head against his shoulder. He stopped. They had had this discussion ever since he had said something about the fountain. She had latched onto the idea, and he had tried to talk her out of it. He couldn't know the greatest attraction, though. He couldn't know because she couldn't explain it.

Rugad had invaded her mind. He had taken her body for his own and used it in his own way. He had woven bits of himself throughout her, and when he had finally been destroyed, those parts of her were destroyed as well.

As strong as she was, as confident as she was, she wasn't sure she would be able to rebuild those parts of herself alone.

The magic of her mother's people couldn't help her. So she was turning to the magic of her father's people before she completely gave up hope.

Arianna listened to the water gurgle. "Carry me down there."

He picked her up and cradled her against his chest, holding her tightly, as if he might never hold her again. She could feel his heart beating against her arm. Such a soothing feeling.

He didn't make another protest, and for that, she was grateful. He carried her carefully down the steps. They went on for a long way and sank into a large bowl. The bloodred color had dripped down the stairs unevenly, so the edges of some of the stairs were still white. Some of the color had trailed to the floor below, but not all of it. The floor at the base of the stairs looked as if someone had spilled wine on it and not yet cleaned it up.

There was a white table in the center, and corridors trailing off to the sides. Between the corridors was the fountain.

Coulter stopped beside it, still cradling Arianna.

She had never been this close to it. Her father hadn't wanted her close, afraid that the water that spilled from it might harm her. She could feel the spray now and she braced herself—half worried that it would melt her like holy water did to the Fey.

But no one knew if holy water harmed Fey who were nonmagical—and at the moment, she was nonmagical. At least, her body was. The light had already drained the magic from her.

The fountain's pedestal had been carved out of the rock

that formed the floor. The bowl had been added later. Water flowed from a crack in the wall, into the basin, and down through the pedestal. Beside the crack were carvings that made no sense to Arianna.

Coulter frowned at them. "We should have brought Matt. He might know what they mean."

"It doesn't matter," Arianna said. "I'm not changing my mind."

Coulter sighed. They had already discussed how they were going to do this. He was to hold her so that she could drink from the fountain and then he was to set her down.

He leaned forward, low enough that she could put her face in the water.

It was cold and fresh, the best she had ever tasted. It slipped into the pores of her skin, chilling them. She drank and drank and drank, unable to get her fill. She had never had water that tasted so good.

Coulter tried to pull her away, but somehow she prevented him. She drank even more, letting the water cover her face, feeling guilty for all that she was taking, but not guilty enough to stop.

The water filled her and spread inside her, and she continued to drink. At some point while she was drinking, she realized she wasn't breathing or blinking or moving.

Coulter finally lifted her out and set her on the floor, and she struggled to get back for more water. Instead, the water within her turned and moved and grabbed her, as if she were part of it, and she felt herself slip into a new state, one she had never been in before.

"Arianna?" Coulter asked.

But she didn't answer him. She couldn't answer him. Her body was still hers, but it wasn't moving. It wouldn't move, even if she wanted it to.

Again? a female voice asked.

Arianna's eyelids were closed, but she could see the inside of the cave. She saw Coulter's concerned face. She saw him step back as he had promised and sit on the step, looking as if he had made the biggest mistake of his life. But she couldn't see the source of the voice.

Another with the Roca's blood, trying to take what she already has. This time the speaker was male.

No, Arianna said. Only the words weren't coming out of her mouth. They were coming out of her as if she were inside of a Link. *I've come to you for help.*

Help? You want more magic? the female voice asked. *How greedy are these creatures?*

My magic has been destroyed, Arianna said. *Please, look. The inside of me has been injured by a dark magic. I need help repairing it.*

Then she saw figures, ghostly figures, floating above her. They were Islanders, pale and round and small. They crowded over her.

Coulter sat up straighter, as if he sensed them.

They touched her with their fingers, gentle upon her forehead. She felt something probe into her mind, saw a male face that looked so much like her father's that she almost cried out to him. But that face was not her father's. It was older and had different lines, lines that were not formed by laughter, like her father's had been. The man touched the black gooey threads and said, *You have been touched by the Lights of Midday, yet you live.*

She nodded. Then she showed him what happened to her, from the baby, through the takeover, and her return. He recoiled as if he felt the pain of it.

Different magic. How strange this is.

Yes, she said. *Please. Can you help me?*

He beckoned, and most of the presences outside her were suddenly inside, touching the damage, grimacing at it, wiping their hands on their ghostly selves as if they had been soiled.

Then, one by one, they left.

Please, Arianna said. *You're my last hope!*

Coulter was wringing his hands and staring at her. She could sense his self-control.

We can repair your physical functions, the man said. *But we cannot give you back the magic you had. We do not know that magic.*

It evolved from a different source, a female voice said.

You are a mixture of two powers. You are unique. We cannot preserve that uniqueness. That was a third voice.

But we can give you the fullest extent of the power that your family should have, said a female voice.

It will not benefit you, said a male voice. *That is the price.*

All magic has a price.

It is a horrible price.

But your children will have a softer version, and their children will be blessed, the man said. *Especially if you unite with the one who brought you here.*

Coulter? Arianna asked.

He comes from a line we once thought would strengthen yours. But there has been no contact between these lines in all of Blue Isle's history. Unite with him, and we will help you.

Arianna looked at Coulter. He seemed so frightened sitting there. Coulter was always frightened, but he always came through for her. And she loved him, more than she wanted to admit.

I will unite with him, she said.

Good, the female voice said. *Then your children will be strong, and your children's children will be blessed.*

You will be the best of all the Isle, the man said.

You must remain its Queen, said another voice.

Blue Isle's Queen? Arianna asked.

But you cannot divide your loyalties any longer. You shall look like your mother's people, but you shall no longer be of them. Do you understand? The man asked.

I'm not going to be Fey anymore? Arianna asked.

Not inside. Our magic cannot repair what was done to you. You will not have the powers you had. Except that which has always been part of you.

My Vision, she said.

It is the only thing that is exactly the same, said the man.

But Coulter's an Enchanter. Isn't that the same? Arianna asked.

You were not gifted with his powers. We are not discussing that, the man said.

You must decide, the woman said. *We give you a moment to consider.*

Arianna felt a pang of sadness. She would never be able to Shift again. Because of what Rugad had done, she would always be a different woman. She couldn't change that. But she could take something from this place. Lose the pain, lose the destruction.

At a price.

Her price. Not the one Rugad had charged her, but one she chose. And the things these presences were asking of her were things she had planned to do anyway.

All right, she said.

The presences swarmed around her, touching her, caressing her. The water moved inside of her and became part of her. She could feel it absorbing into her skin, her bones, her womb. The water became part of her.

And then the presences were gone.

Her eyes were closed, and she couldn't see through her lids any longer.

She sat up. Coulter was beside her. She touched her forehead where the presences had touched her.

"You're moving," he said. "They healed you?"

"In their own way." She put a hand on his cheek, and then pressed her face against his. It would be no sacrifice to marry him or have children with him. She had always wanted that.

But she had to accept the sadness within her. She had to acknowledge the loss. Before she did, she had one more thing to do. One more thing to give up.

She stood slowly, and started up the stairs in search of Gift.

CHAPTER SEVENTY-FIVE

$\mathcal{G}$IFT SAT ON the stone platform leading into the Roca's Cave. He leaned against one of the giant swords. Skya sat beside him. He had his arm around her and was holding her close. His other arm was bandaged and in a sling. The Healers had instructed him not to use it. The damage had been serious and they were worried that any use would ruin the work they had done to repair it.

Dash, Leen, Matt, Scavenger, and, surprisingly, Sebastian, all sat at the edge of the platform overlooking the valley. Leen had helped Sebastian climb to the top when he had said he wanted to be with his sister. It had taken most of the morning, but he had made it up here. He had peered inside the cave, but had decided not to go in.

The decision had relieved Gift. He sensed that Sebastian wouldn't be safe inside, although he didn't know why.

Lyndred had stayed in Jahn with her father. Bridge was exhausted from his injuries and the effort he had put out to defeat Rugad. Lyndred felt she had needed time alone. Con had stayed with her. She had asked him to show her his plans for the Tabernacle, and he was happy to oblige. Arianna's return to power meant Con's dream of reviving the religion—one that would be open to Fey and Islanders—could be realized.

After Gift had left the *Tashka,* he had told Xihu exactly what happened. Xihu finally understood what the changes she had seen in Arianna were. She had brought in Domestics to "clear" the palace of all residue, and she was helping Luke find the Islanders who had worked at the palace so that they could return to their positions. By the time Arianna got back, a lot of the damage Rugad had done to her home would be repaired.

Gift glanced inside the cave. He heard nothing. He hated this idea, but nothing could dissuade Arianna from it. She was so damaged. He wondered if they had let the Lights of Midday ravage her for too long. He had mentioned that to Xihu, but Xihu had said that if they had done it for too short a time, Rugad would not be gone.

Xihu had been intrigued by the fact that the destruction of Rugad had not caused the Blood. She saw it as a sign that the Blood was tied to the physical being, not the essence.

Gift wasn't so sure. Coulter, after all, was the one who held the globe, and even though Gift was directing the heartstone, he didn't touch the weapon. That, too, could have made a difference.

Skya sighed and leaned against him. She was exhausted by all the events, and the pregnancy was beginning to take a toll on her. During the last week, he had spent most of his time with her. The look in her eyes when she had seen his wound told him all he needed to know. Whatever their differences were, she loved him just as much as he loved her.

Young Matt turned and looked nervously at the cave. He had been doing that for the last hour or so. Gift wondered what he felt. The boy had as much magic as Coulter, maybe more. Coulter always said he could feel shifts inside the cave. Gift supposed that Matt could as well.

Matt wasn't completely healed yet either, but he wanted to be here for Coulter. It seemed to Gift that Matt was afraid Arianna would die inside, and that Coulter would not be able to handle the loss.

Gift wasn't sure Coulter could take it either.

Then Gift heard a shuffling from inside. He started to get up, but Skya held him back.

"Let them come to us," she said, and he knew she wasn't saying it out of consideration for them, but out of concern for him. She didn't entirely believe that Gift had lived inside that cave safely. Her Warder's magic had told her to stay away from the interior, and she always followed those warnings. It was, he finally realized, one of the things that made her a good guide.

Finally, Coulter walked out. Alone. Gift felt his heart lurch. He struggled to his feet. Skya clung to his good arm, concern on her face.

The others were standing too.

Coulter continued walking to the center of the platform. He seemed abnormally calm.

"Where . . . is . . . Ari?" Sebastian asked. He sounded panicked. Dear Sebastian, asking what was in everyone's heart.

"Coming," Coulter said.

Gift let out the breath he hadn't realized he had been holding. Coulter faced the cave, and so did everyone else.

At that moment, Arianna walked out.

Gift was surprised by how wonderful it felt just to see his sister walk. He had been afraid he would never see her again. Skya squeezed his arm and then let go, as if she expected him to run and hug Arianna. But that didn't feel appropriate.

His sister came toward him, moving easily. The old fluidity was back in her movements. This was Arianna.

And it wasn't.

Something was different about her face. Her birthmark was gone. And her eyes seemed bluer than they had before.

"Gift," she said, holding out her hand to him. "May I speak to you?"

"Of course," he said, taking her hand. She led him to a place near the rock overhang. Everyone else moved toward the edge of the platform. Coulter, Skya, and Sebastian all looked back as if they were wondering why they were excluded.

Then he and Arianna stepped under the shadow of the rocks.

"Are you all right?" he asked her.

She nodded. "They healed me."

"They?"

"Coulter says they're Powers, but they're not. They're the Islander equivalent, whatever that is."

"They repaired all the damage?" The relief he felt was profound.

"Not all," she said. "I had to make a bargain with them."

He studied her. He remembered his father's stricture that none of them drink from the fountain. Coulter had enforced that for fifteen years. "What bargain?"

"Most of it was stuff I was going to do anyway," she said. "Marry Coulter, have children—"

"Marry Coulter? Does he know?"

She smiled and put a finger on Gift's lips. "Not yet. I'll tell him. It'll work this time."

Gift knew it would. He had seen how protective Coulter was of her and how he didn't want to lose her again. "What was the rest of the bargain?"

The smile left her face. "I'm not Fey anymore."

"Of course you're Fey," he said. "Mother was Fey. You don't stop being Fey just because they say so. You still have the features, the ears—"

"I'm not," she said. "They couldn't give me back my Fey magic."

It took him a moment to understand. "The Shifting and the Vision are both gone?"

"The Vision stays. I never lost it. But the Shifting is gone forever. And my children will be pure Islander."

"How strange," Gift said.

Arianna nodded. She blinked hard, as if her loss hurt her more than she wanted to say.

"So," she said, her voice shaking, "since I'm not Fey, I can't remain Black Queen."

"But you have Vision," Gift said. "That's all you need—"

"It wouldn't be right, Gift. I want to remain Queen of Blue Isle. In fact, that was one of the conditions, but I can't, in good conscience, rule a people I am no longer a part of."

"I don't think you can lose what you are—"

"Gift," she said softly. "I was always more Islander than Fey."

He was silent for a moment. She was raised Islander. Even though their father had tried to keep her in touch with their mother's people, he hadn't known the intricacies of the culture. Neither had Arianna.

And she hadn't gone out and learned about it as Gift had.

"You'll change your mind," he said.

"I won't. This is how it should be. This is how it should always have been. You're the eldest. The Throne is yours."

A shiver ran through him. This, then, was the Vision the Shaman had seen. Arianna giving her scepter to Gift.

They had been right. Gift was to be the Black King.

He shook his head. Was Skya right? Did the Powers manipulate everyone so that their wishes came true? Had he been destined for this from birth? Or from the moment he touched the Black Throne?

"I don't want it, Ari. I've never wanted it."

"Good," she said. "Then you'll never turn into someone like Rugad, someone who wanted to hang on to it even after death."

He sighed, and glanced out at the group still waiting at the edge of the platform. They were consciously trying not to watch Arianna and Gift. Matt was pointing out landmarks, but Coulter kept looking over his shoulder. Once his gaze met Gift's, and he glanced away quickly.

Arianna wasn't going to let him argue with her. And he didn't know how. One of them had to rule the Fey. And if she didn't want to, he had to.

"I have only one request," Arianna said.

Gift looked at her. The brightness of her eyes was beautiful to see. She radiated health now, whereas this morning she had looked near death.

"What's that?" he asked.

"I want Blue Isle to be its own country again. The Fey will be welcome here, both as citizens and as traders. But I don't want the Isle to be part of the Empire anymore. Can you do that, Gift?"

"I take this to mean you don't want me to go on to conquer Leut?"

She didn't laugh. "I suppose you can use the Isle as a launching point if you need it."

"I don't, Ari," he said. "It was a joke."

She smiled, but she was waiting. This was important to her.

"You realize that would make me the first Black King to lose ground," Gift said.

She nodded.

"But I'll do it. It'll show that my reign is different." The words sounded strange to him. His reign. He wondered how Skya would take it. Then he remembered how she had looked at him as she dressed his wound, and realized that however she felt about being his queen, they would be able to manage. Together.

"You'll be the best Black King the Fey have ever known," Arianna said.

"I don't know about that," Gift said.

"You're the only one who has experienced Warrior and Domestic magic. You've been all over the Empire. You know the costs of war and the benefits of peace. You'll be fine."

It was his turn to smile. "Will I be welcome on Blue Isle?"

"You're a citizen of the Isle," she said. "You're the heir to the throne, at least until Coulter and I can do something about that."

He pulled her in close. She hugged him tightly. He understood what she had done. The Places of Power were no longer in the same Empire. They were separate, just as he suspected they were intended to be.

He would never be allowed on this mountainside again, not as long as there were other heirs to Blue Isle's throne. He doubted he would miss this place. But he would come back to the Isle. He wanted to see his sister, his nieces and nephews, and occasionally, the place of his birth.

Slowly she released him from the hug. There were tears in her eyes.

"I'm sorry about the Shifting," he said.

"Me too," she said.

He slipped his good arm around her, and she put her head on his shoulder. The best thing about this was that it made them equals in all ways, something he suspected that they were supposed to be.

"I guess we should tell the others," he said.

"Do you think they'll be surprised?" she asked with a grin. It was the old Arianna, the mischievous one, and he hadn't realized how much he had missed her until she returned.

"I don't know," he said, leading her to their loved ones. "Let's go find out."

ABOUT THE AUTHOR

IN THE PAST year, Kristine Kathryn Rusch's short fiction has won the *Asimov Science Fiction Magazine*'s Reader's Choice Award, *Science Fiction Age*'s Reader's Choice Award, and *Ellery Queen Mystery Magazine*'s Reader's Choice Award. Winning three different Reader's Choice Awards in two different genres in the same year is a feat no other writer has ever accomplished.

She has published six other novels about the Fey, as well as twenty-five unrelated novels. Her novel *Star Wars: The New Rebellion* and several of her Star Trek novels have made the *USA Today* best-seller list. *The Fey: Sacrifice* was chosen by *Science Fiction Chronicle* as one of the Best Fantasy Novels of 1995.